D1598185

Critical Essays on Herman Melville's Pierre; or, The Ambiguities

Critical Essays on Herman Melville's Pierre; or, The Ambiguities

Brian Higgins
and
Hershel Parker

G. K. Hall & Co. • Boston, Massachusetts

Library of Congress Cataloging in Publication Data
Main entry under title:

Critical essays on Herman Melville's Pierre; or, The ambiguities.

(Critical essays on American literature)
Includes bibliographical references and index.
1. Melville, Herman, 1819–1891. Pierre—Collected works.
I. Higgins, Brian. II. Parker, Hershel. III. Title. IV. Series.
PS2384.P53C75   1983   813'.3   83–4385
ISBN 0–8161–8319–8

CRITICAL ESSAYS ON AMERICAN LITERATURE

This series seeks to publish the most important reprinted criticism on writers and topics in American literature along with, in various volumes, original essays, interviews, bibliographies, letters, manuscript sections, and other materials brought to public attention for the first time. The collection compiled by Brian Higgins and Hershel Parker is an exhaustive anthology containing all of the known reviews and early comments. It also contains recent comment by Carl Van Doren, Van Wyck Brooks, Lewis Mumford, R.P. Blackmur, F.O. Matthiessen, Warner Berthoff, and others, most notably the classic essay by E.L. Grant Watson. The introduction is an original essay that presents a thorough review of the scholarship, and the volume ends with a brief original statement by the editors about the future of criticism on *Pierre*. We are confident that this collection will make a permanent and significant contribution to American literary study.

James Nagel, GENERAL EDITOR

Northeastern University

CONTENTS

INTRODUCTION

Pierre; or, The Ambiguities, Herman Melville's seventh book, was a disaster for him personally and professionally.[1] It lost him his English publisher, and reviewers of the American edition (1852) accused the book and the author of being mad. In the remainder of the nineteenth century, *Pierre* was dismissed as Melville's "late miserable abortion"[2] and characterized as repulsive, insane, and unreadable. The book fared little better after it was rediscovered in the 1920s. John Freeman, Melville's first English biographer, found in it "an enormous and perverse sadness, declining to mere madness," and Lewis Mumford saw it as "crude melodrama."[3] Despite his interest in the psychological dimensions of *Pierre*, Henry A. Murray, Jr., judged it "the performance of a depleted puppeteer."[4] Less restrained, another of Melville's modern critics, Newton Arvin, dismissed Pierre as "four-fifths claptrap, and sickly claptrap to boot," while Warner Berthoff characterized it as "freakish," and Edwin H. Miller recently declared that "Pierre is paranoid and so is the book."[5] E.L. Grant Watson has been alone in claiming that *Pierre* is a greater work of art than *Moby-Dick*,[6] and few other critics in the twentieth century have celebrated the book as even a moderately high achievement. Yet despite all the critical uneasiness and outright disdain, *Pierre* is now recognized as one of Melville's most important works, the book nearest to *Moby-Dick* not only in time but also in the ambitiousness of its aims and in the power of at least some passages.

Nonetheless, confusing legends about *Pierre* that grew up in the 1890s, or grew up later, in the 1920s and the 1930s, have since gained such currency as to tinge even the work of careful scholars. It has been commonly assumed, for instance, that the writing of *Moby-Dick* so exhausted Melville that he wrote *Pierre* in a state of physical, emotional, and psychological prostration; that he wrote it after *Moby-Dick* was plainly not going to be a popular, strong-selling book; that he wrote it, moreover, in a mood of defiant candor, or even as a suicidal gesture meant to bring upon him the wrath of the critics; that something happened in late February 1852, after the contract for the book was signed, which caused him to make additions to his manuscript which amounted to some

150 printed pages; that Melville withdrew into reclusiveness as a result of the attacks on *Pierre* in the press; and that the Harpers fire of December 1853 destroyed the plates of *Pierre* along with all or almost all of the unbound sheets and unsold bound copies, so that the book was from that time virtually unobtainable until it was reprinted in the 1920s. In fact, after completing *Moby-Dick*, Melville enjoyed a restful, social, physically active period, free from authorship, which probably lasted as long as four months; and he began *Pierre* not prostrated but feeling (to judge from his letters) buoyant, optimistic, and secure. He began it, too, at a time when he could have seen few, if any, of the reviews of *Moby-Dick* and could have had no knowledge of its sales; far from being a suicidal gesture, *Pierre* was intended to establish his career and reputation more securely than ever before. The "additions" to the manuscript were made after the contract was agreed upon but *before*, not after, it was signed; and, whatever anguish he may have suffered over the reviews of *Pierre* (according to his wife, he made a joke of the reception and said he thought it was just), Melville did not become reclusive till his later years (when his seclusion was never as total as some Melville enthusiasts since the 1880s have claimed[7]). The plates of none of Melville's books were destroyed in the Harpers' fire; but the loss of 494 bound copies of *Pierre* led to a second printing in 1855 (of 260 copies), which (so slow were the sales) made the book available through most, if not all, of Melville's lifetime.[8]

But if the actual facts of the book's history are less melodramatic than legend has held, the experience of writing and publishing *Pierre* was indeed catastrophic for Melville. He began *Pierre* at his farm near Pittsfield, Massachusetts, late in 1851—a critical year in his career. In April, short of money, as always, he had asked for an advance on his whaling book from the Harpers, his American publishers. They gave two reasons for refusing: an "extensive and expensive addition" to their plant in New York City and the fact that Melville already owed them "nearly seven hundred dollars." Borrowing $2050 from T.D. Stewart, an acquaintance from Lansingburgh, Melville made improvements on his farmhouse, Arrowhead, and probably used some of the money to pay for plating his new book (then called *The Whale*), apparently so he would control the plates while he tried to find another American publisher who would offer more for it than the Harpers. Whatever negotiations he may have had with other publishers (his friend Evert Duyckinck, joint-editor of the *Literary World*, lobbied hard for the firm of Redfield), Melville settled with the Harpers on 12 September 1851, receiving no advance for the first time in his dealings with them. Their statement dated 25 November showed that Melville still owed them $422.82, despite the sale of 1535 copies of the new book, retitled in America *Moby-Dick*, and fewer copies of the older books. His luck in England was marginally better, for Richard Bentley paid him £150 in September as an advance against half profits, less than for *Mardi* and *White-Jacket* but more than for *Redburn*.[9]

Melville memorably recorded the debilitating effects of his literary and financial pressures while finishing *Moby-Dick* in his letter of early June 1851 to Nathaniel Hawthorne. At this time he was "so pulled hither and thither by circumstances," that in a week or so he had to go to New York, to "bury" himself in a third-story room and "work and slave" on his "Whale"; that was the only way he could finish it. Financial worries disturbed the peace of mind he needed for writing, and the resulting conflict between financial and artistic considerations injured both his work and his self-respect as an author:

> The calm, the coolness, the silent grass-growing mood in which a man *ought* always to compose,—that, I fear, can seldom be mine. Dollars damn me . . . . What I feel most moved to write, that is banned,—it will not pay. Yet, altogether, write the *other* way I cannot. So the product is a final hash, and all my books are botches.

Thus harried, and further embittered by his sense of the callow unresponsiveness of the book-buying public ("What's the use of elaborating what, in its very essence, is so short-lived as a modern book? Though I wrote the Gospels in this century, I should die in the gutter"), Melville confessed to Hawthorne his presentiments of imminent disintegration and collapse: he would "at last be worn out and perish, like an old nutmeg-grater, grated to pieces by the constant attrition of the wood, that is, the nutmeg"; three weeks had scarcely passed at any time since he was twenty-five that he had not "unfolded" within himself, but now he felt that he had "come to the inmost leaf of the bulb, and that shortly the flower must fall to the mould."[10] Yet for all Melville's continued financial problems (exacerbated by his apparent failure to secure better terms for *Moby-Dick* than the Harpers offered), this ominous mood seems to have been short-lived or intermittent. His next letter to Hawthorne (29 June 1851) records his return to Pittsfield "wearied with the long delay of the printers, and disgusted with the heat and dust of the babylonish brick-kiln of New York"; worse, his *Whale* was still unfinished and "only half through the press." But his earlier mood had abated and he wrote of it now with fleeting self-mockery: for weeks the "most persuasive season" of late spring and early summer had recalled him "from certain crochetty and over doleful chimearas"; he was beginning, moreover, "to come out upon a less bustling time, and to enjoy the calm prospect of things from a fair piazza at the north of the old farm house here."[11] Some three weeks later he was still at least occasionally tormented by "Blue Devils," but was now busy with the haying season and looking forward to being soon "a disengaged man" and to enjoying "some little bit of vagabondism" with Hawthorne on Greylock before autumn.[12]

With *Moby-Dick* off his hands and the haying season over, Melville was free to entertain himself, his sisters, and various visitors and neighbors with picnics and mountain climbing excursions. His mother and one or more of his sisters were there to care for his wife during her confinement and help with the two-year old Malcolm, so Melville had no onerous family obligations. Through the late summer and early fall of 1851 he idled and ruminated over his future writing. These ruminations were serious enough to make him avoid reading two novels his neighbor Mrs. Morewood sent him—novels which might distract him from what he called his "silly thoughts and wayward speculations."[13] As fall deepened, Melville turned to his annual chore of laying in firewood for the winter, all but putting the whaling book out of his mind for a time, and no doubt brooding more and more seriously about the precise nature of his next book, which in the natural course of things would be started at the onset of winter, after the supply of wood was laid up.[14]

While he was finishing *Moby-Dick*, Melville had had a number of future literary projects more or less in mind. For two years or longer he had been thinking of writing up the story of the Revolutionary exile, Israel Potter, and had collected material for that project during his visit to London in the fall of 1849.[15] As early as August 1850 he may have thought of writing not merely some Berkshire scenes for his hero (in reality a Rhode Island boy) but another, different book set in the Berkshires, for while vacationing at his Uncle Thomas Melvill's old farm near Pittsfield, then being run by his cousin Robert as a select summer boardinghouse, he entertained Evert Duyckinck and showed him around the place with such enthusiasm that the visitor reported to his wife that Melville knew "every stone & tree" of the place and would "probably make a book of its features."[16] The next month Melville purchased the Brewster farm, which he named Arrowhead, adjoining his Uncle Thomas's place, which the young John and Sarah Morewood bought in October and subsequently named Broadhall. In the Berkshires Melville's literary plans multiplied so fast that in December 1850 he suggested facetiously that Duyckinck send him "about fifty fast-writing youths," since he had "planned about that number of future works" and couldn't "find enough time to think about them separately."[17] There is no way of knowing how soon the story of Pierre Glendinning took its place among these "future works," but the chances are that any plans for it were inchoate until after Melville was finished with *Moby-Dick*. During the late summer and early fall of 1851, Melville had time for a thoroughgoing assessment of the direction of his career as well as the nature of his next work. In abeyance was the possibility of working up someone's old narrative anew, with *Israel Potter* already in some stage of planning. But he had built a career upon fictionalized autobiography or fiction that was grounded on his own experience and observations, and in the process he had, after six books, all but exhausted the phases of his seagoing experience; if he were to continue to ground his writings on some sort of autobiographical basis while postponing his experimentation with retelling another writer's story, he would have to turn back to his early life. In any case, he was tired of being known as merely the man who lived among the cannibals, as he told Hawthorne in June 1851 ("What 'reputation' H.M. has is horrible. Think of it!")[18] and no doubt eager to establish his own literary reputation upon a basis more like Hawthorne's.

With his review of Hawthorne's *Mosses* in the *Literary World* (17 and 24 August 1850), Melville had helped establish that reputation for his friend, but no one had written a comparable celebration of his own achievements as great American writer rather than fine American sea-writer. More particularly, Melville was irritated that Duyckinck continued to regard him as his Bunsby, the resident authority on things nautical and places exotic, rather than understanding that with *Mardi* (1849) he had made a bid for a high rank among literary immortals. Being asked to contribute a "dash of salt spray" to the Duyckinck's new magazine, *Holden's*, in February 1851, was an annoying reminder of how closed-minded Duyckinck had been to his development over the last several years.[19] Once the paired *Typee* and *Omoo* were behind him, Melville had, in fact, thought—and repeatedly talked to his publishers— in terms of the fresh fields a new venture was taking him into, the newness, the novelty of the manuscript at hand.[20] Along with the commercial need he had felt a psychological need not to duplicate anything he had already done; as he gained awareness of his literary powers, he began to think in terms of making a new book a quantum leap beyond the last. After *Mardi*, he wanted to write something still more ambitious and only through financial pressures buckled down to write the comparatively unambitious *Redburn* and *White-Jacket*, both during a four-month period in mid-1849.[21] In *Moby-Dick* he had made his second bid for literary preeminence, displaying the bold originality he advocated for American authors in his *Mosses* essay[22] by combining adventurous whaling narrative with encyclopaedic cetological lore, elements of Gothic romance and Shakespearean tragedy, and profound psychological and metaphysical exploration, while developing a uniquely rich prose influenced by a range of authors including the translators of the King James Bible, Shakespeare, Sir Thomas Browne, John Milton, Thomas De Quincey, and Thomas Carlyle. After triumphantly sustaining throughout *Moby-Dick* the full powers he had only begun to develop in *Mardi*, Melville wished to experiment still further in a book that would allow his continuing growth: his whale book was ambitious, but, as he told Hawthorne in mid-November 1851, he had "heard of Krakens."[23] Melville was ripe for an attempt at a new, non-nautical genre through which he might make a bid for a high, less specialized literary reputation and through which he might satisfy his internal needs to surpass his previous literary achievements.

To meet these overlapping if not conflicting exigencies and ambitions, Melville apparently thought that he would write what would pass as a "regular romance," as he later called the completed, final version of *Pierre*, "with a mysterious plot to it, & stirring passions at work,"[24] while at the same time he would analyze the ways an explosive tragic revelation may impel an exceptional human being into sudden and ambiguous mental growth. Setting the story in the United States, he would contribute further to the haltingly-emergent national literature he had championed in his review of Hawthorne's *Mosses*; he would explicitly, though playfully, demonstrate the sociological and aesthetic validity of portraying an aristocratic American youth in a rural setting vast as an English dukedom, making his young hero as believable as the aristocratic Englishmen in romances the English (and the American audience for English fiction) were familiar with. He would "poetically establish the richly aristocratic condition" of Pierre's life and character[25] secure in the knowledge, moreover, that his own cousins the Van Rensselaers, were in reality as wealthy and ducal as was his Pierre, however atypical these cousins were in fast-changing American society. Melville's Gansevoort relatives included the great hero of the battle at Saratoga, his mother's father (whom his own Uncle Peter was named for), and he could draw upon his knowledge of the belongings of the Gansevoorts in his depiction of his hero's home. Family portraits, captured British banners and kettledrum, and a Revolutionary camp-bed such as those employed in the novel were all familiar to Melville in his youth. A major plot element was also ready at hand, for at some time (probably after he was twelve) Melville seems to have learned a dark family secret: a surviving letter suggests that his own father, like Pierre's, had had an illegitimate daughter, for two women (mother and daughter) seeking to determine their rights, presented themselves at the house of Melville's paternal grandfather in the interval between the death of Melville's father in January 1832 and that of his grandfather, Thomas Melvill, in September of the same year.[26] The women may of course have had other claims on Allan Melvill, but the obvious inference in probably the correct one, and Melville's device of a secret illegitimate daughter is hardly coincidental. Furthermore, Melville's father, like Pierre's, had become delirious as he was dying. In *Pierre*, the plot involving the sudden appearance of an unknown young woman, supposedly half-sister to the hero, had the great advantage of being easily allegorized within Melville's psychological preoccupations: in the "boundless expansion" of Pierre's life and mind, Isabel would represent the invading Unconscious. Melville must have felt that his mysterious plot and stirring passions in an aristocratic setting would capture the interest of readers and leave him free to explore what really interested him—the awakening of a potentially fine mind to tragedy. He must have felt, in short, that he could become one of the great literary truthtellers he had described in his review of Hawthorne's *Mosses*, those who simultaneously please the many superficial skimmers of pages and the few choice eagle-eyed readers.[27]

In working out his ambitious design, Melville clearly determined to draw upon his recent surroundings and experiences as well as family situations and household paraphernalia. His Berkshire neighbor, Sarah Morewood, very likely figured more largely in the conception of *Pierre* than we can now establish. The archness of Melville's special language in his letters to her is so clearly related to the diction of certain passages early in his book that one suspects they were partly written with her in mind as one potential reader just as passages in *Typee* were obviously written as a way of teasing his household of sisters.[28] Demonstrably, Mrs. Morewood's inveterate socializing is related to the composition of *Pierre*.[29] Reclusive as Melville later seemed to many people, he at this time sought occasions for companionable "vagabondism" with others besides Hawthorne. In 1851 he had a notably sociable August, when Mrs. Morewood took in tow his guests Evert and George Duyckinck, leaving them exhilarated and exhausted. During Elizabeth's confinement before the birth of Stanwix, on October 27, Melville took several outings with members of the Morewood and Melville families into the Berkshire hills. The Berkshire landscape was clearly both "an exhilarative and provocative" (to use the terms he applied in *Pierre* to other sources of creative inspiration) to Melville, for its terrain had been emotion-laden for him since his stays there in his boyhood and was associated now with his profoundly gratifying friendship with Hawthorne; when he took the Old Lenox Road to visit Hawthorne he passed a rocky elevation where as a youth he had climbed to survey the town of Pittsfield and the countryside. Many scenes in the first half of *Pierre* record the hero's perambulations about a landscape obviously based on the stretch of the Berkshires from Mount Greylock to Lenox. The fictional scenes plainly derive from his immediate experiences: in dedicating *Pierre* to "Greylock's Most Excellent Majesty," he was honest in acknowledging that he had received from that sovereign "most bounteous and unstinted fertilizations." One such fertilization was soon clear to many in the Berkshire area. Some time in 1851 (more likely during the August feting of city friends than the family excursions of the fall), Melville and his party had picnicked at the local curiosity, the Balanced Rock, where Mrs. Morewood had placed a music box far under the overhanging stone, so as to make it breathe "mysterious and enchanting music." Melville himself thereupon inscribed "MEMNON" on a nearby tree, and J.E.A. Smith, the recorder of this act of vandalism, coyly linked the occasion to the abandonment of a broken champagne bottle at the foot of the stone.[30] Melville's familiarity with the Balanced Rock certainly led to the creation of the "Memnon Stone" in *Pierre*. But such verifiable use of the Berkshire scenery, while gossip-worthy to Melville's acquain-

tances, is insignificant compared to the profounder fertilizations manifested in the interior landscape of the hero's mind early in the book, as
well as in the later vision of Enceladus.[31]

Probably some weeks elapsed between the fertilizing excursions and
their springing forth in Melville's new manuscript, an interval filled with
nonliterary toil. On 6 November, two weeks after Stanwix's birth,
Melville received from Duyckinck a clipping about the sinking of the *Ann
Alexander* by a whale. On the 7th Melville replied: "For some days past
being engaged in the woods with axe, wedge, & beetle, the Whale had
almost completely slipped me for the time (& I was the merrier for it)
when Crash! comes Moby Dick himself (as you justly say) & reminds me
of what I have been about for part of the last year or two."[32] The whale
had been out of Melville's mind, temporarily, and nothing new of so
obsessive a nature seems to have been on it. Melville's 17[?] November
letter in response to Hawthorne's praise of *Moby-Dick* speaks of literary
plans, but not in terms of a specific work already underway: "Lord, when
shall we be done growing? As long as we have anything more to do, we
have done nothing. So, now, let us add Moby Dick to our blessing, and
step from that. Leviathan is not the biggest fish;—I have heard of
Krakens."[33] All in all, these two letters offer mainly negative evidence:
Melville did not take advantage of two conspicuous opportunities to make
casual mention of any new work in progress. However, any new book was
to be more ambitious than *Moby-Dick*: "I have heard of Krakens."

Once begun, the writing of *Pierre* went steadily and intensely, as we
know from a letter Mrs. Morewood wrote George Duyckinck three days
after the Melvilles had eaten Christmas dinner at her house. This is the
first surviving mention of *Pierre*:

> I hear that he is now so engaged in a new work as frequently not to
> leave his room till dark in the evening when he for the first time during
> the whole day partakes of solid food—he must therefore write under a
> state of morbid excitement which will soon injure his health.—I laughed
> at him somewhat and told him that the recluse life he was leading made
> his city friends think he was slightly insane—he replied that long ago he
> came to the same conclusion himself but that if he left home to look after
> Hungary the cause in hungery would suffer—[34]

However hard he was working, Melville had not missed reports of the
triumphant arrival in New York of the Hungarian patriot Louis Kossuth,
which virtually monopolized space in American newspapers that month.
But his concentration on *Pierre* had indeed been intense, for Mrs. Morewood's rehearsal of his working habits implies a considerable duration:
she would hardly have described him as so engaged that he "frequently"
worked through till dark if he had just begun the routine a week or two
earlier. The routine had gone on long enough for her to think that he
would "soon" injure his health if he continued in it, not the sort of thing
one says about a healthy farmer-writer of thirty-two when he had only

briefly been laboring under extreme conditions. Melville had been writing *Pierre* for at least several weeks, from about the time of the American publication of *Moby-Dick* in mid-November, if not still earlier, establishing a pattern of incessant application from which he was not deflected by any farm or household obligations or any early reviews of *Moby-Dick* which he saw (such as the two-part review in the Duyckincks' *Literary World*, to which he subscribed, or any which his friends and relatives passed on to him). The family supported his routine, with his sister Helen sacrificing an opportunity for a winter-long visit to a cousin in order to be his copyist.[35]

When working at top speed, as he had done in the summer of 1849, Melville could write the equivalent of fifty Harper pages a week. If he began *Pierre* in early November he could have completed some 350 pages by the time he interrupted his schedule in late December for a trip to New York; if he began it in mid-November he could have written 250 or 300 pages by then. In other words, by the post-Christmas trip Melville could have written all of the Saddle Meadows section as we know it, as well as the city section in a short version equivalent to about a hundred printed pages.[36]

This visit to New York has been puzzling to biographers, especially since it seems to have been hastily arranged (otherwise Sarah Morewood would have had no reason for writing George Duyckinck as she did on 4 January 1852: "Were you not surprised to see Herman Melville in Town?"[37]) and since it lasted so long (from the last days of December through the second week of January or into the third). Leon Howard handled the dates and the motive in gingerly fashion, assuming that Melville's rural household routine was upset because Elizabeth had decided that "she needed to go 'home' in order fully to recuperate from her confinement," but that before seeing her off to Boston Melville had "escorted her to New York" and spent a few days with Allan Melville, his brother and his lawyer. Howard continued: "He was too busy to see as much of Duyckinck as he usually did on his visits; but he probably took time to check up on a few city scenes he planned to use in *Pierre* and certainly talked over his literary business with Allan."[38] This is educated guessing. Melville's primary purpose was to arrange for the Harpers to publish his new manuscript, which then was ready to sell (though possibly not yet complete) as a romance of about 360 pages, his shortest book since *Typee* and *Omoo*. The negotiations must have begun soon after his arrival, perhaps as early as the last days of December and surely not later than the first days of January. Around that time all the details of the contract were agreed to, though it was not formally copied out and signed, pending the actual delivery of the manuscript. (This dating is proved by a letter, quoted below, from Allan to the Harpers, 21 January 1852.) Melville had time for other matters, such as writing a lengthy letter to Sophia Hawthorne where he half-facetiously praised her analysis of *Moby-Dick* and promised that his next present to her would be a "rural bowl of milk"—his earliest-known specific allusion to *Pierre*, one which applied better (though ironically) to the manuscript he had brought with him, in which most of the action took place in the country, than to the final book, whose city section he had probably already begun to expand.[39] The Duyckincks had gotten word by their 3 January issue of the *Literary World* that Melville was on a new literary tack[40]—perhaps news Melville provided after he came to town, and a certain amount of social intercourse went on there, Evert Duyckinck giving Melville what the recipient called a "curious" and "duly valued" nutcracker.[41] But business came before whatever social pleasures Melville could enjoy under the circumstances.

The earliest surviving documents concerning the publication of *Pierre* are from very late December 1851 or very early January 1852—two pages from Allan Melville's draft of the contract with the Harpers.[42] A certain amount of negotiation had preceded these notes, for the parties had already agreed that 1,190 copies would be sold before Melville began receiving royalties. Allan evidently thought that if the printed book were to vary much from 360 pages it was going to vary on the light side, not the heavy, and that he should protect his brother's interests in the eventuality that it did run short of the estimate. "Should the number of pages in said work prove to be ~~any considerabl~~ much less than 360" it was agreed that a "corresponding deduction" be made from the number of copies necessary to liquidate the cost of stereotype plates and editors' copies for a book of 360 pages. Allan caretted in "or more" after "much less" ("Should the number of pages in said work prove to be much less or more than 360") but failed to add the words "or addition" after "deduction" and also failed to add "or to" after "from" ("a corresponding deduction shall be made from the number of copies"). Although the interlineation of "or more" at least shows Allan beginning to cover the possibility that the book would run beyond 360 pages, he was apparently expecting the book to be 360 pages or fewer, rather than more than that number.

Soon after these draft pages were written, both parties agreed to the provisions in the form in which they were finally copied and signed on 20 February 1852. Most of the provisions were pretty much the ones customary in some or all of Melville's earlier contracts with the Harpers.[43] Melville would have the copyright; Harper & Brothers would be the sole publisher in the United States; the agreement would continue seven years, after which Melville could purchase the plates at half the original cost, minus depreciation; at the expiration of the agreement the Harpers could dispose of all copies remaining on hand; the contract would apply only to publication of the book in the United States; and the Harpers would provide Melville with corrected proof to offer to an English publisher, then would defer publication until after the time fixed for English publication or after three months from the time corrected proofs were provided, whichever came first. But one provision was greatly altered from the previous contracts: while the publisher would render Melville semiannual accounts, as usual, his royalty was set at 20¢ a copy after expenses rather than at half profits after expenses. Under the old arrangement the Harpers would have split 50/50 with Melville after printing costs were paid, but now the publisher was taking 80¢ on the dollar. The final provision was also new, the first time one of Melville's contracts had set a number of books to be sold before his royalties would begin:

> It is understood that the said work will contain about 360 pages, and it is agreed that the publishing price of said work is to be fixed at one dollar per copy, and that the proceeds of 1190 copies will be required to liquidate the cost of the stereotype plates and of the copies usually given to editors and that the said Harper & Brothers are only to account to the said Herman Melville for the copies of said work which they shall sell beyond the number so required to liquidate the cost of the stereotype plates and of the copies usually given to editors. Should the number of pages in said work prove to be much less or much more than 360 it is agreed that a corresponding deduction or addition shall be made from or to the number of copies which it is agreed will be necessary to liquidate the cost of stereotype plates and editors copies for a book of 360 pages.

Mostly this provision sets up the machinery for activating the contract, but it contains a new and ugly item: whereas the Harpers in earlier years had split the cost of review copies and had even let Melville hand out some of them himself to his acquaintances on newspapers and magazines, now all the review copies were to be charged wholly against his account.[44] This minor retrenchment could hardly have struck Melville as anything but adding insult to injury. Since Melville depended on his annual book for cash (despite whatever help came from his father-in-law or his own recent endeavors as a part-time farmer), the contract was no mere incidental disappointment—it was a somber warning. In January 1852 Melville's long-standing debt to the Harpers was not yet paid off, even by the moderate success of *Moby-Dick* (reflected in the November financial statement), so it was clear that he might ultimately lose more than the publisher's willingness to divide profits generously and to risk a few promotional copies. The way things were going, he might lose the publisher, and thereby jeopardize or lose his literary career.

Ever since the failure of *Mardi* Melville had been postponing what seems to have been inevitable, given the conventionality of the publishing world and literary audience and the reckless unconventionality of Melville's philosophical ideas and literary experiments. In 1851, outwardly unfazed by the Harpers' refusal to give him an advance, he had begun to hedge against the possible failure of his career. To Hawthorne he had talked aloofly about fame, saying calmly that he had come to regard it "as the most transparent of all vanities." Hawthorne's approval of

Moby-Dick had confirmed him in that mood, as Melville's response shows:

> People think that if a man has undergone any hardship, he should have a reward . . . . My peace and my supper are my reward, my dear Hawthorne. So your joy-giving and exultation-breeding letter is not my reward for my ditcher's work with that book, but is the good goddess's bonus over and above what was stipulated for—for not one man in five cycles, who is wise, will expect appreciative recognition from his fellows, or any one of them. Appreciation! Recognition! Is love appreciated? Why, ever since Adam, who has got to the meaning of this great allegory—the world? Then we pygmies must be content to have our paper allegories but ill comprehended. I say your appreciation is my glorious gratuity. In my proud, humble way,—a shepherd-king,—I was lord of a little vale in the solitary Crimea; but you have now given me the crown of India.[45]

But it was one thing to see his career in such exalted perspective and another to face the realities of 20¢ on the dollar instead of 50¢ on the dollar. And it was another thing to face (before, during, and after the negotiations with the Harpers for *Pierre*) the evidence that *Moby-Dick* had failed with an influential part of the literary establishment. For all we know Melville had seen a good many early reviews of *Moby-Dick* before he came to New York City: certainly he saw the two-part essay in the Duyckincks' *Literary World*, to which he subscribed, and Allan may have been saving others for his arrival. He must have seen a number of reviews which appeared in the January magazines just as he arrived in town, reviews which included some of the most scathing ever given to one of his books. In the aftermath of his intense creative labor on the manuscript, which must have left him psychologically and physically vulnerable, and with his hazardously ambitious literary experiment seen now through the skeptical eyes of his profit-minded publishers rather than the haze of the self-delusions under which he had convinced himself that he was writing something which would simultaneously please the populace and the cognoscenti, Melville was in no condition to content himself with cheery auguries such as the praise which laced many reviews of *Moby-Dick*.

In the first days of 1852 Melville's most businesslike course of action would have been to tidy up his manuscript for the press and go home to work on a project more likely to please his publishers—a stirring retelling of the story of Israel Potter, for instance. As he had done before during his short career, Melville took a less practical course.[46] Instead of getting the manuscript to the Harpers and being done with it, Melville began expanding it, at a feverish pace and in an increasingly feverish mood. He stayed on in town through the second or possibly the third week of January working on the newly-conceived enlargement, writing so fast that before 20 January the manuscript had grown far beyond the 360-page estimate. What he was writing and why he wrote it can be guessed easily enough. His first act in the enlargement, very likely, was to give the reader the information, arbitrarily and most belatedly, that Pierre had been a juvenile author with a flourishing career in the magazines. Making Pierre an author allowed Melville the opportunity to satirize the American literary establishment in general and that establishment as embodied in his friend Evert A. Duyckinck, whom he lampooned as the co-editor of the *Captain Kidd Monthly*. Making Pierre an author, more important, allowed Melville the opportunity to work into the manuscript an account of his own career as an American author—an account which was to vary from wryly self-objective satire to miserable self-justification at his failure to make a living as a novelist in America. But in the enlargement Melville's preoccupation with Pierre's juvenile and later heroic authorship has the probably inadvertent effect of blurring the functions of whatever he retained from his original city section, which, the evidence suggests, was much shorter than in the book as published and had presumably focused more steadily on Pierre's relationship with his supposed half-sister, the persistent focus and major strength of the first half of the book.

One of the commonest and most obviously correct assumptions about the book is that in the impudently aggressive joint-editor of the *Captain Kidd Monthly* Melville was portraying his friend Evert Duyckinck. We know for certain that he was betraying his friendship by paraphrasing their correspondence.[47] Ordinary readers would not know who was being satirized, but Duyckinck himself would wince in self-recognition. Even when we acknowledge that Melville's irritation with aspects of Duyckinck's behavior was recurrent and long-standing, we still are at a loss to account for Melville's extraordinary breach of friendship both in working Duyckinck into the manuscript and in addressing on 14 February 1852 this cold letter to the "Editors of the Literary World":

> You will please discontinue the two copies of your paper sent to J.M.
> Fly at Brattleboro' (or Greenbush), and to H Melville at Pittsfield.
> Whatever charges there may be outstanding for either or both copies,
> please send them to me, & they will receive attention.[48]

Nothing in the recent issues of the magazine seems adequate to account for Melville's behavior, and no private communication between him and the Duyckincks has survived from this time, aside from Melville's hasty but polite note written while he was in New York. Scholars have tended to look for some public cause, such as the two-part review of *Moby-Dick* printed in the *Literary World* in November 1851, but the surviving note from January argues against Melville's having taken offense at what is, after all, a favorable review, though one that reproached Melville for his irreverences. Since only a few months earlier, in the late summer of 1851, Duyckinck had argued that the whaling book should go to Redfield, one can reasonably wonder whether or not Melville took Duyckinck the manuscript of *Pierre*, in its short form, when the Harpers were not enthusiastic about it. If so, did Duyckinck react much as he reacted the next year to the published book? There seems no way of knowing, but some such event seems required to account for Melville's reckless violations of the friendship.

As Melville struck out against Duyckinck he struck out against the reviewers of *Moby-Dick* who had condemned him as well as those who had offered perfunctory and irrelevant praise for what he knew should have entitled him to profoundest homage. In this new mood Melville began writing passages relevant only to himself, not to the Pierre he had so consistently characterized in the Saddle Meadows books:

> in the inferior instances of an immediate literary success, in very young writers, it will be almost invariably observable, that for that instant success they were chiefly indebted to some rich and peculiar experience in life, embodied in a book, which because, for that cause, containing original matter, the author himself, forsooth, is to be considered original; in this way, many very original books, being the product of very unoriginal minds.

This section from Book 18 is remarkable as self-analysis, as Melville's own objective sense of why *Typee* had become so popular and what its ultimate worth was, but it is wholly irrelevant to Pierre, who had had no such rich and peculiar experience and who (we are belatedly and distractingly told) had embodied whatever experiences he had had in magazines, not in a book. As he progressed with his expansions, Melville more and more perverted his manuscript into an outlet for his personal anxieties about his career.

Aware that Melville was recalling aspects of his own literary career in Books 17 and 18 of *Pierre*, many modern critics have taken for granted that what the reviewers say of young Pierre is either very like or else patently the opposite of what real reviewers had said of Melville's *Typee, Omoo, Mardi, Redburn, White-Jacket,* and *Moby-Dick*. That turns out not to be altogether accurate. When the phrases attributed to Pierre's critics are compared with the known reviews of Melville's first six books, it becomes obvious that in Book 17 Melville was not reacting *generally* to the reviews of all six of these books (or to a certain segment of them, such as those in religious periodicals).[49] Rather, he was reacting *specifically* to the reviews of his latest book, *Moby-Dick*. Lewis Mumford's impression in 1929 was partly right:[50] it *was* the reviews of *Moby-Dick* which Melville was reacting to, but *not* at the time he conceived and began *Pierre*; rather, his reaction came only during or after his trip to New York, when the manuscript was already thought of as nearly or actually complete. One cannot safely point to particular reviews which Melville must have read before he wrote Book 17, but among the most conspicuous American reviews of *Moby-Dick* and those British reviews of *The Whale* most likely to have reached New York by early January, Melville could have seen many examples of the phrases which he satirizes in *Pierre*. He twists them one way or another for his immediate satirical ends, but the words are readily found in the reviews of *Moby-Dick* as they are *not* found in reviews of his earlier books.[51]

Where Pierre was complimented for *his surprising command of language*, Melville had just been praised for his "mastery over language and its resources" (the *Examiner* [London]), condemned for ravings "meant for eloquent declamation" (the *Southern Quarterly Review* [Charleston]), and denounced for his "rhetorical artifice," "bad rhetoric," and "incoherent English" (the *Democratic Review* [New York]). Where Pierre was commended for *his euphonious construction of sentences*, a reviewer had just condemned Melville for his "involved syntax" (the *Democratic Review*). Where Pierre was praised for *the pervading symmetry of his general style*, Melville had just been praised for his "bold and impulsive style" (*Harper's New Monthly Magazine*, [New York]), tolerated for his "happy carelessness of style" (the *Hartford Daily Courant*) and his "quaint though interesting style" (the *Springfield Republican*), blamed for a style "disfigured by mad (rather than bad) English" (the *Athenaeum* [London]), for his "unbridled extravagance" (the *Atlas* [London]), and for his "eccentricity" in style (the *Britannia* [London]). There is a possibility that by mid-January Melville might have seen a reproach for his not adhering to "the unchanging principles of the truthful and the symmetrical" (the *Morning Chronicle* [London]). While Pierre's writings were praised for *highly judicious smoothness and genteelness of the sentiments and fancies*, Melville had just been condemned for his "forced," "inflated," and "stilted" sentiment (the *Democratic Review*) and for allowing his fancy "not only to run riot, but absolutely to run amuck" (the *Atlas* [London]). Where Pierre was *characterized throughout by Perfect Taste*, Melville had just been condemned for "harassing manifestations of bad taste" (the *Athenaeum*) and for "many violations of good taste and delicacy" (the *New York Churchman*), and called (by Evert Duyckinck) "reckless at times of taste and propriety" (the *Literary World* [New York]) and called also the author of scenes which neither "good taste nor good morals can approve" (the *Washington National Intelligencer*). A reviewer said that Pierre *never permits himself to astonish; is never betrayed into any thing coarse or new; as assured that whatever astonishes is vulgar, and whatever is new must be crude.* Reviewers had just praised Melville himself for his "original genius" and "wildness of conception" (the *Atlas* [London]), for "genuine" evidence of "originality" (the *Leader* [London]), and for his "lawless flights, which put all regular criticism at defiance" (the *New York Daily Tribune*). A critic had just found Melville's materials seemingly very "uncouth" and the Americanisms of *The Whale* charming, although the book might not fall within "the ordinary canons of beauty" (*John Bull* [London]). A reviewer also had found that Melville evinced "originality and freshness in his matter" (the *Worcester Palladium*). A critic declared that *vulgarity and vigor—two inseparable adjuncts—*were *equally removed* from Pierre. Reviewers had just condemned Melville for " 'a too much vigour,' as Dryden has it" in the earlier books but unsurpassed "vigour, originality, and interest" in *The Whale* (the *Morning Herald* [London]), or praised him for "vigor of style" (the *National Intelligencer*), even while condemning him for "vulgar immoralities" (the *Methodist Quarterly Review* [New York]). A clerical reviewer declared that Pierre was *blameless in morals, and harmless throughout,* while real critics had just condemned Melville's "irreverence" (the *Albany Argus*), his "irreverence and profane jesting" (the *Worcester Palladium*), his frequent "profaneness" and occasional "indelicacies" (the *Boston Daily Evening Traveller*), and his "insinuating licentiousness" (the *Democratic Review*), or else deplored his "primitive formation of profanity and indecency" (the *New York Independent*). A religious critic declared that *the predominant end and aim* of Pierre *was evangelical piety*. Melville had just been denounced by clerical critics or pious lay reviewers for his "heathenish, and worse than heathenish talk" and "occasional thrusts against revealed religion" (*John Bull*), for "sneering at the truths of revealed religion" (*New York Commerical Advertiser*), for "a number of flings at religion" (the *Methodist Quarterly Review*), and for "irreligion and profanity" and "sneers at revealed religion and the burlesquing of sacred passages of Holy Writ" (the *Churchman*).[52] Similar parallels abound: these are offered as readily available comments from the reviews and not necessarily the particular comments which Melville read, though he certainly read some of them in New York City as he worked his injured pride and his fears for his career into the outlet most readily available, the story that had been about Pierre Glendinning.

Melville had greatly expanded his manuscript but not completed his alterations when he left for Pittsfield around the third week of January. During that same week, perhaps before Melville left town, Allan first told the publishers that the book would be longer than planned. Before 21 January the Harpers considered the changed length and told Allan that the prospective price would be raised from $1 to $1.25.[53] These minor details are established by the same document which conclusively dates both the drawing-up of the contract and Melville's crucial decision to enlarge the book—Allan's letter to Harper & Brothers on 21 January 1852.[54] The awkward phrasing of the letter is obviously the result of its having been designed to reconfirm in writing a change already agreed upon as well as to remind the publishers of two other necessary changes:

> My brother would like to have his account with your house to the 1st
> Feby made up and ready to render to me, as near that date as will be con-
> venient to you[.]
> Respecting "Pierre" the contract provides that if the book exceeded 360

pages a corresponding addition should be made to the number of copies required to liquidate the cost of the stereotype plates &c, for a book of that size [.] As the book exceeds that number of pages it will of course be necessary to ascertain how many more copies are to be allowed than provided by the contract for a book of 360 pages. The retail price of the book has been also raised beyond the price fixed by the agreement, which was one dollar & of course a corresponding increase per copy should be made to the author.

In this letter the agreement is spoken of as a thing thoroughly settled: "the contract provides. . . ." The letter also establishes the *sequence* of the events already outlined; the coming to terms on a contract for a shortish book, Melville's subsequent decision to enlarge it, his actual composition of many pages beyond the original estimate ("the book exceeds that number"), and Allan's consultation with the Harpers over the change (the obvious reason for the "retail price" being "raised" is to accommodate the new length).

The contract with Harper & Brothers was signed on 20 February. At that time the publisher paid Melville (presumably through Allan) $500, of which two-fifths was already due him from royalties on earlier books (mainly from recent sales of *Moby-Dick*) and three-fifths was an advance on Pierre.[55] In the copy of the contract Allan kept for Herman the interlineation of "or addition" after "deduction" ("it is agreed that a corresponding deduction shall be made") looks like someone's dawning realization, as late as 20 February, that the book might in fact run longer than 360 pages, but in fact the omission of "or addition" was simply a lapse, for the provision had been agreed to, some seven weeks before, and whoever copied the contract properly incorporated the preceding contingency pair ("much less or much more") and the subsequent ("from or to").[56] On 16 April, while visiting New York with Elizabeth after vacationing with her in Boston, Melville was able to send his English publisher, Richard Bentley, a set of the corrected proofs—that is, not merely first proofs with errors marked for correction but later proofs, pulled after the standing type had been corrected. Judging from the time they had taken with *Omoo, Mardi,* and *Redburn,* the Harpers probably needed the entire period between 20 February and mid-April to set the book and provide Melville with "perfect proof."[57]

Sometime between very late December and early February 1852 Melville had offered his English publisher, Richard Bentley, a book about the length of his original estimate to the Harpers. Presumably he wrote Bentley by early January, before deciding to enlarge the manuscript. (One can be sure that the estimate was around the Harper estimate of 360 pages because when Melville sent Bentley the Harper proofs on 16 April 1852—eight pages in roman numerals and 495 in arabic—he wrote: "It is a larger book, by 150 pages & more, than I thought it would be, at the date of my first writing you about it."[58]) If Melville did write Bentley in early January, Bentley was unusually slow in responding: the reply was mailed half-finished on 3 March 1852, so that an apologetic follow-up letter had to be written the next day.[59] There is no way of proving that the offer to Bentley did not take place in late January or very early February, except for the ridiculousness of supposing that Melville knowingly made an out-of-date page estimate, but the offer could not have been made after mid-February, for it normally took seventeen to nineteen days for letters to cross the Atlantic between Melville and Bentley.

In his 4 March letter Bentley reported a loss of £453.4.6 (which "may be lessened in the end by 100") on *Mardi, Redburn, White-Jacket*, and *The Whale*. Melville's books, Bentley feared, were "produced in too rapid succession," and he suggested that the new book be put into his hands "to publish on our joint account; I yielding to you half the profits as they arise." In his letter of 16 April accompanying the Harper "perfect proof" Melville rejected Bentley's terms on the grounds that his previous books might continue to sell and that the success of a new book might also increase their sales; "more especially" he was "impelled to decline those overtures" on the grounds that his new book possessed "unquestionable novelty," compared to his former ones, "treating of utterly new scenes & characters," and, he believed, "very much more calculated for popularity than anything you have yet published of mine—being a regular romance, with a mysterious plot to it, & stirring passions at work, and withall, representing a new & elevated aspect of American life." After offering Bentley the book "for England—out-&-out" for £100 "to be drawn for by me at thirty days' sight, immediately upon my being apprised of your acquiescence," Melville suggested that it be published anonymously "or under an assumed name:—'*By a Vermonter*' say" or (as he added in a footnote) "*By Guy Winthrop*"; several reasons, he said, had prompted this idea, one of them "the rapid succession" in which his books had "lately been published."[60]

After seeing the Harper proofs, Bentley offered on 5 May 1852 to publish *Pierre* at half profits, with no advance, provided that Melville gave him "permission to make or have made by a judicious literary friend" such alterations as were "absolutely necessary" to the book's being "properly appreciated" in England.[61] Melville must not have accepted, for no Bentley edition was published, and the only circulation *Pierre* had in England during Melville's lifetime was in the form of a few copies of the Harper sheets bound with a Sampson, Low cancel title leaf. According to the contract the Harpers were free to publish *Pierre* any time after mid-July, and in fact advance copies were available late that month, although the official publication date was 6 August.

Melville probably did not admit to himself until late in the composition of *Pierre* that he might fail in his attempt to make the book both popular and profound, but in Book 26 the accusatory letter from Pierre's publishers, Steel, Flint, & Asbestos, can hardly be construed as anything but Melville's self-accusation: "SIR:—You are a swindler. Upon the pretense of writing a popular novel for us, you have been receiving cash advances from us, while passing through our press the sheets of a blasphemous rhapsody, filched from the vile Atheists, Lucian and Voltaire." His self-accusatory mood may, nonetheless, have lasted only a short time, and he may even have passed out of it before he finished the book. In the months between the completion of the book and its publication nothing in his recorded behavior suggests that he was weighed down by a sense of guilt and trepidation. Soon after the proofs were sent to Bentley in mid-April, Melville returned with Elizabeth to Pittsfield and the farm work which kept him constantly out of doors for many weeks. During this time it became clear that he had drastically misjudged what Bentley, for one, might be willing to accept, and that he would have to forgo the income from the sale of his book to an English publisher. But whatever Melville's immediate reaction to this fresh blow to his career, by mid-summer he had sufficiently recovered from any lingering self-destructive tendencies of the kind which had marred *Pierre* to be planning in some detail a new literary venture of a remarkably different kind and temper.

In early July, Melville's father-in-law, Judge Shaw, held court in Nantucket, and invited Melville to accompany him, perhaps with a view to his obtaining literary material from the whalingmen he wanted him to meet at Nantucket and New Bedford.[62] During their tour Melville apparently talked little, if at all, about *Pierre*, though he may have expressed his "hopes & expectations" for it.[63] On their travels he seemed unusually serene, inscribing in a guest register on July 13: "Sweet shall be the memory of Naushon," and adding: "Blue sky—blue sea—& almost every thing blue but our spirits."[64] As Shaw reported on July 20, "Melville expressed himself extremely well pleased with the excursion, he saw many things & met with many people, whom he was extremely glad to see."[65] By mid-August all the Judge knew of *Pierre* was that it evidently did not "relate to incidents, or characters, connected with the sea"—information public in Boston since the *Transcript* notice on August 2.[66]

At Pittsfield an advance copy of Hawthorne's *The Blithedale Romance* was waiting when Melville returned on July 16, and the following day he received an invitation to visit Hawthorne in Concord. He excused himself on grounds of his not having written anything for months: "I am but just returned from a two weeks' absence; and for the last three months & more I have been an utter idler and a savage—out of doors all the time. So, the hour has come for me to sit down again."[67] What he planned to "sit down" to write was the story of Agatha Hatch which he had heard in Nantucket. He had not at first thought of "making literary use" of this tale of patience and resignation—qualities so antithetical to those of the heroes of his last two books—but he found himself turning the subject over in his mind "with a view to a regular story" to be founded on the "striking incidents" he had heard of. By August 13 Melville had decided that the Nantucket story was after all more appropriate for Hawthorne than himself, and in a letter offered his friend the raw material and a good deal of his own elaborations on it; on the same day he sent Hawthorne a copy of *Pierre*.[68] Whatever immediate comment Hawthorne may have made about *Pierre* does not survive, and for his part Melville ignored *Pierre* in his surviving letters to Hawthorne that fall.

Apparently neither Melville nor his family were prepared for the overwhelmingly hostile reception of *Pierre*. Both reviews and defamatory news items (such as the one in the New York *Day Book* headlined "HERMAN MELVILLE CRAZY") traduced the book as literary monstrosity and outrage to public morality—and were often explicitly worded so as to discourage its sales.[69] Their influence was reflected in the account the Harpers sent to Melville on March 21, 1853: of the 2,310 copies printed, 1,423 had been sold—a figure which includes whatever sets of the American sheets Sampson, Low, the Harpers' London agent, bought for sale in England. Melville's royalty (25 cents each on the 233 copies sold after the sale of the first 1,190) thus amounted to only $58.25 (so that at this time, because of the $500 given him on 20 February 1852, he still owed his publishers $298.71, even with credit from his other works). By October 6, 1854, 133 more copies had been sold, but the next twelve years brought sales of only another 139; between 1854 and 1887, the year of the Harpers' last report, exactly 300 copies were sold.[70]

We have Mrs. Melville's word, in a letter of 20 September 1901, that the reception of *Pierre* had no part in causing Melville to lead a reclusive life: "in fact it was a subject of joke with him, declaring that it was but just, and I know that however it might have affected his literary reputation, it concerned him personally but very little."[71] Melville's joking, however, must have concealed misery, just as Mrs. Melville's comments are a brave attempt to put the best face toward the world. Melville's real response to the reviews and the disastrously low sales can better be surmised from his comment in *The Confidence-Man* (chapter 33) that "so precious to man is the approbation of his kind, that to rest, though but under an imaginary censure applied to but a work of imagination, is no easy thing." Yet bitter as it undoubtedly was for Melville to rest under the very real censures applied to *Pierre*, the practical consequences of the reviews and the low sales they influenced must have been equally galling. Melville had already defaulted on his interest payments to T.D. Stewart; following the disastrous reception of *Pierre*, he continued to default.[72] Still more serious were the consequences for Melville's literary career, which can be gauged by his failure to publish the book-length manuscript presumably made out of the "Agatha" story (after Hawthorne had urged him to use the material himself),[73] his failure to complete the book of "Tortoise Hunting Adventure" he offered the Harpers in November 1853 and was advanced $300 for in December 1853,[74] and his beginning to concentrate on writing stories for magazine publication rather than book-length works. After the calamitous reception of *Pierre*, the publication and even the planning of bold new advances beyond his previous accomplishments were out of the question for Melville. That ambitious phase of his career was ended.

The hostility of the contemporary reviewers toward *Pierre* clearly influenced the way later readers perceived the book and was echoed in the brief comments it elicited during the remainder of Melville's lifetime and even the first quarter of the twentieth century.[75] After the more thoughtful of the condemnatory reviews, serious discussion of *Pierre* scarcely began till the late 1920s. There was much new ground to explore. With considerable verve and humor, the contemporary reviewers had derided Melville's moral and aesthetic failings, but otherwise they had signally neglected to discuss or even mention crucial parts of *Pierre*. Only three had briefly alluded (with horror) to its central incestuous situation, and only one had mentioned the chapter on "Chronometricals and Horologicals." Presumably out of self-protection, none of the reviewers had mentioned Melville's satire on mid-nineteenth-century publishing and reviewing practices; and none had commented on the powerful passages dealing with Pierre's immature attempt to write profoundly and his Enceladus vision. None had seen *Pierre* as an attempt to extend the domain of romance by employing the form to investigate the subtlest workings of not only a complex individual mind but of the mind in general; and, appalled as they were by the book as a whole, none had perceived how Melville had marred his ambitious design by his decision to air his own preoccupation with the perils entailed in "authorship that is high." To readers after the *Moby-Dick* revival of the early 1920s was left the arduous and exhilarating enterprise of uncovering the awesome, though mutilated, features of an American literary Enceladus.

Brian Higgins
Hershel Parker

Notes

1. This introduction incorporates material in Parker, "Why *Pierre* Went Wrong," *Studies in the Novel*, 8 (Spring 1976), 7–23, and "Contract: *Pierre*, by Herman Melville," *Proof*, 5 (1977), 27–44.

2. [Abel Stevens] "The Editor's Table," *National Magazine*, (New York) 2 (January 1853), 88.

3. John Freeman, *Herman Melville* (London: Macmillan and Co., 1926), p. 111; Lewis Mumford, *Herman Melville* (New York: Harcourt, Brace & Co., 1929), p. 209.

4. "Introduction," *Pierre; or, The Ambiguities* (New York: Hendricks House, Inc., 1949), p. xiv.

5. Newton Arvin, *Herman Melville* (New York: William Sloane Associates, 1950), p. 226; Warner Berthoff, *The Example of Melville* (Princeton: Princeton University Press, 1962), p. 51; Edwin Haviland Miller, *Melville* (New York: George Braziller, Inc., 1975), p. 231.

6. "Melville's *Pierre,*" *New England Quarterly,* 3 (April 1930), 195–234.

7. See Merton M. Sealts, Jr., "A Hermit's Reputation," in *The Early Lives of Melville: Nineteenth-Century Biographical Sketches and Their Authors* (Madison: University of Wisconsin Press, 1974), pp. 20–38.

8. See Hershel Parker, "Historical Note," in *Pierre; or, The Ambiguities,* ed. Harrison Hayford, Hershel Parker, and G. Thomas Tanselle (Evanston and Chicago: Northwestern University Press and The Newberry Library, 1971), pp. 379–80 [hereafter "*Pierre*"].

9. Information in this paragraph is derived mainly from Jay Leyda, *The Melville Log: A Documentary Life of Herman Melville, 1819–1891,* 2 vols. (1951; rpt., With a New Supplementary Chapter, New York: Gordian Press, 1969), I, 410, 420, 428, 438 [hereafter "*Log*"]. In "Two New Melville Letters," *American Literature,* 49 (November 1977), 418–21, Patricia Barber identified the "T.D.S." long known to have made the loan of $2050 to Melville. For details of Melville's earlier contracts see the various "Historical Notes" in the Northwestern-Newberry Edition and for details of his contracts for *Moby-Dick* and *The Whale* see Harrison Hayford, "Contract: *Moby-Dick,* by Herman Melville," *Proof,* 1 (1971), iii–vi, 1–7.

10. *The Letters of Herman Melville,* ed. Merrell R. Davis and William H. Gilman (New Haven: Yale University Press, 1960), pp. 128–30 [hereafter "*Letters*"].

11. *Letters,* p. 132.

12. Letter to Hawthorne, 22 July 1851 (*Letters,* p. 135).

13. *Letters,* p. 138.

14. See his letter to Evert Duyckinck, 7 November 1851 (*Letters,* p. 141), where he writes that he has had his "dressing-gown patched up, & got some wood in the wood-house"— plainly a reference to his chores preparatory to writing and to his actual or figurative writing costume.

15. See Merton M. Sealts, Jr., *Melville's Reading: A Check-List of Books Owned and Borrowed* (Madison: University of Wisconsin Press, 1966), p. 86 (No. 407), and *Log,* I, 315, 350.

16. *Log,* I, 383.

17. *Letters,* p. 117.

18. *Letters,* p. 130.

19. See *Letters,* pp. 119–20, for Melville's echo of Duyckinck's phrase and his own bluff refusal of the request.

20. See Melville's letters to Richard Bentley, 19 June 1847[?]; to John Murray, 29 October 1847, 1 January 1848, 25 March 1848; and to Richard Bentley, 5 June 1849 and 27 June 1850. (*Letters,* pp. 64, 66, 68, 71, 86, 109.)

21. See Melville's letter to Evert Duyckinck, 5 April 1849, where he writes, in reference to *Mardi* and works as yet unwritten: "live & push—tho' we put one leg forward ten miles—its no reason the other must lag behind—no, *that* must again distance the other"; and his letter to Lemuel Shaw, 6 October 1849, where he refers to *Redburn* and *White-Jacket* as "two *jobs,* which I have done for money—being forced to it, as other men are to sawing wood." (*Letters,* pp. 83, 91.)

22. "Hawthorne and His Mosses," in *The Norton Anthology of American Literature,* 2 vols., ed. Ronald Gottesman et al. (New York: W.W. Norton & Co., 1979), I, 2064. (The Melville section is edited by Hershel Parker.) Pending publication of volume 9 of the Northwestern-Newberry Edition of Melville, this text of "Hawthorne and His Mosses" is the best version available.

23. *Letters,* p. 143.

24. *Letters,* p. 150.

25. *Pierre,* p. 12.

26. See, in this volume, Amy Puett Emmers, "Melville's Closet Skeleton: "New Cross-lights on the Illegitimate Daughter in *Pierre*," pp. 237–240.

27. "Hawthorne and His Mosses," pp. 2061, 2067. In his letter of 8 January 1852 to Sophia Hawthorne, Melville claimed that Hawthorne's letter of mid-November 1851, by in-timating to him "the part-&-parcel allegoricalness of the whole," had altered the way he thought about *Moby-Dick* (*Letters*, p. 146). As Harrison Hayford pointed out in "The Signifi-cance of Melville's 'Agatha' Letters," *ELH*, 13 (December 1946), 299–310, Melville had already developed a theory that great works of literature could be simultaneously popular and profound, appealing to the masses while being truly understood only by a select few. Still, Hawthorne's special insight into *Moby-Dick* may have affected Melville's attitude toward *Pierre*: he would—this time by conscious design—work on dual levels, producing a book com-prehensible and salable as a regular romance with stirring passions at work yet susceptible of profounder interpretation by readers such as Hawthorne, whose understanding of *Moby-Dick* had given him a "sense of unspeakable security" (*Letters*, p. 142).

28. See, for example, *Letters*, pp. 137–38, 166–67, 168, 303.

29. There are good accounts of what Evert Duyckinck called Mrs. Morewood's "maelstrom of Hospitality." See especially Luther Stearns Mansfield, "Glimpses of Herman Melville's Life in Pittsfield, 1850–1851: Some Unpublished Letters of Evert A. Duyckinck," *American Literature*, 9 (March 1937), 26–48; Leon Howard, *Herman Melville: A Biography* (Berkeley: University of California Press, 1951), chapters 7 and 8; and Eleanor Melville Met-calf, *Herman Melville: Cycle and Epicycle* (Cambridge: Harvard University Press, 1953), chapter 8. Good coverage of Melville's socializing in October and November 1851, before and after the birth of his son Stanwix, is in Metcalf, pp. 125–26.

30. Godfrey Greylock [J.E.A. Smith], *Taghconic: or Letters and Legends about Our Summer Home* (Boston: Redding and Co., 1852), pp. 42–43, reprinted in Sealts's *The Early Lives of Melville*, p. 195. Published about the end of September 1852, Smith's account was written before he read *Pierre*; otherwise, having mentioned Melville's use of the Pittsfield Elm in *Moby-Dick*, he would surely have mentioned the use of the Balanced Rock in Book 7, as he did in the short biography he wrote for the *Pittsfield Sun* after Melville's death. See, in this volume, pp. 83–85.

31. A striking instance of the fusion of outer and inner landscape is the start of Book 6, "Isabel, and the First Part of the Story of Isabel."

32. *Letters*, p. 139.

33. *Letters*, p. 143.

34. This letter is in *Log*, I, 441 and in Metcalf, p. 133. The passage here is quoted from Metcalf, since the *Log* wrongly omits "so" before "engaged." Later Melville might fairly have been described as a recluse, but the raillery in this letter can be appreciated only if one keeps in mind Sarah Morewood's compulsive socializing.

Earlier in this letter is a passage which ominously parallels the response many reviewers had toward *Moby-Dick* and which suggests that the climate of opinion in the Berkshires may have triggered Melville's aggressiveness toward conventional Christianity in *Pierre*: "Mr. Her-man was more quiet than usual—still he is a pleasant companion at all times and I like him very much—Mr. Morewood now that he knows him better likes him the more—still he dislikes many of Mr. Hermans opinions and religious views—It is a pity that Mr. Melville so often in conversation uses irreverent language—he will not be popular in society here on that account—but this will not trouble him—I think he cares very little as to what others may think of him or his books so long as they sell well—"

35. See *Log*, 467–68.

36. For proof of how short Melville then thought the city section would be, see the following two paragraphs. In visualizing the proportions of *Pierre* it helps to recall that in the Harper edition "The Journey and the Pamphlet" starts on p. 277; Melville anticipated a com-

pleted book of approximately 360 pages, but the last page of the text is p. 495. We are assuming that the Saddle Meadows section was composed pretty much in the final order, or at least that Melville made few additions to it during the last weeks of his work on the book.

37. Metcalf, p. 134. *Log*, I, 443, erroneously prints "Were you surprised. . . ."

38. *Herman Melville: A Biography*, p. 186. The best attempt to trace Melville's movements in late December 1851 and January 1852 is in the *Letters*, pp. 347–48, the editors' note to Melville's letter to Evert Duyckinck conjecturally dated 9 January 1852. Normally precise, Davis and Gilman were not proof against the complexities of this period in Melville's life. The Morewoods did not return to New York on 29 December, as the editors say; they stayed on at Pittsfield for the New Year and returned on Monday, 5 January. (Paul R. Rugen, Keeper of Manuscripts, the New York Public Library, who kindly checked the variants mentioned in footnotes 34 and 37, pointed out to Parker that Mrs. Morewood altered the date of her letter to George Duyckinck from 4 to 5 January. Perhaps she began it in Pittsfield and finished it in New York.) Mrs. Morewood did not expect to see Elizabeth Melville in New York on 5 January, as Davis and Gilman say. Knowing Mrs. Morewood's need for company, one can guess that her mention of remaining "quietly indoors" ever since her arrival on Monday places her at midweek (she clearly finished the letter later than the 5th): probably the following "evening" she hoped to pass with Elizabeth was the eighth or ninth, which would still allow Elizabeth time to reach Boston by the tenth. Also, it was not Elizabeth's brother who recorded her presence with her children in Boston, but her sister-in-law. Furthermore, Melville's saying to Duyckinck that he was "engaged to go out of town tomorrow" does not mean he left for Pittsfield at the same time his wife went to Boston: the note specifies that he was going out of town only for the day. (Maybe he accompanied her and the boys to Boston, then returned immediately to New York.) Finally, "9 December" is a typo for "9 January," and 21 January 1852 fell on a Wednesday, not a Friday! Despite its appealing terseness, the account of this period in the *Letters* has to be disregarded.

We still know very little of what Melville did in town aside from the crucial business dealings discussed below. He gave a copy of *Moby-Dick* to his friend Dr. Robert Tomes on the fifth (see the Supplement to the revised edition of the *Log*, II, 930), wrote Mrs. Hawthorne on the eighth, and wrote Evert Duyckinck on the ninth, apparently, to say that he would be out of town all the next day: "I will be glad to call though at some other time—not very remote in the future, either." (*Letters*, pp. 147–48.) It is quite possible that Melville ensconced himself to work on *Pierre* in the same third-story room (presumably at Allan's) where he had labored on *Moby-Dick* a few months before.

39. *Letters*, pp. 145–47.

40. See Brian Higgins, *Herman Melville: An Annotated Bibliography, Volume I: 1846–1930* (Boston: G.K. Hall & Co., 1979), p. 115 (B21).

41. *Letters*, p. 148.

42. These draft pages of the contract and Allan's letter of 21 January 1852 to the Harpers and the contract itself, discussed below, are in the Houghton Library (MH).

43. See the survey in Hayford, "Contract: *Moby-Dick*, by Herman Melville," pp. 1–7.

44. Hayford explains (p. 3): "For *Omoo* and *Mardi*, 125 review copies were to be charged to joint account; for *Redburn* and *White-Jacket*, the contracts specify that 25 of these were to be turned over to Melville; for *The Whale* and *Pierre*, there is no provision at all for review copies"; actually, while no number of review copies for *Pierre* is specified in the contract, provision for "editors copies" is made. A comprehensive survey of Melville's income from his writing is in G. Thomas Tanselle, "The Sales of Melville's Books," *Harvard Library Bulletin*, 17 (April 1969), 195–215.

45. *Letters*, pp. 130 and 141–42.

46. Melville's compulsion to work his new preoccupations into the manuscript at the cost of lengthening it was at war with his best pecuniary interests. He had reason for thinking that every few pages he added beyond 360 would cause the Harpers to add several copies to the

number they had to sell before he began accruing royalties. If the Harpers were to hold him to the letter of the contract, Melville probably realized, the more he wrote the more he would lose. As it turned out, they did not do so. In *Pierre*, the "Historical Note," p. 378, Leon Howard explains: "Although the contract provided for an increase or decrease in the number of copies required to pay the cost of stereotyping if the book was not of the estimated length, and although a large number of copies (150) were given away, the publishers only claimed the first 1,190 for costs. It was probably a just claim in view of the increased retail price, but, within the terms of the contract, they could have claimed the proceeds from 400 more . . . ."

47. See *Letters*, pp. 120–21, and *Pierre*, pp. 253–54.

48. *Letters*, p. 149. See *Letters*, pp. 122–23, for the reason Melville was uncertain of the address of his old friend Fly.

49. Melville might seem to be recalling the Protestant clerical and lay attacks on *Typee* and *Omoo* in satirizing the clerical compliments paid to Pierre's effusions, and perhaps he is; but even here the language attributed to the fictional reviewers is best seen as precisely the reverse of what was being said of *Moby-Dick*. For quotations from the reviews of Melville's first five books we are still dependent on the *Log* and, especially, Hugh W. Hetherington's unreliable *Melville's Reviewers: British and American, 1846–1891* (Chapel Hill: University of North Carolina Press, 1961), though certain reviews have been reprinted in Hershel Parker, *The Recognition of Herman Melville* (Ann Arbor: University of Michigan Press, 1967) and still more in Watson G. Branch, *Melville: The Critical Heritage* (London and Boston: Routledge & Kegan Paul, 1974). Melville's contemporary reception is also discussed in each of the Northwestern-Newberry Edition's "Historical Notes."

50. *Herman Melville*, pp. 198–200.

51. The quotations in the next paragraph are representative of many that Melville could have seen during his stay in New York City. They do *not* constitute a representative sampling of the range of commentary on *Moby-Dick*, however; Melville was ignoring many points the reviewers were making, especially anything said in praise. The quotations may readily be located in *MOBY-DICK as Doubloon*, ed. Hershel Parker and Harrison Hayford (New York: W.W. Norton & Co., 1970), or (in the case of quotations from the *New York Independent* and *New York Churchman*) in Hershel Parker, "Five Reviews not in *MOBY-DICK as Doubloon*," *English Language Notes*, (March 1972), 182–85. The quotation from *Harper's New Monthly Magazine* is not from the review in the December issue but the commentary on the British reception in the January issue.

52. These accusations, however well grounded, would probably have caused anguish in any household in the country. The anguish in the Melville household may have been intensified by the memory that Elizabeth's father, Lemuel Shaw, the Chief Justice of the Massachusetts Supreme Court, had been the last judge to sentence a man to jail for blasphemy in that state. At the sentencing of Abner Kneeland in 1838 Shaw had offered this as the legal definition of blasphemy: "speaking evil of the Deity with an impious purpose to derogate from the divine majesty, and to alienate the minds of others from the love and reverence of God. It is purposely using words concerning God, calculated and designed to impair and destroy the reverence, respect, and confidence due to him . . . . It is a wilful and malicious attempt to lessen men's reverence of God." (See Leonard W. Levy, *The Law of the Commonwealth and Chief Justice Shaw* [Cambridge: Harvard University Press, 1957], p. 52.)

53. More precisely, the Harpers told Allan that the price would be raised. Presumably they raised it at once to the final price, $1.25. The contract did not have to be redrafted since it contained sliding clauses to cover any such eventuality.

54. Leyda describes this letter in *Log*, I, 445 as Allan Melville's "adjusting the details of the contract for *Pierre*," and quotes the opening words about rendering an account as of 1 February. Leyda may not fully have realized the letter's significance in dating the composition of *Pierre*, and Howard and Parker in preparing the "Historical Note" for the Northwestern-Newberry Edition neglected to question Leyda's description of it or to obtain a

copy. Lacking the complete letter, Howard, the author of section one of the Note, assumed that Melville made a wholesale enlargement after the contract was signed on 20 February 1852.

55. See the "Historical Note" in *Pierre*, p. 379. (Hershel Parker is the author of sections two through four of the Note.)

56. See above for full quotation from this part of the contract.

57. More than six weeks elapsed between Melville's signing the contract for *Omoo* and his sending the proofs to England; the *Mardi* proofs took over ten weeks after the contract was signed; for *Redburn* more than six weeks elapsed between contract and complete proofs; anomalously, proofs of *White-Jacket* seem to have preceded the signing of the contract. (See *Log*, I, 230, 234, 283, 287, 308, 311, 312, 313.) In the United States *Typee* was published by Wiley & Putnam; later Harper & Brothers bought the plates. Melville hired Robert Craighead to stereotype *Moby-Dick* before he negotiated the contract with the Harpers. (See *Moby-Dick*, ed. Harrison Hayford and Hershel Parker [New York: W.W. Norton & Co., 1967], pp. 473–75.)

58. *Letters*, p. 150. Deducting 150 pages and more from around 500 leaves something under 350. It is wrong to try to be precise, since Melville's arithmetic was usually hit-or-miss. He had surely given Bentley about the same figure he gave Allan and the Harpers at year's end or very early January. Of course, it is a simplification to say that Melville added about 150 pages to his manuscript: he must have condensed some sections already planned or actually written, and he may have completed others in altered, if not shortened, form.

59. See Bernard R. Jerman, " 'With Real Admiration': More Correspondence Between Melville and Bentley," *American Literature*, 25 (November 1953), 311.

60. *Letters*, pp. 150–51.

61. Jerman, p. 313. During the weeks Melville spent enlarging the manuscript he must have been conscious that a deadline was approaching—1 May 1852, when an interest payment was due on his loan from T.D. Stewart. As it turned out, his delay left him still involved in negotiations with Bentley (and still hoping to secure £100 for the English rights) when the day passed and he defaulted on the payment. (See Patricia Barber, "Two New Melville Letters," *American Literature*, 49 [November 1977], 418–21.)

62. See *Log*, I, 451.

63. See *Log*, I, 457.

64. See *Log*, I, 453.

65. *Log*, I, 453.

66. See *Log*, I, 457, and p. 31 in this volume.

67. *Letters*, p. 153.

68. *Letters*, pp. 153–61; *Log*, I, 457.

69. See *Pierre*, "Historical Note," pp. 379–92, for discussion (and synopsis) of the book's reception.

70. *Pierre*, "Historical Note," pp. 379, 393.

71. Mrs. Melville's letter, to Mrs. Mary L.D. Ferris, is printed in Dorothy V.B.D.R. McNeilly, "The Melvilles and Mrs. Ferris," *Extracts*, No. 28 (November 1976), p. 6.

72. See footnote 61 and Barber, pp. 418–19.

73. See Melville's letter of late November 1852 to Hawthorne, *Letters*, pp. 162–63. On April 20, 1853, Melville's mother wrote to Peter Gansevoort that Melville was "completely absorbed by his new work, now nearly ready for the press" (*Log*, I, 468); and in his letter of 24 November 1853 to the Harpers Melville makes references to "the work which I took to New York last Spring, but which I was prevented from printing at that time" (*Letters*, p. 164). In the spring of 1853 the Harpers may well have declined the offer of a new book by Melville so soon after their embarrassment with *Pierre*.

74. See *Letters*, pp. 164–65.
75. See *Pierre*, "Historical Note," pp. 393–96.

Section one of the following collection contains all of the known contemporary reviews of *Pierre* (1852); section two contains virtually all of the known commentary on the book from 1853 to 1917, a period in which critics routinely neglected or abused it; section three contains most of the known commentaries, in their entirety or in large extract, from 1919 to 1929, a period in which critics were finally awakening to a sense of the book's importance, even if they were morally and aesthetically repelled by it. In section four, which covers the period from 1930 to the present, we have been more selective, including only pieces which we believe have enhanced understanding and appreciation of the book. (One omission we deeply regret: we originally planned to include extracts from Henry A. Murray's "Introduction" to the Hendricks House edition of *Pierre* [1949] but were unable to secure permission.) At the end of the fourth section we have included a brief prospectus for future scholarship and criticism on *Pierre*.

BH
HP

REVIEWS

New York Herald

29 July 1852

In fiction, Herman Melville has a new book, "Pierre, or the Ambiguities," in which it is understood that he has dressed up and exhibited in Berkshire, where he is living, some of the ancient and most repulsive inventions of the George Walker and Anne Radcliffe sort—desperate passion at first sight, for a young woman who turns out to be the hero's sister, &c., &c., &c. It is conceded that Mr. Melville has written himself out. The book is advertised by the Harpers.

Albany Evening Journal

31 July 1852

HERMAN MELVILLE has been again giving vein to his fine fancy. "Pierre" is an attractive character, and his history is full of stirring incidents. Every one will wish to know him—done up, as he is, in a handsome bound volume of 500 pages.

Boston Daily Evening Transcript

2 August 1852

The author of "Typee" here wholly forsakes the sea, and ventures upon a regular story of life and love and tragic personal adventure on shore. With what success, we cannot know until we have found leisure to read the book. It is received in this city by Ticknor & Co.

Lansingburgh (N.Y.) *Gazette*

3 August 1852

A new work from the pen of Mr. Herman Melville cannot fail of being received with approbation. The author, in this, has chosen a new field wherein to give the rein to his vivid imagination, and unsurpassed beauty of description. "Pierre Glendenning," the hero of this tale, is a fine character, well conceived and admirably sustained. The book is full of sterling incident and abounds in numerous fine passages. The chief disappointment experienced while reading it is in coming to the end. Frailty and vice are delineated with energy and acuteness, and in the most glowing language. Whether Mr. Melville will find more admirers ashore than afloat we know not, but we hold that the work now before us places him indisputably in the highest list of eloquent writers.

Boston Post

4 August 1852

As the writer of the fascinating and *Crusoish* "Typee," Mr Melville has received considerable attention from those whose hard fate it is, to "notice" new books; and as emanating from the writer of "Typee," Mr Melville's subsequent works, ranging from fair to execrable, have been held worthy of lengthy critiques, while critics have been at some pains to state, in detail and by means of extracts, their various merits and defects. But we think it full time to stop this mode of treatment. The author of one good book more than offsets the amusement derived from it by the reading public, when he produces a score of trashy and crazy volumes; and in the present case, and after the delivery of such stuff as "Mardi" and the "White Whale," [we] are not disposed to stand upon much ceremony. Mr Melville's latest books, we are pleased to say, fell almost stillborn from the press, and we opened the volume under notice with the hope and almost the expectation that he would not again abuse the great gift of genius that has been bestowed upon him. We hoped and almost expected that he had sown his literary wild oats, and had now come forth, the vivid and brilliant author that he might be, if he chose to criticise himself, and lop off the puerility, conceit, affectation and insanity which he had previously exhibited. But we reckoned without our host. "Pierre; or the Ambiguities" is, perhaps, the craziest fiction extant. It has scenes and descriptions of unmistakeable power. The characters, however false to nature, are painted with a glowing pencil, and many of the thoughts reveal an intellect, the intensity and cultivation of which it is impossible to doubt. But the amount of utter trash in the volume is almost infinite—

trash of conception, execution, dialogue and sentiment. Whoever buys the book on the strength of Melville's reputation, will be cheating himself of his money, and we believe we shall *never* see the man who has endured the reading of the whole of it. We give the story of the book in a few sentences. Pierre Glendinning and his proud but loving mother are living together, surrounded by everything the world, intellect, health and affection can bestow. The son is betrothed to a beautiful girl of equal position and fortune, and everything looks brightly as a summer morning. All at once, Pierre learns that his father has left an illegitimate daughter, who is in poverty and obscurity. His conscience calls upon him to befriend and acknowledge her—although, by the way, his proof of the fact that the girl is his father's offspring is just nothing at all. On the other hand, he will not discover to the world or to his mother the error of his (supposed) sainted father, and he adopts the novel expedient of carrying off the girl, and giving out that he has married her. His mother discards him and soon dies of wounded love and pride, and his betrothed is brought to the brink of the grave. She finally recovers somewhat, and strange to say, invites herself to reside with Pierre and his sister, who, as far as the world and herself were concerned, are living as husband and wife. The relatives of Lucy, as a matter of course, try to regain her, and brand Pierre with every bad name possible. The latter finally shoots his cousin who had become the possessor of the family estate and a pretender to the hand of Lucy—is arrested and taken to prison. There he is visited by the two ladies, the sister and the betrothed. Lucy falls dead of a broken heart and Pierre and his sister take poison and also give up the ghost. This tissue of unnatural horrors is diversified a little, by the attempts of the hero to earn his living by authorship, and by the "ambiguous" love between Pierre and his natural sister.

Comment upon the foregoing is needless. But even this string of nonsense is equalled by the nonsense that is strung upon it, in the way of crazy sentiment and exaggerated passion. What the book means, we know not. To save it from almost utter worthlessness, it must be called a prose poem, and even then, it might be supposed to emanate from a lunatic hospital rather than from the quiet retreats of Berkshire. We say it with grief—it is too bad for Mr Melville to abuse his really fine talents as he does. A hundred times better if he kept them in a napkin all his natural life. A thousand times better, had he dropped authorship with "Typee." He would then have been known as the writer of one of the pleasantest books of its class in the English language. As it is, he has produced more and sadder trash than any other man of undoubted ability among us, and the most provoking fact is, that in his bushels of chaff, the "two grains of wheat" are clearly discernible.

Hartford Daily Courant

4 August 1852

We rather think, from a slight examination of this work, that it is very exciting. The style is a strange one—not at all natural and too much in the mystic, transcendental vein of affectation that characterizes some of our best writers. Such a style, we suppose, however, belongs to the new era of progress, and so we must submit to it.

Baltimore American & Commercial Daily Advertiser

6 August 1852

Also, from the same [publishers], a new novel by Mr. Herman Melville, entitled *Pierre; or the Ambiguities*. Mr. M. who is well known as the author of "Typee," has hitherto placed the scene of his stories on the sea, but in the work before us he confines himself to the land, and produces a regular romance of love and its dangers and difficulties, and of bold and successful daring. Without having read the book entirely through, we have no reason to doubt that it will be found quite as entertaining as the previous popular works of the author.

Boston Daily Advertiser

7 August 1852

Pierre, or the Ambiguities, is the title of the new Romance by Hermann Melville, Esq., author of Typee, Omoo, &c. The author has taken the Hero of this story from the very highest aristocracy of the country, so high one hardly knows where to look for it, and the scene of it is entirely on land. Published in New York by the Messrs. Harper & Brothers, and in Boston by Messrs. Crosby, Nichols & Co.

New York Journal of Commerce

7 August 1852

The same publishers have issued a volume entitled "PIERRE; OR, THE AMBIGUITIES," by Herman Melville. Its mechanical execution is very fair, and the style of writing vivacious and attractive. It comprises 495 pages.

New York Commercial Advertiser

11 August 1852

We must confess our inability to discover anything admirable in this production, notwithstanding the praises of contemporaries. Mr. Melville seems to have exhausted his literary capacity. His earlier publications were very flatteringly noticed by the British as well as the American critics, and his unusual success in this respect has apparently spoiled his judgment. The highest literary reputation ever achieved would be demolished by the publication of a few volumes of such trash as this "Pierre"—a novel, the plot of which is monstrous, the characters unnatural, and the style a kind of prose run mad.

Philadelphia Public Ledger

11 August 1852

THE PLOT OF A NEW AMERICAN WORK—A critic, in the Boston Post, who appears to have read Herman Melville's new work, says: "Pierre; or, the Ambiguities," is, perhaps, the craziest fiction extant. . . . and we believe we shall never see the man who has endured the reading of the whole of it. The critic of the Post must be the exception, for he gives the following brief plot, from which the reader may see whether it is worth buying or not:

Pierre Glendinning and his proud, but loving mother . . . crazy sentiment and exaggerated passion. What the book means, we know not. [See Boston *Post* review, August 4, 1852, pp. 32–33.]

New York Sun

16 August 1852

We need not wait for time to peruse this new work of Melville's, before we commend it to our readers. His previous efforts have been so completely and almost unboundedly successful, that we hazard little in giving this a full meed of recommendation.—Although a love story to the full it is not, we opine, one of the every day sickening sort, but daintily told and in merry cheerful language. It has something to do, we see, with the Patroons and the anti-renters, and, moreover, with "an immature attempt at a mature book," wherein, perchance, the author has taken a look at his first beginnings.

Springfield Republican

16 August 1852

Dedicated in form to the mountain "Greylock," is this last work of Melville. Dedicated in spirit to the mystical Greylock, is the tangled skein of narrative which the work develops. Of mist-caps, and ravines, and sky piercing peaks, and tangled underwoods, and barren rocks of language and incident, the book is made. Genteel hifalutin, painful, though ingenious involutions of language, and high-flown incidental detail, characterize the work, to the uprooting of our affection for the graceful and simple writer of Omoo and Typee. Melville has changed his style entirely, and is to be judged of as a new author.—We regret the change, for while the new Melville displays more subtleness of thought, more elaborateness of manner, (or mannerism), and a higher range of imagination, he has done it at a sad sacrifice of simplicity and popular appreciation. His present story, although possessing the characteristics we have ascribed to it, is readable to all those who, like us, possess a forgiving spirit, and who entertain the hope that the author, seeing his exceeding sinfulness, will return to the simple and beautiful path of authorship so graced by his early footsteps.

Boston Daily Evening Traveller

17 August 1852

In the present work our author has forsaken the distant regions of the South Sea islands and the ever changing ocean for a firmer surface and a region much more real to most readers. But his work is even more unnatural and improbable than either of his previous productions, whilst the interest is extremely disagreeable and tragical in its character. The plot is complex and involved, but on the whole skilfully managed. The characters, though exceedingly unnatural and bearing but little resemblance to living realities, are held with a firm grasp. The style is easy but discursive; and throughout the book bears the marks of the writer's unquestionable genius. Still we have not been much interested in it; and we think it will add little if anything to Mr. Melville's previous reputation.

Washington National Era

19 August 1852

Truly is there "but one step from the sublime to the ridiculous," and as truly hath Mr. Melville herein accomplished it. Such a mass of incongruities, "ambiguities," heterogeneities, absurdities, and absolute impossibilities, as the two covers of this volume enfold, it has rarely been our fortune to light upon. Now and then we strike upon something that reminds us of Typee, Omoo, &c., but it is speedily swallowed up in the slough of metaphysical speculation, which constitutes the largest portion of the work. The characters are absurdly paradoxical and greatly overdrawn; the incidents are impossible, in real life, and the whole book is utterly unworthy of Mr. Melville's genius. It unquestionably contains a vast deal of power, but it amounts to nothing, and accomplishes nothing but a climax too horribly unnatural to be thought of.

Mr. M. has evidently taken hold of a subject which has mastered *him*, and led him into all manner of vagaries. He is more at home in the manifold intricacies of a ship's rigging than amid the subtleties of psychological phenomena.

Albion (New York)

NS 11 (21 August 1852), 405

Ambiguities there are, not a few, in this new work by a popular author; but very little doubt can there be, touching the opinion which the public will entertain of its merits. It must, we regret to say, be pronounced a dead failure, seeing that neither in design or execution does it merit praise, or come within any measurable distance of Mr. Melville's well-deserved reputation. And sorely goes it against the grain with us to venture so harsh a judgment; but whilst we would pass lightly over the errors and short-comings of unknown writers, with whom it is sufficient punishment that their books drop still-born from the press, we deem it the bounden duty of an honest critic to speak out the plain truth when public favourites go palpably astray. Such is now the case; "Pierre" is an objectionable tale, clumsily told. Let us try to sketch briefly its contents.

The volume (a closely printed one of nearly five hundred pages) introduces you at the start to the hero, whose name it bears. Master Pierre Glendinning—for so is he fantastically called—is an aristrocratic young American, brought up on his patrimonial estate by a widowed mother, who is lovely, loveable, and haughty, doting on her son, lady patroness of her neighbourhood, exemplary in her doings, and carrying it bravely through the sunshine of life. Pierre, the object of her fond idolatry, is gifted with all those graces of person and mind that are usually found in heroes of romance. Between the pair an almost romantic affection exists, having an additional bond in the devoted regard entertained by the widow for the memory of the husband of her youthful days, and in the reverential attachment with which Pierre clings to his own ideal of his unremembered father. As the climax of all the enjoyable blessings with which they are endowed, Pierre, with his mother's full approbation, is on the point of marriage with a certain Lucy Tartan, a very charming Lucy of course, but not differing much from some scores of Lucies in your book acquaintance, if it be extensive.—And so in short every thing wears a smiling aspect; when down upon Pierre, like a clap of thunder, comes the intimation that he has a living sister. The model husband, the gentleman, the Christian, the pattern of all the moralities—alas! he had left behind him, in the person of a certain Isabel Banford, proofs of a little juvenile peccadillo, of which neither wife or son could ever have suspected him. Hereupon, you may well believe, all pleasance ceases. Isabel, studiously concealed hitherto and known only as a serving dairy-maid at a farm, has accidentally discovered the secret of her relation to Pierre, and herself communicates it to him at a most inauspicious moment. But the generous young enthusiast at once determines that she shall be recognized, moved partly thereto by his impulsive sense of right, and partly by the mysterious influence immediately exercised over him by Isabel. Concerning her, by the way, we cannot determine whether she be more ridiculously sublime or sublimely ridiculous. The patient reviewers will probably settle that point; but be it as it may, she throws poor Pierre into a terrible quandary. Righted the wronged one must be; but shall the fair fame of his sainted father be dashed down before the eyes of the world? Shall his mother's joy and pride in the memory of the deceased be all converted into shame and grief? As for any hope that Mrs. Glendinning would acknowledge poor Isabel, or help to raise her from social and individual degradation—that is altogether out of the question. The author (and here is our first serious quarrel with him) drags in a bit of episodical and gratuitous seduction, in order that any such vague idea in Pierre's mind may be quietly knocked on the head. Delly Ulver, a daughter of the farmer with whom Isabel has been serving, is abominably made to have a little convenient mishap. Mrs. Glendinning and the clergyman of the parish talk the matter over, in the presence of Pierre, when the lofty dame calls the lowly sinner by such ugly names, and wraps herself up so inexorably in the garments of her own immaculateness, that the doubting Pierre is satisfied that his illegitimate sister must not hope for recognition in that quarter.

Now the candid reader will probably agree with us (and we are quite serious) that the situations so far are wrought up cleverly enough. What a fine dramatic starting point would this have been for the hero of a play! Imagine Pierre having to choose between all this contrarity of duties, and feelings, and interests. Just think of an attempt to reconcile his respect for his living mother, his jealousy for his dead father's good repute, his passion for his intended Lucy, and his sense of duty to his new-found sister Isabel, to say nothing of the infallible loss of his inheritance, which has been left at his mother's disposal. A clash and a catastrophe are foreseen at the moment. Would that Mr. Melville had hit upon a less Frenchified mode of carrying us through the one, and bringing about the other! What fatality could have tempted him to call upon the spirit of Eugène Sue, to help him in such extreme emergency! For, what doth the romantic Master Pierre? He determines to pass off Isabel as his already secretly married wife, and to live with her *nominally* as her husband. Good bye to astounded Mrs. Glendinning, who of course turns him out of doors, maddened into speedy death by her son's dishonest breach of faith with Lucy and his presumed degrading match with a low-born substitute! Adieu to the gentle Lucy herself, who should have quite died outright of a broken heart, instead of being reserved to add another absurdity to the monstrous conclusion of the tale! Farewell to the ancestral mansion, and to the esteem of men, and to all cheerful ways of life, to all usefulness, to all honour, to all happiness. Pierre, with his sham-wife and the Magdalen Delly, hies him to New York. There he passes through scenes of poverty and wretchedness, physical and moral, such as you can scarcely read without thanking God that if woe and want do produce unutterable misery, such additions to it as Master Pierre voluntarily made can scarcely have existence, save in the diseased brain of a romancer.—But to conclude; heaping up horrors and trash to the last, our author positively brings the gentle and loving Lucy to her lover's abode, and there, during a few pages, Lucy and Isabel, each ignorant of the other's real position towards Pierre, dwell with him and Delly in a state of inconceivable and incongruous propinquity. Finally, and after forcible efforts on the part of Lucy's friends to extricate her, Pierre's bodily and mental faculties fail him. He can no longer eke out subsistence by his embittered attempts at authorship. He determines to commit suicide; but his intention is changed into the commission of murder. He shoots his cousin who had disinherited him and made vain love to Lucy, and is arrested and carried to the Tombs. There he is visited by the *nun*-such damsels. Lucy falls dead at his feet, whilst he and Isabel mutually take poison!—Reader, we have not been sketching a Porte St. Martin tragedy, but condensing the newest work of one of our favourite novelists. We wish we could close here, but we regret to add that in several places the ambiguities are still further thickened by hints at that fearfullest of all human crimes, which one shrinks from naming, but to which the narrative alludes when it brings some of its personages face to face with a copy of the Cenci portrait.

In noticing that bold, original work "Moby-Dick," we remember showing that Mr. Melville never could make his characters talk. It is the same here. Almost every spoken word reminds you of the chorus of the old Greek Tragedies. With the exception of some few sentences very naturally suited to the mouth of the Revd. Mr. Falsgrave, a sleek, smooth-tongued clergyman, there is scarcely a page of dialogue that is not absurd to the last degree. It would really pain us to give extracts, and we decline doing so; but the truth is as we state it. We allow the greatest stretch to the imagination of an author, so far as situations and persons are concerned; but if they can't speak as such men and women would be likely to speak,

under such and such circumstances, the reader cannot sympathise with them. We repeat our opinion that this is an objectionable tale, clumsily told; and if we had any influence with Mr. Melville, we would pray him to wash out the remembrance of it by writing forthwith a fresh romance of the Ocean, without a line of dialogue in it. Thereon is he at home; thereon he earned his literary laurels; thereon may he regain his literary standing, which he must have perilled by this crazy rigmarole. Do, Sir, give us something fresh from the sea; you have power, earnestness, experience, and talent. But let it be either truthful or fanciful; not an incoherent hodge-podge. Peter Simple is worth a ship-load of your Peter the Ambiguous.

Literary World (New York)

No. 290 (21 August 1852), 118–20

The purpose of Mr. Melville's story, though vaguely hinted, rather than directly stated, seems to be to illustrate the possible antagonism of a sense of duty, conceived in the heat and impetuosity of youth, to all the recognised laws of social morality; and to exhibit a conflict between the virtues. The hero of the tale is Pierre, a fiery youth full of love and ardor. He is the last of the Glendinnings, a family that can boldly face the memory of at least two generations back without blushing, which is a pretty fair title to an American nobility. He is an only son, the pride of his mother and his house, and the expectant heir of its wide domains. A warm affection unites Mrs. Glendinning, an aristocratic dame, and Pierre, and the heart of the proud woman is all content in the responsive love of her son. A certain Lucy Tartan, with all the requisite claims for a novelist's beauty, wins the affection of and in due course of time is betrothed to Pierre. All appears smooth and prosperous to a future of happiness, when a mysterious dark-eyed, dark-haired damsel, Isabel, proves herself to the satisfaction of Pierre, though on testimony that would not pass current in any court of law, to be his sister, the natural child of his father. Here is a sad blot upon the memory of a Glendinning, a living testimony of the sin of one who had been embalmed in the heart of Pierre, as pure and without reproach. Pierre, tortured with this damning fact that pollutes his filial ideal of a virtuous parent, conceives and rightly, that he has two duties to perform: to screen his dead father's memory and give to a living sister her due, a brother's affection. Pierre impetuously decides that the only way of reconciling these two duties is by the expedient of a pretended marriage with Isabel, and thus shield the memory of his father while he protects and unites himself in brotherly affection with his sister.

Mark the tragical result. The proud mother's proudest hopes are blasted by this supposed marriage; she drives Pierre from her house, disinherits him and dies a maniac. Pierre, an outcast, seeks in the company of his sister, his pretended wife, a refuge with his cousin, a rich denizen of the city, is totally ignored by him and repelled from his door. He is compelled to seek his livelihood with his pen. While he is thus engaged, struggling with poverty and misery, Lucy Tartan, who has survived the first shock from the agony of Pierre's abandonment and supposed marriage, unable to live without Pierre and instinctively justifying his infidelity on a principle, by no means clear to the reader, of abstract faith to her former lover, resolves to live with him, and joins the household of Pierre and Isabel. Lucy is followed to Pierre's dwelling by her brother and Pierre's cousin, who has succeeded Pierre as a suitor of Lucy. They attempt to force Lucy away, but she is rescued by Pierre with the aid of his fellow lodgers. Vengeance is sworn by the brother and cousin. An insulting letter is written to Pierre, denouncing him as a seducer and liar. To add to the agony of Pierre he receives at the same time a letter from his publishers, rejecting his novel. Pierre is outrageous, and arming himself with two pistols, seeks out his cousin, finds him, is struck by him, and in return shoots his cousin doubly dead with the two pistols. He is thrown into prison. He is sought out there by Isabel and Lucy. Lucy learning for the first time, from an agonizing cry of "brother" from Isabel, that she was Pierre's sister and not his wife, swoons away and dies. While Isabel and Pierre, conjointly help themselves in a fraternal way, to a draught of poison that Isabel has concealed upon her person, and they also die—*felo de se.* Nor is this the end of the casualty, the full list of the dead and wounded, for the surviving Tartan family must be necessarily plunged in irretrievable agony, leading to the probable result of some broken and various wounded hearts, on account of the death and supposed dishonor of Lucy.

Mr. Melville may have constructed his story upon some new theory of art to a knowledge of which we have not yet transcended; he evidently has not constructed it according to the established principles of the only theory accepted by us until assured of a better, of one more true and natural than truth and nature themselves, which are the germinal principles of all true art.

The pivot of the story is the pretended marriage of Pierre with his sister, in order to conceal her illegitimacy and protect his father's memory. Pierre, to carry out his purpose, abandons mother, home, his betrothed, all the advantages of his high social position, wealth and its appointments of ease and luxury and respect, and invites poverty, misery, infamy, and death. Apart from the very obvious way of gaining the same object at an infinitely smaller cost, is it natural that a loving youth should cast away the affection of his mother and his betrothed and the attachment of home to hide a dim stain upon his father's memory and to enjoy the love of an equivocal sister? Pierre not only acts thus absurdly, but pretends to act from a sense of duty. He is battling for Truth and Right, and the first thing he does in behalf of Truth is to proclaim to the whole world a falsehood, and the next thing he does is to commit in behalf of Right, a half a dozen most foul wrongs. The combined power of New England transcendentalism and Spanish Jesuitical casuistry could not have more completely befogged nature and truth, than this confounded Pierre has done. It is needless to test minutely the truth and nature of each character. In a word, Pierre is a psychological curiosity, a moral and intellectual phenomenon; Isabel, a lusus naturæ; Lucy, an incomprehensible woman; and the rest not of the earth nor, we may venture to state, of heaven. The object of the author, perhaps, has been, not to delineate life and character as they are or may possibly be, but as they are not and cannot be. We must receive the book, then, as an eccentricity of the imagination.

The most immoral *moral* of the story, if it has any moral at all, seems to be the impracticability of virtue; a leering demoniacal spectre of an idea seems to be speering at us through the dim obscure of this dark book, and mocking us with this dismal falsehood. Mr. Melville's chapter on "Chronometricals and Horologicals," if it has any meaning at all, simply means that virtue and religion are only for gods and not to be attempted by man. But ordinary novel readers will never unkennel this loathsome suggestion. The stagnant pool at the bottom of which it lies, is not too deep for their penetration, but too muddy, foul, and corrupt. If truth is hid in a well, falsehood lies in a quagmire.

We cannot pass without remark, the supersensuousness with which the holy relations of the family are described. Mother and son, brother and sister are sacred facts not to be disturbed by any sacrilegious speculations. Mrs. Glendinning and Pierre, mother and son, call each other brother and sister, and are described with all the coquetry of a lover and mistress. And again, in what we have termed the supersensuousness of description, the horrors of an incestuous relation between Pierre and Isabel seem to be vaguely hinted at.

In commenting upon the vagueness of the book, the uncertainty of its aim, the indefiniteness of its characters, and want of distinctness in its pictures, we are perhaps only proclaiming ourselves as the discoverers of a literary mare's nest; this vagueness, as the title of the "Ambiguities" seems to indicate, having been possibly intended by the author, and the work meant as a problem of impossible solution, to set critics and readers a wool-gathering. It is alone intelligible as an unintelligibility.

In illustration of the manner of the book, we give this description of a gloomy apparition of a house, such as it was conjured up by the vague confused memory of Isabel. There is a spectral, ghost-like air about the description, that conveys powerfully to the imagination the intended effect of gloom and remote indistinctness:—

" 'My first dim life-thoughts cluster round an old, half-ruinous house
. . . . some dark bread and a cup of water by me.' " [Bk.6, ch.3, paras.
1–2]

All the male characters of the book have a certain robust, animal force
and untamed energy, which carry them through their melodramatic parts
—no slight duty—with an effect sure to bring down the applause of the
excitable and impulsive. Mr. Melville can think clearly, and write with
distinctness and force—in a style of simplicity and purity. Why, then,
does he allow his mind to run riot amid remote analogies, where the chain
of association is invisible to mortal minds? Why does he give us incoherencies of thought, in infelicities of language? Such incoherency as this:—
"Love is both Creator's and Saviour's gospel to mankind . . . . All this earth
is Love's affianced; vainly the demon Principle howls to stay the banns."
[Bk.2, ch.4, paras.10–12] Such infelicities of expression, such unknown
words as these, to wit: "human*ness*," "heroic*ness*," "patriarchal*ness*,"
"descended*ness*," "flushful*ness*," "amaranthi*ness*," "instantaneous*ness*,"
"leapingly acknowledging," "fateful frame of mind," "protecting*ness*,"
"young*ness*," "infantile*ness*," "visible*ness*," *et id genus omne*!
The author of "Pierre; or, the Ambiguities;" the writer of a mystic
romance, in which are conjured up unreal nightmare-conceptions, a confused phantasmagoria of distorted fancies and conceits, ghostly abstractions and fitful shadows, is certainly but a spectre of the substantial
author of "Omoo" and "Typee," the jovial and hearty narrator of the
traveller's tale of incident and adventure. By what *diablerie*, hocus-
pocus, or thimble-rigging, "now you see him and now you don't" process,
the transformation has been effected, we are not skilled in necromancy to
detect. Nor, if it be a true psychological development, are we sufficiently
advanced in transcendentalism to lift ourselves skywards and see clearly
the coming light with our heads above the clouds. If this novel indicates a
chaotic state of authorship,—and we can distinguish fragmentary
elements of beauty—out of which is to rise a future temple of order,
grace, and proportion, in which the genius of Mr. Melville is to enshrine
itself, we will be happy to worship there; but let its foundation be firmly
based on *terra firma*, or, if in the heavens, let us not trust our common
sense to the flight of any waxen pinion. We would rejoice to meet Mr.
Melville again in the hale company of sturdy sailors, men of flesh and
blood, and, strengthened by the wholesome air of the outside world,
whether it be land-breeze or sea-breeze, listen to his narrative of a
traveller's tale, in which he has few equals in power and felicity.

Morning Courier and New-York Enquirer

21 August 1852

LA ROCHEFAUCAULD, we believe it was, who said that no man ever yet exercised his faculties to the full extent of which they were capable. We are sure this is the case with Mr. MELVILLE. His works, especially his recent one, are unsatisfactory, not so much because of *themselves*, as because of *himself*. He has powers, it is believed, to which he does not do justice. There are passages in this book that absolutely glitter with genius. There are scenes and portraitures that nothing but the most extraordinary skill could execute. And yet the work is strangely unequal, and abounds with defects and even positive deformities. Mr. MELVILLE is not content to let his mind bravely and yet soberly work out a production of symmetrical shape and high single purpose, but takes delight in wild fantastic irregularities that seem to have no other design than to offend all correct judgment and taste. It would be hard to match such extravagant ideas and such absurd forms of expression as may be found in this book. The author is capable of better things. One sees it at a glance. Wherefore then does he not abjure his affectations, curb his fine powers into correct working discipline, and more worthily vindicate his title to a place in the very first rank of American writers?

Church's Bizarre for Fireside and Wayside (Philadelphia)

NS part 10 (21 August 1852), 307

This author's name has been blown widely on this side the water, and partially on the other, for several works which possessed the attribute of originality by consent of all, however opinions might otherwise differ. We have read none of them, as a whole, before this, and to speak our opinion of this, would require pages instead of a paragraph. It is an original book; it has depth, passion, even genius, but it is wild, wayward, overstrained in thought and sentiment, and most unhealthy in spirit. And for the style, it is barbarously *outré*, unnatural and clumsy beyond measure. It was no true, fluent inspiration which produced these five hundred pages, and we would heartily wish the author, if he again draws pen, a better mood and purer taste!

New York Evening Mirror

27 August 1852

We take the following outline of Melville's new work from the *Literary World:*

> "The hero of the tale is Pierre, a fiery youth, full of love and ardor. . . . leading to the probable result of some broken and various wounded hearts, on account of the death and supposed dishonor of Lucy." [See *Literary World* review, August 21, 1852, pp. 40–41.]

We will only add that we have read these "Ambiguities" with alternate feelings of pleasure and disgust. The book contains a good deal of fine writing and poetic feeling, but the metaphysics are abominable. The whole *tone* of the work, from beginning to end, is morbid and unhealthy; and the action, as well as the plot, is monstrously unnatural. Mr. Melville should feel almost as much ashamed of the authorship of "Pierre," as he has a right to be proud of his "Typee." And yet we concede that the book is marked by great intellectual ability; while some of the descriptive portions are transcendantly beautiful. It reminds one of a summer day that opens sweetly, glittering with dew-drops, redolent of rose-odors, and melodious with the singing of birds; but early clouded with *artificial smoke*, and ending in a terrific display of melo-dramatic lightnings and earthquakes. There is no natural sequence in the accumulated misery that overwhelms every character in the tragedy. Insanity, murder and despair sweep their Tartarean shadows over the scene; and we close the volume with something of the feeling, and just about as much benefit as we experience on awakening from a horrid fit of the night-mare.

Spirit of the Times (New York)

22 (28 August 1852), 336

Every work written by this author possesses more than common interest, and abounds in strange and wild imaginings, but this book outstrips all his former productions, and is quite equal to "Moby Dick, or the Whale." It is certainly one of the most exciting and interesting ever published, and it must be read to be clearly appreciated, but none will regret the time spent in its perusal.

Southern Literary Messenger (Richmond)

18 (September 1852), 574–75

We know not what evil genius delights in attending the literary movements of all those who have achieved great success in the publication of their first book; but that some such companion all young and successful authors have, is placed beyond dispute by the almost invariable inferiority of their subsequent writings. With strong intellects, there is little danger that the influence of this unhappy minister will be lasting, but with far the greater number it continues until their reputation is wholly gone, or as the phrase runs,—*they have written themselves out.* Mr. Melville would really seem to be one of this class. Few books ever rose so rapidly and deservedly into popular favor as Typee. It came from the press at a time when the public taste wearied and sickened of didactic novels and journals of travel through fields explored many hundred times before. It presented us with fresh and delightful incidents from beyond the seas, over which was thrown an atmosphere soft and glowing as that hung above the youthful lovers in the enchanting story of St. Pierre. In a word, it was a novelty, and a novelty in literature, when it offends not against rule, is always to be commended. But from the time that Typee came from Mr. Melville's portfolio, he seems to have been writing under an unlucky star. The meandering nonsense of Mardi was but ill atoned for even by the capital sea-pieces of Redburn and White Jacket; Moby Dick proved a very tiresome yarn indeed, and as for the Ambiguities, we are compelled to say that it seems to us the most aptly titled volume we have met with for years.

The purpose of the Ambiguities, (if it have any, for none is either avowed or hinted,) we should take to be the illustration of this fact—that it is quite possible for a young and fiery soul, acting strictly from a sense of duty, and being therefore in the right, to erect itself in direct hostility to all the universally-received rules of moral and social order. At all events, such is the course of Pierre the hero of the story, from the opening chapter, without one moment's deviation, down to the "bloody work" of the final catastrophe. And our sympathies are sought to be enlisted with Pierre for the reason that throughout all his follies and crimes, *his sense of duty* struggles with and overcomes every law of religion and morality. It is a battle of the virtues, we are led to think, and the supreme virtue prevails.

To show how curiously Mr. Melville proceeds in his purpose, (supposing him to have one,) it will be necessary for us to give some hurried sketch of the story. Pierre, then, the hero, is the sole male representative of the family of Glendinning, a sprig of American Aristocracy, the idol of his proud and accomplished mother and the plighted lover of Lucy

Tartan, who is every thing that she should be, either in or out of a story-book. The course of true love runs without a ripple for these pleasant young people, until one day there appears an obstacle in the person of a fair unknown, with eyes of jet and tress of raven hue, who demonstrates to the entire conviction of Pierre that she is his sister—the illegitimate off-spring of the paternal Glendinning. To Pierre then, here was a dreadful disclosure—a bar sinister upon the family escutcheon—an indisputable and living reproach upon the memory of a sainted father. Pierre was therefore perplexed. How to reconcile the obligation which rested upon him to protect his father's fame with the equally binding obligation to love his newly found sister, was indeed a puzzle, and one which he proceeded to solve in a very extraordinary manner. Pierre affects to marry the dark-eyed one, the sister, by name Isabel; by which agreeable device he accomplishes three things—

1st. He drives his mother to the horrors of lunacy, in a paroxysm of which she dies.

2nd. He brings upon himself and sister penury and anguish, while endeavoring to live by literary labor; and

3rd. He involves in wholesale assassination by pistols, poison and other diabolical means, the rest of the characters, making as much work for the Coroner as the fifth act of Romeo and Juliet, or the terrific melodrama of the Forty Thieves.

This latter state of things is thus brought about. Pierre having been driven off by his relatives, sets up a small establishment of his own. Lucy Tartan, recovering from the earliest burst of grief into which she had been thrown by Pierre's pretended marriage, and still, most unaccountably, clinging to the belief that Pierre is not wholly unfaithful, determines to live in his presence at all hazards. But her brother, and a new suitor to her hand, a cousin of Pierre, attempt to wrest her by violence from Pierre's household. Frustrated in this, they write to Pierre, calling him some rather hard names, such as liar and seducer, whereupon Pierre,—in no very good humor from having received a communication from his publishers, declining to purchase his last novel,—arms himself, seeks his cousin, and kills him several times with two pistols. But Pierre is "no sooner out than taken by the watch" and escorted to jail. Here he is visited by Isabel and Lucy, and the latter discovering that Isabel is the sister and not the mistress of Pierre, there ensues a fainting scene, after which these amiable ladies, for no adequate motive that we can see, proceed to drink each other's healths in prussic acid, though not exactly with the air of Socrates pouring off his hemlock to immortality. Here fitly ends the volume, for surely in its 'shocking department' we have "supped full of horrors," and yet the tragic effect of its perusal does *not* end here, for Lucy's fate, and supposed infamy 'leave to the imagination of the reader' any desired quantity of despair among the surviving relatives.

Such is the outline of the Ambiguities, hurriedly given. The observant reader will see at once the absurdity of the principle upon which it has been constructed. Pierre discovers a sister whose very existence is evidence of a father's sin. To treat that sister with kindness and to cover over the father's shame, is without doubt a most laudable thing. But to accomplish it, Pierre is led to do things infinitely worse than it would be to neglect it. He not only acts like a fool in severing the most sacred ties and making the dearest sacrifices to purchase what he might have obtained at a much lighter expense, but he justifies his conduct by a sense of duty, false in the extreme. He wishes to uphold the just and true, and to do this he commences by stating a lie—his marriage with Isabel. It is in the cause of affection and consanguinity that he is content to suffer, and for this cause, he breaks off the closest and holiest bond that exists on earth, the bond of filial love, thus causing the mother that bore him to die a maniac. For every duty he performs, he is compelled to commit a dozen outrages on the moral sense, and these are committed without hesitancy or compunction. The truth is, Mr. Melville's theory is wrong. It should be the object of fiction to delineate life and character either as it is around us, or as it ought to be. Now, Pierre never did exist, and it is very certain that he never ought to exist. Consequently, in the production of Pierre, Mr. Melville has deviated from the legitimate line of the novelist. But badly as we think of the book as a work of art, we think infinitely worse of it as to its moral tendency. We have not space left us to enter upon this view of the volume, and we must therefore leave it with the remark that if one does not desire to look at virtue and religion with the eye of Mephistopheles, or, at least, through a haze of *ambiguous* meaning, in which they may readily be taken for their opposites, he had better leave "Pierre or the Ambiguities" unbought on the shelves of the bookseller.

We have received the volume from A. Morris.

From "The Editor's Shanty,"
Anglo-American Magazine
(Toronto)

1 (September 1852), 273

THE LAIRD.—I say lads, hae ony o' ye read Herman Melville's new wark?

THE DOCTOR.—You mean *"Pierre; or the Ambiguities"* I presume?

THE LAIRD.—Just sae! I saw it on Scobie's counter this morning, and wad ha'e coft it if I had had siller eneuch in my spleuchan!

THE DOCTOR.—It was just as lucky, that your exchequer was at so low an ebb, else thou might have been a practical illustration of the old saw which declares that a fool and his money are soon parted!

THE LAIRD.—You astonish me! I wad ha'e judged that in this age o' commonplace, a production frae the pen o' the author o' *Mardi* wad ha'e been a welcome addition to the stores o' our booksellers!

THE DOCTOR.—Melville unquestionably is a clever man, but in the present instance he has sadly mistaken his walk. *"Pierre"* from beginning to end is a gigantic blunder, with hardly one redeeming feature.

THE MAJOR.—What is the nature of the story?

THE DOCTOR.—You might as well ask me to analyse the night-mare visions of an Alderman who after dining upon turtle and venison had wound up by supping upon lobsters and toasted cheese! The hero is a dreamy spoon, alike deficient in heart and brains, who like Hamlet drives a gentle confiding maiden crazy by his flatulent caprices, and finally winds up by drinking poison in prison to save his neck from a hempen cravat!

THE MAJOR.—The affair, I presume belongs to the German school?

THE DOCTOR.—Yes! *"Pierre"* is a species of New York Werter, having all the absurdities and none of the beauties of Goethe's juvenile indiscretion!

THE MAJOR.—Strange that a really able man like Herman Melville should have compromised himself so egregiously by giving birth to such a production!

THE DOCTOR.—'Tis passing strange!

THE SQUIREEN—Men of genius will occasionally be guilty of such freaks. I remember Liston once playing Richard III. for his benefit in the Theatre Royal, Dublin, and though his most tragic passages were received with shrieks of laughter from box, pit, and gallery, the besotted comedian could not be convinced that it was with himself and not the public where the error lay!

New York Home Journal

4 September 1852

"Pierre; or, the Ambiguities." Under this mysterious title—which carries with it a certain fascination—Herman Melville has adventured in a new sphere of writing. We can imagine certain professed novel readers provoked by the small gratification it affords to their appetite for a continuous narrative of perilous adventures, or a series of every-day characters; but the original power of the author is manifest in the very eccentricity of his invention. The story is not artistically contrived, but it is psychologically suggestive. It is subtle, metaphysical, often profound, and has passages of bewildering intensity.

New York Day Book

7 September 1852

HERMAN MELVILLE CRAZY.—A critical friend, who read Melville's last book, "Ambiguities," between two steamboat accidents, told us that it appeared to be composed of the ravings and reveries of a madman. We were somewhat startled at the remark; but still more at learning, a few days after, that Melville was really supposed to be deranged, and that his friends were taking measures to place him under treatment. We hope one of the earliest precautions will be to keep him stringently secluded from pen and ink.

New York Herald

18 September 1852

Ambiguities, indeed! One long brain-muddling, soul-bewildering ambiguity (to borrow Mr. Melville's style), like Melchisedeck, without beginning or end—a labyrinth without a clue—an Irish bog without so much as a Jack-o' th'-lantern to guide the wanderer's footsteps—the dream of a distempered stomach, disordered by a hasty supper on half-cooked pork chops. Verily, books spring into life now a days, by a strange Cæsarian process. Our ancestors, simple folk, used to fancy it incumbent on an author to nurse the germ in his fecundated brain till the fœtus assumed a definite shape, and could be marshalled into existence, safe from the brand of monstrosity. Modern writers miscarry 'ere the embryo hath shapen limb or nerve, or blood, and mid-wives and doctors in droves pledge their willing faith that it will live. Potent elixirs and cordials elicit some reluctant spark of animation; but reaction soon follows, and 'mid the feigned astonishment of foster-mothers and wet-nurses, the emasculated bantling expires a miserable death.

What can be more conclusive evidence of immature conception than the planting on the social stage of this nineteenth century, of a man like Pierre—brimful of noble passions—silly weaknesses—lordly power of mind and warmth of heart—the petted child of a tender mother, who, yielding to her son's craving after sisterly love, calls him "brother"—thrusting him into contact with a timid, fragile girl, who turns out to be an illegitimate daughter of his father's, and firing him with such a chivalrous devotion for this new found sister, *par la main gauche*, that he resigns, without a pang, home, mother, betrothed, rank, and even the necessaries of life, to roam the world, knight-errant like, in her company; reversing, with less show of reason, Abraham's white lie, and proclaiming publicly that the daughter of his father is his wife? Where did Mr.

Melville find an original for the portrait of Isabel? Where for Mrs. Glendinning? or where for the fond, but unwomanly Lucy? Alas! those pork chops! Sore must have been the grapple between the monster indigestion and the poor suffering epigastrium. Frantic the struggle between the fiend nightmare and our unfortunate friend the author.

We do not object to a canvas well laid with weird horrors, fantastic sprites gushing from out some misty cloud, and playful imps, dancing and chattering in the foreground, to the ruin of the composition of the picture, and to the speechless agony of the severe classic. But, good Mr. Melville, your dream has overstepped the bounds of our impressibility. We long to give you one good shake, to have you rub your eyes, and favor us with the common sense word of the enigma. Is Pierre really a candidate for the distinguished honor of a latticed chamber at the Brattleborough asylum? Would a mild infusion of hellebore, and a judicious course of treatment in some sunny vale, calm his phrenzy, and cool his calcined brain? or are his erratic habits—his wondrous *épanchement* for a full-blown sister—his reckless disregard of filial duty, plighted love, and public esteem—mere forms of eccentricity, outward symptoms of the genius latent within? We confess that we should like to be correctly informed on these points. We own to a sneaking partiality for Pierre, rough and unnatural as he is, and share his fiery rebellion against the yoke of conventional properties, and the world's cold rules of esteem. Weep we, too, with gentle Isabel; poor bud, blighted by a hereditary canker. And, need we blush to avow that our pulse beat faster than our physician in ordinary would have sanctioned, when the heartless Stanly disclaimed his poverty-stricken cousin, and strove to wrest his reluctant bride from the arms of her chosen lover? But that shot—was it manly? was it honorable? was it fair? to requite a hasty blow, well warranted, *du reste*—for who would not strike to the earth one who passed for the seducer of his mistress?—with a pistol ball, fired from an arm's length on a defenceless man? This, Mr. Melville, is murder. For a murderer in cold blood—a wretch who cooly loads his arms, rams the charge home, and sallies forth with the set purpose of taking the life of his rival—we have no thrill of sympathy, no bowels of compassion. Let him hang like a dog! A harmless madman in the first chapter, he is a dangerous poet in the last. Let him hang! And those ill starred girls! Ill became it their pure maidenhood to drench the fatal phial, and drown the spark of heavenly virtue and earthly sense in one corroding draught of poisonous passion. Sadly, too sadly—but, as we said, we cannot wholly eradicate every trace of compassion for the erring impulse of confiding girlhood—do we see Lucy relax her hold of the flask, and reeling forward, fall heavily across the prostrate form of her lover. These three—the murderer, the child of fractious whim and ungovernable passion, the self denying woman, to whom infamy is pleasant, so it be the price of her lover's society—the pariah, clinging, cerement-like, to the only hand that has ever clasped hers in friendly grasp—stiffening horridly in the rack of death, and clenching, in the last throe, the hem of each other's garment— oh! 'tis a mournful, a sickening picture!

Why did Mr. Melville desert "that bright little isle of his own," in the blue waters of the Pacific? Is Polynesia used up? Has the vulgar herd of authors penetrated the fastnesses of those primitive tribes, whose taboo has become naturalized among us, and whose aquatic nymphs have fired the imagination of many a future Bouganville or Cook? Is there not a solitary whale left, whose cetaceous biography might have added another stone to the monumental fame of the author of Moby-Dick? If our senses do not deceive us, Mr. Melville will rue his desertion of the forecastle, and the virgin forest, for the drawing room and the modest boarding-house chamber. The former was the scene of victories of which no young author need be ashamed; the latter, we fear, has some defeats to witness. Social life is not, perhaps, more difficult to paint than pleasant excursions into Mahomet's paradise; but it requires a different order of talent. Mere analytical description of sentiment, mere wordy anatomy of the heart is not enough for a novel to-day. Modern readers wish to exercise some little judgment of their own; deeds they will have, not characters painted in cold colors, to a hairbreadth or a shade. We are past the age when an artist superscribed his *chef d' oeuvre* with the judicious explanation, "this is a horse." Mr. Melville longs for the good old times when the chorus filled the gaps between the acts with a well-timed commentary on the past, and a shrewd guess at the future.

But we have a heavier charge than this to advance. Mr. Herman Melville, the author of "Typee" and "Omoo," we know; but who is Mr. Herman Melville, the copyist of Carlyle? Most men begin by treading in the wake of a known author, and timidly seeking for shelter under the cover of his costume. Mr. Melville ventured his first flight on his own unaided pinions, and now that their strength has been fully tested, voluntarily descends to the nursery, and catches at leading-strings. No book was ever such a compendium of Carlyle's faults, with so few of his redeeming qualities, as this Pierre. We have the same German English—the same transcendental flights of fancy—the same abrupt starts—the same incoherent ravings, and unearthly visions. The depth of thought—the unerring accuracy of eye—the inflexible honesty of purpose, are wanting; at least, nothing outwardly reveals their presence. Like many other people, Mr. Melville seems to have attributed a large share of Carlyle's popularity to his bad English; whereas, in point of fact, his defects of form have always proved a drawback to his success, and nothing short of his matchless excellence of matter, would have introduced him into literary society. A much higher rank would have been held to-day by the author of "Sartor Resartus," had he clad his striking and brilliant ideas in a less barbarous garb. The fault was original and "catching." Herds of pretenders to literary fame have ranged themselves under the banner of the Edinburgh reviewer, and, fancying they were establishing a Carlyle-ist school, have borrowed their master's hump, without stealing a single ray from the flashing of his eye, or a single tone from the harmony of his tongue. Sorry, indeed, are we to class Mr. Melville among these. Could he but sound the depths of his own soul, he would discover pearls of matchless price, that 'twere a sin and a shame to set in pinchbeck finery. Let him but study the classic writers of his own language—dissect their system—brood over their plain, honest, Saxon style—not more French than German—the search would soon convince him that he might still be attractive, though clad in his homely mother tongue. *Soyons de notre pays*, says the poet-philosopher of Passy, it will satisfy our wants, without borrowing tinsel imagery of a Lamartine, or the obscure mysticism of a Goethe or a Kant.

Yet a single admonition. Nature, Mr. Melville, is the proper model of every true artist. Fancy must be kept within proper bounds, and the eye must never be suffered to wander from the reality we are striving to paint. No poetical license can justify such departures from the style of ordinary dialogue as abound in this book. The Tireis-and-Phillis tone of conversation is long since dead and buried; trouble not its ashes. Passion can excuse incoherency, but not fine drawn mannerism, or gaudy *conceits*. For instance, what can be in worse taste than the following reply of Isabel, when Pierre entreats her not to demur to Lucy's living with them?

"Thy hand is the castor's ladle, Pierre, which holds me entirely fluid. Into thy forms and slightest moods of thought thou pourest me; and I there solidify to that form, and take it on, and thenceforth wear it, till once more thou mouldest me anew. If what thou tellest me be thy thought, how can I help its being mine?"

How false this coloring! How far from the sweet simplicity with which Sterne or Tennyson would have robed the timid Isabel!

As we said above, we can trace many of the faults of the book to the deleterious influence of deep, untempered draughts of Carlyle. This particular one may perhaps be laid to the charge of a man who has done no good to our literature—Martin Farquhar Tupper. We want no such *réchauffé*, though the hot dish were, at its first appearance on table, worthy the palate of an epicure; we want our own author, in his own unborrowed garb, adorned with his own jewels, and composing his features into that countenance and expression which nature intended they should wear.

Southern Quarterly Review (Charleston, S.C.)

22 [NS 6] (October 1852), 532

That "Typee," "Omoo," and other clever books, should be followed by such a farrago as this of "Pierre" was not surely to be predicted or anticipated. But, verily, there is no knowing when madness will break out, or in whom. That Herman Melville has gone "clean daft," is very much to be feared; certainly, he has given us a very mad book, my masters. His *dramatis personæ* are all mad as March hares, every mother's son of them, and every father's daughter of them; and that too, without needing that we should take any pains to prove their legitimacy. The sooner this author is put in ward the better. If trusted with himself, at all events give him no futher trust in pen and ink, till the present fit has worn off. He will grievously hurt himself else—or his very amiable publishers.

Hunt's Merchants' Magazine (New York)

27 (October 1852), 526

Melville's reputation as a writer is widely spread. The reception of his earliest works by the public has been of the most flattering kind. This volume is more imaginative in its character than the former ones, and aims to present the workings of an over-sensitive spirit. The story is well told as usual, although not perhaps equal in interest to some of the other volumes from the same pen.

Godey's Magazine and Lady's Book (Philadelphia)

45 (October 1852), 390

We really have nothing to add to the severity of the critical notices which have already appeared in respect to this elegantly printed volume; for, in all truth, all the notices which we have seen have been severe enough to satisfy the author, as well as the public, that he has strangely mistaken his own powers and the patience of his friends in presuming to leave his native element, the ocean, and his original business of harpooning whales, for the mysteries and "ambiguities" of metaphysics, love, and romance. It may be, however, that the heretofore intelligible and popular author has merely assumed his present transcendental metamorphosis, in order that he may have range and scope enough to satirize the ridiculous pretensions of some of our modern literati. Under the supposition that such has been his intention, we submit the following notice of his book, as the very best off-hand effort we could make in imitation of his style: Melodiously breathing an inane mysteriousness, into the impalpable airiness of our unsearchable sanctum, this wonderful creation of its ineffable author's sublime-winging imagination has been fluttering its snow-like-invested pinions upon our multitudinous table. Mysteriously breathing an inane melody, it has been beautifying the innermost recesses of our visual organs with the luscious purpleness and superb goldness of its exterior adornment. We have listened to its outbreathing of sweet-swarming sounds, and their melodious, mournful, wonderful, and unintelligible melodiousness has "dropped like pendulous, glittering icicles," with soft-ringing silveriness, upon our never-to-be-delighted-sufficiently organs of hearing; and, in the insignificant significancies of that deftly-stealing and wonderfully-serpentining melodiousness, we have found an infinite, un-bounded, inexpressible mysteriousness of nothingness.

Graham's Magazine (Philadelphia)

41 (October 1852), 445

This work is generally considered a failure. The cause of its ill-success is certainly not to be sought in its lack of power. None of Melville's novels equals the present in force and subtlety of thinking and unity of purpose. Many of the scenes are wrought out with great splendor and vigor, and a capacity is evinced of holding with a firm grasp, and describing with a masterly distinctness, some of the most evanescent phenomena of morbid emotions. But the spirit pervading the whole book is intolerably unhealthy, and the most friendly reader is obliged at the end to protest against such a provoking perversion of talent and waste of power. The author has attempted seemingly to combine in it the peculiarities of Poe and Hawthorne, and has succeeded in producing nothing but a power-fully unpleasant caricature of morbid thought and passion. Pierre, we take it, is crazy, and the merit of the book is in clearly presenting the psychology of his madness; but the details of such a mental malady as that which afflicts Pierre are almost as disgusting as those of physical disease itself.

Lantern (New York)

2 (2 October 1852), 127

FATAL OCCURRENCE.

ABOUT ten o'clock, yesterday, an intelligent young man was observed to enter the store of STRINGER and TOWNSEND, the well-known publishers, and deliberately purchase a copy of HERMAN MELVILLE's last work.

He has, of course, not since been heard of.

Lantern (New York)

2 (16 October 1852), 153

But to our more immediate task—a night's sleep, with a page of HALLECK, had somewhat dissipated the nausea we had incurred by reading the "Unpublished Fragments," and we felt sufficiently recovered to turn over the leaves of HERMAN MELVILLE's Ambiguities.

Our Owl had told us the subject, and we were, therefore, prepared for the peculiarity of its plot.

The book is a mistake, even the name is a blunder—it should be called the *double entendre*. There is nothing equivocal in it; the moral is unmistakeable.

We hereby commend our friend, HERMANN, either to resign his pen altogether or to choose different subjects. He must not dance on the tight rope between morality and indecency longer—dullness is better than meretriciousness.

American Whig Review (New York)

16 [NS 10] (November 1852), 446–54

A bad book! Affected in dialect, unnatural in conception, repulsive in plot, and inartistic in construction. Such is Mr. Melville's worst and latest work.

Some reputations seem to be born of accident. There are commonplace men who on some fine day light, unknown to themselves, upon a popular idea, and suddenly rise on the strength of it into public favor. They stride the bubble for a little while, but at last its prismatic hues begin to fade; men see that the object of their applause has after all but an unsubstantial basis, and when at length the frail foundation bursts, they fall back into their original obscurity, unheeded and unlamented. Mr. Melville has experienced some such success. A few years back, he gave to the world a story of romantic adventure; this was untrue in its painting, coarse in its coloring, and often tedious and prolix in its descriptive passages. But there was a certain air of rude romance about it, that captivated the general public. It depicted scenes in a strange land, and dealt with all the interests that circle around men whose lives are passed in peril. Nor were appeals to the grosser instincts of humanity wanting. Naked women were scattered profusely through the pages, and the author seemed to feel that in a city where the ballet was admired, "Typee" would be successful.* Mr. Melville thought he had hit the key-note to fame. His

---

*Mr. Cornelius Mathews was, we believe, the first to designate this prurient taste under the happy and specific head of "the ballet-feeling."

book was reprinted in all directions, and people talked about it, as much from the singularity of its title as from any intrinsic merit it possessed.

This was encouraging, and Mr. Melville evidently thought so, for he immediately issued a series of books in the same strain. Omoo, Mardi, White-Jacket, Redburn, followed one another in quick succession; and the foolish critics, too blind to perceive that the books derived their chief interest from the fact of the scenes being laid in countries little known, and that the author had no other stock in trade beyond tropical scenery and eccentric sailors, applauded to the very echo. This indiscriminating praise produced its usual effect. Mr. Melville fancied himself a genius, and the result of this sad mistake has been—"Pierre."

As a general rule, sea-stories are very effective, and to those versed in nautical lore, very easy writing. The majority of the reading public are landsmen, and the events of an ocean-life come to them recommended by the charm of novelty. They cannot detect the blunders, and incongruity passes with them for originality. The author can make his vessel and his characters perform the most impossible feats, and who, except the favored few that themselves traverse the sea professionally, will be one bit the wiser? The scope for events is also limited, and this very limitation renders the task of writing a sea-tale more simple. A storm, a wreck, a chase and a battle, a mutiny, desertions, and going into and leaving port, with perhaps a fire at sea, form the principal "properties" of a salt-water artist. Considerable descriptive powers are, we admit, necessary to the management of these materials. The storm must be wild, the battle fierce, and the fire terrible; but these, after all, are broad outlines, and require little delicacy of handling to fill them in. Sometimes, as in the Pilot, one finds a veil of pathetic tenderness and grace flung over the characters, but as a general rule in nautical fictions, the wit is coarse, the pathos clumsy, and the most striking characters are invariably unnatural.

It is when a writer comes to deal with the varied interests of a more extended life; when his hand must touch in harmonious succession the numberless chords of domestic sorrows, duties and affections, and draw from each the proper vibration; when he has to range among the ever-changing relations of every-day humanity, and set each phase of being down in its correct lineaments; it is then he discovers that something more is necessary for the task than a mere arrangement of strong words in certain forms,—or the trick of painting nature, until, like a ranting actress, she pleases certain tastes according as she deviates from truth.

Mr. Melville's previous stories, all sea-born as they were, went down the public throat because they were prettily gilt with novelty. There are crowds of people who will run after a new pill, and swallow it with avidity, because it is new, and has a long Greek name. It may be made of bread, or it may be made of poison; the novelty of the affair renders all considerations of its composition quite immaterial. They learn the name, eat the bolus, and pay the doctor. We have a shrewd suspicion that the uncouth and mysterious syllables with which Mr. Melville baptized his books had much to do with their success. Like Doctor Dulcamara, he gave his wares an exciting title, and trusted to Providence for the rest. The enchantment worked. The mystic cabala of "OMOO, *by the author of* TYPEE," was enough in itself to turn any common novel-reader's brain, and the books went off as well as a collection of magic rings would in Germany, or the latest batch of *Agnus Deis* in an Italian village. People had little opportunity of judging of their truth. Remote scenes and savage actors gave a fine opportunity for high coloring and exaggerated outline, of which Mr. Melville was not slow to avail himself, and hence Fayaway is as unreal as the scenery with which she is surrounded.

We do not blame Mr. Melville for these deviations from truth. It is not much matter if South Sea savages are painted like the heroes of a penny theatre, and disport themselves amid pasteboard groves, and lakes of canvas. We can afford Mr. Melville full license to do what he likes with "Omoo" and its inhabitants; it is only when he presumes to thrust his tragic *Fantoccini* upon us, as representatives of our own race, that we feel compelled to turn our critical Ægis upon him, and freeze him into silence.

Pierre aims at something beyond the mere records of adventure contained in Mardi and Omoo. The author, doubtless puffed up by the very false applause which some critics chose to bestow upon him, took for granted that he was a genius, and made up his mind to write a fine book; and he has succeeded in writing a fine book with a vengeance. Our experience of literature is necessarily large, but we unhesitatingly state, that from the period when the Minerva press was in fashion, up to the present time, we never met with so turgid, pretentious, and useless a book as "Pierre." It is always an unpleasant and apparently invidious statement for a critic to make, that he can find nothing worthy of praise in a work under consideration; but in the case of Pierre we feel bound to add to the assertion the sweeping conclusion, that there we find every thing to condemn. If a repulsive, unnatural and indecent plot, a style disfigured by every paltry affectation of the worst German school, and ideas perfectly unparalleled for earnest absurdity, are deserving of condemnation, we think that our already expressed sentence upon Pierre will meet with the approval of every body who has sufficient strength of mind to read it through.

Mr. Pierre Glendinning, the hero of the book, and intended by the author to be an object of our mournful admiration, supports in the course of the story the arduous characters of a disobedient son, a dishonest lover, an incestuous brother, a cold-blooded murderer, and an unrepentant suicide. This *repertoire* is agreeably relieved by his playing the part of a madman whenever he is not engaged in doing any thing worse.

This agreeable young gentleman is the only son of a widow lady of large fortune, who coquets in her old age with suitors about the same age as Pierre. And to render the matter still more interesting, Pierre by mutual consent sinks the son, and deports himself by word and look towards his mother as a lover; while she, charming coquette of fifty that she is, readily imitates this delightful *abandon*. The early character of Mr. P. Glendinning, as traced by our author, is exceedingly fine; we will, however, spare it to our readers, merely stating on Mr. Melville's authority, that in him might be observed "the polished steel of the gentleman, girded with Religion's silken sash;" which sash, his great-grandfather had somehow or other taught him, "should, in the last bitter trial, furnish its wearer with glory's shroud." Setting aside the little incompatibility of religion having any thing to do, even in sashes, with martial glory, we cannot help thinking that the mere mention of making a shroud out of so scanty an article as a sash, is quite sufficient to scandalize any respectable undertaker.

Well, this be-sashed young gentleman, who lives alone with his mother at the family place of Saddle Meadows, is engaged formally to a very flighty young lady named Lucy Tartan. If there is any thing to which we object particularly in this young couple, it is the painful habit they have contracted of *tutoyer*-ing each other through whole pages of insane rhapsody. We cannot believe that the indiscriminate use of "thee" and "thou" makes the nonsense with which it is generally connected one atom more readable. On the contrary, it has a most unpleasant effect, for it deprives the mad passages in which it occurs of the only recommendation that can palliate insanity, that is, simplicity.

Notwithstanding Mr. P. Glendinning's being already supplied with a mother and a mistress, he is pursued by indefinite longings for a sister. His reason for this imperious craving is rather a pugnacious one, and almost inclines us to believe that the young gentleman must have had some Celtic blood in his veins. If he had but a sister, he alleges he would be happy, because "it must be a glorious thing to engage in a mortal quarrel on a sweet sister's behalf!" This, it must be confessed, is a strange fancy, but we suppose it is to be accounted for by the fact of Saddle Meadows being rather a dull place, and Mr. Pierre believing that a little fighting was the best thing in the world for the blues.

By a chain of the most natural circumstances in the world—we mean in Mr. Melville's books—this sister is most unexpectedly supplied. In fact, though the author says nothing about it, we are inclined to think that he imported her direct from a lunatic asylum for the occasion. She proves to be an illegitimate daughter of Pierre's father, and judging from her own story, as well as we could understand it, appears to have been dry-nursed by an old family guitar; an allegory almost as fine as that of Romulus and Remus. If we suppose this paternal instrument to have been out of tune at the time that it assumed the responsibility of the little Isabel, that young lady's singular turn of mind is at once accounted for; but if we go a little farther, and suppose the worthy instrument to have been cracked, we explain still more satisfactorily the origin of her very erratic conduct.

"Sister Isabel," being an illegitimate Glendinning, is of course inadmissible to the refined atmosphere breathed by the aristocratic Mrs. Glendinning, who has rather strong ideas upon such subjects. Accordingly, Pierre, who is afraid to mention to his mother the discovery he has made, and moved to compassion by the forlorn state of the young lady, who lives with her faithful guitar in a charming cottage on the edge of a beautiful lake, takes compassion on her desolate condition, and determines to devote his life to her. He therefore conceives the sublime idea of obviating all difficulties—for difficulties there must have been, or Mr. Melville would not say so, though we confess that we have not been so fortunate as to discover them—by presenting her to the world as his wife! The reasons alleged by this virtuous hero are detailed at some length by Mr. Melville, as if he knew that he could not apologize too much for presenting such a picture to the world. Firstly, Pierre wishes to conceal the fact of Isabel's being the offspring of his father's sin, and thereby protect his parent's reputation. Secondly, he is actuated by a desire not to disturb his mother's mind by any disclosure which would destroy the sacredness of her deceased husband's memory; and lastly, he entertains towards this weird sister feelings which Mr. Melville endeavors to gloss over with a veil of purity, but which even in their best phase can never be any thing but repulsive to a well constituted mind.

Now, in this matter Mr. Melville has done a very serious thing, a thing which not even unsoundness of intellect could excuse. He might have been mad to the very pinnacle of insanity; he might have torn our poor language into tatters, and made from the shreds a harlequin suit in which to play his tricks; he might have piled up word upon word, and adjective upon adjective, until he had built a pyramid of nonsense, which should last to the admiration of all men; he might have done all this and a great deal more, and we should not have complained. But when he dares to outrage every principle of virtue; when he strikes with an impious, though, happily, weak hand, at the very foundations of society, we feel it our duty to tear off the veil with which he has thought to soften the hideous features of the idea, and warn the public against the reception of such atrocious doctrines. If Mr. Melville had reflected at all—and certainly we find in him but few traces of reflection—when he was writing this book, his better sense would perhaps have informed him that there are certain ideas so repulsive to the general mind that they themselves are not alone kept out of sight, but, by a fit ordination of society, every thing that might be supposed to even collaterally suggest them is carefully shrouded in a decorous darkness. Nor has any man the right, in his morbid craving after originality, to strip these horrors of their decent mystery. But the subject which Mr. Melville has taken upon himself to handle is one of no ordinary depravity; and however he may endeavor to gloss the idea over with a platonic polish, no matter how energetically he strives to wrap the mystery in a cloud of high-sounding but meaningless words, the main conception remains still unaltered in all its moral deformity. We trust that we have said enough on this topic. It is a subject that we would gladly not have been obliged to approach, and which we are exceedingly grieved that any gentleman pretending to the rank of a man of letters should have chosen to embody in a book. Nor can we avoid a feeling of surprise, that professedly moral and apparently respectable publishers like the Messrs. Harper should have ever consented to issue from their establishment any book containing such glaring abominations as "Pierre."

But to return to the development of this chaotic volume. Mr. P. Glendinning, actuated by this virtuous love for his sister, informs his proud mother that he is married. She, knowing not the true relationship that binds them together, spurns her unworthy son from her house for having degraded the family name so far by making a *mésalliance*; and the worthy young gentleman, after having nearly killed Miss Lucy Tartan, his betrothed, with the same intelligence, and left his mother in a fit of indignation which has every chance of becoming a fit of apoplexy, sets out with—we really do not know what to call her, for Mr. Melville has so intertwined and confused the wife with the sister, and the sister with the wife, that we positively cannot tell one from the other; so we may as well compromise the matter by calling her simply Isabel. He sets out then with Isabel, in a perfect enthusiasm of virtue, for the city, having first apprised a fashionable cousin of his, one Mr. Glendinning Stanly, that he was on his way, and requesting him to prepare his house for his reception. This fashionable cousin, however, takes very little trouble about the matter; and accordingly, when Pierre and Isabel arrive accompanied by a young lady of loose morals named Delly, they find no house or welcome. A series of incidents here follow, which are hardly worth reciting. They consist of Pierre's quarrel with Stanly, a scene in a police station, a row with a cabman, and ending by Pierre's taking rooms in some out-of-the way place, inhabited by a colony of poor authors, who bear the general denomination of Apostles. Just in this part of the book it comes out suddenly that Pierre is an author, a fact not even once hinted at in the preceding pages. Now the reader is informed, with very little circumlocution, and as if he ought to have known all about it long ago, that Mr. P. Glendinning is the author of a sonnet called the "Tropical Summer," which it seems has called forth the encomiums of the literati, and induced certain proprietors of certain papers to persecute him for his portrait. All this is told in a manner that proves it very clearly to be nothing more than an afterthought of Mr. Melville's, and not contemplated in the original plan of the book, that is, if it ever had a plan. It is dragged in merely for the purpose of making Pierre a literary man, when the author had just brought him to such a stage that he did not know what else to do with him.

Of course, under such circumstances, Mr. P. Glendinning, having the responsibility upon his back of Mrs.—Miss Isabel, his wife-sister, (as Mr. Melville himself would express it,) and the young lady of loose morals, and having no money wherewith to support them, can do nothing better than make his living by writing. Accordingly he writes away in his garret; and we cannot help thinking here, that if he wrote at all in the same style that he speaks, his MSS. must have been excessively original and amusing. Here in this poor place he starves his time away in company with Isabel and the young lady of loose morals. Meanwhile he hears of his mother's death, her bequest of all the property to his cousin Stanly, and the betrothal of that gentleman to his late mistress, Lucy Tartan. This intelligence, however, is soon followed by a remarkable event. Miss Lucy Tartan, true to her old habits of flightiness, conceives the resolution of coming to live with Pierre and Isabel, whom she believes to be his wife. Accordingly, she arrives at the haunt of the Apostles, and takes up her abode with her old lover, very much to the disgust of Madam Isabel, who acts much more like a jealous wife than a sister. In this comfortable state they all live together until Mr. Glendinning Stanly and Miss Lucy Tartan's brother arrive at Pierre's domicile to reclaim the fugitive. She refuses to go, however, and Mr. Pierre thrusts them out of the house. Immediately after he receives two notes: one from a bookseller, for whom he was writing a work, informing him that he is a swindler; the other from Messrs. Stanly and Tartan, putting him in possession of the fact that he is a liar and a scoundrel—all of which conclusions the reader arrives at long before this epoch.

Mr. P. Glendinning on reading these notes immediately proceeds to stand on them. This operation is minutely described by our author, and is evidently considered by him as a very effective piece of business. Putting a note under each heel of his boots, appears to be with Mr. P. Glendinning the very climax of vengeance. Having stood for a sufficiently long time upon the epistles, he proceeds to enter an Apostle's room, and burglariously abstract from thence a pair of pistols, which he loads with the unpleasant letters. Then marching into the street, he meets with, and is cowhided by, Mr. Stanly, and in consequence thereof shoots that individual with two distinct pistols. One would have been meagre, but two bullet-holes make the thing dramatic.

Mr. P. Glendinning now makes his appearance in prison; a place that, if fitness were any recommendation, he ought to have been in long ago. Here he raves about as usual in compound words and uncompounded ideas, until Lucy and Isabel enter, when there is a terrific amount of dying, and the usual vial of poison makes its appearance. How many persons give up the ghost in the last chapter of this exciting work, we are really unable to decide. But we have a dim consciousness that every body dies, save and except the young lady of loose morals.

Previous to entering more closely upon the singular merits of this book, we have endeavored, we fear but feebly, to give the reader some idea of the ground-work on which Mr. Melville has strung his farrago of words. If we have succeeded, so much the better, for our readers will perhaps appreciate more fully our approaching remarks. If we have not, it matters but little, for the reader will have lost nothing that is worth a regret.

We have already dismissed the immorality of Mr. Melville's book, which is as horrible in its tendency as Shelley's Cenci, without a ray of the eloquent genius that lights up the deformity of that terrible play; but we have yet another and less repulsive treat in store for the reader. Mr. Melville's style of writing in this book is probably the most extraordinary thing that an American press ever beheld. It is precisely what a raving lunatic who had read Jean Paul Richter *in a translation* might be supposed to spout under the influence of a particularly moon-light night. Word piled upon word, and syllable heaped upon syllable, until the tongue grows as bewildered as the mind, and both refuse to perform their offices from sheer inability to grasp the magnitude of the absurdities. Who would have believed that in the present day a man would write the following, and another be found to publish it!

> "Now Pierre began to see mysteries interpierced with mysteries, and mysteries eluding mysteries; and began to seem to see the mere imaginariness of the so supposed solidest principle of human association. Fate had done this for them. Fate had separated brother and sister, till to each other they somehow seemed so not at all"—Page 193.

There, public! there's a style for you! There, Mr. Hawthorne, you who rely so much upon the quiet force of your language, read that and profit by it! And you, Mr. Longfellow, who love the Germans, and who in "Hyperion" have given us a sample of an ornate and poetical style, pray, read it too, and tell us if it is a wise thing to bind 495 pages of such stuff together, and palm it off upon the public as a book! But here is a string of assertions that we think are not to be surpassed; it is positively refreshing to read them:

> "Of old Greek times, before man's brain went into doting bondage, and bleached and beaten in Baconian fulling mills, his four limbs lost their barbaric tan and beauty; when the round world was fresh, and rosy, and spicy as a new-plucked apple; all's wilted now! In those bold times, the great dead were not, turkey-like, dished in trenchers, and set down all garnished in the ground to glut the damned Cyclop like a cannibal; but nobly envious Life cheated the glutton worm, and gloriously burned the corpse; so that the spirit up-pointed, and visibly forked to heaven!"— Page 269.

We pause here. And when our readers have sufficiently recovered their senses to listen, we will remark that until now we were quite unaware that it was the modern practice to bury people in cover dishes or soup tureens, after having garnished them with parsley. Mr. Melville however asserts it, so it *must* be correct. Neither do we see what the Cyclop has to do with the funereal ceremonies alluded to. A church-yard is the last place in which we should think of looking for Polyphemus.

It is rather a curious study, that of analyzing a man's style. By a little careful examination and comparison, we are always able to hunt out the lurking secret of a writer's diction. We can discover Bulwer's trick of culminating periods, and Dickens's dodge of impossible similes and startling adjectives. A perfectly plain and pure style is the only one which we cannot properly analyze. Its elements are so equally combined that no one preponderates over the other, and we are not able to discover the exact boundary line that separates the art of the author from the nature of the man. But who writes such a style now-a-days? We feel convinced that echo will *not* answer, "Mr. Melville."

The author of Omoo has his own peculiarities. The English language he seems to think is capable of improvement, but his scheme for accomplishing this end is rather a singular one. Carlyle's compound words and Milton's latinic ones sink into insignificance before Mr. Melville's extraordinary concoctions. The gentleman, however, appears to be governed by a very distinct principle in his eccentricities of composition, and errs systematically. The essence of this great eureka, this philological reform, consists in "est" and "ness," added to every word to which they have no earthly right to belong. Feeling it to be our duty to give currency to every new discovery at all likely to benefit the world or literature, we present a few of Mr. Melville's word-combinations, in the hope that our rising authors will profit by the lesson, and thereby increase the richness and intelligibility of their style:

Flushfulness,	page	7	Solidest,	page	193
Patriarchalness,	"	12	Uncapitulatable	"	229
Humanness,	"	16	Ladylikeness,	"	235
Heroicness,	"	do.	Electricalness,	"	206
Perfectest,	"	41	Ardentest,	"	193
Imaginariness,	"	193	Unsystemizable	"	191
Insolubleness,	"	188	Youngness,	"	190
Recallable,	"	186	Unemigrating,	"	470
Entangledly	"	262	Unrunagate,	"	do.
Intermarryingly,	"	151	Undoffable,	"	do.
Magnifiedly,	"	472			

After such a list, what shall we say? Shall we leave Mr. Melville to the tender mercies of the Purists, or shall we execute vengeance upon him ourselves? We would gladly pursue the latter course if we only knew how to accomplish it. As to destroying or abusing the book, we cannot make it appear worse than it is; and if we continue our remarks upon it, it is simply because we have a duty to perform by every improper work, which we have no right to leave unfinished. We shall, then, instead of turning executioners, simply assume the post of monitors, and warn all our little authors who are just now learning to imitate the last celebrity, to

avoid Mr. Melville and his book, as they would some loathsome and in-
fectious distemper.

Perhaps one of the most remarkable features in Pierre, is the boldness
of the metaphors with which it is so thickly studded. Mr. Melville's imagination stops at nothing, and clears a six-barred simile or a twenty-word
antithesis with equal dexterity and daring. It is no light obstacle that will
bring him up in his headlong course, and he scoffs alike at the boundaries
of common sense and the limits of poetical propriety. We have just caught
an image which will serve our purpose, and transfix it, butterfly-like, on
our critical pin, for the admiration of scientific etymologists. It is a fine
specimen, and quite perfect of its kind. Fortunately for the world,
however, the species is very rare:

> "An infixing stillness now thrust a long rivet through the night, and fast
> nailed it to that side of the world!"—Page 219.

This is a grand and simple metaphor. To realize it thoroughly, all we
have to do is to imagine some Titantic upholsterer armed with a gigantic
nail, and hammer to match, hanging one hemisphere with black crape.

His description of a lady's forehead is equally grand and incomprehensible. He says, "The vivid buckler of her brow seemed as a
magnetic plate." Trephining is rather an uncommon operation, but we
fancy that this lady's head must have undergone some such treatment, in
order to warrant her forehead being likened to a "vivid buckler."

Mr. Melville, among other improvements, has favored us with a new
substantive of his own invention. We are very grateful to him for this little
attention, but our thankfulness would be rendered still more willingly if
he had appended a little note explaining the meaning of this—no doubt
very forcible—word. At page 252 we find the following sentence: "Thy
instantaneousness hath killed her." On a first reading of this we hurriedly
came to the conclusion that "instantaneousness" must be either some very
old or some very new weapon of destruction. We judged simply from the
fatal results attributed to it in the sentence. Can it be possible, thought we
to ourselves, that the reign of the sanguinary Colt is over? that revolvers
are gone out of fashion and "instantaneousnesses" come in? What can these
new weapons be like? Have they six barrels, or are they worked by steam?
In the midst of these perplexities we were still further bewildered by coming suddenly upon this passage, at page 248:

> "The strange, imperious *instantaneousness in* him."

Here in an instant was our whole theory upset. The hieroglyph on the
Rosetta stone was not more puzzling than this noun of Mr. Melville's. It
was evident from the context in the last sentence that it could not be a
weapon of destruction, so we immediately formed a conception that it
must be some newly discovered magnetic power, which resided *in* the
man, but could be used with fatal effect if necessary. Upon this hypothesis

we were proceeding to build another theory, far more magnificent than our first, when we lit upon a *third* sentence that sent to the winds all previous speculations. It ran as follows:

"That *instantaneousness* now impelled him."—Page 252.

Eureka! we shouted, we have it. Success has crowned our toil, and the enigma is for ever solved. "Instantaneousness" is a new motive power! We leave our readers to brood over this discovery.

Mr. Melville's lingual improvements do not stop here. He discards all commonplace words, and substitutes much better ones of his own in their stead. He would not for the world call the travelling from one place to another "a journey"—*that* would be far too common. In Mr. Melville's refined diction it becomes "a displacement." Every thing that is dim is with him "nebulous." Hence we have nebulous stories, nebulous landscapes, nebulous meanings, and though last, not least, Mr. Melville himself has given us a very nebulous book!

His descriptive passages are very vivid. The following "night piece" is somewhat after the manner of Callot:

"The obscurely open window, which ever and anon was still softly illumined by the mild heat-lightning and ground lightning, that wove
their wonderfulness without, in the unsearchable air of that *ebonly warm*
and most noiseless summer night."—Page 203.

In the same page, a little further on, we find that

"The casement was suddenly and *wovenly* illumined."

This is no doubt fine to those that understand, but, strange as the confession may appear, we are foolhardy enough to acknowledge that we have not the remotest conception of what it all means. We cannot, by any mental process hitherto discovered, induce our reasoning faculties to accept "ebonly warm" and "wovenly illumined" as conveying any tangible idea. The first two words we do not recognize as belonging to any known language, and we have a shrewd suspicion that the idea—if the author intended any—is quite as undiscoverable.

Again, he hits off a lady's eyes after the following fashion. It may be poetical, but we cannot call it complimentary:

"Her dry burning eyes of long-fringed fire."—Page 202.

This young lady must have been the original performer of the "lightning glance" and the "look of flashing scorn," once used so freely by a certain class of novel-writers.

At page 60 we find the following singular expression:

"It was no wonder that Pierre should flush a bit, and *stammer in his attitudes* a little."

It was an old-fashioned idea that the disease of stammering was usually confined to the organs of speech. In modern times, however, it seems to embrace a wider sphere; and we shall, no doubt, soon hear of "stuttering legs" and "a man with a hesitation in his arm." Nor do we see why the converse should not be adopted, or why a man should not have a "club tongue," or "bunions upon his conversation!"

We have been so far particular in pointing out Mr. Melville's faults. We have attached a certain degree of importance to each of them, from the fact that we are obliged to look upon him in the light of an experienced author, and cannot allow him that boyish license which we are always ready to grant to tyros who lose themselves for the first time amid the bewildering paths of literature. Mr. Melville has written good books, and tasted largely of success, and he ought to have known better. We regret that we are not able to temper our criticism with some unalloyed praise. Critics too often gain the reputation of deriving pleasure from the depreciation of others, but it is those who are ignorant of the art that say so. The true critic rejoices with a boyish enthusiasm when he meets with a work worthy of his admiration. The very nature of his avocation enhances the pleasure he feels at the recognition of original beauty. He that has been travelling for many a weary day over dry and dusty tracks of letterpress, strewn thickly with withered commonplaces, and enlivened only with newly-feathered platitudes, must experience a thrill of strange delight when he suddenly emerges from the desolate path he has been pursuing, and comes upon a rich and pleasant pasture of thought. Believe not, fair Public, that this weary critic will not do the fresh mead justice. Believe rather that in his wild pleasure at lighting upon this pure untrodden ground, where things do not smell of second-hand nature, he will rush madly into the extreme of praise, and search as sedulously for the hidden flowers of beauty as he did before for faults. Critics are not envious or malicious—they are simply just; and being just, they are obliged to condemn three fourths of the books that are submitted to their notice. It is not by any means with a view of proving our magnanimity that we quote the following passage from Pierre as a specimen of Mr. Melville's better genius. Even this very passage is disfigured by affectations and faults, which, in any other book, would condemn it to exclusion; but in a work like Pierre, where all else is so intensely bad, and this is probably the only passage in it that could be extracted with advantage, we feel that we would be doing our author an injustice if, after setting forth all his sins so systematically, we did not present to our readers some favorable specimen of his powers. The passage we subjoin is a description of old Pierre Glendinning, the grandfather of the young Pierre, our ambiguous hero:

> "Now this grand old Pierre Glendinning. . . . steeds whose great-great-great-grandfathers grand old Pierre had reined before."—Pages 38–41.
> [Bk. 2, ch. 3, paras. 3–9]

We have dwelt long enough upon these "Ambiguities." We fear that if we were to continue much longer, we should become ambiguous ourselves. We have, we think, said sufficient to show our readers that Mr. Melville is a man wholly unfitted for the task of writing wholesome fictions; that he possesses none of the faculties necessary for such work; that his fancy is diseased, his morality vitiated, his style nonsensical and ungrammatical, and his characters as far removed from our sympathies as they are from nature.

Let him continue, then, if he must write, his pleasant sea and island tales. We will be always happy to hear Mr. Melville discourse about savages, but we must protest against any more Absurdities, misnamed "Ambiguities."

National Magazine (New York)

1 (November 1852), 476

The papers, secular and religious, are very severe on Herman Melville's last work, called "Pierre; or the Ambiguities." A Boston paper pronounces the volume "abominable trash—an emanation from a lunatic rather than the writing of a sober man."

Athenæum (London)

No. 1308 (20 November 1852), 1265–66

THE brilliant success of some recent American fictionists makes us turn with more than common interest to any new work coming from transatlantic authors. This volume is a would-be utterance of 'Young Yankee' sentimentalism:—but beyond that its writer may be a subject of the States, we can discern nothing either American or original in its pages. It reads like an "upsetting" into English of the first novel of a very whimsical and lackadaisical young student at

the U——
niversity of Gottingen.

It is one of the most diffuse doses of transcendentalism offered for a long time to the public. When he sat down to compose it, the author evidently had not determined what he was going to write about. Its plot is amongst the inexplicable "ambiguities" of the book,—the style is a prolonged succession of spasms,—and the characters are a marrowless tribe of phantoms, flitting through dense clouds of transcendental mysticism. "Be sure," said Pope to a young author, "when you have written any passage that you think particularly fine—*to erase it*." If this precept were applied to 'Pierre; or, the Ambiguities,'—its present form would shrink into almost as many pages as there are now chapters. German literature with its depths and shallows is too keenly appreciated in this country for readers to endure Germanism at second hand. We take up novels to be amused—not bewildered,—in search of pleasure for the mind—not in pursuit of cloudy metaphysics; and it is no refreshment after the daily toils and troubles of life, for a reader to be soused into a torrent rhapsody uttered in defiance of taste and sense.

Love has often driven wise men mad, and the workings of that subtle passion have given rise to many strange effusions even from men of genius:—but what do our readers think of a passage like this?—

> "No Cornwall miner ever sunk so deep a shaft beneath the sea, as Love will sink beneath the floatings of the eyes. . . . on many a distant shore the gentler west wind persuades the arid east." [Bk.2, ch.4, paras. 10–11]

Pierre finds a rocking stone in the woods, and thus apostrophizes.—

> " 'If the miseries of the undisclosable things in me . . . as he owed thanks to none, and went his moody way." [Bk. 7, ch. 5, paras. 2–3]

That many readers will not follow "the moody way" of Pierre, is in our apprehension not amongst the "ambiguities" of the age. The present chaotic performance has nothing American about it, except that it reminds us of a prairie in print,—wanting the flowers and freshness of the savannahs, but almost equally puzzling to find a way through it.

ARTICLES AND ESSAYS

Neglect and Abuse, 1853-1917

[An Unhealthy Mystic Romance]

Anonymous*

Mr. Melville has published already (1852) six works. The first, entitled "Typee, or a Peep at Polynesian Life, during a Residence of Four Months in a Valley of the Marquesas," was published in London, early in 1846. It immediately appeared in the United States, and was soon translated into some of the European languages. It met with marked success, and the writer suddenly acquired a substantial reputation. "Omoo, or Adventures in the South Seas," appeared in 1847, in London. In 1849, "Mardi, and a Voyage thither," and "Redburn, or the Adventures of the Son of a Gentleman," were published; in 1850, "White-jacket, or the World in a Man-of-War;" and in 1851, "Moby-Dick, or the Whale." His latest production is "Pierre, or the Ambiguities," an unhealthy mystic romance, in which are conjured up "unreal night-mare conceptions, a confused phantasmagoria of distorted fancies and conceits, ghostly abstractions, and fitful shadows," altogether different from the hale and sturdy sailors and fresh sea-breezes of his earlier productions. It met with a decided non-success, and has not been reprinted in this country.

[The Late Miserable Abortion]

[Abel Stevens]†

Mr. Hawthorne's position in our literature has become quite determinate, and will unquestionably be permanent. . . . With the prestige of his past decided success, the mature strength of life before him, and original and abundant resources within him, he stands forth *the* American author of his day. Such both foreign and domestic authorities pronounce him.

With these views of his merits and prospects, we cannot but regret some of his faults . . . . We have space here to notice but one of them, and

*Reprinted from "Melville, Herman," in *Men of the Time or Sketches of Living Notables* (London: David Bogue, 1853), pp. 310-11.
†Reprinted from "The Editor's Table," *National Magazine* (New York), 2 (January 1853), 87-88.

that, to us, is the most serious one. We refer to the unhealthy tone of his works. They tend, as our critic asserts, to make the reader better, but they do so by a most ungenial process. Hawthorne shows a morbid propensity for morbid characters—bizarre anomalies of human nature. A strong predilection for this sort of writing seems to be developing itself in our national literature. Poe's best poems and his prose tales are rife with it. Some of Miss Cheesebro's volumes are sad examples of it. "Pierre, or the Ambiguities," the late miserable abortion of Melville, is another. In the name of all that is good or beautiful, why should art of any kind be prostituted to such moral deformities? As well might the sculptor reproduce the horrors of Dupruytren's Pathological Museum. Dupruytren's specimens have their place and their uses unquestionably, but are fit only for the eyes of medical men. The morbid facts and characters of this kind of literature may be real, and have their appropriate place of record; but it is in the annals of crime, or, more frequently, in the annals of insanity, not in the productions of genius and beautiful letters—the common and health-giving food (as they should be) of the common mind. . . .

. . . The *London Atlas* says:—"It is a melancholy sign for the prospects of rising American literature that some of its most hopeful professors should have, in recent works of fiction, been evidently laying themselves out for that species of subtile psychological romance, first introduced to the reading world by such authors as Balzac and Sand. Abandoning the hearty and wholesome tone which has almost always characterized English literature—giving up the painting of real human manners and human actions—Mr. Nathaniel Hawthorne and some others of his countrymen have adopted the style of a bastard French school, and set themselves to the analysis and dissection of diseased mind and unhealthy and distorted sentiment. Anything more sad and foul than this change it would be impossible to imagine. Instead of conveying to us on this side of the Atlantic a true idea of American society—society in the great seaboard city or in the far West settlement—instead of presenting us with stories, racy of the soil and instinct with its vigorous and aggressive theories, the misguided party in question select some half-dozen morbid phases of mind, bring before us three or four intellectual cripples or moral monsters—personages resembling in their spiritual natures the calves with two heads or the cats with five legs exhibited at fairs—and then proceed with the dryest minuteness to describe the pathology of the morbid structure, to trace and dissect the anatomy of the monstrous moral and intellectual abortion, and, instead of laying before us a wholesome story of natural character and motive, to let us into the secret turnings and windings of unhealthy and abnormal mental power and promptings."

[Inexcusable Insanity]

[Fitz-James O'Brien]*

It is no easy matter to pronounce which of Mr. Melville's books is the best. All of them (and he has published a goodly number, for so young an author) have had their own share of success, and their own peculiar merits, always saving and excepting Pierre—wild, inflated, repulsive that it is.

. . . In every thing he [Sir Thomas Browne] says there is a deep meaning, although sometimes an erroneous one. We cannot always say as much for Mr. Melville. In his latest work he transcended even the jargon of Paracelsus and his followers. The Rosetta stone gave up its secret, but we believe that to the end of time Pierre will remain an ambiguity.

. . . Typee, his [Melville's] first book, was healthy; Omoo nearly so; after that came Mardi, with its excusable wildness; then came Moby-Dick, and Pierre with its inexcusable insanity. We trust that these rhapsodies will end the interregnum of nonsense to which Keats refers, as forming a portion of every man's life; and that Mr. Melville will write less at random and more at leisure, than of late. Of his last book we would fain not speak, did we not feel that he is just now at that stage of author-life when a little wholesome advice may save him a hundred future follies. When first we read Pierre, we felt a strong inclination to believe the whole thing to be a well-got-up hoax. We remembered having read a novel in six volumes once of the same order, called "The Abbess," in which the stilted style of writing is exposed very funnily; and, as a specimen of unparalleled bombast, we believed it to be unequalled until we met with *Pierre*. . . . Now Pierre has all the madness of Mardi, without its vague, dreamy, poetic charm. All Mr. Melville's many affectations of style and thought are here crowded together in a mad mosaic. Talk of Rabelais's word-nonsense! there was always something queer, and odd, and funny, gleaming through his unintelligibility. But Pierre transcends all the nonsense-writing that the world ever beheld.

Thought staggers through each page like one poisoned. Language is drunken and reeling. Style is antipodical, and marches on its head. Then the moral is bad. Conceal it how you will, a revolting picture presents itself. A wretched, cowardly boy for a hero who from some feeling of mad romance, together with a mass of inexplicable reasons which, probably, the author alone fathoms, chooses to live in poverty with his illegitimate sister, whom he passes off to the world as his wife, instead of being respectably married to a legitimate cousin. Everybody is vicious in some way or other. The mother is vicious with pride. Isabel has a cancer of morbid, vicious, minerva-press-romance, eating into her heart. Lucy Tartan is viciously humble, and licks the dust beneath Pierre's feet

*Reprinted from "Our Young Authors—Melville," *Putnam's Monthly* (New York), 1 (February 1853), 155–64.

viciously. Delly Ulver is humanly vicious, and in the rest of the book, whatever of vice is wanting in the remaining characters, is made up by superabundant viciosities of style.

Let Mr. Melville stay his step in time. He totters on the edge of a precipice, over which all his hard-earned fame may tumble with such another weight as Pierre attached to it. He has peculiar talents, which may be turned to rare advantage. Let him diet himself for a year or two on Addison, and avoid Sir Thomas Browne, and there is little doubt but that he will make a notch on the American Pine.

[From "American Authorship, No. IV—Herman Melville"]

"Sir Nathaniel"*

Speaking of the passengers on board Redburn's ship *Highlander*, Mr. Melville significantly and curtly observes, "As for the ladies, I have nothing to say concerning them; for ladies are like creeds; if you cannot speak well of them, say nothing." He will pardon us for including in this somewhat arbitrary classification of forms of beauty and forms of faith, his own, last, and worst production, "Pierre; or, the Ambiguities."

O author of "Typee" and "Omoo," we admire so cordially the proven capacity of your pen, that we entreat you to doff the "non-natural sense" of your late lucubrations—to put off your worser self—and to do your better, real self, that justice which its "potentiality" deserves.

[Frightful Nightmare]

Anonymous†

The readers of Omoo and Typee will be rejoiced to learn, that their favorite Hermann Melville has awakened from that uneasy sleep, during which his genius was disturbed by such distempered dreams as Mardi, and frightful nightmares like the ambiguous Pierre. We are again promised a prospect of another of those Pacific elysiums, which the oriental imagination of the author of Typee can so richly reproduce, in a series of articles for one of our New York monthlies. It is said that the next number of Putnam is to contain "The Encantadas, or The Enchanted Isles," a reminiscence of life among a group of islands on the equator, somewhere in the wide Pacific, one of those oases of the desert sea, where, under the pilotage of Melville, all readers will be sure of falling in with refreshing fountains of pleasure and delight.

*Reprinted from the *New Monthly Magazine* (London), 98 (July 1853), 300–08.
†Reprinted from the *New York Evening Post*, 14 February 1854.

[From a Review of *Israel Potter*]

Anonymous*

"Israel Potter" is well known to the readers of Putnam's Magazine. It is now published as the work of Herman Melville, whose earlier productions placed him high among our writers of fiction, but whose late works have been unsatisfactory, not to say ridiculous. . . . Mr Melville has made a most interesting book from the facts at his command—a book, not great, not remarkable for any particular in it, but of a curt, manly, independent tone, dealing with truth honestly, and telling it feelingly. Its *Paul Jones* and *Benjamin Franklin*, to be sure, are not without a spice of Melville's former "humors," as they used to be called; but upon the whole, its style, sentiment and construction are so far above those of "Pierre" and some of its predecessors, that we dislike to say one word against it. It is a readable book, with passages and descriptions of power. We trust its successor will be quite as sensible, but be of wider scope and a larger subject.

[From a Review of *Israel Potter*]

Anonymous†

This very simple yet graphic recital of interesting adventure is republished in attractive form from the pages of *Putnam's Magazine*, its appearance in which we have noticed with more or less favor for many months past. As a literary performance it is equal to anything which Mr. MELVILLE's pen has produced, although it is in quite a different vein from that in which he has heretofore worked with so much success. Its style is remarkably manly and direct, and is in this respect in pleasant contrast to that of Mr. MELVILLE's last book.

[From "American Authors— Melville"]

Anonymous‡

Who is this rough "sailor before the mast," in jacket and tarpaulin, with rolling gait and tarry aspect, who intrudes so unceremoniously upon the grave and black-coated fraternity of American Authors, and boldly

*Reprinted from the *Boston Post*, 15 March 1855.
†Reprinted from the *Morning Courier and New-York Enquirer*, 17 March 1855.
‡Reprinted from the *New York Christian Intelligencer*, 22 January 1857.

elbows his way to a front seat among the best of them? Who is this new Rasselas, who runs away from a happier valley than the Prince of Abysinia ever saw, to beguile civilised ears with glowing pictures of life among the gentle savages of Typee? Who is this pleasant, witty, dashing companion, who in "Omoo," "White Jacket," and "Redburn" has given us some of the most brilliant and high-colored, though not always reliable, salt-water books ever published? Who is this madman, who in "Moby Dick, or the Whale," has mingled the coolest and calmest matter-of-fact with the wildest midsummer lunacy—who in one chapter scientifically cuts up Leviathan, and stows away his oil with an eye to dollars, and in the next, out-Carlyles Carlyle in some wild rhapsody, some insane Babel-talk, in which nothing can be clearly made out save that there has been a woeful waste of learning and genius in its concoction. Who is this imitator of the worst French school, who in "Pierre" has poured out a flood of lurid nonsense which, it is to be hoped, no one save the devoted proof-reader has ever had the patience to wade through? . . . .

These books are certainly among the most remarkable productions of our literature. The author wields a wondrous and witching pen, and once under their influence, the reader cannot easily shake off his spells. There is a perennial vigor and vitality in his writings. They fascinate, startle, astound. He is so wealthy in imagination, and so profuse in the expenditure of his treasures, that in reading him one is apt to labor under what our Gallic neighbors call an "embarrassment of riches." He is a bundle of incongruities. Sometimes he will coil up delicate little bits of beauty in out-of-the-way places, where they are scarcely appreciable by any but a spirit of sympathetic criticism, and anon, he will shock both the æsthetic and moral sense by some broad, coarse, glaring *ad captandum* effect. Sometimes he is fresh, wholesome, and natural—at others, he is morbid, fantastic, spectral. But whatever else he may be, he is never weak—he never fails to leave an impression of power. His genius is original, and creative; he has struck out a new path for himself; he is always thoroughly in earnest, and here lies the real secret of his popularity.

[From A Review of *The Confidence-Man*]

Anonymous*

It will be seen that Mr. Melville can still write powerfully when it pleases him. Even when most wayward, he yet gives evidence of much latent genius, which, however, like latent heat, is of little use either to him or to us. We should wish to meet him again in his legitimate department, as the

*Reprinted from the *Literary Gazette* (London), No. 2099 (11 April 1857), 348–49.

prose-poet of the ocean; if, however, he will persist in indoctrinating us with his views concerning the *vrai*, we trust he will at least condescend to pay, for the future, some slight attention to the *vraisemblable*. He has ruined this book, as he did 'Pierre,' by a strained effort after excessive originality. When will he discover that—

> "Standing on the head makes not
> Either for ease or dignity?"

[From A Review of
The Confidence-Man]

Anonymous*

The author of *Typee* has again come upon us in one of his strange vagaries, and calls himself *The Confidence Man*. His publishers are Dix, Edwards & Co., who seem to have an affection for our young authors. Mr. Melville's *Confidence Man* is almost as ambiguous an apparition as his *Pierre*, who was altogether an impossible and ununderstandable creature. But, in the *Confidence Man* there is no attempt at a novel, or a romance, for Melville has not the slightest qualifications for a novelist, and therefore he appears to much better advantage here than in his attempts at story books. . . .

[More Akin to the Modern Novel]

Anonymous*

Mr. Herman Melville has been well known for a dozen years past, both in this country and Europe, as the author of a number of tales, the most popular and best of which are stories of the sea, such as "Typee," "Omoo," and "Moby Dick." Of late years, Mr. M. has turned his attention to another species of composition more akin to the modern novel. "Pierre, or the Ambiguities," is an example of this; highly extravagant and unnatural, but original and interesting in its construction and characters. His last production, "The Confidence Man," is one of the dullest and most dismally monotonous books we remember to have read, and it has been our unavoidable misfortune to peruse, in the fulfillment of journalistic duty, a number of volumes through, which nothing but a sense of obligation would have sustained us. "Typee," one of, if not the first of his works, is the best, and "The Confidence Man" the last, decidedly the worst. So

*Reprinted from the *New York Daily Times* [Supplement], 11 April 1857.

*Reprinted from a review of Melville's lecture on Roman statuary, *Cincinnati Enquirer*, 3 February 1858.

Mr. M's authorship is toward the nadir rather than the zenith, and he has been progressing in the form of an inverted climax.

[Unfettered by Ordinary Precedents]

Anonymous*

    Those who have read Herman Melville's "Omoo," "Typee" and "Pierre," need not be told that a strong vein of poetic feeling pervades passages of these works, expressed sometimes rather wildly and even vaguely, but nevertheless real and unquestionable. . . . His style in verse is as unfettered by ordinary precedents as in such of his prose works as "Pierre." His accounts of the impressions produced by the various reports from Fort Donelson—about the time of its surrender—is a specimen of this, yet it presents a faithful picture of the times, and recalls them vividly to the mind of the reader.

[From "Literary Invalids"]

Anonymous†

    A New York correspondent of the Cincinnati *Times* writes: The custom house appears to be a kind of hospital for literary invalids who retain their positions through all changes of administration. Among the litterateurs there are Richard Grant White [and Charles F. Briggs, Richard Henry Stoddard, and Robert Barry Coffin]. . . .

    Herman Melville, who delighted the publick with his "Typee" and "Omoo," and ended with such trash as "Pierre" and the "Confidence Man," has enrolled himself in the service of Uncle Sam. He is thoroughly written out, and so very unpractical that he needs some such position to live.

    How the scribblers manage to retain their situations there year after year, and term after term, I do not understand. They may be trimmers—I hope they are not—or they may be deemed incapable of earning a living in the ordinary way, on account of their literary tastes and pursuits. Possibly they are considered geniuses in the popular sense—men who can't do anything worth doing, and who need to be taken care of by persons of common sense.

---

*Reprinted from a review of *Battle-Pieces*, *New York Evening Post*, 10 October 1866.
†Reprinted from *Richmond Southern Opinion*, 4 July 1868.

[The Most Impossible of All his Books]

Julian Hawthorne*

But in what manner have our other writers of fiction treated the difficulties that were thus dealt with by Hawthorne?—Herman Melville cannot be instanced here; for his only novel or romance, whichever it be, was also the most impossible of all his books, and really a terrible example of the enormities which a man of genius may perpetrate when working in a direction unsuited to him. I refer, of course, to "Pierre, or the Ambiguities."

[From "Herman Melville's Funeral"]

Arthur Stedman†

. . . Mr. Melville always has been an interesting figure to New-York literary circles. So far from being forgotten, he was among the very first to be invited to join the Author's Club at its founding in 1882. His declination of this offer, as well as his general refusal to enter into social life, are said to have been chiefly due to natural disposition, and partly to the very adverse critical reception afforded his novel, "Pierre, or the Ambiguities," published in 1852.

[A Stupid Book]

Anonymous‡

Do boys between the ages of 10 and 70 read his books now? I fear not, for some of them are out of print; and yet I was mightily pleased at finding the copy of "Moby Dick"—and what a queer yarn it is—thumbed beyond repair, and with broken back, the testimony of the appreciation of frequenters of the Public Library. What a grand fellow that harpoon-man was—I have forgotten his name—who, when he was in the New Bedford inn, began dressing by putting on his stove-pipe hat.

Then there was "Typee," and who would not have lived among such cannibals and watched the maidens bathing in the surf? Then came

*Reprinted from "The American Element in Fiction," *North American Review* (New York), 139 (August 1884), 175.
†Reprinted from the *New York Daily Tribune*, 1 October 1891.
‡Reprinted from "Here in Boston," *Boston Post*, 2 October 1891.

"Omoo," the book that made the missionaries so mad with anger. "Mardi" I never understood: it was an olia podrida, compounded of transcendentalism, Rabelais, hashish and tar. "White Jacket" was thoroughly delightful, and from "Redburn" I learned the interesting fact that certain members of the English aristocracy had a coronet stamped upon their boot heels. "Pierre" was a stupid book. "The Confidence Man" baffled my conjecture. I never could read his poetry, but the short stories—they came out in the old Putnam's Magazine—were dear to me, even the grotesque "Lightning Rod Man."

[From "Herman Melville"]

Anonymous*

The most important of his other books [after *Typee* and *Omoo*] were *White Jacket, or the World in a Man-of-War; Moby Dick, or the White Whale; Pierre, or the Ambiguities; Israel Potter; The Piazza Tales; The Confidence Man*; and a volume of poems published the year after the close of the war. After 1866 Mr. Melville withdrew from the world, and lived in the strictest seclusion, prompted perhaps by natural melancholy of temperament, and his anger possibly at the bitter and persistent attacks of the critics consequent on the publication of *Pierre*.

[A Repulsive, Insane and Impossible Romance]

Julian Hawthorne and Leonard Lemmon†

"Moby Dick, or The Whale" takes up the whole subject of whaling, as practised in the '30's and '40's, and is, if anything, more interesting and valuable than "White Jacket"; the scenes are grouped about a wildly romantic and original plot, concerned with the chase round the world of an enormous white whale—Moby Dick—by a sea-captain who has previously lost a limb in a conflict with the monster, and has sworn revenge. This is the most powerful of Melville's books; it was also the last of any literary importance. "Pierre, or The Ambiguities" is a repulsive, insane and impossible romance, in which the sea has no part, and one or two later books need not be mentioned. But Melville's position in literature is secure and solitary: he surpasses Cooper, when Cooper writes

*Reprinted from *Harper's Weekly Magazine* (New York), 35 (10 October 1891), 782.
†Reprinted from "Herman Melville, An Early Sea-Novelist," in *American Literature: A Text-Book for The Use of Schools and Colleges* (Boston: D. C. Heath, 1892), pp. 208–09.

of the sea; and no subsequent writer has even challenged a comparison
with him on that element.

[From "Herman Melville: A Great Pittsfield Author—Brief Biographical Sketch"]

[J.E.A. Smith]*

The volume of Battle Pieces was received by the press without harsh
criticism; but also without the favor which it merited as its author must
have well known and felt. The same was true of some other of his later
works which had merit that would have been recognized by the critics
and the public,[1] had not the shadow of that unhappy Pierre come between them and the splendor of his early fame. We cannot deny that sen-
sitiveness to this criticism had much to do with his retirement from
literary work, although other circumstances which we have mentioned
also contributed to it. . . .

But, whatever influence—be it what it may—the general criticism of
his later works had upon Mr. Melville's withdrawal from literary work,
those who attributed it to the unlimited censure of Pierre, show a strange
forgetfulness of dates, for that work was published in 1852, and he continued to write with energy for 12 years afterwards. As for Pierre itself its
condemnation was just; but Herman Melville was not the first great
author who ever made a single lapse. Among the greatest there are
writings to which oblivion would be the best charity. That charity should
have been bestowed upon Pierre, and its memory not preserved to cloud
judgment of the author's later works. That it was not done is an exceptional case in literary history. Yet there are keen and just thoughts scattered here and there through the book, and at least a score of pages of
local interest which we of Berkshire could ill afford to lose. First comes
the dedication to "King Greylock" in which the author in his own peculiar
quaintness proclaims the devoted loyalty of himself and his fellow subjects
to that great monarch of all he surveys; sitting in regal—or rather as Mr.
Melville describes it in imperial—majesty upon a throne whose everlasting stability is so grandly in contrast with the tumble-down things
which human monarchs mount and call eternal. We transcribe it. . . .

Even better than this is the pen picture of our pet local monster and
geological mystery

The Balanced Rock.

in Lanesboro on the edge of Pittsfield. The description in "Pierre" of this

*Reprinted from the *Pittsfield Evening Journal*, 16 and 25 January 1892.

wonderful natural problem for the learned and of marvelling curiosity for all, is the best ever written; and for that reason we copy it.

> "Pierre plunged deep into the woods, and paused not for several miles
> . . . . that spot first menaced by the Terror Stone should it ever really
> topple." [Bk 7, ch. 4, paras. 1–3, 6–7]

As a picture this is perfect. It is as realistic as a photograph, with the addition of whatever interpretation a poetic artist could give it. But the story attached to it is purely imaginary, as is also what is said of the location and its surroundings. The portion whose omission is indicated by stars is only one of the irrelevant rhapsodies which mar many of Mr. Melville's later works; and Pierre most of all. Even in books where he was not avowedly his own hero, he often idealized himself in portions of the story of some of his characters; or it may be more correct to say that he often, and sometimes very closely, modelled incidents in his stories upon real ones in his own experience; very often in cases where he had been magna pars. Of course he did not incorporate these incidents literally and bodily into the story; and still less was his idealization of himself a portrait of what he was in his own eyes. Like other novelists, he adapted both to the exigences of the plot. Unfortunately, in Pierre, the exigences of the plot were—in the author's own estimation, "ambiguous." The book itself was simply a freak of genius, and should have been so regarded by the world. We catch here and there in it, glimpses of the family portraits,— there is one by the bye, in the Athenæum, which is valuable, but not as a work of art. There is also a shadowy vision of the author's maiden aunt. But Greylock and Balance Rock are what chiefly interest Berkshire readers. In the case of the rock, aside from its photographic likeness the variations were wide; Pierre, even in fiction, was not "the first known publishing discoverer of the stone," for it was early known to geologists like Professors Emmons and Dewey, and already had its place in story. Nor was the surrounding population so indifferent to its wondrous character as the story would indicate. Lanesboro society at that time and for years before, was as refined and intelligent as that of any town or city in the commonwealth, and its members were fully alive to the beauties and wonders with which nature surrounded them; and, after the nearer Constitution hill and Pontoosuc lake, the first to which they invited their friends from abroad, was the Balanced Rock—or as they called it "The Rolling Rock," probably because it would not roll. To reach it Pierre had no occasion to plunge madly or otherwise, through miles of original forest, for there had not been a forest within a mile of it for more than a century. The last relics of one were a few beeches, chestnuts and maples, whose bark was thickly inscribed with the names or initials of generations of visitors. Sorry are we to say it, but these too have mostly disappeared.

The true story of the Memnon naming is this: One charming summer day, Mr. Melville, passing with his accustomed party of merry ladies and gentlemen, over smooth roads, came to the rock, and there had their usual picnic. While the party were enjoying their woodland meal one of the ladies crept into that fearful recess under the rock into which no man dare venture. And soon there issued from its depths sweet and mysterious music. This cunning priestess had hidden there a magnificent music box whose delicious strains must still be remembered, by some in Pittsfield and New York. This mysterious music completed in Mr. Melville's mind the resemblance to the Egyptian Memnon suggested by the size and form of the rock. And voila—Pierre's Memnon!

Note

1. The *Evening Journal* prints "the cities and the public"; the correction appears in Smith's *Biographical Sketch of Herman Melville, 1891* (1897), a reprinting of the *Evening Journal* article, which appeared in nine installments between October 1891 and January 1892. [Ed. Note.]

[Mere Bombast and Rhetoric: A Fatal Climax]

The increasing transcendentalism of Melville's later thought was accompanied and reflected by a corresponding complexity of language, the limpid simplicity so remarkable in "Typee," and "Omoo," and "White Jacket" being now succeeded by a habit of gorgeous and fantastic word-painting, which, though brilliantly effective at its best, degenerated, at its worst, into mere bombast and rhetoric, a process which had already been discernible in the concluding portions of "Mardi," while in "Pierre" (or "The Ambiguities," as it was appropriately designated) it reached the fatal climax of its development. This unfortunate book, published in 1852, was to a great extent the ruin of its author's reputation; for the critics not unfairly protested against the perversity of "a man born to create, who resolves to anatomise; a man born to see, who insists upon speculating." Of "The Confidence Man" (1857), and Melville's later books in general, it is not necessary to speak; though it is noticeable that in his narrative of "Israel Potter" (1855), and one or two of the short stories in "The Piazza Tales" (1856), he partly recovered his old firmness of touch and delicacy of workmanship.

For, in spite of all the obscurities and mannerisms which confessedly

*Reprinted from " 'Marquesan Melville,' " *Gentleman's Magazine* (London), 272 (March 1892), 248-57.

deform his later writings, it remains true that *naturalness* is, on the whole, Melville's prime characteristic, both in the tone and in the style of his productions.

[All But Unreadable]

Ernest Rhys*

"Moby Dick" was the last book in which the balance between transcendentalism and reality in Melville was maintained with any effective control of his art as a romancer. Some of his books, such as "Pierre; or, The Ambiguities," an ominous sub-title, 1852, and "The Confidence Man," are all but unreadable.

[Hopelessly Frantic]

Carl Van Doren†

Too irregular, too bizarre, perhaps, ever to win the widest suffrage, the immense originality of *Moby Dick* must warrant the claim of its admirers that it belongs with the greatest sea romances in the whole literature of the world. . . . Although he [Melville] did not cease to write at once, *Moby Dick* seems to have exhausted him. *Pierre* (1852) is hopelessly frantic; *Israel Potter* (1855) is not markedly original; neither are *The Piazza Tales* (1856), and *The Confidence Man* (1857).

[A Sailor's Theory of Ethics]

Edwin E. Slosson‡

"Smell I the flowers or thee?" cried Pierre.

"See I lakes or eyes?" cried Lucy, her own gazing down into his soul as two stars gaze down into a tarn.

That was the way lovers talked to each other in the fifties according to Herman Melville, or else that was the way he thought they ought to

*Reprinted from "Editor's Note," in *Moby Dick*, Everyman's Library (London: J. M. Dent & Co.; New York: E. P. Dutton & Co., 1907), pp. vii–viii.

†Reprinted from "Contemporaries of Cooper," in *The Cambridge History of American Literature*, ed. W. P. Trent et al. (New York: G. P. Putnam's Sons; Cambridge, England: University Press, 1917), I, 323.

‡Reprinted from 'A Number of Things," *Independent* (New York), 89 (8 January 1917), 84.

talk. From this sample of the dialog it is no wonder that his novel of "Pierre or the Ambiguities" never attained the popularity of "Typee" and "Omoo." Most of the admirers of Melville believe that after writing "Moby Dick"—some would say before—his mind flew the track and went off on a tangent for the remaining forty years of his life. But embedded in the "Ambiguities"—to give the strange romance its most appropriate name—there is fragment apparently brought down from some earlier mental epoch. It is entitled "Chronologicals and Horologicals," and contains an original theory of local morality based upon the idea of local time, especially pertinent just now when countries are shifting their clocks back and forth to save daylight or rather gaslight. It is a theory of ethics that would naturally occur to a sailorman, if a sailorman theorized on ethics at all, for as he went from port to port he would find them all with different times and with different codes of morality, and he would have to adopt both while in the port if he wanted to get along smoothly with the people there. Yet above all the ports he would see the stars which somehow must be eternally right.

Melville considers the case of a ship which sets its chronometer by Greenwich and carries it to China where it is wrong and yet it has guided the vessel aright across the trackless deep. Then he applies his analogy in this fashion:

> Now in an artificial world like ours, the soul of man is further removed from its God and the Heavenly Truth, than the chronometer carried to China is from Greenwich. As that chronometer, if at all accurate, will pronounce it to be twelve o'clock high noon, when the China local watches say perhaps it is twelve o'clock midnight, so the chronometric soul, if in this world true to its great Greenwich in the other, will always in its so-called intuitions of right and wrong, be contradicting the mere local standards and watchmaker's brains of this earth.
>
> Bacon's brains were mere watchmaker's brains; but Christ was a chronometer; and the most exquisitely adjusted and exact one, and the least affected by all terrestrial jarrings, of any that have ever come to us. And the reason why his teachings seemed folly to the Jews, was because he carried Heaven's time in Jerusalem, while the Jews carried Jerusalem time there. . . . But whatever is really peculiar in the wisdom of Christ seems precisely the same folly today as it did 1850 years ago. Because in all that interval his bequeathed chronometer has still preserved its original Heaven's time, and the general Jerusalem of the world has likewise carefully preserved its own. . . . Nor does God at the Heavenly Greenwich expect common men to keep Greenwich wisdom in this remote Chinese world of ours; because such a thing were unprofitable for them here and indeed a falsification of himself in as much as in that case, China time would be identical with Greenwich time, which would make Greenwich time wrong.
>
> But why then does God now and then send a heavenly chronometer (as

a meteoric stone) into the world, uselessly as it would seem, to give the lie to all the world's time-keepers? Because he is unwilling to have men without some occasional testimony to this: that tho man's Chinese notions of things may answer well enough here, they are by no means universally applicable and that the central Greenwich in which he dwells goes by a somewhat different method from this world.

From this Melville reaches the conclusion "that this world's seeming incompatibility with God absolutely results from its meridional correspondence to him." This conclusion is as convenient as it is ingenious for it enables one to postpone to Heaven any precepts that prove impracticable on earth. Which anyway is what we all do even without hearing of his justification.

A virtuous expediency, then, seems the most desirable or attainable earthly excellence for the mass of men, and is the only earthly excellence that their creator intended for them. When they go to Heaven, it will be quite another thing. There they can freely turn the left check, because there the right cheek will never be smitten. There they can freely give all to the poor, for *there* there will be no poor to give to.

It is lucky Melville lived before Michelson's interferometer abolished the ether, for with the ether would have been swept away the last remnant of his orthodoxy. For according to the now fashionable theory of relativity there is no such thing as absolute time and simultaneity is a simulacrum dependent upon the motion of the observers. What the theory of relativity will do to ethics when it gets in there is appalling to contemplate.

Discovery 1919-1929

[Melville's Failures]

F.C. Owlett*

Mr. Shorter and others have styled Melville the American Borrow. To a certain extent the implied comparison is just. Both were vagabonds, in the sense of Alexander Smith's delightful essay of that title; both knew how to turn their vagabondisings to good account in the weaving their experiences into fascinating narrative; both had the poetic vision; both had humour.

Melville, however, was much more of the idealist than Borrow, who at bottom was a realist. Melville's idealism frequently became transcendentalism. In transcendental mood he conceived and fashioned "Moby Dick." It is the finest sea story in the world. In transcendental mood he wrote "Mardi," "Pierre," and other books equally unreadable. The robuster humour of Borrow saved him from perpetrating a "Pierre"; his greater matter-of-factness prevented his ever giving to the world a "Moby Dick."

Melville's humour is of a subtler and more intimate quality than Lavengro's. It permeates his work—is, indeed, the vital essence of it—charging it through and through, and playing on it from without as it were, lambent always save in those great moments when it breaks and surges in riot. His style is spontaneous, buoyant, rich—with the richness of seventeenth century prose (Mr. Strachey has pointed out the literary kinship of Melville with Sir Thomas Browne). His best descriptive passages reach the highest level of impassioned prose, and even in those books where he falls farthest from literary grace, he never loses his sense of the force and the colour of words. It may even be contended that the badness of his worst work is due to an over-development of this same sense, which, in its relation to our author's other excellent qualities, exhibited at times the dangerous tendencies of an Aaron's rod. . . .

The great books, then, are "Typee" (1846), "Omoo" (1847), "White Jacket" (1850), and "Moby Dick, or The Whale" (1852)—these four. Melville's other books, e.g., "Mardi" (1848), "Pierre" (1852), "Israel

*Reprinted from "Herman Melville (1819-1891): A Centenary Tribute," *Bookman* (London), 56 (August 1919), 166-67.

89

Potter" (1855), "Piazza Tales" (1856), and "The Confidence Man" (1857) must be accounted failures, in spite of some excellent writing (particularly in "Mardi" and in "Israel Potter," the latter of which was praised by Hawthorne for its delineations of Franklin and Paul Jones), because, in them, the transcendentalist and metaphysician too often triumphed over the artist and poet. The difference between "Typee" and "Pierre" is the difference between Philip drunk and Philip sober. That Philip should ever have been drunk is unfortunate; that Philip in his cups, as it were, should have wielded the pen, is hard lines on Philip sober. Had Melville's masterpieces, indeed, been less masterly they would hardly have availed to save their writer's memory from the oblivion which at one time seemed to threaten it.

[Like a Transcendentalist's Ravings]

Philip Hale*

It is a singular fact that those writing about Herman Melville whose centenary is now celebrated have nothing to say about two of his books that are to be ranked with "Typee" and "Moby Dick." Some have dwelt on the "unintelligibility" of "Pierre" and "The Confidence Man," which, to say the least, are queer, reminding one at times of a transcendentalist's ravings. Due praise has been awarded "Typee," "Omoo," "White Jacket," "Moby Dick". . . .

"The Piazza Tales" and "Israel Potter" have passed unnoticed, yet these books alone would give Melville a high and honorable position in American, yes, English literature.

. . . How Melville became imbued with the mysticism that crops out even in "Moby Dick," the one great prose epic of the sea, has never been explained. There is no life of him, to our knowledge. The biographical sketches are inadequate. We are told in them that he married the daughter of Chief Justice Lemuel Shaw, to whom he dedicated "Typee"; but why did Melville suddenly become lonelier in New York city than he was on any island in the Pacific? What mental transformation led him to unite [write?] "Pierre" and "The Confidence Man?"

*Reprinted from "As the World Wags," *Boston Herald,* 1 August 1919.

[An Evil French Influence]

Anonymous*

When "White Jacket" appeared in 1850, and "Moby Dick" a year later, his fame had reached its zenith, and a point by no means unenviable. Both books were perceived at the time by sound judges to be what they are, admirable specimens of combined narrations and exposition. Unfortunately, there had begun creeping upon the now quiet inhabitant of the spacious Pittsfield farmhouse the "morbid state of mind"—as his neighbor, Hawthorne called it—which was to be his literary ruin. Its encroachments may be clearly seen in "Moby Dick," greatest of Melville's books as that is commonly estimated. His next book, "Pierre," a melodramatic work showing an evil French influence, bore the truly sinister sub-title of "The Ambiguities." He had a sufficiently large public to be welcomed to the pages of *Harper's* and *Putnam's Magazines*; there are excellent passages in his historical novel of the Revolution, "The Refugee"; but in general his books became more and more, as he himself humorously put it, "adapted for unpopularity."

[Subtle and Merciless Analysis]

Raymond M. Weaver†

Melville's later novels mark a deepening of despair. "Pierre, or the Ambiguities" (1852), while worthily comparable to Meredith's "Egoist" in elaborate subtlety and mercilessness of pyschological analysis, is a prophetic parody of Hardy's most poisonous pessimism. The intention of this dark, wild book of incest and death seems to be to show the impracticability of virtue: that morality is a luxury occasionally to be indulged in by a strolling divinity, but for man a dangerous form of lunacy. "Pierre" is a book to send a Freudian into ravishment.

*Reprinted from "An American Romancer: Centenary of Herman Melville, Writer of Sea Tales," *New York Evening Post*, 2 August 1919.

†Reprinted from "The Centennial of Herman Melville," *Nation* (New York), 109 (2 August 1919) 146.

[Repellent, Overwrought, Yet Powerful]

Frank Jewett Mather, Jr.*

Melville, in prose, for he was also no mean poet, had three styles, like an old master. The swift lucidity, picturesqueness, and sympathy of "Typee" and "Omoo" have alone captured posterity. Melville lives by his *juvenalia*. "Redburn" and "White Jacket" are straightforward manly narratives, less colorful than their predecessors. They have not stood the competition with Dana's quite similar "Two Years Before the Mast." They are not quite as solid as that classic, but their chief fault was merely in being later. Then Melville developed a reflective, mystical, and very personal style, probably influenced by Carlyle, which the public has from the first eschewed. It asserts itself first in the strange allegory, "Mardi, and a Voyage Thither," 1849, it pervaded "Pierre, or the Ambiguities," 1852, and other later books. "Moby Dick" shows an extraordinary blend of the first and the last style—the pictorial and the orphic; is Melville's most characteristic and, I think, his greatest book. Still, for the average reader Melville is merely the author of "Typee" and "Omoo." Chronology and the popular will, if it can be at all invoked in Melville's case, alike bid us slur his single historical novel, "Israel Potter," 1855, and his middle-western character sketches in "The Confidence Man," 1857, and even the excellent "Piazza Tales," 1856, in favor of the Marquesan idyl and the picaresque account of Tahiti. . . .

In a sense "Moby Dick" exhausted Melville's vein. At thirty-two he had put into a single volume all that he had been in action, all that he was to be in thought. The rest is aftermath, yet it, too, is considerable. The year after "Moby Dick," 1852, appeared "Pierre, or the Ambiguities." Legend assigns the author's swift obscuration to the dispraise "Pierre" aroused. It is too simple an explanation, as we shall see. The book is repellent and overwrought, yet powerful. The theme is the endeavor of a long-parted brother and sister, a mere lad and lass, to cut loose and lead their own lives, as nominal husband and wife. The ambiguity of their situation leads to misery, madness, and ruin. Convention triumphs over a boy's genius and chivalry, as over a girl's unmeasured tenderness. The struggle is painful, without winning much sympathy. The moral that one must somewhat bend to things as they are is almost common-place. The demonstration is powerful, but without much sequence; reflection and satire burgeon over the mishaps of the luckless brother and sister, as if the red, red rose and the briar should finally conceal the twin tombs of the ballad lovers. Yet as a literary curiosity "Pierre" is worth reading, and it is at least a curious coincidence that it completely anticipates in wire-drawn

*Reprinted from "Herman Meville," *Review* (New York), 1 (9 August 1919), 277, and (16 August 1919), 299.

fashion what was soon to be the leading motive of "The Ordeal of Richard Feverel." The parallel is commended to would-be doctors of philosophy.[1]

Note

1. Later in his essay (p. 300), Mather adds, " 'Pierre' is one long parable of living too intensely, morbidly, and individually. It probably reflects a personal struggle of the author for a mental equipoise which he attained at the cost of surrender of old activities and ambitions," and " 'Pierre' is perhaps the only positively ill-done book, and it is stuffed with memorable aphorisms." [Ed. Note.]

[From "A Comparison of Manners"]

Arthur Johnson*

It would be tempting, to say the least, when everybody is attributing to the work of The Younger Generation the influence of Henry James, to attribute to the work of Henry James the influence of Herman Melville—if one only could. But one alas can't. No. Fabulous, orgic, as such a turn of the tables would be, I am not meaning even to lend a hand to it. I wish simply to point out an entertaining discovery. . . .

Henry James, perhaps, did not know even as much about his father's contemporary. Still, it is certainly possible that he did. He may have known him personally, not unlikely. Melville was living in New York when James was a child, and they both came later to Massachusetts at approximately the same time, as it happened. But one wonders not so much about these details—or about old-world points of view they may have had in common; one wonders rather, for instance, if James, on rainy days of his boyhood, wouldn't have been irresistibly attracted by things in stray Melville volumes he chanced to espy standing dusty on the shelves of libraries he was brought up among. Bartleby is not so far from a short story in the early James manner, despite its occasional flatness, and though it concerns itself somewhat with "the base rattle of the foreground." Benito Cereno could, by a stretch of the artistic sense, be compared not so lamentably with a tale of Joseph Conrad. But I don't intend to argue. Anything like a real matching of the merits involved is too far fetched even for me. What I do intend is to call your attention to the "manner," here and there, of Herman Melville.

We have heard so often the explanation of James's "later manner"—not to say latest. (Just where the dividing line is, I don't know; a friend of

*Reprinted from *New Republic* (New York), 20 (27 August 1919), 113–15.

mine traces it to a certain chapter and paragraph toward the end of the second volume of The Tragic Muse.) We have listened to the improvisation about the stenographer, who wrote down not only what Mr. James said but also what he thought; and we've smiled at the comment: "Yes, and what the stenographer thought, too." And we've read The Great Good Place, said to be a distilled objectification of the author's reflections on the luxury of dictating,—of which the preface to the New York edition only vouchsafes, however: "It embodies a calculated effect, and to plunge into it, I find, even for a beguiled glance—a course I indeed recommend—is to have left all else outside." We have believed, moreover—had scarce a doubt.

But now crops up disconcertingly this out-of-date popular author who wrote in a manner which, though it falls wretchedly short in beauty and revelation of that with which I am daring to compare it, nevertheless is, I submit, as "manners" go, almost uniquely comparable. Not always—he had his other manner, too. The "lively sea-tales" are as crystal clear as one could wish—as crystal in their clarity, at least, as the James of those years before he forgot, presumably, if he ever knew, precisely what sort of author Herman Melville was. But consider patiently, please—my pièces de resistance—the sentences I shall lay before you from Pierre, or The Ambiguities (Harper & Brothers, 1852). It appeared when Henry James was nine years old—before typewriters or stenographers existed. (Bartleby, to which I've referred, and which "came out" four years afterwards, is about a scrivener in New York.) ["Bartleby" was first published in *Putnam's* in November and December, 1853. Ed. Note.] The plot or theme of it, let me interpolate, were it not so "done" as to be hardly decipherable, would be today considered rather "advanced." D.H. Lawrence hasn't exceeded it for morbid unhealthy pathology. But I am concerned mostly with sentences here. I attach specimens of them, like exhibits, in support of my case—not so many, I trust, as will overtax the least jaded enthusiast; though Pierre, or The Ambiguities, is a long novel, and, similarly to some novels of Henry James's, is divided into twenty-six "Books," each of a half dozen chapters, more or less. The punctuation is obtrusively mid-Victorian. But substitute commas for semi-colons, now and then, if you will.

Page 481–482.

"Setting aside Aunt Dorothea's nebulous legend, to which, in some shadowy points, here and there Isabel's still more nebulous story seemed to fit on—but uncertainly enough—and both of which thus blurredly conjoining narrations, regarded in the unscrupulous light of real naked reason, were anything but legitimately conclusive; and setting aside his own dim reminiscences of his wandering father's death bed; (for though, in one point of view, those reminiscences might have afforded some degree of presumption as to his father's having been the parent of an unacknowledged daughter, yet were they entirely inconclusive as to that presumed daughter's identity; and the grand point now with Pierre was, not the general question whether his father had had a daughter, but whether, assuming that he had had, *Isabel*, rather than any other living being, *was that daughter*;)—and setting aside all his own manifold and inter-enfolding mystic and transcendental persuasions—originally born, as he now seemed to feel, purely of an intense procreative enthusiasm—an enthusiasm no longer so all-potential with him as of yore; setting all these aside, and coming to the plain, palpable facts—how did he *know* that Isabel was his sister?"

Page 352.

"Even so, it may possibly be, that arrived at this quiet retrospective little episode in the career of my hero—this shallowly expansive embayed Tappan Zee of my otherwise deep-heady Hudson—I too begin to long-ingly expand, and wax harmlessly sad and sentimental."

Page 239.

"This preamble seems not entirely unnecessary as usher of the strange conceit, that possibly the latest germ of Pierre's proposed extraordinary mode of executing his proposed extraordinary resolve—namely, the nom-inal conversion of a sister into a wife—might have been found in the pre-vious conversational conversion of a mother into a sister; for hereby he had habituated his voice and manner to a certain fictitiousness in one of the closest domestic relations of life; and since man's moral texture is very porous, and things assumed upon the surface, at last strike in—hence, this outward habituation to the above-named fictitiousness had insensibly dis-posed his mind to it as it were; but only innocently and pleasantly as yet."

Page 187.

"So, also, in a good degree, did he endeavor to drive out of him, Isabel's reminiscence of the, to her, unnameable large house, from which she had been finally removed by the pleasant woman in the coach."

Page 458-459.

"Certain that those two youths must be plotting something furious against him; with the echoes of their scorning curses on the stairs still ring-ing in his ears—curses, whose swift responses from himself, he, at the time, had much ado to check;—thoroughly alive to the supernaturalism of that mad frothing hate which a spirited brother forks forth at the insulter of a sister's honor—beyond doubt the most uncompromising of all the social passions known to man—and not blind to the anomalous fact, that if such a brother stab his foe at his own mother's table, all people and all juries would bear him out, accounting everything allowable to a noble soul made mad by a sweet sister's shame caused by a damned seducer;—imagining to himself his own feelings, if he were actually in the position which Frederic so vividly fancied to be his; remembering that in love matters jealousy is as an adder, and that the jealousy of Glen was double-addered by the extraordinary malice of the apparent circumstances under which Lucy had spurned Glen's arms, and fled to his always successful and now married rival, as if wantonly and shamelessly to nestle there;—remembering all these intense incitements of both those foes of his, Pierre could not but look forward to wild work very soon to come."

Page 447.

"And when it so chanced, that—owing perhaps to some momentary jarring of the distant and lonely guitar—as Lucy was so mildly speaking in the presence of her mother, a sudden, just audible, submissively answering musical, stringed tone, came through the open door from the adjoining chamber; then Isabel, as if seized by some spiritual awe, fell on her knees before Lucy, and made a rapid gesture of homage; yet still, somehow, as it were, without evidence of voluntary will."

The technique and texture of it are, of course, essentially different to the master's. In relation to his, it is as crude and stark as warp without any woof. Melville ramified along the way to elementary goals, punctilious to leave no stone unturned that should add to the complexity of what he fancied was to him alone obvious; whereas James, exploring and groping ahead, coped with inspiration upon inspiration, and concentric inspirations, so to speak, the very poignancy and multiplicity of which, and his zeal not to miss an impression, absorbed the least dread of obscurity. Yet their thoroughness, thus dissimilarly acquired perhaps, involved devices and idiosyncracies grotesquely alike—all quite aside, I mean, from whatever in their methods of presentation I've hinted may appear rather to tally. Melville, it is told, had a proclivity to metaphysics, and James's inheritance possibly included an aptitude for the elaborations which such a field seems inevitably to engender. At any rate, one queries if there isn't a something about the convolutions of both that savors of philosophers' painstakingness.

[Going on Beyond Greatness]

Viola Meynell*

Moby Dick is the high-water mark of Herman Melville's achievement. Its narrative and record of fact are superior to those of the earlier works, *Typee* and *Omoo*; and on its inventive side it is superior, at any rate to ordinary understanding, to the later books, *Mardi* and *Pierre, or the Ambiguities*, and others. It will not surprise readers of *Moby Dick* to think that after it was written its writer passed from them, in a sense. Already in this book one is carried to the comprehensible limits of marvellous imagination. There the mere reader and follower can stay in safety, transfigured with the great gifts that have been added to him, even

*Reprinted from "Introduction," in *Moby-Dick*, The World's Classics, No. 225 (London: Oxford University Press, 1920), pp. v–vi.

while not being of the nature that conceived them. But the nature that conceived them has its course still to run. Herman Melville has here endowed human nature with writing that I believe to be absolutely unsurpassed. To read it and absorb it is the crown of one's reading life,—but from the laws of mind that made it the reader is still apart and immune. It is the wildest farthest kind of genius. Herman Melville could not have been so great as this if he had not been going on beyond greatness as we know it. Many deep divers may fail to reach a spot marked at a great depth, and when one of them reaches it at last it is because he sinks on beyond it to return no more. In the works that followed this, he is called transcendentalist and metaphysician, writing of 'exotic philosophies, with an echo of gargantuan laughter.'

[Plagiarised from Melville's Own Psychology]

Raymond M. Weaver*

In *Pierre*, Melville coiled down into the night of his soul, to write an anatomy of despair. The purpose of the book was to show the impracticability of virtue: to give specific evidence, freely plagiarised from his own psychology, that "the heavenly wisdom of God is an earthly folly to man," "that although our blessed Saviour was full of the wisdom of Heaven, yet his gospel seems lacking in the practical wisdom of the earth; that his nature was not merely human—was not that of a mere man of the world"; that to try to live in this world according to the strict letter of Christianity would result in "the story of the Ephesian matron, allegorised." The subtlety of the analysis is extraordinary; and in its probings into unsuspected determinants from unconsciousness it is prophetic of some of the most recent findings in psychology. "Deep, deep, and still deep and deeper must we go," Melville says, "if we would find out the heart of a man; descending into which is as descending a spiral stair in a shaft, without any end, and where that endlessness is only concealed by the spiralness of the stair, and the blackness of the shaft." In the winding ambiguities of *Pierre* Melville attempts to reveal man's fatal facility at self-deception; to show that the human mind is like a floating iceberg, hiding below the surface of the sea most of its bulk; that from a great depth of thought and feeling below the level of awareness, long silent hands are ever reaching out, urging us to whims of the blood and tensions of the nerves, whose origins we never suspect. "In reserves men build imposing

*Reprinted from *Herman Melville: Mariner and Mystic* (New York: George H. Doran Co., 1921), pp. 341–44.

characters," Melville says; "not in revelations." *Pierre* is not conspicuous for its reserves.

Pierre aroused the reviewers to such a storm of abuse that legend has assigned Melville's swift obscuration to this dispraise. The explanation is too simple, as Mr. Mather contends. But there is, doubtless, more than a half truth in this explanation. The abuse that *Pierre* reaped, coming when it did in Melville's career, and inspired by a book in which Melville with tragic earnestness attempted an apologia of worldly defeat, must have seemed to him in its heartlessness and total blindness to his purpose, a definitive substantiation of the thesis of his book.

Pierre has been very unsympathetically handled, even by Melville's most penetrating and sympathetic critics. Mr. Frank Jewett Mather, Jr., for example, in the second of his two essays on *Herman Melville* (*The Review*, August 9 and 16, 1919), says of *Pierre* that "it is perhaps the only positively ill-done book" of Melville's. Mr. Mather grants power to the book, but he finds it "repellent and overwrought." He recommends it only as a literary curiosity. And as a literary curiosity Mr. Arthur Johnson studied its stylistic convolutions in *The New Republic* of August 27, 1919. It is certainly true, as Mr. Johnson has said, that "the plot or theme, were it not so 'done' as to be hardly decipherable, would be to-day considered rather 'advanced.' " Mr. Johnson contends that for morbid unhealthy pathology, it has not been exceeded even by D. H. Lawrence. All this may be very excellent ethics, but it is not very enlightening criticism.

Melville wrote *Pierre* with no intent to reform the ways of the world. But he did write *Pierre* to put on record the reminder that the world's way is a hypocritic way in so far as it pretends to be any other than the Devil's way also. In *Pierre*, Melville undertook to dramatise this conviction. When he sat down to write, what seemed to him the holiest part of himself—his ardent aspirations—had wrecked itself against reality. So he undertook to present, in the character of Pierre, his own character purged of dross; and in the character of Pierre's parents, the essential outlines of his own parents. Then he started his hero forth upon a career of lofty and unselfish impulse, intent to show that the more transcendent a man's ideal, the more certain and devastating his worldly defeat; that the most innocent in heart are those most in peril of being eventually involved in "strange, *unique* follies and sins, unimagined before." Incidentally, Melville undertakes to show, in the tortuous ambiguities of *Pierre*, that even the purest impulses of Pierre were, in reality, tainted of clay. *Pierre* is an apologia of Melville's own defeat, in the sense that in *Pierre* Melville attempts to show that in so far as his own defeat—essentially paralleling Pierre's—was unblackened by incest, murder, and suicide, he had escaped these disasters through accident and inherent defect, rather than because of superior virtue. Pierre had followed the heavenly way that leads to damnation.

Such a thesis can be met by the worldly wisdom that Melville slanders in *Pierre*, only with uncompromising repugnance. There can be no forgiveness in this world for a man who calls the wisdom of this world a cowardly lie, and probes clinically into the damning imperfections of the best. His Kingdom is surely not of this world. And if this world evinces for his gospel neither understanding nor sympathy, he cannot reasonably complain if he reaps the natural fruits of his profession. Melville agreed with the Psalmist: "Verily there is a reward for the righteous." But he blasphemed when he dared teach that the reward of virtue and truth in this world must be wailing and gnashing of teeth. Like Dante, Melville set himself up against the world as a party of one. A majority judgment, though it has the power, has not necessarily the truth. It is theoretically possible that Melville, not the world, is right. But one can assent to Melville's creed only on penalty of destruction; and the race does not welcome annihilation. Hence this world must rejoice in its vengeance upon his blasphemy: and the self-righteous have washed their feet in the blood of the wicked.

After *Pierre*, any further writing from Melville was both an impertinence and an irrelevancy. No man who really believes that all is vanity can consistently go on taking elaborate pains to popularise his indifference. Schopenhauer did that thing, it is true; but Schopenhauer was an artist, not a moralist; and he was enchanted with disenchantment. Carlyle, too, through interminable volumes shrieked out the necessity of silence. But after *Pierre*, Melville was without internal urgings to write. "All profound things, and emotions of things," he wrote in *Pierre*, "are preceded and attended by silence." "When a man is really in a profound mood, then all merely verbal or written profundities are unspeakably repulsive, and seem downright childish to him." Infinitely greater souls than Melville's seem to have shared this conviction. Neither Buddha nor Socrates left a single written word; Christ wrote once only, and then in the sand.

[Verbal Curiosities]

Philip Hale*

The judicious collector of Melville's books, already having "Moby Dick"—the first reprint was in 1892, with the table of contents omitted—would choose "Typee," "Omoo," "White Jacket," "Israel Potter," "The Piazza Tales," and probably "Mardi." He would not be in a hurry to secure "Redburn," "The Confidence Man," "Pierre; or, the Ambiguities," or the volumes of verse. . . .

"The Confidence Man" and "Pierre" may be purchased as verbal

*Reprinted from "As the World Wags," *Boston Herald*, 22 June 1921.

curiosities, though the former is not without humor. "Pierre" is a morbid story: Melville in his most extravagant mood, writing pages that might have appealed to the readers of the N.Y. Ledger in the days of Mrs. Southworth and Mrs. Stephens. Nor is "Redburn," a story of a voyage to England, wholly worthy of Melville.

[A Tragic Trinity: *Mardi, Moby-Dick*, and *Pierre*]

Carl Van Vechten*

It is a pleasure, moreover, to find that Mr. Weaver has a warm appreciation of "Mardi" and "Pierre," books which have either been neglected or fiercely condemned since they first appeared, books which are no longer available save in early editions. They are not equal to "Moby Dick," but they are infinitely more important and more interesting than "Typee" and "Omoo," on which the chief fame of the man rests. It is to his credit that Mr. Weaver has perceived this, but a great deal more remains to be said on the subject. "Mardi," "Moby Dick," and "Pierre," as a matter of fact, form a kind of tragic trinity: "Mardi" is a tragedy of the intellect; "Moby Dick," a tragedy of the spirit, and "Pierre," a tragedy of the flesh. "Mardi" is a tragedy of heaven; "Moby Dick," a tragedy of hell, and "Pierre," a tragedy of the world we live in.

[A Book for Freudians]

Carl Van Vechten†

From now on Melville wrote inner rather than outer books and from now on he lost credit with public and critics both. His very next work, indeed, "Pierre or The Ambiguities," infuriated the reviewers and drove them to dreadful tongue-lashings. The ecclesiastics and the hundred per cent Americans helped to castigate the man. It may be said, in extenuation, that the performance was strange enough, even from the writer of "Mardi," to have wrung astonishment from stout hearts. Yet I cannot help believing that had "Pierre" been written today by James Joyce or D. H. Lawrence, its reception would have been far different. Either, with certain personal alterations, might have conceived the book. The subject, in-

*Reprinted from "A Belated Biography," *Literary Review* (New York), 2 (31 December 1921), 316, a review of Raymond M. Weaver's *Herman Melville: Mariner and Mystic*.
†Reprinted from "The Later Work of Herman Melville," *Double Dealer* (New Orleans), 3 (January 1922), 9–20.

deed, would have delighted the soul of Henry James, had he hit on it. In its consideration the subtitle must be stressed. Ambiguity is Melville's theme.

Pierre, a happy son, living with his widowed mother, betrothed to Lucy Tartan, whom, apparently, he dearly loves, learns, or thinks that he learns, that he has an illegitimate sister. On the instant (indeed, a little before, for his first strange meeting with Isabel is anonymous), he is seized with an embracing adoration for this new demi-kinswoman, an adoration which to the reader certainly appears to be sexual, but which to Pierre himself is always ambiguous in its nature. His instinct at first demands a public recognition of the girl, a tardy restitution of her ambiguous rights, but more sober reflection convinces him that his mother will never receive this symbol of the bar sinister, of whose very existence she is quite unaware. Further, it is necessary to consider his dead father's good name, quite unbefouled so far as public scandal goes. In his ambiguous dilemma this hero hits on the expedient of a white marriage. During the ceremony, "the surplice-like napkin dropped from the clergyman's bosom, showing a minute but exquisitely cut cameo brooch, representing the allegorical union of the serpent and dove." Now Pierre bids his Lucy farewell and is turned from his home by his proud mother whom he never sees again. Dying within a few months, she disowns him by testament, leaving her property to his cousin, Glen Stanly, also in love with Lucy. Pierre and Isabel go to New York, where he tries to make his living as a novelist. In the meantime, Lucy, through some mystic visitation, has arrived at the belief that Pierre has acted quixotically but nobly (she is entirely unaware of his reasons), and insists on coming to live with the possibly incestuous pair. Glen and her brother attempt to drag her away but fail. So does her mother. Nunlike, she occupies an adjoining chamber to the guilty (?) couple. The ensuing chapters are blood-curdling in their implications. There are passages which seem to suggest that this amazing marriage was truly consummated. There are passages which seem to suggest that Lucy . . . but let the author speak:

> As a statue, planted on a revolving pedestal, shows now this limb, now that; now front, now back, now side; continually changing, too, its general profile; so does the pivoted, statued soul of man, when turned by the hand of Truth. Lies only never vary; look for no invariableness in Pierre. *Nor does any canting showman here stand by to announce his phases as he revolves. Catch his phases as your insight may.*

The plot hastens towards its catastrophe, in which Pierre's novel is rejected as Voltairean and atheistic, and in which he is insulted by Glen, whom he kills in a street brawl. Led to prison, he is visited by Lucy and Isabel. The sister-wife drinks poison and Pierre and Lucy drain the bottle. The three ambiguous corpses clutter the stage as the curtain swiftly falls. Towards the close, there is a curious scene in which the very evidence that

Pierre had urged to make himself believe that Isabel was his sister is discovered to be worse than circumstantial. The book, indeed, is a study of a man who commits an ignoble act by convincing himself that he is committing a noble one. It depicts the danger of idealization. Pierre is so difficult to come by at present (only the first edition exists and that was very largely depleted by a fire at the Harpers' in the early fifties) that it is by no means as well-known or as much admired as it would be if it could be reprinted. Whoever republishes it should send advance copies to Drs. Freud and Brill, and to Mr. D. H. Lawrence. They will be entranced. I prophesy that a new cartload of Freudian literature will grow up around this book, the peripeteia of which occurs in a dream.

Both in "Pierre" and in "Moby Dick" critics have protested against the author's use of Gothic dialogue. That this was a perfectly conscious device on Melville's part, I think there can be no question, for when he wished, as in "Bartleby", he could be as convincingly colloquial as the next man. This Gothic dialogue serves to remove "Captain Ahab" and "Pierre" from any particular environment or period. It gives them a strange air of nowhere, no place, very apposite to his general purpose in the creation of these masterpieces. . . .

From "Pierre" I have culled the following:

> In the inferior instances of an immediate literary success, in very young writers, it will be almost invariably observable, that for that instant success they are chiefly indebted to some rich and peculiar experience in life, embodied in a book, which because, for that cause, containing original matter, the author himself, forsooth, is to be considered original.

This may be regarded, in a sense, as a rather bitter criticism of his own "Typee."

[An Obligation to Read]

Van Wyck Brooks*

So much for the objective books, the simple tales, transcripts, for the most part, of the author's experience. What is to be said of the metaphysical novels which, apart from "Moby-Dick," represent Melville's serious aspirations as a man of letters? A handful of readers will always delight in "Mardi" and "Pierre"; still more will be obliged to examine them, from generation to generation, because they help to explain a mind that had its moments of supreme greatness. "The Confidence Man," singularly interesting in conception, is an abortion: it is broken off in the middle, apparently, but not before the author has lost the thread of his original

*Reprinted from "A Reviewer's Notebook," *Freeman* (New York), 7 (9 May 1923), 215.

idea. . . . "Pierre" is a novel which, interesting still, might once have been regarded as great: it is one of the penalties of a delayed fame in a world of changing fashions that so many elements of an author's work which ought to have given pleasure in their time are seen too late to be admired. But let me make two preliminary comments on this book. Whoever enjoys Balzac's "Seraphita" will enjoy the story of Pierre and Isabel; and the chapters dealing with Pierre as a struggling author are incomparably more powerful than anything of the kind in Gissing's "New Grub Street."

[Solitary as at the Pole]

Van Wyck Brooks*

Melville was not a thinker; worse still, the only reality that he knew, far from stimulating his curiosity, repelled him. It is probably true, in the first place, that a youth of excessive adventure is the most unfavourable preparation for a patient intellectual life, which inevitably presents itself to the mind as insipid by contrast. It is reasonable to suppose, too, that impressions as violent as those which Melville had received during his early voyages and in the South Seas may have deadened his sensibilities, or at least rendered pallid in his eyes the scenes of the more familiar world. Aside from this, aside from his failing eyesight, we gather that his personal life was in every way a drab disappointment: he who reveals himself in "The Paradise of Bachelors" as by nature a lover of "good living, good drinking, good feeling and good talk" was all too evidently condemned to the grim, colourless, monotonous round of a small provincial existence. "One in a city of hundreds of thousands of human beings, Pierre," he says, "was solitary as at the pole. In his deepest, highest part he was utterly without sympathy from anything divine, human, brute or vegetable." He himself had had but one literary friend; and Hawthorne was no man to communicate a lively sense of terrestrial realities. As for the literati of New York, Poe had sufficiently taken their measure; and who can blame Melville for having found them wanting in flavour? If he had encountered other men, men whom he could respect and who were intensely interested in writing, if he had been able to exchange the merest commonplaces of the craft, if he had been able to count upon a handful of understanding readers, he might have learned how to check and manipulate the flow of his mind, how to nurse his talent, he might have remained a man of this world and an artist: it was not without good reason, it was in response to a profound instinct of self-preservation that Whitman, condemned to a similar isolation, surrounded himself with disciples and

*Reprinted from "A Reviewer's Notebook," *Freeman* (New York), 7 (23 May 1923), 263.

made a cult of his ego. Renan was right; talent is a frivolous vice. We cease to believe in it when no one shares our belief. Melville at thirty-five had outlived the literary illusion; he had come to despise the written word. We see in all this a little of the contempt of the physical man for the work of the brain, the *malaise* of the barbarian chained to a desk; but more still, the suffocation of a mighty genius in a social vacuum. Melville touched the uttermost note of pathetic irony when, for want of a sole articulate companion, he dedicated "Pierre" to Mount Greylock and "Israel Potter" to the Bunker Hill Monument.

[Product of Reading and Transparent Autobiography]

Van Wyck Brooks*

I have said very little in these pages about "Mardi" and "Pierre," after "Moby-Dick" the most ambitious of Melville's books. They seem to me—except for the latter chapters of "Pierre"—rather the products of his reading than of any intense personal experience. . . . In "Pierre" we find still another set of influences at work. Were it possible we should suppose that Melville had read "Seraphita," for the conception of Isabel, who "seemed moulded from fire and air, and vivified at some voltaic pile of August thunder-clouds heaped against the sunset," strikingly resembles that of Balzac's figure of mystery. We can only conclude that he had read the writers whom Balzac himself had read, Maturin, Mrs. Radcliffe and Monk Lewis. However this may be, we know that "Vathek" and "The Castle of Otranto" were among the books that he brought back from England in 1850. To these may be traced perhaps the magniloquent, high-flown style in which he cast the story of Pierre and Isabel.

As I have already said, the latter chapters of this book are transparently autobiographical: they give us what we may fairly regard as a picture of the circumstances under which "Moby-Dick" was written. A complete change takes place in the style when it appears that the romantic Pierre is a writer, that he has undertaken to write an immense book, a "comprehensive compacted work," an Inferno, as it soon turns out to be; the vaporous atmosphere of the story suddenly clears, we are confronted with a scene of the most convincing reality, we feel that the author has abandoned the uncongenial task of invention, that he is speaking to us directly, that he is describing a personal experience. As a matter of fact, the material circumstances that surround the composition of Pierre's book are precisely those that accompanied the composition of Melville's. He too was obliged

*Reprinted from "A Reviewer's Notebook," *Freeman* (New York), 7 (30 May 1923), 286–87.

to send the manuscript to the printer while he was still at work on it, he too struggled against failing eyesight, he too was a victim of "clamorous pennilessness"; and we have only to recall his remark to Hawthorne that "Moby-Dick" was "broiled in hell-fire" to lose any fear of pressing the analogy too close. "All creation," said Amiel, "begins with a period of chaotic anguish. The chaos that is to give birth to a world is vast and dolorous just in proportion as the world is to be one of grandeur." Never was this better exemplified than in the case of Melville's masterpiece.

I can only recount a few details of this remarkable passage. Melville describes Pierre, in the first place, as "goaded, in the hour of mental immaturity, to the attempt at a mature work." He feels that he possesses immense inner resources; he speaks of the "Switzerland of his soul," of the "overawing extent of peak crowded on peak, and spur sloping on spur, and chain jammed behind chain." It appals him when he looks within; for equally great is the difficulty which he experiences in formulating his thoughts. He feels that there are two books being written of which only the bungled one will ever reach the world. The larger book "whose unfathomable cravings drink his blood" can not be drawn forth; it has a soul "elephantinely sluggish, and will not budge at a breath." Doubts assail him, a feeling of hopelessness and despair. His physical instincts, the instincts of the primitive man, revolt against this victimization of his lungs and his life. He feels that he has assassinated the natural day; he begins to loathe his food; he can not sleep—"his book, like a vast lumbering planet, revolves in his aching head." Then the time comes for the first pages to go to the printer.

> Thus was added still another tribulation; because the printed pages now dictated to the following manuscript, and said to all subsequent thoughts and inventions of Pierre—Thus and thus; so and so; else an ill match. Therefore was his book already limited, bound over, and committed to imperfection, even before it had come to any confirmed form or conclusion at all. . . . Now he began to feel that in him the thews of a Titan were forestallingly cut by the scissors of Fate. He felt as a moose, hamstrung. All things that think, or move, or lie still, seemed as created to mock and torment him. He seemed gifted with loftiness, merely that it might be dragged down to the mud. Still, the profound wilfulness in him would not give up. Against the breaking heart and the bursting head; against all the dismal lassitude, and deathful faintness and sleeplessness, and whirlingness and craziness, still he like a demigod bore up. His soul's ship foresaw the inevitable rocks, but resolved to sail on, and make a courageous wreck. Now he gave jeer for jeer, and taunted the apes that jibed him. With the soul of an atheist, he wrote down the godliest things; with the feeling of death and misery in him, he created forms of gladness and life. . . . And everything else he disguised under the so conveniently adjustable drapery of all-stretchable Philosophy.

In the midst of this comes a final disaster—the failure of his eyesight:

But man does never give himself up thus, a doorless and shutterless house for the four loosened winds of heaven to howl through, without still additional dilapidations. Much oftener than before, Pierre lay back in his chair with the deadly feeling of faintness. Much oftener than before, came staggering home from his evening walk, and from sheer bodily exhaustion economized the breath that answered the anxious inquiries as to what might be done for him. And as if all the leagued spiritual inveteracies and malices, combined with his general bodily exhaustion, were not enough, a special corporeal affliction now descended like a sky-hawk upon him. His incessant application told upon his eyes. They became so affected, that some days he wrote with the lids nearly closed, fearful of opening them wide to the light. Through the lashes he peered upon the paper, which so seemed fretted with wires. Sometimes he blindly wrote with his eyes turned away from the paper: thus unconsciously symbolizing the hostile necessity and distaste, the former whereof made of him this most unwilling state's-prisoner of letters. . . . And now a general and nameless torpor—some horrible foretaste of death itself—seemed stealing upon him.

But enough of this most mournful exhibition of what Flaubert described as the "quaint mania of passing one's life wearing oneself out over words." I have left no room to speak of the other devils that beset our author, the presentiment of the decay of his powers, the disgust at his own aspirations, the feeling that all things human and divine are combined against him. Melville "supped at black broth with Pluto" when he wrote "Moby-Dick."

[Melville's Lonely Journey]

[J. W. N. Sullivan]*

The recent emergence of a large public for Melville's work, as testified by these collected editions, is one of the most interesting indications of the change which is taking place in the general mind. Melville's complete lack of popularity in his own time was due to the great dissimilarity between his personal vision and the general *Weltanschauung*. The world of the Victorians was hardly a mysterious world. Their material world was a perfectly clear-cut and comprehensible affair, and everything that was not material was merely moral. Every aspect of their world, as it seems to us now, was most strangely finite and most strangely clear; their most comprehensive schemes left out so much. Perhaps it was only in that age that the biological theory of evolution

*Reprinted from "Herman Melville," *Times Literary Supplement* (London), No. 1123 (26 July 1923), 493–94. This review essay was occasioned by the publication of the Constable and Cape editions of Melville.

could have been welcomed as a world philosophy; when it was objected to, it was objected to as "degrading." Important people felt their dignity to be outraged, but the entire irrelevance of the theory to the central mystery of man himself seems hardly to have been remarked either by the antagonists or the supporters of the theory. The severer science of that time, splendid as it was, was equally naïve. "Matter," it was accepted everywhere, was the sort of stuff that made up the stone Dr. Johnson kicked—and obviously there was no mystery about that. To the kind of awareness possessed by Herman Melville it must have seemed that his contemporaries understood hardly anything. Even to us there is often something invisibly superficial about their outlook. They were islanders who lived unconscious of the sea. No murmur from far-off regions could reach their ears. The rumblings of "Moby Dick" were quite inaudible to them, and even that most mystical of composers, Beethoven himself, became somebody remarkable for the elevation of his style and the nobility of his sentiments. This is not to say that there were no exceptions. But to the general consciousness of that age Melville probably had less to say than he would have had in almost any other age, and certainly much less than he has to say to us. And it may be mentioned, incidentally, that the complete lack of comprehension he encountered was hardly a good thing for Melville. A kind of recklessness in fantasy, the growing lack of a sense of proportion, observable in Melville's later work, sprang, we think, from the complete lack of public understanding of his essential purpose. He became more and more content to make less and less effort to communicate to others the profundities of his inner life. It is not without significance that whereas "Moby Dick" is dedicated to Nathaniel Hawthorne, "Pierre" is dedicated to no human being, but to Greylock, the mountain near which Melville lived. And it is in "Pierre" that Melville shows a more bitter scorn for his contemporaries than it is good for a man, so little shallow, to have.

> So beforehand he felt the unrevealable sting of receiving either plaudits or censures, equally unsought for, and equally loathed ere given. So beforehand he felt the pyramidical scorn of the genuine loftiness for the whole infinite company of infinitesimal critics. His was the scorn which thinks it not worth the while to be scornful. Those he most scorned never knew it.

But worse things come of this lonely and implacable voyaging than loss of contact with one's fellows. As Melville says later, "But man does not give himself up thus, a doorless and shutterless house for the four loosened winds of heaven to howl through, without still additional dilapidations."

As we say, we think there has been a change in the general mind. It would seem that there is a *Zeitgeist* swaying peoples as a whole; it seems that man's consciousness develops, or at least acquires a new direction. Things which were dark become clear; there is a perpetual shifting up and down of great ones on their thrones; the region of the possible becomes enlarged, and more and more adventurous spirits are driven to peep over the edge of the world. In our own time we think that science has been the chief agent in liberating men from the clear but too finite world of the Victorians. There is a great difference between the random collocations of atoms which were supposed to produce us and the modern universe whose matter, space, and time, it appears, are largely creations of our own. Such ideas do not nestle isolated in the mind. They subtly modify the whole of a man's outlook; they make a sensitive surface where there was nothing but a blind integument: they create dim centres of vision for what was before total darkness. It is characteristic of our time that there is a sense of unprecedented possibilities; the firm lines of our accustomed world are growing indistinct. In science and philosophy, chiefly, we feel that the soul of man has started on new adventures. We get glimpses of greater and perhaps more lonely seas than man has ever adventured on before. And although the general consciousness may have no more than the dimmest apprehension of what is being attempted, it is aware that something is afoot. It stirs, a little blindly, but not much more blindly than the most far-sighted man amongst us. These troubled waters may presage some great tidal movement, but no man can yet say what the direction will be. And we are now sufficiently tremulous, sufficiently sensitive, for that strange class of writers to which Melville belongs to be, not perhaps intelligible, but certainly not meaningless. We are aware of possibilities; man is once more a mystery to us, and a greater mystery than ever before. We feel that Melville's oceans and leviathans are credible symbols. That man hunts through a great deep who looks into himself. . . . By the time Melville came to write "Pierre" he seems wholly concerned with the inner life. The disparity between the symbolism of this story and the meaning that Melville forces his symbols to carry is so great as to be occasionally ludicrous and even repulsive. An ardent young man who wishes to spare his father's name the stigma of having had an illegitimate daughter; the extravagant device, therefore, of pretending to marry his unacknowledged sister, rejecting the girl he had promised to marry and breaking his mother's heart—none of this produces the slightest illusion of reality. The book has been dismissed as unintelligible, as the work of a man too abnormal to be called sane. But it is sane enough. It is profound. But Melville, either perfunctorily or through that curious lack of a sense of proportion which he exhibits in all his writings, has tried to embody his thoughts in a vehicle which cannot contain them. Isabel, the unacknowledged sister, is Melville's last and subtlest presentment of the white whale. But Isabel, beautiful and mysterious, is as attractive as any angel of light. And perhaps the deepest point at which Melville had arrived is his conviction that it was the very nobility of Pierre, his faultless and unswerving grasp of the good, which led him to abandon Lucy and marry Isabel. Isabel is no siren; if she be the principle of evil, then evil is not to be distinguished from good. Is there good and evil? Melville seems to ask. Are we aware of anything but ambiguities? Isabel herself, so far as any human insight can pierce, is wholly good. In cleaving to her Pierre unfalteringly obeyed the god within him. And his end is the hopeless, pointless, irremediable destruction of himself and those he loves. The world is a lie, through and through a lie, is Melville's final conclusion. In this world it is hopeless to distinguish good from evil, or even to know whether there is any distinction. There is nothing but ambiguities. There is despair in this book and much bitter wisdom. Melville's lonely journey has taken him into a deeper and deeper night. There is no room here for heroic purpose or unyielding pride. For there is no foe, except in the sense that the whole context of things is at enmity with the soul of man, poisoning his virtue and giving heavenly radiance to his vice, entangling him in ambiguities, leaving him with nothing indubitable, no loyalties and no aspirations. It is a comfortless last word, but we must take Melville as we find him. He is one of the men who have adventured far; perhaps one has to go farther yet to find light. We are convinced that Melville's knowledge was no empty fantasy. He has a high place amongst those who adventure even if we believe, as we prefer to believe, that there are others who have adventured farther and passed through Melville's night.

[Trying to Reveal a Mystery]

John Middleton Murry*

In 1851 Herman Melville published "Moby Dick"; in the next five years "Pierre," which was received with cold hostility, "Israel Potter," and the "Piazza Tales." Then, to all intents and purposes, there was silence till the end, which did not come till thirty-five years later. The silence of a great writer needs to be listened to. If he has proved his genius, then his silence is an utterance, and one of no less moment than his speech. The silence of a writer who has the vision that Melville proved his own in "Moby Dick" is not an accident without adequate cause; and that we feel that silence was the appropriate epilogue to Melville's masterpiece is only the form of our instinctive recognition that the adequate cause was there. After "Moby Dick" there was, in a sense, nothing to be said, just as after King Lear there seemed nothing for Shakespeare to say. Shakespeare did find another utterance in Antony and Cleopatra: then he too was silent. For, whatever names we may give to the "romantic" plays of his final period, and however high the praises we sincerely heap upon them, they belong to another order and have a significance of another kind than the great tragedies. They are, essentially, the work of a man who has nothing

*Reprinted from "Herman Melville's Silence," Times Literary Supplement (London), No. 1173 (10 July 1924), 433.

more to *say*, but who is artist and genius enough at last to contrive a method of saying even that.

Herman Melville could not do that, but then nobody save Shakespeare has been able to work that miracle. Probably Melville knew exactly what Shakespeare had achieved in the faint, far reflection of *The Tempest*; for in the "Battle-pieces, and other Poems," with which he made scarce so much as a ripple in his own silence in 1866, is this strangely irrelevant verse on Shakespeare:—

> No utter surprise can come to him
> Who reaches Shakespeare's core;
> That which we seek and shun is there—
> Man's final lore.

Melville knew where Shakespeare had been: no doubt he also knew where Shakespeare at last arrived; but he could not communicate those mysterious faint echoes of a certitude—that certitude "which we seek and shun"—which are gathered together into *The Tempest*.

Yet Melville was trying to say more during his long silence. How much he struggled with his dumbness we cannot say; perhaps during most of those thirty-five years he acquiesced in it. But something was at the back of his mind, haunting him, and this something he could not utter. If we handle the clues carefully we may reach a point from which we too may catch a glimpse of it; but then, by the nature of things, we shall be unable to utter what we see. We can only indicate the clues. They are to be found, one at the beginning and one at the end of the silence. "Pierre" is at the beginning. It is, judged by the standards which are traditional in estimating a "work of art," a complete failure. The story is naive, amateurish, melodramatic, wildly improbable, altogether unreal. Let those who are persuaded that a novel is a good story and nothing more avoid "Pierre." But those who feel that the greatest novels are something quite different from a good story should seek it out: to them it will be strange and fascinating, and they will understand why its outward semblance is clumsy and puerile. Melville is trying to reveal a mystery; he is trying to show that the completely good man is doomed to complete disaster on earth, and he is trying to show at the same time that this must be so, and that it ought to be so. The necessity of that "ought to be so" can be interpreted in two ways: as Melville calls them, horologically or chronometrically. Horologically—that is, estimated by our local and earthly timepieces—the disaster of the good ought to be so, because there is no room for unearthly perfection on earth; chronometrically—that is, estimated by the unvarying recorder of the absolute—it ought to be so, because it is a working out, a manifestation, of the absolute, though hidden, harmony of the ideal and the real. In other words, Melville was trying to reveal anew the central mystery of the Christian religion.

He did not succeed. How could he succeed? Nobody understood

"Pierre"; apparently nobody had even a glimmering understanding of it. And the thirty-five years of silence began. At the extreme end of them, moved perhaps by a premonition of coming death, Melville wrote another "story." "Billy Budd" is carefully dated: it was begun on November 16, 1888, the rewriting began on March 2, 1889, and it was finished on April 19, 1891. In the following September Melville was dead. [As Harrison Hayford and Merton M. Sealts, Jr., indicate, "the manuscript was in a heavily revised, still 'unfinished' state when he died." *Billy Budd, Sailor* (Chicago: University of Chicago, 1962), p. 12. Ed. Note.] With the mere fact of the long silence in our minds we could not help regarding "Billy Budd" as the last will and spiritual testament of a man of genius. We could not help expecting this, if we have any imaginative understanding. Of course, if we are content to dismiss in our minds, if not in our words, the man of genius as mad, there is no need to trouble. Some one is sure to have told us that "Billy Budd," like "Pierre," is a tissue of naivety and extravagance: that will be enough. And, truly, "Billy Budd" *is* like "Pierre"—startlingly like. Once more Melville is telling the story of the inevitable and utter disaster of the good and trying to convey to us that this must be so and ought to be so—chronometrically and horologically. He is trying, as it were with his final breath, to reveal the knowledge that has been haunting him—that these things must be so and not otherwise.

[Interesting Diagnosis of Melville's Mind]

H. P. Marshall*

After the high ecstasy of *Moby Dick*, Melville did not go back to simple story-telling, but being wound up, he proceeded to run down. The result was that strange lonely affair *Pierre or the Ambiguities*.

I have classed *Pierre* among the interesting books, for it is as impossible to claim that it is good as to blame it for being dull. Melville was not careful to choose titles which would describe the content of his books, but when he added "The Ambiguities" after *Pierre*, he was being extremely explicit and truthful.

The book is an astonishingly frank revelation of personality, so obviously autobiographical that few men would have dared to write it;

*Reprinted from "Herman Melville," *London Mercury*, 11 (November 1924), 65–66.
Earlier in his essay (p. 60) Marshall writes: "It must be admitted that *Typee* and *Omoo* are better constructed than *Mardi* and *Pierre*, but they are also far less ambitious; I would rather have a few paragraphs of the sayings of Old Bardianna, or the lecture of Plotinus Plinlimmon on 'Horologicals and Chronometricals,' than the whole of *Typee*, *Omoo* and *White Jacket*."

but though its foundation is clear, it is hard to draw from it any conclusion. It is not essential, of course, that conclusions should be drawn from a book; to what certain knowledge do we attain by reading *The Crock of Gold* or *The Wallet of Kai-Lung*? For a little while our outlook upon life may become more kind; we may realise, until reality forces us to forget, that even if men are all fools, they are not all malicious fools; we may, in fact, allow ourselves to fall under the spell of cunning and kindly words, but we shall have gained no knowledge. We shall not know if the authors of these most cherished books have a message for the age, or if they use safety razors, and, here is the point, we shall not care. Between us and the author there is a barrier of magic words, but between us and Melville there is no such barrier. There is, instead, always an element of personal struggle. To read *Pierre* is like listening to some friend talking, and trying to understand what vague and indefinable terror is troubling him. His mother, in the story, feels the same as we do. "And some deed of shame," she says "or something most dubious and most dark is in thy soul, or. . . . What can it be? Pierre, unbosom. Answer, what is it, boy?" She also felt the need for some answer to the riddle—but she did not realise, as we must, that it is useless to ask Pierre—it is only possible to share with him the awful disaster to which he is brought by his idealism.

The critics unmercifully abused the book when it appeared, and I am not sure that they were entirely wrong. That ecstasy and enthusiasm which gives to *Moby Dick* a great deal of its wonder becomes in *Pierre* an alarming lack of restraint; a sensation is caused like that which accompanies an inferior film. I had the misfortune a little while ago to see Jackie Coogan on the screen in a film where for some reason he creeps away from hard-faced workhouse officials to place a withered flower on the neglected grave of his mother. There is no reason why he should not creep away and be sentimental if he pleased, but there is every reason why he should do so strictly in private, and it was because Melville, by writing *Pierre*, aroused similar thoughts in the minds of the critics that they attacked him. All through the book the conversation is stilted and slightly absurd; it is hard to imagine a maid even eighty years ago, expressing anger like this:

"Monster! Incomprehensible fiend! Depart! See! She dies away at the sight of thee—begone! Woulds't thou murder her afresh? Begone!"

Because of the genuine feeling behind the hysterics, it seems petty to stress so much the blemishes of style in the book, but, however earnest a man may be, any speech he makes will carry less conviction than it should if he interrupts himself by alternately gnashing his teeth and weeping bitterly. And yet, just as that man may be interesting, since behind his demonstrations must lurk some feeling, so Pierre is extremely interesting for the diagnosis it gives us of Melville's mind. It was a mind that was always probing to find what lay behind the terms Destiny, Chance, and Fortune. Hawthorne, in his *English Notebook* says:

> Herman Melville came to see me at the Consulate. On Wednesday we took a pretty long walk together, and sat down in a hollow among the sand-hills. Sheltering ourselves from the high cold wind, Melville, as he always does, began to reason of providence and futurity, and of everything else that goes beyond human ken . . . .

There is the Melville of *Pierre*—wrestling incessantly with the Ambiguities of Life, and coming to the conclusion that the Heavenly Justice varies as much from earthly justice as Greenwich time from Chinese time. It is the disillusionment that W. B. Yeats put into the mouth of Fergus:

> I see my life go dripping like a stream
> From change to change; I have been many things,
> But now I have grown nothing, being all,
> And the whole world weighs down upon my heart.

But it was those uncertainties that lie over the furthest hill, and are hidden beyond the deepest sky, that weighed upon Melville's heart; it was not this world, but the power that drives it onward that drove him to despair, and Pierre was his last desperate effort to express the mystery that obsessed him.

I say it was his last effort, though he published subsequently three volumes of prose, and four of verse, as well as some contributions to *Harper's New Monthly Magazine*, and *Putnam's Monthly Magazine*; but *Pierre* was his "flurry," as he would have said.

[The Spiritual Counterpart of *Moby-Dick*]

John Freeman*

How great was his discouragement at this time is clearly seen in *Pierre*, published about a year after *Moby-Dick*. It is a book of raptures and glooms, in which all the artillery of circumstance is turned against the innocence and foolishness of youth, to sink it into the mud. Dostoieffsky never wrote a more desperate book, nor the author of *Jude the Obscure* a more depressing. It is written out of an exhausted imagination and an inflamed nervous system. His eyesight had troubled him, and Mrs. Melville said that they all felt anxious about the strain on Herman's health in the spring following the issue of *Pierre*; and this must have been due partly to an inevitable reaction from the inhuman tension of composition, and partly to the abuse which *Pierre* provoked. The strain on his physical

*Reprinted from *Herman Melville* (London: Macmillan and Co., 1926), pp. 59–60; 108–113; 180–81.

health was cause and effect of the strain on his spiritual health, as shown in his apprehension of the world. His judgement of his readers failed, or he saw and defied it with a fierce surge of the perversity that heaved within him. No book was less likely to conciliate readers than *Pierre*, and he found that the vast idealism of one part and the abhorrent realism of the other, and the distressing gulf between the two, revolted them all. In a later chapter we shall be looking at *Pierre* more closely, but it must be said here that this novel is one of the most powerful of all the books neglected by readers avid of an easier delight than Melville offers. *Pierre* is the spiritual counterpart of *Moby-Dick*, and like that written from within, with desperate pulse and bitter returns of hope and defeat. . . .

Pierre, the story of a challenge ending in disaster—to justify the label is easy, but it will convey small sense of the significance of the novel that followed *Moby-Dick*. The sub-title is "The Ambiguities", and is essential to an understanding of the book. . . .

The chief justification of the sub-title, "The Ambiguities", is seen not in Pierre's relation to his mother, a playful one, but in his response to his new-found sister. Her beauty, her strangeness, her remoteness from all but the hungers of affection, play upon him powerfully, and incestuous passions seize him when most he pities her. When he explains that without gratuitous dishonour to his father's memory he cannot be an open brother to her, and whispers untold words of his intention to assume a union which cannot be a real one, "the girl moved not; was done with all her tremblings; leaned closer to him, with an inexpressible strangeness of an intense love, new and inexplicable. Over the face of Pierre there shot a terrible self-revelation; he imprinted repeated burning kisses upon her; pressed hard her hand; would not let go her sweet and awful passiveness.

"Then they changed; they coiled together, and entangedly stood mute."

More painful, and far from ambiguous, is another passage in which, confessing the disappointment of his hopes as an author, he finds his torments displaced by worse torments, and in burning, extravagant phrase cries out, as Isabel clings to him in the twilight: "If to follow Virtue to her uttermost vista, where common souls never go; if by that I take hold on hell, and the uttermost virtue, after all, prove but a betraying pander to the monstrousest vice,—then close in and crush me, ye stony walls!" And when Pierre sallies forth to the last bloody act he bids Isabel and Lucy farewell in the like frenzy: "For ye two, my most undiluted prayer is now, that from your here unseen and frozen chairs ye may never stir alive; the fool of Truth, the fool of Virtue, the fool of Fate, now quits ye forever!" And yet again, when he seizes the fatal drug he cries to Isabel, for whom his life has been lost, "Wife or sister, saint or fiend", ambiguity clinging still to his words, but disappearing in his action—the fool of Virtue.

The unique quality of *Pierre* is found in its violent disillusion. The brilliant young man, the high-hearted idealist, confronts a difficulty, chooses dishonour for honour's sake, challenges the world and is doubly defeated; first and most deeply by his own masculine passion, secondly by conflict with unrealized circumstances. A worm writhes in the heart of this Galahad. His idealism becomes his undoing, his relation with Isabel is corrupted, and that which began pure and bright ends in the treachery of the senses. And as for that drear, fore-doomed conflict with the world, there is something at once crass and sad in the silliness of the challenge; and here it is plain enough that the author is speaking not simply for Pierre Glendinning but also for Herman Melville. Pierre is his Hamlet, and Hamlet not alone in his exposure of himself to the world but even in his odd and curt dealing with his mother and her pastor when the fatal secret is out.

Less fantastic than *Mardi* in its conception, *Pierre* is scarcely less remote from reality, and yet at times it touches the sharpest of realities far more clearly than *Mardi* does. But in *Mardi* there is something sweet, aspiring and undefeated in the pursuit of the inexpressible idea, while in *Pierre* there is an enormous and perverse sadness, declining to mere madness. Melville rose to his greatest when he turned from the allegory of *Mardi* to the symbolism of *Moby-Dick*; he sank into perversity when he conceived *Pierre*. It expresses his own disenchantment in a way that makes him seem like an Apostate of the imagination, turned from his allegiance not for mercenary reasons but for a reason no less deplorable— a lack of faith in himself, in his privilege, in his calling. He is satirizing not his mother, not his friends, but his soul, himself.

There is something of the beauty and the strangeness of shadows in *Pierre*. A strict aesthetic might insist that the beauty of shadows, however rare, cannot surpass the beauty of the shape which is shadowed; another, that even what is void of beauty may cast a shadow which, by the merciful cunning of a single beam, itself becomes a shape of beauty. Even the gloom of *Pierre*, in the intense light of Melville's genuis, is figured with shadows of beauty that rejoice the heart and almost justify the darkness.

Yet, nevertheless, who will not deplore the waste of beauty! There are passages of lovely prose in *Pierre*, leisured, deep-breathed prose; there are tender and gentle episodes—but all wasted. Pierre Glendinning, says Melville, "had not as yet procured for himself that enchanter's wand of the soul, which, but touching the humblest experiences in one's life, straightway it starts up all eyes, in every one of which are endless significancies. Not yet had he dropped his angle into the well of his childhood." He had thrown aside the enchanter's wand when he finished *Redburn*, and now bore a serpent. The psychology is intolerably followed, with the sly and thirsty fury of a stoat; nothing outside the Russians could be more subtle or less scrupulous. "I write precisely as I please," he cries, breaking in on the narrative; and in this scorn of others he has written a book which may move deeply but cannot please any one.

And a principal reason for this failure is clear. Granting the subject, Melville's aim could only be achieved in verse. The theme is, essentially, one for an Elizabethan play, in which every emotion is exalted and the large movement of blank verse is ready to sustain vast incredibilities. In a verse-drama Melville would have achieved what he needs but cannot achieve—remoteness; his desperate imagination, hanging above and apart from a creeping reality, might have taken on another reality, that of the poetry which is as remote, as real, and as necessary as the sun. But the faculty was denied to him, and he attempted to do in elaborate prose what he could not do in native verse; and he failed as clearly as Pierre Glendinning failed, and as greatly. . . . Part of Melville's character, as I have suggested, is to be read in what he wrote, but another part in what he refrained from. No one can read his work extensively without noticing the almost complete absence of women and his almost complete silence about sex. A cold nature his assuredly was not, and passages in *Pierre* have a power so unholy that one reads shrinkingly. But excepting *Pierre* and one or two of the lesser books, and also *Clarel* among the poems, there is scarce a hint that Melville was aware of what it is that teases, exalts, ennobles and destroys men. The sharpest sexual passion anywhere in his work, and it is an all but solitary instance, is incestuous. Was it perhaps the upgathered impulses of his puritanic heritage that warred with his natural passion and made out of that strife a silence, a desolation? Of all modern imaginative writers Melville is the least obviously troubled by the struggle that Blake seraphically viewed as a part and an image of spiritual life. Here, indeed, the analogy between Blake and Melville suddenly fails. For Blake, as for other mystics, the sexual strife was a rehearsal of the unending vaster conflict between the forces of man and God, Time and Eternity; but Melville saw it as something only to be annulled. Save for the abundance of masculine passion expressed in other books and other ways, and the normality revealed in nearly all of them, it might have seemed that he was deficient in humanity; but against this all his writing, and all his life so far as it is recorded, is clear evidence.

It is indeed a singular character, thus viewed in its suppressions. Melville is like nobody else, and perhaps if any verdict of posterity could give him pleasure it would be simply that.

[One of the Most Important Books in the World]

Anonymous*

The most interesting fragments of literary comment are always those not intended for publication; so, without permission, I reprint part of a letter from a correspondent abroad who wants to know if Herman Melville's "Pierre" and "Piazza Tales" are in print over here, except as members of a de luxe set. He writes;

> Melville, it is supposed, has been re-discovered recently. Actually, folk here rave hysterically about "Moby Dick," principally, and apparently lack the wit to know that "Pierre" is one of the most important books in the world, profound beyond description in its metaphysic: in fact, I believe that you yourself would find something to keep your mind hard at work for many a day if you read that philosophically dramatic or dramatically philosophical novel, for it *is* a philosophical novel, reaching to heaven and down to hell in its march to a tragic culmination, a consummation; and there is one short story in the other book, "Bartleby" by name, which ought to fascinate you in its psychology like a theological mystery, since you are built and designed to be snared and decoyed in the theological nets.

[*Mardi*, *Moby-Dick*, and *Pierre*: A Trilogy and a Crescendo]

Anonymous†

This latest addition to the "English Men of Letters" series seeks to fulfil a crying need, being the first English book on perhaps the most astonishing literary figure of the last century. Professor Raymond Weaver led the way in America with his "Herman Melville, Mariner and Mystic"; and certainly Melville was a spiritual mariner, his sharp, peering eye ever on the human compass. The facts of the life are yet sparse, and several "tease the sense with unconfirmed significance," to quote from "Clarel," the interminable strange poem published toward the end of Melville's days. In "Pierre" he wrote that not to know gloom and grief is not to know anything an heroic man should learn: an aphorism that comes pat to the mind reflecting on Melville, who, as a thinker, is even more heroic than his valiant Ahab; and, like Paracelsus, at once longs to trample on and to save mankind. In his maturity he produced two great prose tragedies,

*Reprinted from Christopher Morley, "The Bowling Green," *Saturday Review of Literature* (New York), 2 (1 May 1926), 755.

†Reprinted from "Herman Melville," *Times Literary Supplement* (London), No. 1268 (20 May 1926), 337, a review of John Freeman's *Herman Melville*.

"Moby Dick" and "Pierre," and a short one, "Bartleby" in the "Piazza Tales," works without parallel; and if Hawthorne spoke truth, there was a deep, dark tragedy in Melville's own life, for he could neither believe nor accept unbelief. He too strove angrily with God for a blessing and probed far into the mystery of iniquity.

August 1, 1919, was the hundreth anniversary of his birth, and from that hour, in the incalculable giddy dance of public favour and criticism, his renaissance as an author began: he literally arose from the dead to enchant and to puzzle the world. A thick harvest of reviews and articles followed promptly, the many rhetorical, a few hysterical, concerned in the main with "Moby Dick"; in fact, Melville was paraded and trumpeted as a one-book man, an author of romantic sea tales, who damned himself finally and drowned his genius in a metaphysical vat. The standard English edition of his works revealed another Melville, notably in "Mardi," "Pierre" and "Bartleby." His greatness, standing four-square for inspection, appeared vast and obscure enough to promote a new literature; his life-work offered a labyrinth for anyone with sufficient temerity and patience to blaze paths here and there. One path only has been cleared and can be taken with a relative ease; and though Mr. Freeman, in his short study, glances to right and left, makes tentative steps, loiters with his eye on this and that sombre, entangled byway, he is content generally to follow rather than boldly to lead, though he amplifies and extends the analysis of "Moby Dick," making skilful use of Blake's Good and Evil doctrines to help him by analogy in his exposition of that mighty human synthesis. Melville, however, reaching as he did to the opaque core of life, demands a critic as doughty and indomitable as his own Ahab; for he fascinates and imperils like the White Whale. . . .

Hawthorne was the only man of genius with whom Melville seems to have been friendly, a fact attributable perchance as much to Melville's reticence and stern pride as to neglect from others. He reared his family under financial and more subtly distressing circumstances, if the parable of "I and my Chimney" is autobiographical, though Mr. Freeman ignores such a probability. Melville lived in an old farmhouse at Pittsfield, within hail of Hawthorne, and racked himself in a fever of work and thought. "Since you have been here," he wrote to Hawthorne, "I have been ploughing and sowing and raising and printing and praying. . . . Dollars damn me; and the malicious Devil is for ever grinning in upon me, holding the door ajar." He had succeeded with his early books, failed memorably with "Mardi" and foresaw gloom and despair awaiting him. The public banned what he felt most moved to write, he said; it would not pay; yet he would not write otherwise. Let him be infamous, there was no patronage in *that*. Always he had been unfolding within himself, now reached the inmost leaf of the bulb, and shortly the flower must fall into mould. Mr. Freeman assumes that this "inmost leaf" was "Moby Dick"; other close readers may think of "Pierre." There is a reference somewhere, missed by Mr. Freeman, to Melville's having suggested that, though he had dealt with Leviathan, meaning his White Whale, and climbed an apparent summit in life and work, there was yet the Kraken, that mythical enormous sea-monster greater than Leviathan. This too may point to "Pierre"; which followed close on "Moby Dick," provoked a tempest of rage from a startled public, and at length smothered Melville to seeming extinction as a writer formerly popular, one "who had lived among the cannibals," he says, passionate and scornful. Mr. Freeman ascribes Melville's so-called pessimism to a reaction of mind against the task of incessant composition: surely a trivial notion to account for an in-born and developed habit of mind, a predisposition of temperament, dif-fused throughout Melville's big works and affining him spiritually to Dante, Shakespeare, Ecclesiastes, Schopenhauer, Hartmann and the like masters of a profound and unflinching philosophy of life. Mr. Freeman makes part amends later when, after again referring the aforesaid pessimism to the exhaustion of authorship, he adds, "and the mysteries of the world metaphysically considered." . . .

Mr. Freeman examines the works in detail, doing his duty as critic and expositor faithfully and well, until he comes to "Mardi"; and here, and specifically in "Pierre," either because his peculiar prejudice is too stubborn, or because his critical equipment is too narrow, he is less suc-cessful; and unquestionably his difficulties were great. He fails to see a trilogy and a crescendo in "Mardi," "Moby Dick" and "Pierre," and is therefore hampered at the outset; nor does a fear of or a distaste for metaphysics separate him from many of his fellows. He sees allegory in "Mardi," but will not allow its place in "Moby Dick" or in "Pierre," though he stresses the symbolism of the White Whale; and he has a plaguey suspicion that there may be something of the kind in the tragic story of young Glendinning. He makes no effort to trace the spiritual resemblances between the shadowy women in "Mardi" and the two heroines in "Pierre." "Mardi," to him, is a perversely imperfect allegory of eternal and obscure things and he classes it among "hapless might-have-beens." He admits that "Pierre" moves deeply, but says it cannot please anyone, either overlooking or discounting Melville's own views ex-pressed in Father Mapple's amazing sermon: "Woe to him who seeks to please rather than to appal! . . . Woe to him who would not be true, even though to be false were salvation." He does not imitate Professor Weaver, who declares that "Pierre" is Melville's most frankly poisonous book, a work almost destroyed "by divine incitation" in the Harper fire of 1853, and accordingly reduced to a safely limited edition; but he can find little beyond a morbid tale of incest in that astonishing work, and insists upon the failure of the form, such a theme, he suggests, being fit only for an Elizabethan play wherein, by the large movement of blank verse, in-credibilities can be sustained and "remoteness" attained.

Other readers may see in "Mardi" a prefatory review of human experience and endeavour and collapse, a survey of all philosophies and creeds and myths, at times reminding one of Flaubert's "Saint Antony"; in "Moby Dick" yet another search for the Absolute, limited by mundane law and leading to disaster; in "Pierre" a cosmic drama worked out in vividly human symbols involving enemy-impulsions and the primordial urge of the whole universe. Perhaps the key to "Pierre," or rather, a key—for there is the chapter on Chronometrical and Horoscopical Time, likewise the vision of the Titans, to help those who do not necessarily run when they read—lies in Schopenhauer and Hegel; and there is evidence to prove that Melville had read widely in the former, and probably in the latter, reaching metaphysical conclusions similar to those advanced by Hartmann in "The Philosophy of the Unconscious," printed in 1869, seventeen years after the publication of "Pierre." Mr. Freeman might reply that any work of art which deals with the conflict of Will and Idea by means of created character fails integrally: later adventurous critics may rank the appalling "Pierre" with Dante's "Inferno" and Goethe's complete "Faust." Mr. Freeman is more happy when dissecting Melville's poems, yet he does not draw attention to the slight though intensely tragic story of the sea captain—Ahab, even a Melville, in miniature—one of the few redemptive passages in "Clarel"; nor does he cope fully with that strange, haunting, excessively vital short tale "Bartleby," which, like "Pierre," may become a touchstone for the critics of the next age. However, most readers will be grateful to Mr. Freeman, notwithstanding his imposed limitations; for it is the excellency of a writer to leave things better than he found them, and undeniably Mr. Freeman has done this.

[A Great Book *Manqué*]

Arnold Bennett*

Wednesday, June 2nd. [1926]
. . . I had ordered the complete works of Herman Melville on Monday. They arrived yesterday in three large parcels, of which I only opened two, because I didn't want to begin reading *Pierre* (which was in the third parcel) immediately—not until I had assimilated *An American Tragedy* a bit. So I went on with Macauley's "Essay on Frederick the Great," which is very good reading.

Sunday, June 27th. [1926]
    I finished reading *Pierre*. This novel is not equal to *Moby Dick*; but it is full of very fine things, and a most remarkable book. Melville's idea was

*Reprinted from *The Journal of Arnold Bennett, 1896-1928* (New York: The Viking Press, 1933), pp. 877, 882.

the grand romantic manner, and when he succeeded in it, he *did* succeed. His humour too is very rich. I think he must have been influenced by Rabelais, though there is nothing Rabelaisian in the book. The pity is he gets so many incidents improbable, when with a little more invention and trouble he might have made them quite probable. Nevertheless, I think it is entitled to be called a great book—even if *manqué* here and there.

[Nightmare Nonsense, Outcome of Disease]

Julian Hawthorne*

In my boyhood and youth Herman Melville was so good a playmate of mine that I was resentful at his disappearance from the later scene. But many years passed—thirty, forty, fifty—and no one knew him or spoke his name, except Clark Russell and one or two others who had followed the sea and written of it, who acknowledge him as their pioneer and master. It might be partly because steam had supplanted sails; or that real or fictitious tales of adventure in far places had become common: be that as it might, no one knew him or spoke of him any more, and his books, which had the flow and freedom of the sea that inspired them, were forgotten. "Redburn," "Omoo," "Typee," the first chapters of "Mardi," and much of "Moby Dick," seemed sunk fathom deep in the ocean of oblivion. It was as if a section of one's favorite landscape had vanished. That the latter part of "Mardi," and the extravaganzas of "Moby Dick" should be cast off and set adrift caused me neither surprise nor regret; but the rest was pure literature; and "White Jacket," too, bore imaginative and thoughtful touches, in addition to its sterling value as record of a lost phase of sea-faring, which should have been preserved in men's memories.

As for the nightmare nonsense of "Pierre," I was glad that it had gone down with the rest: it was the outcome of disease, distorted and repulsive: the sweet bells jangled out of tune and harsh. And the poems were disordered doggerel; let them pass. "Israel Potter" might have been written by any publishers' hack. Other fugitive pieces might remain fugitive: the beauty of the original Melville had ceased to be; he was crippled, pitiful, but undesirable. Midway through his "Mardi" the evil spirit which had already threatened him in "Moby Dick," settled down upon him like a vulture: and the true Melville ended. . . .

Little is known of Melville's conditions in boyhood, but an uneasy

*Reprinted from "When Herman Melville was 'Mr. Omoo,' " *Literary Digest International Book Review* (New York), 4 (August 1926), 561–62, 564. Occasioned by publication of John Freeman's *Herman Melville*.

mind rather than a genuine impulse to adventure was the cause of his leaving home, and once afloat he accomplished nothing, and after his return did nothing but write of what he had experienced. In spite of the excellence of the descriptive ability which he thus discovered in himself, at times rising to genius, he could not see that his proper function was description of things seen and known; he wanted to probe and solve the moral universe. For this, he was equipped neither by nature nor education, and he drifted upon the rocks. The catastrophe inflamed his malady, and brought it from latent to positive disease. His case was plainly pathological; he had already begun to succumb to it in the latter chapters of "Moby Dick," and in "Pierre" it became rampant. The ruin was accompanied by fitful blazings-up of passion and even of insight, which produce a powerful and even splendid impression, tho never an agreeable one; insanity must always be a painful spectacle, tho the normally hidden faculties may be at moments brilliantly in evidence, like explosions of gunpowder in a sinking hull. They achieve a sensation in the beholder, but it leads to nothing. It was otherwise with a mind such as Goethe's, which can pass untroubled through the visions of the Second Part of Faust: the fruits of his journey are a better understanding of human limitations and possibilities. Imagination holds its wholesome integrity, and knows its course. . . .

A few years ago, Mr. Raymond Weaver, and after him several other pious zealots, filled so large a balloon with hot air in regard to Melville that the loom of it was seen across the Atlantic, and was brought to the attention of the present Mr. John Freeman, with the consequence of his little monograph. Balloons do not last long; the hot air cools, and they collapse. And, to be serious for a moment, there is no harm in recounting facts; the mischief begins when their discoverers, or rediscoverers, erect upon them a superstructure of inferences and deductions. Mr. Freeman, for example, has allowed himself to select characters, or incidents, from Melville's books, and to assume that they may be revelations, more or less veiled, of his actual personal experiences. Is the Mother in "Pierre" Melville's own mother? Because Pierre was tempted to incest with his sister, was Melville so tempted? He doesn't pretend to decide the question; but merely to suggest the possibility casts a portentous gleam upon the poor man's figure, and leads us to dilate him to Byronic or Mephistophelian proportions. If literary criticism be justified in this, the sooner writers abolish their imaginations, the better for them; and, to be sure, as things are going now, that ought not to prove a difficult or prolonged undertaking.

Melville's own era appraised him justly enough. As long as he did good and sane work, he was widely read and extolled; when he fell to metaphysical rubbish, his audience turned to more agreeable books. Why should we be asked to share his crazy resentment at what was inevitable? I return to my appreciation of Mr. Freeman's conscientiousness, method and diligence, but discerning literary criticism does not weave ropes out of sand. Melville, in his young manhood, was a likable, even lovable man, and richly endowed as a writer: it was his infirmity, not his fault, that beguiled him into mistaking the true nature and limitations of his gifts.

[Melville's Last Real and Audible Word]

Percy H. Boynton*

The book *Pierre* is an intriguing production and a chaotic one. Though it has a carefully devised plot and moves toward its tragic end with a relentless inevitability, it is not a good story, for it does not contain a single thoroughly human major character; and it is not a good allegory because it is not sufficiently detached from life, nor clearly enough superimposed upon it. It deals with the conflict between the claims of the conventional social order and the duties and claims of the individual. A young and wealthy aristocrat is adored by his mother and by a lovely and eligible girl to whom he is betrothed. Suddenly he becomes aware of the existence of an illegitimate sister, beautiful and poverty stricken. Without explaining fact or motive, in an evasive effort to protect his mother's pride, he wounds it to death by befriending the sister as her nominal husband. The mother dies after disinheriting him, and he lives out his last miserable days before suicide, with the sister for whom he now feels an overwhelming passion, and with the abandoned love who has now abandoned all to join the two outcasts in unhappy platonic devotion.

It is too much and too little to ask anyone to read. The characters are waxwork figures. They put Mme Tussaud's chamber of horrors to the blush. They are less convincing than hers because they are made to move and talk, ornately rhetorical talk with the strides and gestures of clumsy mechanisms. If the theme were overwhelmingly big, it might somehow overshadow the characters. But it is not. Pierre is a blundering and melodramatic ninny. His mother's alleged colossal pride is only a futile vanity. Pierre's first love is too stupid to see through him. His sister, though she is a duskily alluring beauty who serves often as the author's spokesman, is in the story no more than the occasion for the blunders and the futilities of the others. Yillah; unattainable beauty? Yes, but not the disheveled Isabel. Captain Ahab, incarnate hatred? Yes, he is a splendid madman; but Pierre is a quixotic lunatic. And yet one cannot climb Rock Rodondo or understand Melville without making *Pierre* a step in the ascent.

Melville at thirty-three was through with the life of the world and through with effective authorship. *Israel Potter* was to come, but it was a

*Reprinted from "Herman Melville," in *More Contemporary Americans* (Chicago: University of Chicago Press, 1927), pp. 43–47.

perfunctory piece of work not as interesting as the book it was based on. *Piazza Tales* were to come, pallid lotos-island reveries; *The Confidence Man*, an ineffectual pseudo-narrative treatise; and some metaphysical verses privately printed. But *Pierre* was Melville's last real and audible word, and even *Pierre* was an epilogue. He was done with story-telling or with the kind of criticism that is called "allegory." He was headed for a life of speculation in solitude; and *Pierre*, though to a degree autobiographical, had in it more of the future than of the past. He called the book in subtitle *The Ambiguities*. He wrote it in scorn of the conventional novels which were spinning intricate veils of mystery only to unravel and spool them neatly at the end, and in scorn of the compensation school of philosophy which held that clouds are provided solely for the making of rainbows. He was a skeptic as to the ways of the philistine world, more or less of an agnostic as to the detailed operations of Providence, but as much of a mystic in his ultimate optimism as the "compensationist" Emerson himself. He saw that "human life doth come from that which all men are agreed to call by the name of *God*, and that it partakes of the unravellable unscrutableness of God." "We live in nature very close to God." "From each successive world the demon principle is more and more dislodged; he is the accursed clog from chaos. . . . Want and woe, with their accursed sire, the demon principle, must back to chaos whence they came."

In another mood he wrote that for the enthusiastic youth there must surely come the time when faith enters into conflict with fact, "and unless he prove recreant, or unless he prove gullible, or unless he can find the talismanic secret, to reconcile this world with his own soul, then there is no peace for him, no slightest truce for him in this life." The talismanic secret, he went on to say, has never been found, and in the nature of things never can be found. Melville was neither recreant nor gullible. There is little to tell whether he ever found peace. But he disappeared from the life of men. He stopped writing for the public, though he left behind, written at the end of his long silence, a last story of the sea, *Billy Budd*, which was full of the sweep and vigor of his greatest work, a final resurgence of his energies not without parallel in the histories of genius. But long before this he had set down in the pages of *Pierre* the saddest of passages, which in the light of all we know can be taken as a self-revelation and a valedictory. It is part of a solid paragraph. I hope it is not an undue liberty to print it thus:

> I say, I cannot identify that thing which is called happiness;
> That thing whose token is a laugh,
> Or a smile,
> Or a silent serenity on the lip. . . .
>
> Nor do I feel a longing for it, as though I had never had it;
> My spirit needs different food from happiness. . . .
> For I think I have a suspicion of what it is.

I have suffered wretchedness,
But not because of the absence of happiness;
And without praying for happiness.

I pray for peace—
For motionlessness—
For the feeling of myself,
As of some plant, absorbing life without seeking it,
And existing without individual sensation.
I feel that there can be no perfect peace in individualness.
Therefore I hope one day to feel myself drunk up
Into the pervading spirit animating all things. . . .

I feel I am an exile here.

[For the Adventurous and the Fearless]

Arnold Bennett*

My second important large work [the first was Dreiser's *An American Tragedy*] read this year is Herman Melville's *Pierre*, which ought to be issued separately—at present it can only be had in the standard edition of Melville's works in heaven knows how many volumes. Melville was once famous as the author of those rather second-class (at any rate as bowdlerized for print) South Sea romances, *Typee* and *Omoo*. Then, much later, he became known as the author of *Moby Dick*—a great novel. He may still later become famous as the author of *Pierre*.

Pierre is transcendental, even mystical, in spirit. The basic idea of its plot is entitled to be called unpleasant. It contains superb writing, and also grotesque writing, which its author mistakenly thought to be superb. It is full of lyrical beauty which the veriest sentimentalist could not possibly confuse with ugliness. It is conceived in an heroical, epical vein, and executed (faultily) in the grand manner. It has marked originality. In it the author essays feats which the most advanced novelists of to-day imagine to be quite new.

Melville was an exalted genius. *Pierre*, though long, is shorter than *An American Tragedy*; but it is even more difficult to read. I recommend it exclusively to the adventurous and the fearless. These, if the book does not defeat them, will rise up, after recovering from their exhaustion, and thank me. I intend to pursue my researches into Herman Melville.

*Reprinted from *The Savour of Life: Essays in Gusto* (Garden City: Doubleday, Doran & Co. Inc., 1928), pp. 305–7.

[A Book Out of Soundings]

H. M. Tomlinson*

Pierre was published in 1852, in New York, by Messrs. Harper and Brothers; in London, by Messrs. Sampson Low. It was the book to follow *Moby Dick*, and our curiosity to learn what could follow so remarkable an adventure is natural. *Pierre* was issued a year after *Moby Dick*, and readers who are now about to read it for the first time will soon discover, and perhaps with little alarm, that it is not quite normal, as reading matter. To those readers of it who know it already, and so must be respectful admirers of Herman Melville, let me say that this attempt of mine to introduce this book is no proof at all of that assurance which is wisdom's when bearing a lamp and leading the labyrinthine way in knowledge to a central and hidden matter, because I do humbly confess there are things hidden which we shall never see with full understanding.

The *White Whale* sank the audacious ship which hunted it. That, of course, was the inevitable end of the story. Only the crack of doom will end that monster; nevertheless we know literature is ennobled by the fate of men who challenge the gods. But among Melville's letters you will find one which answers an admirer who had congratulated him on the magnitude of his whale. Melville disparages the size of it. He refers cryptically to something greater still—to a kraken. The kraken, by all accounts, was a fearful thing, more a primary terror than a form, so it could take any shape it chose, as the bestiaries show. When you have read *Pierre* you can make a guess at what Melville meant by something greater than a symbolical whale, something worse than the anger of gods who were too closely beset by importunate men. Though Moby Dick sank the ship which hunted him, he could not founder the book which described the heroic chase. In *Pierre*, however, you will see that Melville himself was overcome by the terror of a shadow much more ominous than the quarry Captain Ahab hunted in the other book. The subtitle of this novel, you will have noticed, is "The Ambiguities." Melville means the ambiguity of both good and evil. He attempts, in the character of Pierre, his hero, to follow a noble aim to its ultimate in the nature of man, and yet, with so good a purpose, he comes to dire disaster. He found that nobility had changed its face to evil; he found that instead of the everlasting light he looked into the bottomless pit.

The whale, let us remember, was an objective target. That enemy was not of man's making, any more than an earthquake or a typhoon. The hunt in this book is of a different nature. We shall understand *Pierre*—I mean we may more easily surmise what it is about—if we recall a certain fairy tale which tells of a hunter who shot at an enchanted beast, and then

---

*Reprinted from "Preface," in *Pierre*, ed. John Brooks Moore (New York: E. P. Dutton & Co., 1929), pp. vii–ix, xii–xvii.

found in horror that he had put an arrow into the heart of his love. So how, if a man should, like Pierre, aim to redress an evil in the world, the work of other men, and find that his crusading shaft has gone into his very soul and put death there?

The ambiguities. Well, they appear to have overcome even Melville's attempt to resolve them. His hero perishes in the effort and brings the book down to failure with him, for this novel is a failure. Yet do not let us suppose that *Pierre* is the less important because of that. It is hard to write a successful novel, but it is done fairly frequently today, and often in inadvertence, apparently. This unsuccessful *Pierre* is another affair. When I was reading it again, perplexed and troubled by the vision of the Laocoön, I put down the volume and took to read for relief a most successful work of recent fiction, which all the town knows. But the light had gone out of its cleverness. The little tragedy that was in it seemed ridiculous. It was assured and witty, it was complete in itself and successful, but *Pierre* had given it an unexpected valuation. I had then to return again to this introduction, under a compulsion I would have avoided, had it been possible, in an effort, which I felt was hopeless, to keep unwary and inexperienced readers of it within soundings, as a sailor would say, yet I know I cannot do it.

The story, you will find, is sufficiently disturbing to scare all who shrink from great heights and deeps and vacant outer space. I am forced now to confess that it is impossible for any reader, however wary he may be, to keep within soundings when reading *Pierre*. This book is bottomless. It is out of soundings. A reader of it is poised over an abyss of darkness most of the time, to the ultimate depth by which no sounding by man will ever be made. It is useless to attempt to explain what Herman Melville himself could but shadow forth, as of omens, rumblings, hints and stifled cries, out of the Valley of the Shadow. . . . As a rule, readers do not enjoy having their settled and comfortable opinions disturbed. They want them confirmed. They prefer a soothing hand. Christ himself never performed a greater miracle than that which Christians have worked with his message. They made a Church to give divine authority to their desires out of the material of his cross. Something had to be done with a symbol and sacrifice so inimical to authority and tradition, and intuitively they did the right thing before the challenge went too far. They sacrificed Christ again and more securely. We refuse to be disturbed; but if disturbance seems likely to come, then we can be trusted to transmute even Calvary into what will beautifully accord with guns, usury, and the other phenomena projected from the common opinions of our society. We resist change, for it is unknown danger to the kind of life we find it easier to understand; and a book like *Pierre* which so indecently reveals the relativity of what we have called virtue, the ambiguous and even awful possibilities in what we call love, the cheat in sacrifice, the evanescence of parental affection, the granite nature of pride and vanity, and the pit which may yawn suddenly in this world at the touch of an idealist resolute in his pure innocence to serve but his noblest impulse, a pit to engulf him, such a book rocks the verities on which we have built our abode. We do not read to have our verities rocked; we want to keep our place. The relativity of Good and Evil? Is it likely we are going into that? Well, that is what *Pierre* invites. We prefer, however to read for the confirmation of what we like, for entertainment, refreshment, ease of mind. We can stand tragedy, of course, if it has been boiled in sweet comfort; but the suggestion of inevitable doom inherent in our acts, however innocent they may seem to us, a fate self-induced on a day of sunshine, but as irrevocable as an astronomical certitude when menacing facts are arrayed in the last act—no, not that; we want Destiny to look upon our palmed half-crown as genially as an amiable policeman.

The facts of life which we do not like are not there. We have to remember, for example, that we would listen to nothing about our own great tragedy of twelve years ago unless that funny figure of a soldier, Old Bill, made it amusing, or as we would say, human. We were aware—for so it had been whispered to us—that our war had features which were not human at all as we understood humanity; but, as we have witnessed, they could be left out, could be ignored, buried, shut up in asylums, slums, and secluded institutions, or left quietly to sink to oblivion in the memory of the multitude of survivors who knew, but who dared not or could not confess. Human impulses, their springs and their consequences, quite often will not bear looking at, however noble their seeming. But never mind. Regard Old Bill, not Tolstoy. We do not want to hear what we do not want to know, more especially when we fear we ought to know it. Yet doubtless a time will come when we shall be able to look steadily and faithfully at ourselves as we were in war-time, and not only at the face of the horror, but to its origins and ancient heart beating in the dark and ugly body of the beast. For that is our saving grace; a generation of men can never be persuaded to round ruthlessly on itself, yet the next generation will turn on its fathers cheerfully, and abolish the revered and ancestral home, handsomely admitting the bats in its belfry and its fraudulent foundations. Consider us as now we read with sympathetic understanding the pursuit of a legendary monster by Captain Ahab and his men of the whaler "Pequod" though the people of 1851, more profitably occupied with the cosy romance of domesticity, refused to see anything in the world which remotely resembled Herman Melville's dire suggestions and images; they were left to us to interpret after seventy years.

Mr. John Freeman, in his excellent little study of Herman Melville, says fairly of *Pierre* that "the psychology is intolerably followed, with the sly and thirsty fury of a stoat; nothing outside the Russians could be more subtle or less scrupulous. . . . a book which may move deeply but cannot please anyone." This critic uses also another epithet "unholy." And certainly it is not without significance that Melville, whose books hitherto had ignored women, should in *Pierre* portray a mother, a bride-to-be, and a half-sister, and thereupon, out of the motive of love in its several appearances, even the love which leads to renunciation and sacrifice, have developed the relative nature of evil. I think "the thirsty fury of the stoat" is too small an image to give us the idea of Melville in this dreadful quest. There is, of course, for those whose traditions permit, something "diabolical" or "unholy" in it, but to me it seems merely that a man of sombre imaginative genius too much alone, and with a magnanimity inverted by the indifference of a generation utterly alien from his mind, had explored human conduct in desperation, with even a malign ruthlessness far beyond that point where safe novelists politely turn about through a deference for our susceptibilities. That a good man like Pierre, when following an exalted mission, should presently find his conscience seared, and in a hideous change in the elements of his thoughts see no way to distinguish his pure motive from the look of incest. Pierre cries out at the end; "If to follow Virtue to her uttermost vista, where common souls never go; if by that I take hold on hell, and the uttermost virtue, after all, prove but a betraying pander to the monstrousest vice—then close in and crush me, ye stony walls." He calls himself in his extremity, this Pierre, "the fool of Truth, the fool of Virtue, and the fool of Fate." He is undone by a high-hearted ideal. And then Melville, as Shakespeare did with his puppets in Hamlet, swept them all off the board.

I have called *Pierre*, as a novel, a failure. But what a tragic and noteworthy failure it is. It compels a reader, repels him, draws him to it again, shocks and disturbs in a way we never expect of the latest of our literary successes. It seems to me that Melville, except in *Moby Dick*, never did control his genius throughout a book. He had not the restraint and impartial eye which give balance and proportion to a work. There is a vulgar phrase: a loose fly wheel. By some fortunate coincidence of events the bewildering urge of his genius completed *Moby Dick* without once faltering or sprawling. In most of his other works it ran away with him. He seemed, at times, to abandon himself to mere impulse, and wantoned with words and ideas in an extravagance of Byronic melodrama. Mr. Freeman thinks that the reason for the failure of *Pierre* is clear, and says that, granting its theme, Melville's aim could have been achieved only in verse. The form of verse-drama would have given Melville what the story needs, remoteness, because "the large movement of blank verse is ready to sustain vast incredibilities." There is something in the suggestion, but with the success of *Moby Dick* before us I do not see how it can be maintained. Prose will do anything which a writer has the ability to demand of it, just as will verse. It was not that Melville demanded too much of prose, but that his genius worked unequally. He had, in *Pierre*, a daunting task, and at times his powers failed him or betrayed him. The truth simply is that some of *Pierre* is badly written, is even ridiculous, and that the course of the narrative is occasionally compelled along by coincidences which are incredible only because a reader observes that they are necessary, or the narrative would have to stop before its end. The reader should not be able to see that; he sees it only because the construction of the story is faulty. There is nothing incredible in *Moby Dick*, nothing irrelevant, all is swept naturally into the vast broad tide of the story. But listen to this:

> "Pierre was the only son of an affluent and haughty widow; a lady who externally furnished a singular example of the preservative and beautifying influences of unfluctuating rank health and wealth, when joined to a fine mind of medium culture, uncankered by any sordid grief, and never worn by sordid cares."

That is incredible if you like. It occurs early in the book. A great theme cannot be maintained by English of that quality; and more examples like it could be given. Melville declaims at times. He makes magnificent gestures when he is saying very little. His story is ungoverned. It is not intrinsically incredible nor somewhat mad; it is not modulated. When he was writing it, Melville appears to have been too dour and congested, his scorn of his casual and foolish but confident fellow creatures was too acute, to allow him a little humour, with which he could have gone aside to consider the proportions of his growing work. "I write precisely as I please," he exclaims, angrily in the book itself. That is all very well, but he should have asked himself whether what pleased him—or what gave him relief at the moment—was in accord with what he proposed to accomplish. After all, even an author should confess that he expects to have more than one reader.

Yet all that is written by a man of Melville's significance is important, and certainly *Pierre* is an important book. I have quoted from it a displeasing example of English. But if you want to make sure that Melville must take his place with the masters, then turn in this book to the passages he calls Enceladus, and to the discourse by Plotinas Plinlimmon on Chronometricals and Horologicals. Why, Melville could write a Christian sermon—though the Church seems not to have heard of it—better than any dean except Donne, better than any master of prose except Sir Thomas Browne. Strange that Christians should be unaware of so remarkable an apology for their faith as that of the non-benevolent Plinlimmon; but it was very like Melville to stow that sermon in a dark barque, built in the eclipse, with a bit of a gibbet post about her somewhere, and a tragic figure aboard who had to brood over even unmentionable sins.

[One of the Greatest Themes of Nineteenth Century Literature]

John Brooks Moore*

There are writers occasionally to be found (writers perhaps of many volumes) who may still be properly regarded as one-book men:—take Blackmore, "the author of *Lorna Doone*," as we appropriately think of him, despite his many other novels. Melville, on the contrary, has unfortunately been lately re-baptized "the author of *Moby Dick*," though he was thought of by his contemporaries as the author of *Typee*, and though he can scarcely be thought of as a one-book writer by any person who has read four or five of his stories. The chief interest of Melville's books derives from the account there found of evolution—or, better, the rebellion and disillusion—of a remarkable man of the nineteenth century. Perhaps this interest lies even more in his development as a man than as a man of the nineteenth century, for here is more than a touch of the inescapable disenchantment of mere ordinary existence. *Moby Dick*, with its sinister protest, is extremely confusing unless read as a chapter in the work of Melville, not the most important chapter necessarily, however masterful; a singular exposition of whaling, but a more singular account of the throes of an idealist almost undone in his idealism. How can this be understood if the reader of *Moby Dick* does not know the preceding experiences of the man, chronicled in *Typee, Redburn*, and *White Jacket*, and the later experiences shadowed in *Pierre*. The novels of Melville may be said, in general, to present a crescendo of protest, rebellion, disillusion, quiescence—the end of all incurable anguish. The steps in what was certainly the almost intolerable process of development to Melville can be fairly well represented by four books of his: *Redburn*, the first questioning of the world and the first disgust for its ways; *Typee*, the partial escape from that repulsive world; *Moby Dick*, the indictment of life and of things as they are; *Pierre*, the revulsion complete and refusal to make any terms of concessions—a book of death, the only solution. Those four are essential. The development can be followed still farther in *The Confidence Man*, *Clarel*, and *Billy Budd*, farther into the realm of passivity, that period from 1857 to 1891, when (despite some inconsequent writing) Melville seems to have indicated that for such as himself the rest must be silence.

Pierre is one of the lost novels of Melville. Melville as a writer and person was almost lost himself in the later nineteenth century. Finally *Typee, Omoo*, and *Moby Dick* were revived and rather widely circulated, as they still are, but *Pierre* is unread, unknown, like a newly discovered MS. Who has read it? A dozen people, here and there, for the book has utterly disappeared, not from men's minds (where it never really gained

*Reprinted from "Introduction," in *Pierre*, ed. John Brooks Moore (New York: E. P. Dutton & Co., 1929), pp. xxi–xxvii.

entrance in those genteel times of its publication), but from libraries. The world has been against it hitherto. Condemned on two counts by the reviewers of that day—(1) as being incomprehensibly transcendental, and (2) as being truly immoral and vicious—it never has had a hearing on its own merits. The long list of histories of American literature contains the name, I believe, of only one important volume that gives a first-hand estimate of *Pierre*, while the average volume never mentions the lost book, or simply names it, in total ignorance repeating the ancient charge of incomprehensibility and vice. Strange that any reader of *Moby Dick* should credit the tradition that Melville could write a really nasty or debased book! Yet such is the repute (only repute is too strong a word) of *Pierre*. Up to the present year (1928) of the twentieth century, this, certainly the second in power and personal significance of Melville's works, has been out of reach of practically all readers. Unthought of from the eighteen-fifties till the nineteen-twenties, when it appeared as volume nine in Constable's English edition of Melville, it has still remained unseen by, and unknown to, and nearly unobtainable to, Americans.

A student of twentieth century fiction may be imagined in perusal of *Pierre*, a book pronounced by everyone who mentioned it for seventy years morbidly vicious and metaphysically foggy. He may well marvel at his forefathers! The theme and development, the mood and the whole intent of the story are so powerfully and explicitly enforced that no mistake would seem possible: so much for foggy metaphysics. Of course, Melville was always interested in philosophic speculation, but *Pierre* is not in the least overloaded or obscured by such material. What, then, about the obscenity and vice in the book, those unspeakable things that made it not only a failure but also a scandal? There can be no mistake on that score, for Pierre, the hero, does indubitably feel pangs of incestuous affection for his illegitimate sister (discovered quite by chance when both brother and sister were full-grown young man and young woman) on more than occasion. These incestuous yearnings are presented by Melville as frightful and half-repulsive to Pierre, as full of horror. There is no condonement of incest that the most righeous might attack. But think: *Pierre* was published in 1852. No time to mention incest. To print the word in a book was such a breach of refinement that it could never be overlooked. Even Hawthorne's *Scarlet Letter*, printed not far from a year before *Pierre*, had been denounced as a vile and indecent affair—and that was only adultery, whereas this was incest and this author, Melville, made his hero passionately sympathetic and great of heart though rebellious against society, against his mother, against his betrothed, against the ways of the world; a true hero yet a hater of the genteel and refined world; a true hero assailed by incestuous desire in trying gallantly to save a sister. Surely a good young man could never in the nineteenth century have suffered so appallingly because he was trying to do ideal justice! One must not write nor even think such things. If Melville took the ultimate success of

Hawthorne's novel of adultery as warrant for the production of a novel of incest and social rebellion, he failed to sense the delicate bounds of the "possible" and the "impossible."

Melville's best known books—*Typee, Omoo, Redburn, White Jacket*, and *Moby Dick*—are concerned prevailingly with adventures by sea. In them, he capitalizes the unusual experiences of his two early voyages (one to Liverpool and back from New York; the other to the South Seas and finally back again). In *Pierre* we have Melville's only book which depends not at all on any novel or exotic background, a sort of quadrilateral love story involving Pierre, his mother, Lucy, his betrothed, and Isabel, his illegitimate sister. For once Melville enters the usual field of the long story, depending altogether on the interest of his characters and their peculiar strivings. The plot sounds melodramatic. In brief, Pierre Glendinning, the son of parents as aristocratic as were to be found then in America, living a joyous life with his widowed, gently domineering mother and in prospect of marriage with Lucy Tartan, a girl of both his mother's choice and his own, this Pierre strangely stumbles upon an illegitimate sister in the immediate vicinity of his home. It was a spiritual thunderbolt. Could his father of revered memory, the household god of his mother and himself, have thus begotten a child and left the child unprovided, too, at his death? Pierre's world rocks and heaves about him at the discovery. He longs for the sister, Isabel; feels her to be the one most wronged, the one to whom some restitution is owing. But his mother, who is wholly absorbed in him and in whom he has been even more absorbed, to tell the truth, than in his genuinely beloved Lucy! An abnormally close bond has tied son to widowed mother. He must never let her know the disgrace of his father—never let her hear of the illegitimacy of Isabel. Pierre's heart is in turmoil. Of the three precious women, two, at least, must be frightfully wounded whatever course he may take. But Isabel, the abandoned sufferer, to him her rights seem greatest: and, besides, he is drawn powerfully, incestuously; his kisses for her have some heat of passion, his embraces are more than brotherly. Not that his affection for his mother is lost nor his desperate love for his betrothed, Lucy, not that, but rather it appears to his inexperienced idealistic soul that not too much can be sacrificed to atone to Isabel for her desolate existence. He cannot reveal Isabel's true circumstances to his mother or Lucy. He comes to the final scheme, astonishing in anyone except a magnanimous-souled Pierre, of slipping away with Isabel under pretense of a secret marriage, thus putting himself in a position to cherish her forever, and thus taking all the load of opprobrium for leaving his mother and jilting his betrothed upon his own head. Everyone abjures him and casts him off. He flees with Isabel to the city to suffer frightfully in the attempt to earn a living by writing. No; not everyone casts him off. Lucy Tartan still has faith in him and, with a magnanimity surpassing even his own, she insists on coming to the aid of Pierre and Isabel. Lucy's relatives view Pierre as a seducer.

They hound him until suicide and murder bring a bitter end to Pierre, Lucy and Isabel.

The twentieth-century student, invoked above, will not find the book obscure; the incest hinted will not shock him; but he will be astounded at Pierre's attempt to face down the world, at his magnificent idealism, at his foregone ruin. He will look wonderingly, this student, at the title-page of the book:

Pierre;

or,

The Ambiguities.

What does the wild, passionate, distressing tale signify in the light of that sub-title, "The Ambiguities"? Certainly Pierre's attitude in his pretended marriage is ambiguous; his father's life and repute were also ambiguous in the light of this illegitimate Isabel. Are the multiple misconceptions arising from Pierre's yearning to follow his lofty idea of rectitude, are they the ambiguities? Why has this book been so roundly denounced or so tacitly disregarded for seventy years? Something more than a few hints of incest is needed to account for that. Perhaps the clue lies in this (to quote from Weaver's biography—*Herman Melville, Mariner and Mystic*)—that "Melville set himself up against the world as a party of one." Whatever else *Pierre* may be, it is the most powerful denunciation of mid-nineteenth century American society yet written, and it was written at that time, not in easy retrospect. Melville's fellows could not have remained themselves, have followed their daily lives if they had read this book and taken it to heart. It was the book of death for the whole order of life of the period. A book to be secretly somehow got rid of. Accordingly, the eighteen-fifties effectively did overwhelm both *Pierre* and its author.

Pierre, like almost all of Melville's stories, is unmistakably symbolic, the meaning goes far beyond the mere tale. It expresses the desperation of the noble individual surrounded by a world of comfortable compromises and snobberies. Either the individual or his nobility or both must be annihilated; it is the rule most sacred to such a world to crush noble unyielding protest and intolerable criticism like Pierre's. Melville is dealing with one of the greatest and one of the most insistent themes of nineteenth-century literature. Think of Balzac's *Lost Illusions*, of Tolstoi's two great novels, of Gorky's *Foma Gordyeef*, of Hardy's *Jude the Obscure*. *Pierre* belongs to that company, not first of the group but not last either.

[From "Amor, Threatening"]

Lewis Mumford*

Moby-Dick was done. In the fall of 1851 it appeared, first in England, then, a few weeks later, in America. Melville was exhausted, exhausted and overwrought. In the prodigious orchestration of Moby-Dick, Melville had drained his energies, and, participating in Ahab's own pursuit and defiance, he had reached a point of spiritual exasperation which, like Ahab's illness after Moby-Dick had amputated him, was increased by his lowered physical tone, by his weak eyes. Books like this are written out of health and energy, but they do not leave health and energy behind. On the contrary, the aftermath of such an effort is irritation, debility, impotence.

Melville was worked up, in the writing of Moby-Dick, to the highest pitch of effort; and he was harried, no doubt, by his ever-present necessity to keep his public and add to his income. The spiritual momentum remained, but the force behind it dwindled away. With no time for recuperation, he plunged into his new work: an unwise decision. Melville was not without his weaknesses, and they rose to the surface in his new book, Pierre, or The Ambiguities. Moby-Dick had disintegrated him: by some interior electrolysis, its sanative salt was broken up into baneful chemical elements. In this disintegration, Pierre rises at times as high as Moby-Dick, and sinks lower than any of Melville's other books. It contains passages that are the finest utterances of his spirit; it also has passages that would scarcely honour Laura Jean Libbey.

What caused this break-up? What value has Pierre in the sum of Melville's work? Neither of these questions admits of a quick and facile answer. One cannot dismiss the novel high-handedly as Melville's contemporaries did; and since the relation of the personal life of the artist to his art is still one of the major ambiguities in psychology, one cannot give a decisive or confident answer to the first question.

2

Melville's situation at the time of writing Pierre might have upset him even in a period of completer poise and more abundant health. He had written a great book: of that he could not possibly have had any doubt. Minor writers may think their rhinestones are diamonds, but rarely does a Shakespeare, a Swift, a Melville make the contrary mistake: if he speak lightly of his own work, or affect to disregard it, it is only for the reason that once he has reached the utmost depths of consciousness and realizes that vast and myriad interior which can never be fully

*Reprinted from Herman Melville (New York: Harcourt, Brace & Co., 1929) pp. 196–202, 206–222.

reported, he begins to realize that diamonds, too, are only another kind of rhinestone: they are mined too cheaply.

Melville knew that Moby-Dick was bound to be his chief title to fame. In 1849 he had written to Mr. Duyckinck: "Would that a man could do something and then say It is finished—not that one thing only, but all others—that he has reached his uttermost and can never exceed it." Melville had done this: he had mined and tunnelled through every part of his experience to produce this book. "There is a sure, though secret sign in some works," he wrote in 1850, "which proves the culmination of the powers . . . that produced them," and he recognized this secret sign in Moby-Dick: his letters to Hawthorne announce it. Mid all the tribulations and vexations of his life, there was, as in the heart of the whale Armada, a quiet place of calm and inward peace; within that spot, he had no reason to doubt or be dissatisfied with his work.

Still, what a writer articulates is always, though his words stay in a private diary, an effort at communication; the very nature of language makes this inevitable. Melville was necessarily not without his curiosity as to how the world would greet this magnificent product of his maturity, the first book in which he was in full command of his powers. And what was the world's answer?

The world's answer was no doubt what was to be expected; but it was no less discouraging for this reason. The Literary World indeed treated Moby-Dick with respect, and with as much understanding as a purely bookish man, like Mr. Duyckinck, could be expected to show: though it wasted most of the first review telling about the parallel fate of the Ann Alexander, it made up for this adventitious journalism by a second article which acknowledged Moby-Dick's manifold powers and excellences. "An intellectual chowder of romance, philosophy, natural history, fine writing, good feeling, bad sayings . . . over which, in spite of all uncertainties, and in spite of the author himself, predominates his keen perceptive faculties, exhibited in vivid narration." In the light of other contemporary reviews, this was fairly handsome. The Dublin University Magazine, with steady opacity, said Moby-Dick was quite as eccentric and monstrously extravagant in many of its incidents as even Mardi, but was a valuable book because it contained an unparalleled mass of information about the whale. As for the Athenaeum, it righteously reminded Mr. Melville that he "has to thank himself only if his horrors and his heroics are flung aside by the general reader as so much trash"—criticism which reached a pinnacle in the New Monthly Magazine, which described the style of Moby-Dick as "maniacal—mad as a March hare—mowing, gibbering, screaming, like an incurable Bedlamite, reckless of keeper or strait-waistcoat." [July 1853. Ed. Note.]

One need not go into all the forms under which the contemporary critic disclosed his insensitiveness to great prose and his servile compliance with the idola of the market; but one must note a singular fact:

from Fitz-James O'Brien's first criticism of Melville's work as a whole in 1853 down to Mr. Vernon Parrington's commentary in 1927, Moby-Dick, the keystone of Melville's work, has frequently been left out of account. The book that triumphantly smothers all the contradictory opinions about Melville—that he was a romantic, that he could only portray external scenes, that he was a pure introvert, that he was an adventurous ne'er-do-well, never happy or at home in a settled community, that he was irresponsive to the life around him, that he was a sheer realist who could only record what he had seen—the book that makes these generalizations silly suffered something worse than antagonistic criticism: it met with complete neglect. It is only since 1914 in America that this neglect has been even partly atoned for.

Such obtuseness, such flat stupidity, must have had a dismaying effect upon Melville. The writer begins to doubt the possibility of literature in a world that so flagrantly misunderstands or ignores its higher manifestations. Faced with such contemporaries, the artist may retire within himself, as Bach or Ryder or Cézanne did; but it will only be a miracle that will keep him from taking into his retirement a deep contempt for the people around him. That contempt is worse than isolation; it brings isolation without hope. "I write to please myself," exclaimed Melville in one passage in Pierre. In that mood of wilful defiance, a man may revolt from the good sense of his contemporaries as well as from their deficiencies. There was nothing in the reception of Moby-Dick that would have lessened Melville's scorn, or helped him to fortify himself against his own weaknesses. Quite the contrary. Like Pierre himself he was to learn "and very bitterly learn, that though the world worship mediocrity and commonplace, yet hath it fire and sword for contemporary grandeur."

Moby-Dick was too much for them, was it? Well: it was a mere pencilling of the ultimate blackness that was his to paint: if one were going to tell the truth at all, one could go much further and be much plainer. "Henceforth," proclaimed Pierre, "I will know nothing but Truth; Glad Truth or Sad Truth; I will know what *is*, and do what my deepest angel dictates." And again: "I am more frank with Pierre than the best men are with themselves. I am all unguarded and magnanimous with Pierre: therefore you see his weakness, and therefore only. In reserves, men build imposing characters; not in revelations. He who shall be wholly honest, though nobler than Ethan Allen that man shall stand in danger of the meanest mortal's scorn."

It was in some such mood of defeat, foreboding, defiant candour, that Pierre was conceived and written. Meanwhile, in November, 1851, the Hawthorne family had moved away from the Berkshires and Melville settled to his work, in the spring of 1852, on the north porch that faced Mt. Monadnock [actually, in the fall of 1851, indoors, facing Mount Greylock. Ed. Note.], with an intense feeling of human isolation which brought the mountain closer to him, as his only friend. The one possibility of a friendly, rapturous union of spirits was behind him: no longer could he write to Hawthorne, as he had done just a few months before: "Whence came you, Hawthorne? By what right do you drink from my flagon of life? And when I put it to my lips—lo, they are yours, and not mine. I feel that the Godhead is broken up like the bread at the Supper, and that we are the pieces. Hence this infinite fraternity of feeling." No: already that was over: dead. If the spirit burned now, it burned as ice does to the human touch. It was not altogether in irony, or in wild whimsy, that Melville dedicated his next book, Pierre, to his one solitary and steadfast companion, Mt. Monadnock. [Actually, Mount Greylock. Ed. Note.]

3

There is a sense in which Pierre is an abortive complement to Moby-Dick. Moby-Dick, great fable that it is, contains a good part of human life under one figure or another; but it does not contain everything. I would claim much for it; I would claim much for Melville's work as a whole; but there is still a great segment that remained unexplored till Melville wrote Pierre, and that, to the end, he never satisfactorily penetrated or freely brooded upon.

All Melville's books about the sea have the one anomaly and defect of the sea from the central, human point of view: one-half of the race, woman, is left out of it. Melville's world, all too literally, is a man-of-war's world. Woman neither charms nor nurtures nor threatens: she neither robs man of his strength nor rouses him to heroic frenzy: she is not Circe: she is not Rosalind or Francesca or even the Wife of Bath—she simply does not exist. When the Pequod spreads sail, woman is left behind: she is the phantom of home for Ahab and Starbuck. The whales dally in Moby-Dick and beget offspring; but all the trouble, beauty, madness, delight of human love, all that vast range of experience from the mere touch of the flesh to the most enduring spiritual loyalty, all that is absent. One looks for some understanding of woman's lot and woman's life in Moby-Dick; and one looks in vain. One looks for it again in Pierre, and one is disappointed, although its ambiguities are concerned with nothing else. With experience of woman in every relationship, daughter, girl, sister, wife, mother, matron, he described her in only one aspect—that of the remote and idealized mistress of romantic courtship. Mother, sister, sweetheart, all appeared to Melville's hero in this brief and peculiar aspect.

There was, one is driven to believe, something in Herman Melville's life that caused him to dissociate woman from his account of man's deepest experience. Mr. Waldo Frank has suggested, in general social terms, that the quest of power, which has preoccupied Western man since the Renaissance, has incapacitated him as a lover and kept him from understanding woman and all her essential concerns. If that is true, Melville pushed his aberration to a logical extremity; and he, who captured to the full the poetry of the sea, became as bashful as a boy when he beheld Venus, born of its foam, rising from the waters he knew so well, the most unexpected of monsters, and the only denizen of the sea he dared neither snare nor harpoon nor otherwise dispose of, except by flight. . . .

5

This story of Pierre, hard to accept in bald summary, is no less difficult to accept in detail. The plot is forced: the situations are undeveloped: the dominant colours are as crude as the lithograph advertisements of a melodrama, although there are subordinate parts which are as delicately graded as a landscape by Corot. There is no passage between the various planes of action and mood, as there is in Moby-Dick: Melville slips from prose into poetry, from realism into fantasy, from the mood of high tragedy into that of the penny dreadful.

For the moment, Melville had lost the power to fuse these discordant elements, to reject what could not be fully absorbed: he was at the mercy of his material. All that lives with a vital unity in Moby-Dick has become a corpse in Pierre: there is life in the dead members, but it does not pertain to the body as a whole. The fragments of Pierre are sometimes marvellous, as the broken leg or arm of a great piece of sculpture may be: but the whole is lost. From the moment the story opens to the fatal lines that bring it to a close, one is in an atmosphere of unreality. I do not mean that the facts are untrue to life; I mean that the work as a whole is untrue to the imagination. One accepts Ahab as a demi-god: one cannot accept Pierre as a human being, although Pierres are plentiful, while one might dredge the five seas without bringing up the carcass of another Ahab.

The style itself is witness to this psychal disruption, quite as much as the fable. Pierre is quarried out of the same quarry as Moby-Dick; but whereas there the texture is even and firm, here it is full of flaws and intrusive granulations. Moby-Dick, to use another figure, slides down a long runway before it plunges into its poetic passages: by the time one reaches Ahab's great apostrophes, one is all prepared for the immersion; one's imagination has reached the same pitch of intensity and concentration, and nothing but the most rhythmic patterns will satisfy the mood itself. The common prose in Moby-Dick is but an interval for breathing: it sustains and carries forward the movement of the more expressive passages; and as for the words themselves, they are the exact equivalent for the mood and purpose: distended though the envelope may be, they never burst outside it.

In language, Pierre is just the opposite of this: from the first pages, it is perfervid and poetical in a mawkish way. With the disclosure of the two lovers, Pierre and Lucy, in the opening chapter, the style becomes a perfumed silk, taken from an Elizabethan chamber romance: it sounds exactly like Melville's first effusion in the Lansingburgh Advertiser: " 'Truly,' thought the youth, with a still gaze of inexpressible fondness, 'truly the skies do ope: and this invoking angel looks down. I would return these manifold good-mornings, Lucy, did not that presume thou hadst lived through the night; and by heaven, thou belongst to the regions of an infinite day!' " This is a fair sample of what happens in Pierre whenever Melville approaches romantic passion; his reflections were tied with the same ribbons and furbelows, as in his description of love as "a volume bound in rose-leaves, clasped with violets, and by the beaks of humming-birds printed with peach juice on the leaves of lilies." In style, Melville had suddenly lost both taste and discretion. He opened on a note that could not be carried through. Lovers may indeed once have used such silly rhetoric, but it would take a more careful hand than Melville's to persuade us that the rest of the world adopted these affectations: when scene after scene is conducted in the same tone, the style becomes tedious, intolerable, ridiculous. It would be bad if the characters were in the Renaissance costume of Daphnis and Chloe: it is even worse in a novel that contains realistic caricatures of the slums of New York and satiric commentaries upon the bizarre habits of the transcendentalists. Occasionally, by some happy concentration of emotion, Melville either drops these flabby phrases or permits the reader to forget them, and there are passages which, when read as poetry, are almost as fine as Whitman's verses. But these intervals of good writing do not overcome the main impression; and the main impression is of hectic and overwrought language. With the powerful control he had over Moby-Dick, Melville could never have written in the style that characterizes a large part of Pierre. In Pierre he was no longer the cool rider of words, but the flayed and foaming horse, running away.

There is still another unfortunate lapse in Pierre; and that is the disproportion between stimulus and effect. When Pierre is first beheld by Isabel, then completely a stranger to him, she shrieks and faints away. Her own action was not improbable; but there is no reason why Pierre, healthy, robust, ignorant, should be so profoundly disturbed by this exhibition. The same is true of Pierre's heroic resolution to shield Isabel under the form of wedlock: it is a wild and dangerous leap out of a much less pressing difficulty. When Pierre finally comes to town, the disproportion is so broad it is grotesque, almost comical: his cousin's turning upon him and cutting him, before a group of strangers, with a frigid stare and a command to take that fellow away, does not belong to anything but the pages of crude melodrama. The turning against Pierre is not the subtle, devious series of rebukes and frigidities he would actually receive: such an affront as Melville pictures occurs only in raw dream.

In Moby-Dick, Melville carefully prepared, a hundred pages in advance, for the final effect: Mr. E. M. Forster has even suggested that the emphasis upon "delight" in Father Mapple's sermon is related to the encountering of a ship called the Delight just before the final catastrophe. In Pierre all this subtle preparation is lacking: Melville's impatience turned a genuine theme, the conflict of adolescent purity of purpose with the apologetic compromises and sordid motives of the world, into a crude melodrama. Melville was so immersed in the dilemma of his hero that he did not observe how often he failed to satisfy the demands of art, which require that the very incoherencies of life somehow hang together and be acceptable to the mind.

Finally, Pierre's emotional reaction to Isabel is entirely out of proportion to the fact that he has found a sister whose existence he had never before suspected. For a young man, filially tied to his mother, and by active courtship to Lucy, the entrance of another young woman should not have had such a volcanic effect, since, under the most ancient of social taboos, the relationship between them precludes further intimacy. Kindness and fellow feeling might easily arise there: but what Melville pictures is sudden and violent passion. "Fate," he observes, "had separated the brother and sister, till to each they seemed so not at all. Sisters shrink not from their brother's kisses. And Pierre felt that never, never would he be able to embrace Isabel with the mere brotherly embrace; while the thought of any other caress, which took hold of any domesticness, was entirely vacant from his uncontaminated soul, for it had never consciously intruded there. Therefore, forever unsistered for him by the stroke of Fate, and apparently for ever, and twice removed from the remotest possibility of that love which had drawn him to his Lucy; yet still the object of the ardentest and deepest emotions of his soul; therefore, to him, Isabel soared out of the realm of mortalness and for him became transfigured in the highest heaven of uncorrupted love."

The ambiguity that Melville finally brought his hero to confront in Pierre is that this highest heaven is not necessarily a heaven at all: such a transcendental displacement of earthly emotions and experiences is not the way of "willing, waking love": it is the mood of dream, and by continuous dissociation, it may eventually become the mood of madness. The highest heaven of love does not come with such romantic fixation upon an unapproachable deity: it comes rather with diffusion, when all men are brothers, when all women are sisters, when all children are just as dear as one's own issue. The fixation on a remote figure or symbol is in fact just the opposite of this generous suffusion of love, and of all love's corruptions it is possibly the most dangerous. In the thirteenth century, the Queen of Heaven had such a place, and her almost exclusive worship is perhaps as much a sign of the breakup of the mediaeval synthesis as any more obvious emblem of disintegration.

Man's roots are in the earth; and the effort to concentrate upon an ideal experience, that seeks no nourishment through these roots, may be quite as disastrous to spiritual growth as the failure to push upwards and to rise above the physical bed in which these roots are laid. In Pierre, Melville explored and followed such a fixation to its conclusion: disintegration and suicide. Had this been Melville's purpose in writing the book, Pierre might, in a decisive figure, have ended an epoch—the epoch of the romantic hero; for he had probed that hero's nobility and virtue and disclosed their deeper ambiguities, their conflicts, their irreconcilabilities. Pierre might have been a sort of anti-Werther. Unfortunately, this is just what it is not; for Melville identified himself with Pierre and defended his immaturity. How this came about we will inquire later; for we have not yet done justice to Pierre as a work of art.

6

What did Melville consciously set himself to do when he wrote Pierre? He sought, I think, to arrive at the same sort of psychological truth that he had achieved, in metaphysics, in Moby-Dick. His subject was, not the universe, but the ego; and again, not the obvious ego of the superficial novelist, but those implicated and related layers of self which reach from the outer appearances of physique and carriage down to the recesses of the unconscious personality. "The novel will find the way to our interiors, one day," he wrote in Pierre, "and will not always be a novel of costume merely." [Unlocated. Ed. Note.] Melville, to use his own words, had dropped his angle into the well of his childhood, to find out what fish might be there: before Mardi, he had sought for fish in the outer world, where swim the golden perch and pickerel: but now he had learned to dredge his unconscious, and to draw out of it, not the white whale, but motives, desires, hopes for which there had been no exit in his actual life. Men had been afraid to face the cold white malignity of the universe; they were even more reluctant to face their own unkempt, bewrayed selves. Even Shakespeare, deep as he was, had had reserves: Melville would set an example.

Melville was not concerned to portray "real life," for the unconscious is not for most people part of this reality: in a later book he gave an explanation of his own literary method. He describes readers after his own heart who read a novel as they might sit down to a play, with much the same expectation and feeling. "They look that fancy shall evoke scenes different from those of the same old crowd round the Custom House counter, and the same old dishes on the boarding house table, with characters unlike those of the same old acquaintances they meet in the same old way every day in the same old street. And as, in real life, the proprieties will not allow people to set out themselves with that unreserve permitted to the stage, so in books of fiction, they look not only for more entertainment, but, at bottom, for more reality, than real life itself can show. Thus, though they want novelty, they want nature, too; but nature unfettered, exhilarated, in effect transformed. In this way of thinking, the people in a fiction, like the people in a play, must dress as nobody exactly dresses, talk as nobody exactly talks, act as nobody exactly acts. It is with fiction as with religion: it should present another world, and yet one to which we feel the tie." For this conception of literary method, there is much to be said, and had Pierre carried it out with plausibility and consistency it might have made an even more important contribution to the art of the novel than George Meredith and Henry James were to make. If Melville met failure here, it was not because he had chosen a poor method, but because he lacked adeptness in using it.

As concerns his psychological purpose, however, Pierre for all its weaknesses will stand comparison with the pioneer works of its period. Pierre is one of the first novels in which the self is treated as anything but a unit, whose parts consist of the same material, with the grain, as it were, running the same way. Pierre's double relation towards his father's image and towards his mother's actual presence, his mixed attitudes towards Lucy and Isabel, the conflict between his latent interests and his actions and rationalizations, all these things are presented with remarkable penetration: if there is slag at the entrance of this mine, there is a vein of exceptionally rich ore running through it. Pierre's identification of his mother's love with a supreme form of egotism, Pierre being the mirror in which she beholds her own proud grimace, is no less penetrating than Melville's account of the relation between Pierre and his cousin, which runs from romantic love into apathy and enmity. While the action of Pierre is full of harsh and even absurd contrasts, the psychological mood is portrayed with infinite retirement and with relentless surgical skill: Melville does not hold the pulse of his characters: he X-rays their very organs.

The supreme quality of Pierre is its candour. Like Pierre, the more Melville wrote, "and the deeper and deeper that he dived, [he] saw that everlasting elusiveness of Truth: the universal insincerity of even the greatest and purest written thoughts. Like knavish cards, the leaves of all great books were covertly packed." Melville did his best to avoid playing a foul hand: he dealt his cards as they slipped from the fingers of Fate, Chance, Necessity, Truth; and in this grave honesty of his the greatest of thinkers seemed little better than fictioneers. "Plato, Spinoza, and Goethe, and many more belong to this guild of self-impostors, with a preposterous rabble of muggletonian Scots and Yankees whose vile brogue still the more bestreaks the stripedness of their Greek or German Neoplatonic originals." Not exactly a kind criticism; but, in Melville's exacerbated state, he went even further: not merely did the "compensationists" or the "optimists" seem shallow: literature itself was a hollow business, too. The ultimate, the final truth was inexpressible, and even the mere hinting of it was inadequate: the intensest light of reason did not shed such blazonings upon the deeper truths in man as the profoundest gloom. Utter darkness is the wise man's light; silence his highest ut-

terance. Catlike, one sees in the dark distinctly objects that are erased by
blatant sunshine; indeed, one calls to one's aid senses and instincts that
are dormant when one can move and see. "Not to know Gloom and
Grief," said Melville, in the midst of this illumination, "is not to know
aught that an heroic man should learn."

But if the gold of the transcendentalists was pewter and brass,
Melville was equally honest about his own treasures. "By vast pains we
mine into the pyramid; by horrible gaspings we come to the central
room; with joy we espy the sarcophagus; but we lift the lid—and nobody
is there!—appallingly vacant, as vast as the soul of man." One threw
away literature and philosophy, yes, language itself, only to find oneself
without visible support. One eliminated not merely the debris and muck:
one got rid of the miner, and the very purpose of his occupation. "In
those hyperborean regions to which enthusiastic Truth and Earnestness
and Independence will invariably lead a mind fitted by nature for profound and fearless thoughts all objects are seen in a dubious uncertain
and refracting light. Viewed through the rarefied atmosphere, the most
immemorially admitted maxims of men begin to slide and fluctuate and
finally become wholly inverted. . . . But the example of many minds
forever lost, like undiscoverable Arctic explorers, amid those treacherous
regions, warns us entirely away from them and we learn that it is not for
man to follow the trail of truth too far, since by so doing he entirely loses
the directing compass of his mind, for, arrived at the Pole, to whose barrenness only it points, there, the needle indifferently respects all points of
the horizon alike."

Within the heap of fragments in Pierre that mark the thrust and
power of Melville's mind, there is one fragment, fallen at random in the
mass, that remains embedded in the memory. It is the message of the
pamphlet that comes by accident into Pierre's hand when he is making his
escape to New York: in his overwrought state, the words have a peculiar
significance for his own purposes; and they are remarkable enough, in
their enigmatic quality, to consider by themselves. The title of the pamphlet is Chronometricals and Horologicals: in it the fictitious lecturer pur-
ports to set forth his own heretical philosophy. The moral is embroidered
in a single trope: the notion that there are two kinds of time in the world,
that which is established at Greenwich and kept by chronometers, and
that which prevails in other longitudes, recorded by the local watches. It
is a parallel of the philosophic and practical aspects of life, or rather, of
ideal and working morality; and I know no better exposure of the identity, yet dualism, of thought and action, ideal and practice.

The philosophic or religious minds are always correcting their
watches by Greenwich time; and, by continuous observation of the
heavens, they are always trying to make Greenwich time itself more correct. They know that the compromises and conveniences of society are
useful: but they also know that these things have no ultimate reason for

existence, and that one's employment of them must always be modified by reference to a scale of values alongside which they are false or meaningless. Shallow people never make such a correction: they believe in "dress" or "family" or "prestige" or "success" as if these were the vestments of eternity. Melville's error, at least Pierre's error, was just the opposite of this: he did not see that watches and local time are necessary, too, that there is no truth so cruelly meaningless as to give a person Greenwich time without telling him his longitude and enabling him to make his correction: that way lies disaster, confusion, shipwreck. A belief in ideal standards and values with no *via media* is scarcely better than a superficial life with no standards or insights at all.

The passage from the universal perception to the common life is difficult to make: it is the point at which religions and philosophies perpetually flounder. Melville saw this paradox; and he was plagued and puzzled by it; he even attributes it to Plotinus Plinlimmon, the leader of the transcendentalist sect, who drinks wine he forbids to his disciples, and, following supernal ideas, seems to prize cigars and food far more; Plinlimmon, whose non-benevolent stare seems to tell Pierre that all that he does is done in vain; Plinlimmon, the very embodiment of these ambiguities. Melville tended, with Pierre, to regard horologicals as a dubious frailty instead of what it actually is—the way that Greenwich time is universalized and incorporated in local practice. Human ideals are, as Melville saw, like the points of the compass: one does not seek the north by going northward: one seeks to reach a humanly important part of the earth, like Pekin or Paris; and ideals are the means by which a life that more fully satisfies our human potentialities can be lived. To observe this paradox without falling into the rôle of Mr. Worldly Wiseman is the essence of an active morality. Melville confronted the paradox; but the point of it eluded him. He idealized ideals as he idealized sexual passion: he wished both to remain for him in that adolescent state in which they are pure, remote, untouchable—forgetting that life is impossible in that sterile and clarified medium. Though Melville had anatomized many human impulses and probed in many sore and hidden places, one part of the personality remained sacred to him in Pierre: the sanctum of adolescence. All the values in the book are distorted, its very purpose is deflected, by Melville's unconscious assumption that the romantic purity of adolescence, the purity that arises not through experience and fulfilment, that is, through continuous purification, but through an ignorance and stagnation within sealed vials—that this purity is central to all the other values. That chronometer was correct enough at nineteen: at thirty-three it was no longer accurate, for a single reason—it had stopped. That, we shall see, was the chief ambiguity of Melville's personal life.

Melville was not alone in parading these fundamental ambiguities. In the dissociation of society in America, the American writer was able to examine all the premises and established truths which a European ordinarily takes so much for granted that he is not aware of taking them at all; and he could separate the essence of our human institutions from their conventional overlayers. Emerson, in Uriel, gives pithy expression to the same insidious ideas one finds in Pierre: but in Melville's novel they are on every page. His mother's love for her son is self-love and her admiration for him is vanity. His father's rectitude leads to a cold marriage, where an unclerked love had shown him a little radiant and a little finer at the core. Pierre's purest love is a disguised incest; his nobility is a worldly crime— while a lack of generous impulses would have led to wealth and honour. Melville's whole life, indeed, had taught him these ambiguities: Jack Chase was the real captain of the ship, not Captain Claret: the surgeon who amputated a living man, Surgeon Cuticle, with his glass eye, his false teeth, his wig, was more dead than the flesh he carved into: the cannibals of the South Seas were civilized, and the civilization of the New York slums was lower than cannibal gluttony: the missionary of Christ inflicted servitude, and the chief goods introduced by the trader were diseases: finally, the one civilization which thoroughly disregards the precepts of Christian morality is that of the Western world, which professes it.

These paradoxes were disturbing enough; but the fundamental ones were even worse. "The uttermost ideal of moral perfection in man is wide of the mark. The demi-gods trample on trash, and Virtue and Vice are trash!" Vice might lead to virtue; virtue might beget vice: the prostitute may teach purity and the holy man blasphemy! Where is one left when Melville and Emerson are through? One is left amid a debris of institutions and habits. Nothing is safe; nothing is secure: one no longer looks for the outer label, or believes in it. If north be the direction of one's ideal, the virtuous captain may have to tack back and forth from east to west in order to reach that destination: for no chart or compass ever enabled a ship to steer blindly for its port without paying close attention to wind and weather.

Had Pierre, as an imaginative work, been a more sufficient demonstration of these ambiguities, the book would have had a high destiny. But although the ideas are clear enough, they remain a potentiality in Pierre, since the story itself lacks integrity of form. The book is a precious crystal smashed out of its natural geometrical shape. Only by a chemical analysis of its elements do we discover what its primal character might have been.

7

The failure of Pierre as a work of art gives us a certain licence to deal with it as biography, all the more because Melville identified himself with the hero, giving him the initials and the Christian name of his beloved grandfather, Peter Gransevoort, and attaching him to objects like the portrait of his father which correspond to things about whose existence there is no doubt. If, as a work of art, Pierre was whole, we should have no good reason to suspect Melville's wholeness. It is the failure of Pierre as literature that draws our attention to Melville's predicament as a man; for in this particular way, he had not erred before. The young Melville who wrote Typee is not in Pierre; instead, a much younger self is there, a self erotically immature, expressing itself in unconscious incest fantasies, and capable of extravagant rationalizations in its effort to sustain them. Pierre is not a demonstration because it is a betrayal—and the person it betrays is Melville. In Pierre, he was an Iago, driven by his own frustration to betray the Othello who had been such a valiant captain in all his previous battles.

The significant question for us is what event, or series of occurrences, caused a hiatus in Melville's emotional and sexual development; and this question cannot be lightly answered by pointing to the obvious symbols in Pierre—for a symbol describes a tendency, rather than an objective event. We know that Melville's earliest associations of sex had been with vice and sexual disease; and in a sensitive lad, this introduction to passion may place bit and bridle on his own development. We know, too, that sexual relations in the United States among respectable people in the fifties were in a starved and stunted state: Stanley Hall, a boy in this very decade, recalled that he had never witnessed the slightest passage of affection between his father and his mother. It may be that Elizabeth, patient as a wife, was timid and irresponsive as a lover: in short, there are a dozen possible circumstances occurring long after childhood, which may have contributed to Melville's regression: and the incest-attachment, so far from being the cause of this, may in Pierre only serve as its emotional equivalent. Wherever sex is mentioned in other passages in Melville's books, it is referred to in a mood of disillusion. In Clarel, for example, he says:

> May love's nice balance, finely slight,
> Take tremor from fulfilled delight?
> Can nature such a doom dispense
> As, after ardor's tender glow,
> To make the rapture more than pall
> With evil secrets in the sense,
> And guile whose bud is innocence—
> Sweet blossom of the flower of gall?

And in one of the few passages in Moby-Dick where sex is referred to, the Sicilian sailor implies that sexual joy is in swayings, touchings, cozenings, and that when one tastes it directly, satiety comes. That, I submit, is not the experience of a healthy and well-mated man, or of a mature erotic state: to long for the pre-nuptial condition, to wish for fixation in court-ship, is the mark of an immature, or at least an incomplete, attachment.

When one says that Melville longed for the pre-nuptial state one does not merely imply that he found his sexual relations difficult or unsatisfactory: this earlier condition meant something more: it meant irresponsibility, freedom to roam, carelessness about health and daily bread, the opportunity to do his work without foreboding and anxiety. Sex had brought disillusion not merely because the first ardour and glow had vanished suddenly with the first physical contact: it had increased all his burdens and threatened to curtail that inner development which he had come to prize above all things—even more than the robust outer experience that had produced Typee. Sex meant marriage; marriage meant a household and a tired wife and children and debts. No wonder he retreated: no wonder his fantasy attached him to a mother who could not surrender, to a half-sister who could not bear children! The ardent impulse remained; he sought only to make it innocuous to his own spiritual life.

In view of the terrific pressure upon Melville, one can sympathize with his retreat; but one sees that, so far from aiding his spiritual development, it halted a good part of it at a critical point: for he did not carry over into his thought and his work the experiences of a husband and a father and a happy lover. He does not speak about these experiences as a mature man: he speaks as an adolescent. At this point, his self did not grow and expand; rather, it became ingrown and withdrawn; and the symbol of incest is perhaps the symbol of this shrinkage, this defeat, and the ultimate blackness of mood that resulted from it. He associated his career with the deep well of adolescent purity, instead of with the running stream of maturity, turbid perhaps, but open to the sunlight, and swift. Doing so, he blocked his own development instead of releasing it: towards later experience he said No: No: and again No. For almost a decade after this, Melville's principal characters are tired, defeated, harassed, tormented, lonely men; and to the end of his days children, the last symbol of maturity, do not, directly or indirectly, enter his imaginative life.

So closely were Melville's sexual impulses and his intellectual career bound up that I am tempted to reverse the more obvious analysis of Pierre, and to see in its sexual symbols the unconscious revelation of his dilemmas as a writer. Lucy, then, may signify the naïve writings of his youth, which promised him happiness, and Isabel, the mysterious child of a foreign mother, lost in an obscure youth, may stand for that darker consciousness in himself that goads him to all his most heroic efforts, that goads him and baffles him, leaving him balked and sterile, incapable of going further in literature, and yet unable to retreat to the older and safer relations with Lucy—the Lucy of Typee and Omoo. We must recall that in writing Moby-Dick Melville had premonitions of his own final flowering and of his sudden falling into mould; and if this prospect haunted him, the relationship with Isabel would be a perfect symbol of it, since it showed him making an effort to go on with his literary career, living under the form of marriage with Isabel, but unable, through the very nature of their relationship, to enjoy the fruits of marriage. In spite of his confidence in Moby-Dick, a doubt might still lurk: suppose Isabel were an impostor! He had given up everything for her: he had abandoned the prospects of a happy literary career, such a career as his family, Elizabeth's family, all his friends and relatives, and the reviewers and society generally would approve of—abandoned it for a mad, chivalrous espousal of his inner life. He had defied the world for this dark mysterious girl; and what she was ready to give him in return the world regarded as an abominable sin. Very well: so much the worse for virtue, if virtue meant Mrs. Glendinning's pride or Lucy's lovely shallowness. Melville was not without hopes that success might join the unsanctified household, that Lucy and Isabel might live side by side; but when the reviewers told him, upon his publishing Mardi and Moby-Dick, that he had espoused a girl of the streets and seduced a virtuous maiden, he saw that there was no way out, except to shoot them and take the consequences.

Pierre itself, then, was a blow, aimed at his family with their cold pride, and at the critics, with their low standards, their failure to see where Melville's true vocation lay, and their hearty recommendation of "virtuous" courses that promised so little. Melville anticipated defeat: Lucy dies of shock, and Pierre and Isabel make away with themselves by poison; for he saw no way to go on with his deepest self, and still continue obedient to the conventions of society and the responsibilities of a married man. His failure to mature with his actual marriage contributed, I think, to his failure to go further with his spiritual union; but how much it contributed, and by what means the injury was done, we can still only speculate. There is no doubt about the final result. The mood of Pierre, the work of art, became the mood of Herman Melville, the man, for almost a decade. Before another year was over, he recovered his grip in writing, and his art became whole and sufficient once more: but his life suffered, and his vision as a whole suffered: Pierre disclosed a lesion that never entirely healed.

[The First Novel Based on Morbid Sex]

S. Foster Damon*

This bit of mad romanticism constitutes the visible plot; had that been all (as the early critics thought), the book could easily be forgotten. But that was not all: the real plot is invisible. The cause of all this intense behavior is a sexual complication involving living and dead, the real facts of which are unknown to all four agonists. This hidden motive is incest,

*Reprinted from "Pierre the Ambiguous," Hound & Horn (Cambridge), 2 (January–March 1929), 112–16.

and Melville's treatment of it is such that *Pierre* takes its place in literary history as the first novel based on morbid sex.

Incest, of course, was nothing new in literature, but never before had there been any attempt whatsoever to analyse it. The Elizabethans had accepted it as a legitimate dramatic complication. One may recall Shakspere's *Pericles*, Beaumont and Fletcher's *King and No King* (also a scene from their *Captain*), Middleton's *Women Beware Women*, Massinger's *Unnatural Combat* and *Bondsman*, Ford's *'Tis Pity She's a Whore*, and Arthur Wilson's *Switzer*, besides doubtful cases such as Lyly's *Galathea* and Tourneur's *Revenger's Tragedy*. The tone was always dramatic, whether tragic, comic, or romantic—but never psychological; and the best solution was to discover that the lovers were not really related at all. The Restoration dramatists had no qualms on any subject: they used incest frequently[1] for the sake of the thrill.

In the novels of the eighteenth century, incest was still treated as naturally repulsive to human instinct, though no one seems to have asked why. The Age of Reason could not get below the surface. Moll Flanders, discovering that she had married a half-brother, breaks up the marriage, though her silence would have left their happiness undisturbed—and heavens knows, Moll had no prudery about her, or such lack of experience as to forfeit happiness for a mere scruple! Tom Jones is equally horrified to discover that he has lain with his mother; but fortunately (as in so many of the plays) she turns out not to have been his mother at all. Fielding includes this episode simply as a final jolt to shake Tom free of his wild oats forever.

Then Walpole—as usual, the awkward pioneer—introduced the romantic attitude with his drama, the *Mysterious Mother*, based on a local tale (which later he found in the *Heptameron*, 30th day); it had also been dramatized previously as *The Fatal Discovery, or Love in Ruins* (anon., 1698) and as *Innocence Distressed, or the Royal Penitents*, by Robert Gould (1737). Marguerite of Navarre recorded the tale originally because of the ingenuity of the epitaph; Horace Walpole saw a chance for a neo-classical drama with unusually heavy atmosphere.

Then came the Radicals. Chateaubriand and Byron aroused the public by the personal idiosyncracies so freely expressed in their writings. Shelley, of course, had contributed his fling against public taste with his *Laon and Cythna* and his *Cenci*. But all this preoccupation never got at the heart of the subject. The problem seemed too simple: prejudice was mere prejudice, nothing more; incest should be as natural as ordinary marriage. Thus the Radicals passed over the whole mystery: incest had sunk to the ordinary symbol of an act blindly and unreasonably condemned by Church and State.[2]

That, of course, was the attitude of the "Satanic School"; in New England there was already that slight difference which eventually accounted for Melville's penetration. The first novel written by an American and published in America was Mrs. Norton's *Power of Sympathy; or, the Triumph of Nature; Founded in Truth* (Boston, 1789). What with a form from Richardson, a sensibility from Sterne, quotations from Milton, and a finale from *Werther*, one might expect little original in the book; yet it was so far "founded in truth" that it caused a scandal, whereby the interested parties (whose names are known) almost succeeded in destroying the entire edition. So rare is the first edition that the editor of the 1894 reprint could find but one copy only. The opening situation is not unlike that of *Pierre*: a fashionable young man falls in love at sight with a fine young woman who has, however, no social standing. Just before their marriage, they learn that she is his illegitimate half-sister. She soon goes mad and dies, whereupon he shoots himself. The authoress recognizes something unusual about their attachment, and insists that their love sprang from their unsuspected blood-relationship; here and here only is the originality of her novel.

Hawthorne, in the *Marble Faun*, chose incest for the secret sin. But he missed his chance; his own inherent decency prevented his examining his subject too closely. Miriam and her mysterious follower are merely Astarte and Manfred again. But Hawthorne made no plea either for personal or social justification; he never analysed it in any way; it was merely SIN—made specific only because incest was literary, unreal, and mystifying; and even so, it was only hinted at by references to the Palazzo Cenci, that "spot of ill-omen for young maidens," and to Guido's portrait of the unfortunate Beatrice. Hawthorne, in short, used incest for theological dramatics only.[3]

Melville, however, was interested in the thing for its own puzzle; and that one shift of emphasis makes all the difference. His book is no longer drama but psychology; the gap between him and his contemporary, Hawthorne, is the gap that separates Calvin and Freud. Melville had learned that the problems of the soul are not to be analysed horizontally in the Conscious, but vertically in the Subconscious. He had learned that dreams are worth fishing for. Thus, guessing at the subtle roots and far-entangled consequences of incest, he made it the secret motivation of the whole moral knot of *Pierre*. "Some nameless struggles of the soul," he wrote, "can not be painted, and some woes will not be told. Let the ambiguous procession of events reveal their own ambiguousness."

Pierre Glendinning is the victim of a profound psychosis of which today we are learning a little under the misnomer, "Oedipus complex."

Notes

1. For lists of titles, see Allardyce Nicoll: *Restoration Drama* (Cambridge, England, 1923), p. 24, and Walpole's *Castle of Otranto*, ed. Montague Summers (London, 1924), pp. xlvii–lvi.

2. Meanwhile Monk Lewis, with his usual lack of taste, added incest to the horrors of his *Monk*; Scott, on the other hand, used incest for comic relief in *Redgauntlet*. The hero, Darsie

Latimer, falls into a violent adoration of an unknown charmer, but conveniently falls out again, just before learning that she is his sister. *Manfred* might never have been written!

3. Two other cases, out of the vast limbo of American literature, may be mentioned. George Lippard's *succès de scandale*, that stew of Hugo, Sue, and Poe, called *The Quaker City; or, The Monks of Monk Hall* (Philadelphia, 1845), depicts in Book III Parson Pyne attempting the virtue of a daughter, who turns out to be no daughter; and the highly respectable Mrs. S. Anna Lewis, in her neo-Byronic *Child of the Sea* (New York, 1848), describes a love-affair that proves non-incestuous before the close of the poem.

Catnip and Amaranth

Lewis Mumford*

"Pierre" is the last important work of Herman Melville to be made available to the general reader. For the sake of all that is valid in "Pierre," one trusts that no new reader of Melville will approach this novel until he has read "Moby-Dick" and "White-Jacket" or "Typee." For "Pierre" is a volcanic fragment of Melville's personality, an uncontrolled eruption, splendid and spectacular at one moment, but obscure and sulphurous and ashen at another. It is without doubt his most ambiguous achievement— so good that it cannot be neglected, and so verbose, high-flown, hectic, weakly theatrical, that one is at loss to pick out a romantic work, from Byron onward, that can rival it in loud ineptitude.

The first person to see any literary merit in "Pierre" was, I think, Mr. Arthur Johnson. In 1921 [1919. Ed. Note.] he published an essay on Herman Melville as a stylist in which he made an ingenious comparison of the prose in parts of "Pierre" with the later manner of Henry James, and suggested, with some show of plausibility, that James might have read "Pierre" as a youth and been unconsciously influenced by it. Later, Professor Percy Boynton discovered a number of prose poems in "Pierre," and aranged them as free verse. "Pierre" is, indeed, a book of fragments, and the fragments are worth mining and extracting. In his very wise preface to the present edition, Mr. H. M. Tomlinson says: "I have quoted from it a displeasing example of English. But if you want to be sure that Melville must take his place with the masters, then turn in this book to the passages he calls Enceladus, and to the discourse by Plotinus Plinlimmon on Chronometricals." For the sake of such passages, and many minor ones on the way, and for the sake of the intention that broods over the whole book, "Pierre" deserves to be read.

What was that intention? Of what platonic idea is "Pierre" the blurred and distorted counterpart?

*Reprinted from *Saturday Review of Literature* (New York), 5 (29 June 1929), 1141. Occasioned by publication of the Dutton edition of *Pierre*.

"Pierre" is a complicated symbol of Herman Melville's dilemmas as a man and his explorations as an imaginative writer and a philosophic thinker. Much of the materials of "Pierre" are plainly autobiographical: the hero's patrician background, his relation to his father and mother, the effect of his father's image, his attachment to his cousin, his career as a writer: the novel, in fact, is full of identifiable landscapes and people, and, according to Dr. Henry Murray, Jr., whose researches into the ac- tualities of Melville's life have gone farther than either Mr. Weaver's or my own, there is even a certain amount of evidence which might link the dark, mysterious Isabel, half-sister to Pierre, with the real sister who dur- ing the early part of his literary career had so patiently made fair copies of his manuscripts.

Melville pictures Pierre's disenchantment with the conventional world of his youth, his revolt against his mother's worldliness, and his chivalrous protection of his half-sister under the form of marriage. With the insight and medical directness of Freud, Melville discloses the am- biguity of Pierre's sexual relations; there is courtship and flirtation in Pierre's relations with his mother, and in his espousal of Isabel he is driven by an unconscious physical passion—in both cases a disguised incest- relation. When Pierre becomes aware of the ultimate bearings of his "pure" and "noble" conduct, when he acknowledges to himself that a crippled or ugly half-sister would not have wrenched him so easily from his plighted love to Lucy, he is horrified; and Melville himself par- ticipated in that feeling. His mental health was shattered when he fin- ished "Pierre"; in the book the hero and all who are involved in his career either die of shock or are murdered. The story is plainly autobiographical even in its fantastic melodramatic conclusion. So much for its sources.

These facts, however, are not themselves free from ambiguities: if they are facts in one relation, they may in turn serve as symbols in another: for the incest, the sterility, the black despair of the fable point to the impasse Melville had reached as a writer and thinker. The chief im- portance of "Pierre" for us today lies not in the adolescent revolt of the hero, a revolt which discloses chiefly Melville's failure to achieve com- plete sexual maturity, but in the insight into certain ultimate truths that had come forth as by-products of his personal dilemma. If the autobio- graphical parts show Melville at his weakest, a poet in the fashion of Thomas Moore, a romantic like Byron, a hopeless adolescent like Wer- ther, there are other sections that reveal to us the great mind that con- ceived "Moby-Dick," and that now turned back into the ego with the same heedless audacity that it had attacked man's external relation to the universe.

The principal moral of "Pierre," perhaps, is the relativity of Vice and Virtue, and, what is even more vexing to one who wants plain signposts and hard-and-fast directions, their strangely interchangeable rôles. Melville had grown up in the hard Protestant conviction that Good and

Bad, Right and Wrong, Virtue and Vice had separately embodied existences: each had an intrinsic character, each was readily identifiable. Was not he himself a "good" man: did he not honorably cleave to his wife, strive to gain a livelihood for his family, fulfil all his duties as a son and a citizen? On the surface, yes: but when he peered below the surface, honestly, remorselessly, holding back nothing and unconcerned about his reputation, he was amazed at his discoveries. Was not all that was valid in his career a defiance of "virtue"? His experiences had come as a vagabond and a deserter; his happiest love affair had not been sanctioned by church or state; his deepest book was one that he had broiled in hellfire and baptized in the name of the Devil. Vice and virtue were indeed the supreme ambiguities. No honest man could pretend to be a virtuous one. What passed for goodness and righteousness was a convention, like eating with a knife and fork. The convention was useful to society, but in the recesses of his soul Melville realized that Vice and Virtue could not be parcelled out in this fictitious manner. Virtuous courses might lead to ruin, and the "virtuous" man might be driven to madness and suicide. The signposts were down: the identities of Virtue and Vice were dissolved: Virtue was the full and unimpeded flow of life, and Vice was the opposite, and at any moment, if one watched carefully, one quality might turn suddenly into the other.

But what, Melville seems to ask himself in "Pierre," what if thought itself is just as dubious in isolation as virtue: may not the loftiest courses be more baneful than men suppose? He began to suspect this, I think, while making his furthest exploration in "Moby-Dick": perhaps the highest, the least human and earthly truth, was mere destruction and nothingness. The white amaranth that grew in the upland pastures was the symbol of the intellectual life: so pure, so austerely beautiful, but so sterile: it ruined the pastures and gave no sustenance to any beast. In contrast, consider the catnip; it was a domesticated plant and it clung even to the ruins of old houses, testifying to life, family, habitations, institutions. "Every autumn the catnip died, but never an autumn made the amaranth to wane. The catnip and the amaranth—man's earthly household peace, and the ever-encroaching appetite for God."

The appetite for God might usurp the place that should be open to other appetites, and in becoming a philosopher or seer one might become something less than a man. Thought that displaced all other form of experience was sterile, as blackly ineffectual as those incestuous wishes that spoiled one's married love. Was not Melville's own mind, particularly his unconscious, his dark half-sister Isabel? That was the final ambiguity. He who quitted the earth, assaulted the sky, sought the ultimate truth, uncontaminated by the local and accidental and personal might, instead of disclosing a more precious realm, discover a wall of blackness. The last reach of thought was emptiness; the final word of literature, silence. Was this profundity—having nothing to say? Mathematically, it was the equivalent of asserting that infinity equals zero. If that be the ultimate destination of thought, wisdom might urge that one tarry at the half-way stations.

"Pierre" suggests, in more than one pregnant passage, the ultimate reaches of Melville's thinking. Mr. Tomlinson does not exaggerate when he says: "This book is bottomless. It is out of soundings. A reader is poised over an abyss of darkness most of the time, to the ultimate depth of which no sounding by man will ever be made." That is true of its core; and in a sense, Melville penetrated in "Pierre" farther than he himself was aware: the book perhaps means more to us, in the light of what modern science has taught us of physics and psychology, than it did to its own author: his hints and dim intuitions come to us now clarified by appropriate concepts. One may view with tolerance the patent, the almost laughable defects in "Pierre." The wreckage of a great mind has more valuable treasures than the tidy bulk of a small one. If in "Pierre" Melville often seems one of the last and weakest of the Romantics, he is also one of the first, and surely one of the most profound, of the moderns.

Modern Criticism, 1930–1983

[An Experiment in Fiction]

Robert S. Forsythe*

Melville's pictures of the scenery about Saddle Meadows, as has been said, owe something to his recollections of the Gansevoort mansion at Saratoga and much to his surroundings at Arrowhead. Other scenes in the book evidently are drawn from life, such as those laid in the police station on the night of Pierre's arrival in New York. It seems hardly possible that the careful and vivid description of the metamorphosed Church of the Apostles and its annex, wherein Pierre lived in the city, with Isabel and Delly, is wholly invented. So far, however, the original has eluded positive identification. There is a mere possibility that the French Protestant Church in Pine Street, L'Église du Saint Esprit, which the congregation sold in 1834, was the original of the "Apostles'."

The tenants of the Apostles' are very certainly to some degree drawn from living models. They personify the fads and fancies of cultists and reformers of the day; and as such, they are amusingly presented by the healthy meat-eating, wine-drinking, tobacco-loving Melville, whose picture of Heaven was completed by a bottle of champagne! Although the names of the vegetarian Shelley and of the food-reforming Dr. Graham are mentioned, in all probability, it was Amos Bronson Alcott and his associates at Fruitlands who furnished Melville with the greater part of the remarkable practices recorded of the Apostles. The dietetic eccentricities, as well as other unconventional doings of the Fruitland communists, are almost exactly paralleled by the customs of Pierre's neighbors.

The suggestion has been made that the chief of the Apostles, the philosopher Plotinus Plinlimmon, whose pamphlet fell into Pierre's hands on the way to New York and whose proximity later so powerfully affected the youth, was intended to portray Hawthorne. There is exactly as much likelihood in this as in the other singular notions that Hawthorne drew Melville as Ethan Brand (in a story written before the two had met!) or as Hollingsworth, the philanthropist (!), in *The Blithedale Romance*. Perhaps Plinlimmon is a satiric portrait; very surely his original is not Hawthorne.

*Reprinted from "Introduction," in *Pierre*, ed. Robert S. Forsythe (New York: Alfred A. Knopf, 1930), pp. xxv–xxvi, xxvii–xxviii, xxxiv–xxxviii.

Probably, however, Plinlimmon is based, at least to some degree, upon his creator's reading. Like Carlyle's philosopher, Professor Teufelsdröckh, Plinlimmon dwells in a high-situated lodging whence he may survey the activity about and below him. Like Teufelsdröckh, too, Plinlimmon is "so sly and still, so imperturbably saturnine; shows such indifference, malign coolness toward all that men strive after; and ever with some half-visible wrinkle of a bitter sardonic humor, if indeed it be not mere stolid callousness,—that you look upon him almost with a shudder, as on some incarnate Mephistopheles . . ." In fact, Pierre could not endure Plinlimmon's steady "non-benevolent" gaze upon him in his room, and so was fain to curtain his window. The manner in which Plinlimmon's cogitations were disseminated and preserved for the edification of posterity is no less precarious than the six famous paper bags of Teufelsdröckh inscribed with the zodiacal signs and stuffed with odds and ends of laundry-bills, philosophizings, autobiography, and what you will.

Nor should we forget, in this connection, the "philosophical professor" whom Longfellow introduces at Heidelberg in his *Hyperion*. A descendant of Teufelsdröckh, he is a remote cousin of Plinlimmon. Another of Longfellow's characters, his Kavanagh, in the romance of that name, like Plinlimmon, has a study in a church tower, whence alone and aloof, he views the scene below him, and where he is secure from molestation. . . .

It is true that there is much in *Pierre* that is factual in origin. A large part of this, is autobiographical or relating to Melville's family history. Yet it must be observed that these are almost always mere details used in heightening character or rendering settings more vivid: hardly ever do they enter into the plot. And they are employed with Melville's usual disregard for painstaking accuracy, being twisted and distorted to suit his purpose as a novelist. Representative of this is his endowing Pierre with Peter Gansevoort as a paternal grandfather, who replaces his own grandfather, Major Thomas Melville of the Boston Tea-Party. Perhaps it is Major Melville who serves as Mary Glendinning's father, although promoted to the rank of general.

The plot of *Pierre* in itself can hardly be considered of especial interest or importance. It is sensational and unconvincing. The action is, however, only a necessary structure erected upon the foundation of Melville's ideas of life. To the reader of to-day, it is these ideas and the problems which arise from them that constitute the most valuable part of the novel. It is not, then, as a mere story that *Pierre* should be regarded, but as the expression of its author's questionings as to life and manners and of his answers to his self-put interrogations. . . .

The modern reader is not shocked by Melville's showing that society is not governed by the Golden Rule. He has met this notion before in literature, and he has observed its truth in life. He is charitable toward the division of Pierre's affections between Lucy and Isabel. He will accept, perhaps with some reservations, the doings of the characters. Symbolism will not deter him. His great objection is to Melville's style, as it occurs in much of *Pierre*. And this objection is hard to meet.

Already Melville had ventured, in *Mardi* and in *Moby-Dick*, into what adverse contemporary criticism termed the "rhapsodical." But in those novels there is comparatively little of this, and each of them is patently not realistic nor meant to be. *Pierre* deals, however, ostensibly with the life of the day. But the language of the book is not of that period or of any other.

The style of *Pierre*, in general, is extraordinary. It is often rhythmical, even metrical. Much of the book seems written in something approaching blank verse. Singular figures of speech—sometimes too striking to be effective—are not infrequent. Certain of these are, in elaborateness and ingenuity, better fitted for a "metaphysical" lyric of the seventeenth century than for a novel of nineteenth century society. An abundance of allusions occurs—not many of them obscure. A tendency toward the stilted is noticeable. Coined words are numerous, many of them awkward or cacophonous adverbs or abstract nouns. Sentences of surprising length—although of perfect clarity—now and again stretch down a page.

But it is the dialogue which especially jars upon the twentieth century reader. There are two sharply differentiated types. The language of those characters who are in the lower social groups—hackmen, policemen, draymen, servants,—usually is realistic, as if recorded from life, and so with such a semi-comic personage as Charlie Millthorpe. The principal figures of the novel are, however, made to speak a dialect of their own, not Melvillese, but, rather, Pierreian, for in no other prose work does Melville sustain, as in *Pierre*, this highly mannered style.

Pierre, Mrs. Glendinning, Isabel, Lucy, and the other characters of their station in life, save, for some occult reason, Pierre's Aunt Dorothea, habitually use the second person singular in conversation. From this fact arises, in part, the unreality of the dialogue. Still less convincing are those speeches which, as many are, are over-figurative or bookish in construction and vocabulary.

Why Melville should have chosen for *Pierre*, what can only be called an unhappy type of prose is a problem, the solution of which is yet in the realm of the speculative. It seems not unlikely that the element of experiment enters here again into the matter. For a novel differing from its predecessors as did *Pierre*—an experiment in plot—an appropriately distinctive style might be essayed. Already in two pieces of what are predominantly inventions, Melville had laid aside to some degree the simple direct prose of his autobiographical romances in favor of a more complicated and individual mode of expression. In *Pierre*, he went far beyond anything in *Mardi* or *Moby-Dick*, carrying the experiment to its very extreme. Inasmuch as criticism had not been generally favorable to the style of these earlier novels, it is not inconceivable that some degree of defiance—"I write precisely as I please," he says in *Pierre*—enters into Melville's persistence in employing a type of prose condemned by timid conventionalists. It must not be forgotten either that *Pierre* is modelled upon a verse tragedy and that its essentials do not necessarily call for ordinary prose expression. That Melville knew this is not improbable, and it is not more improbable that he was influenced by the knowledge to utilize for his novel-tragedy a sort of prose which is often frankly metrical and is seldom for long very far from blank verse. Possibly indeed, like Poe in his *Eureka*, Melville essayed in *Pierre* (and with more success) a "prose poem."

The sources upon which Melville drew for the style of *Pierre*, for models to some degree he had, require brief consideration. From the publication of Fitzjames O'Brien's essay upon Melville, it has been repeated over and over that the novelist's later prose was modelled in style after that of Sir Thomas Browne. That Melville knew and esteemed Browne and, to some degree, was influenced by him, is indisputable; but Melville had other prose masters, and in *Pierre*, it is not the Norwich physician but writers of Melville's own day or of the more immediate past whom he chiefly followed.

First of these is Carlyle, whose *Sartor Resartus* and *French Revolution* are impressed upon many a page of *Pierre*. In common with Carlyle, Melville has grammatical eccentricities—the second personal singular pronoun and the German compounded phrasal adjective, for example;—unusual words, rare or coined, some of the former of which both use; multitudinous verbal compounds; frequent abstract terms; unconventionalities in sentence structure; a leaning toward much capitalization; and an inverterate use of the dash in punctuation.

Closely associated with Melville's stylistic imitation of Carlyle in *Pierre* is his borrowing, perhaps unconsciously, of ideas. The historian's praises of silence in *Sartor* and in *The French Revolution* are adapted by the novelist. The description of the mood wherein Pierre has his vision of the Titans has its original in *Sartor* (and, interestingly enough, a parallel in Longfellow's *Hyperion*, that reflection of an amiable spirit!)

The metrical tendencies of *Pierre*, of course, cannot be traced to the rough jagged prose of Carlyle. Perhaps, indeed, they are an overdevelopment of Browne's sonorous and marching periods. Yet a contemporary of Melville, one whose work he knew and admired, a prosewriter who himself was a disciple of Browne, possibly served to inspire the American to smooth and regularize his expression. This is De Quincey, many traces of whose *Suspiria de Profundis* are to be found in *Pierre*. It may, in fact, be De Quincey whose country nurture is compared to that of Pierre. But one must not forget that Longfellow wanders, in his *Hyperion*, into polyphonic prose.

Whether or not the cause with Melville was the same as with Pierre

and his book—hasty and imperfect correction of the proofs of an unre-
vised manuscript—is uncertain; but, in any case, it is true that the novel is
by no means without positive errors in style. Nor does one need to be a
mere "entomological critic" to notice them. Misused words, careless diction, grammatical slips, badly built sentences,—more than one example
of each of these are to be met in *Pierre*. To over-rapid composition and
under-careful revision are also due a part, no doubt, of the errors of fact
and the inconsistencies which are to be found in the novel. Most of these
are of no great importance but simply jar upon the close and critical
reader: there would be, therefore, little point in enumerating these imperfections here.

From what has been said, it is evident that as a mere novel, *Pierre*
cannot be called a masterpiece. It has grave defects of structure,
characterization, and style. These to some degree, however, are atoned
for by the character of the book—a revelation by Melville of one of the
important problems of life and of the way in which one solution failed. As
a serious and thoughtful work, as a literary experiment, as a novel by Herman Melville, *Pierre* demands attention. Through even the least promising pages, furthermore, are scattered passages showing Melville in his
strength; keen satire, biting irony, vivid realism, picturesque landscapes
and sonorous eloquence,—these and a dozen more types of characteristically Melvilleian achievement reward the reader of *Pierre*.

Melville's *Pierre*

E. L. Grant Watson*

I

In those Hyperborean regions, to which enthusiastic Truth and
Earnestness, and Independence, will invariably lead a mind fitted by
nature or profound and fearless thought, all objects are seen in a dubious,
uncertain, and refracting light. Viewed through that rarefied atmosphere
the most immemorially admitted maxims of men begin to slide and fluctuate, and finally become wholly inverted; the very heavens themselves
being not innocent of producing this confounding effect, since it is mostly
in the heavens themselves that these wonderful mirages are exhibited.

This paragraph might well have been placed as the first introductory
lines of *Pierre*; for those Hyperborean regions, to which Truth,
Earnestness, and Independence lead, are the lands which this uniquely
penetrating and profound book seeks to discover. And certain it is that in

*Reprinted from *New England Quarterly*, 3 (April 1930), 195–234.

this rarefied atmosphere the admitted maxims of men slide and fluctuate, and that the heavens themselves are not innocent of producing this
confounding effect.

In his earlier works, until the very last chapters of *Moby Dick*, the
symbolical, transcendental stuff of Melville's expression has been always
intermixed with a large proportion of realistic description and narrative,
but now, in *Pierre*, the book which is dedicated to the mountain
Greylock, and not to any mortal consciousness, the book of which he had
hinted in a letter to Hawthorne, as of a kraken more monstrous and of
profounder habitation than any leviathan; in *Pierre* (with the exception of
those inserted chapters of satirical commentary on American literature)
there is all symbolism, and no realism at all.

To many readers of past years this book has seemed gloomy and
obscure; but to those who had the key to the supersensual experience of
which Melville writes, who had within themselves the interior experience
necessary for its comprehension, it was then, as it still remains, a work of
surprising loveliness, of most accurate and delicate perception. Any man
who has looked under the surface-seeming of life will be aware of a vast
undiscovered region, on the very fringe of which his faint and intermittent consciousness exists, as does grass on the earth's surface, putting
down short roots, waxing for a while and fading, yet always renewing
itself so as to seem the same, though changing with the years. In this
region of mystery spring the founts of existence; here Death and Life are
merged.

Pierre is a record (for a certain period) of Melville's mystical experience. It is the story of the coming of the knowledge of good and evil,
of the fall from innocence and the paradisaical, unconscious spell of
childhood; it is placed in a deliberately artificial setting, borrowed from
the New England of 1850. It is more than the story of the fall, for with the
fall from innocence of this modern Adam, comes a soul-shaking increase
of consciousness, which could only come to one who has the legend of
Christianity as his spiritual inheritance.

As in *Moby Dick*, Melville created Ahab as the Man-god; "That
Godlike godless man": a consciousness, which in the face of the universe,
must seek for an absolute value, finding (or seeming to find) that value in
his own will; so now Melville creates Pierre as the God-man, one who, im-
aginatively conscious of the tragedy of life, would offer himself as a
sacrifice to right the wrongs which Life—the father-life from which he
himself has sprung—has, in moods of truculent unheedingness, created.
But there is much besides, and if the reader's intuition can penetrate
beneath the surface value of the symbols, he will find, recreated in the
substance of this story of the soul, the fine, ambiguous threads of the warp
and woof of good and evil.

Melville, in this work, more directly than in any other, attempts to
formulate what he has apprehended of the mystery of life; and what is

particularly interesting and remarkable is that he has placed all his apprehendings within the scope of those symbols offered by the *domestic* human circle, thus indicating that the spiritual advancement of man still exists and has its origins within the bonds of the family. Or in other words the world-images created from within outward are all sexual objects. The elements of the soul are divided into the mother and her son, the father and the son, the brother and sister, and the young man and his betrothed. These are not simple in their relationship; the brother and sister have different mothers; the boy calls his mother, sister; and later, with the coming of the consciousness of the tragedy of life, takes his sister to be his wife. The situation becomes thereby immensely complicated, and to the end it remains so, and, as a true picture of life, unresolved.

II

From the first page with its emotional appreciation of the trance-like quality of the dawn, we are led into a conventional realm, which to the most casual reader is far from actuality. This convention Melville has created, as will be recognized later, as the best setting for the transcendental values he is about to reveal. It would be absurd to imagine that the man who in earlier works could describe in unsentimental and vivid terms the life of actuality, should intend the artificial coloring of Saddlemeadows and its inmates to be taken at its face value. There is a viscous and somewhat cloying quality about the style, which like the substance of the subconscious world, with which it deals, is at first repellent. Like some alien particle, unable to fuse or to accommodate itself to this deliberate artifice, the mind, which can not at once shake off the values of normal existence, rebels against the exaggerated virtuousness of the Glendinning family.

There are Pierre Glendinning and his mother. Pierre is the hundred-per-cent American as seen in the most favorable picture of himself. He is of old family, his forebears distinguished in the war of liberation; he is the son of democracy, yet possessing aristocratic descent; he is the owner of broad lands, paid for, in the early history, in blood spilt in battle. He has all the virtues. He is pure, unselfish, vastly inexperienced, and delicate in his sensibilities. He shows the white, glittering side of the bright coin of Puritan America. Not only is he gentle and good, a considerate and dutiful son, loving his mother, and reverencing, even idealising the memory of his dead father, but he is not lacking in the manly virtues. He swims, he shoots, he hunts, is physically strong, and, as a manly man should, eats a good breakfast. In these first chapters he is absurd and unreal; only his love of truth saves him from complete artificiality; and yet Melville though he mocks him, loves him, as he mocks and loves his own Puritan, American soul; and, reading, one feels that the poor boy is a good boy at heart, and a very gentleman in the word's original sense.

His mother is all that has conditioned Pierre's up-bringing. It is she who has filled him with artificial values. She dominates him with pride and will. She is the idealised mother in all the sentimentality of that conception. Pierre and his mother are immensely, fantastically artificial. To hide her dominating and contracting sway, there is invented a device of assumed equality; they call each other brother and sister, and with a false sportiveness, she seeks to make impossible the awakening of Pierre to manhood. Mrs. Glendinning symbolises that part of the Puritan American inheritance which is compounded of pride, of respectable goodness, of power, and of possessive affection; and later, when the hour of his initiation and his trial has come, Pierre too plainly sees: "that not his mother had made his mother; but the Infinite Haughtiness had first fashioned her; and then the haughty world had then further moulded her; nor had a haughty ritual omitted to finish her."

Besides claiming the possession of Pierre as her son, she chooses for him a most docile bride, so that though married, they shall remain under her own sway. Lucy Tartan, fair-haired, blue-eyed, beautiful, refined, richly-endowed, and seemingly submissive, has from his childhood been the companion of Pierre; the parents on both sides have wished their union, and as the two children have grown older, it has seemed natural and inevitable that they should be engaged. As his mother symbolises those elements of his environment that have fashioned his life; so does Lucy Tartan symbolise those *conscious* elements of his soul that appear as yet all purity and goodness. And, for this, that she is, he loves her, or thinks he loves her. He is developed only on one side, on that white shining side which is called goodness and is what society would have us believe that we wish ourselves to be. He is waiting for the destruction of that conscious self, waiting for the lightning stroke which shall come from *beneath*, from the underground of the unconscious, waiting for the dark side, which is to be the compensation of his brightness, and for what is feared as evil and is rejected as unclean. Half of his soul, he vaguely feels, has, in the purity of his upbringing, been left unregarded. This yet undiscovered portion of himself he uncertainly apprehends, and it is not long before there are premonitions of its awakening.

There is a girl's face, dark-haired, dark-eyed, suffering, and beautiful, which by chance he sees but for a few moments; it strangely disquiets him and fills him with vague longings. This girl, though he then knows it not, is his half-sister; she is dark, and sad, and poor, an outcast from society, with none of the golden fortune which has been Pierre's. She and not Pierre knows of the tie of blood, and at a chance meeting, cries out in recognition, without declaring herself. Pierre, attracted by that cry of the heart, looks with a half-conscious recognition at her pale face. The face haunts him. Amid the branches of the great fir-tree, the only one which had been left standing on those smoothed meadows, in this tree of his life, the face appears with premonitions of a possible great sorrow. He longs for, yet shrinks from the unknown, believing still that he can, uninterrupted, continue the superficial and constrained life that his mother, in the haughtiness of her tradition, has planned.

Daily the strange face haunts him, claiming more and more of his thoughts, and in a short while, he learns to know this face as that of his illegitimate sister, Isabel. She comes as the first manifestation of the dark half of his soul. She and Lucy form the two opposite parts of the soul. And as Lucy is the bright, the pure, the conscious part of himself, that part approved by his mother, though far superior to his mother, so Isabel is the angel of the dark, and the hitherto unapprehended, which now for the first time arises into part-consciousness; she comes trailing behind her clouds both of glory and of ignominy, of mystery and of overwhelming, mastering attraction. She is no earthly or physical representation, but is a soul-image, an image, too, of an awakening universe. She is a symbol of the consciousness of the tragic aspect of life; she is his angel of experience as contrasted with Lucy, who is his angel of innocence. As a symbol of the Tragic Muse, blood-related to himself, born of the same life-spring, Pierre must accept from her the wider vision that in her complete purity she brings; he must descend into the depths of the underworld; she is the gate and the way; and at the first uncomprehending sight of her, his fate, though he knows it not, is already sealed.

> But Pierre's profound curiosity and interest in the matter did not so much appear to be embodied in the mournful person of the olive girl, as by some radiations from her, embodied in the vague conceits which agitated his own soul. *There* lurked the subtler secret: *that* Pierre had striven to tear away. From without, no wonderful effect is wrought within ourselves, unless some interior, responding wonder meets it. That the starry vault shall surcharge the heart with all rapturous marvellings, is only because we ourselves are greater miracles, and superber trophies than all the stars in universal space. Wonder interlocks with wonder, and then the confounding feeling comes. No cause have we to fancy that a horse, a dog, a fowl, ever stand transfixed beneath yon skyey majesty. But our soul's arches underfit into it, and so prevent the upper arch from falling on us with unsustainable inscrutableness. "Explain ye my deeper mysteries," said the shepherd Chaldean king, smiting his breast, lying on his back upon the plain; "and then I will bestow all my wonderings upon ye, ye stately stars!" So, in some sort with Pierre. Explain thou this strange integral feeling in me myself, he thought—turning upon the fancied face—and then will I renounce all other wonders, to gaze wonderingly at thee. But thou hast evoked in me profounder spells than the evoking one, thou face! For me thou hast uncovered one infinite, dumb, beseeching countenance of mystery, underlying all the surfaces of visible time and space.

Thus does Pierre apprehend the approaching phase of his initiation. The story is veiled in mystery as by the dark hair of this fatal girl, and in places is illuminated by a mystic loveliness from the scintillations which emanate from her being.

III

The suspicion of a connection between himself and the strange girl is confirmed by a letter. Isabel declares herself his sister; in her forlornness and desertedness asks his help and gives a *rendezvous* for the following night. Pierre never for a moment doubts the truth of her claim, though it shatters at one blow all his illusions about his father; the letter at once proclaims its truth, and confirms suspicions which have been latent in his mind, for he has already suspected that his father was not always like the picture that his mother has presented.

Still haunted by the face, and overwhelmed as he was by the interior revolution which the letter and its disclosure has wrought in his inner life, he now contemplates a portrait of his father which hangs in his own room. Pierre had been brought up to worship the memory of his father as a man without blemish, unclouded, snow-white, and serene—Pierre's fond personification of perfect human goodness:

> Before this shrine he has poured out the fullness of his young life's most reverential thoughts. Not to God had Pierre ever gone in his heart, unless by ascending the steps of that shrine, and so making it the vestibule of his abstractest religion.

His father is in the image of God, and as God he had known him as the original source. In his innocence, he had looked on his father as *un-clouded, snow-white* and *serene*, as indeed many others have been brought up to look upon the mystical father of their being.

The particular portrait that he now examines is one his mother has always disliked, it being in her estimation unlike her husband. It was painted before his marriage by a cousin who took the occasion of stealing the portrait while the sitter was unaware. It is a *life-like* representation, having, like Life, an ambiguous smile, which in its care-free, morning expression is both frank and sly. Looking at the portrait, Pierre now remembers hints and stories told him by an old aunt about how and why the portrait was painted, and about a certain young *foreign* lady that his father was at that time supposed to be paying court to; as he looks at the portrait it seems to say to him:

> Look, I am thy father as he more truly was . . . In mature life we abdicate ourselves and take unto ourselves another self, in youth we *are*, but in age we *seem* . . . Look, do I not smile with an unchangeable smile? And thus have I unchangingly smiled for many years gone by . . . Consider, for a smile is the chosen vehicle of all ambiguities, Pierre. When we would deceive we smile; when we are hatching any nice little artifice, only just a little gratifying to our own sweet appetites, then watch us and out comes that odd little smile.

Thus the portrait seems to speak, and Pierre knows that his father was different from the pure being his mother has painted. His father takes on that changed and ambiguous aspect that Life has suddenly assumed.

And as his father changes, so his mother changes under the stress of his ordeal. He imagines himself going to her and saying: "Dearest Mother, God hath given me a sister, and unto thee a daughter, and covered her with the world's extremest infamy, so that I and thou, *thou*, my mother, mightest gloriously acknowledge her, and . . ." But he knows that his mother, who represents the complex of the social instinct, which till now has dominated him, could never suffer that repulse to her pride. By this test she is become known to him for what she is, for "a creature formed chiefly for the gilded prosperities of life, . . . bred and expanded under the influence of hereditary forms and world-usages."

Melville's analysis is deep and unsparing. As the disguises have been torn from the father and the mother, so is Pierre in all his earnestness shown captured by the face of his mysterious sister. Because she is for him growth and enlargement, though in herself sad and clothed in ignominy, she is *beautiful*; and because she is beautiful, he will give up father and mother and even his own bright, simple innocence, which had found its image in Lucy. The dark is more strange and wonderful than the light; the tragic aspect of life kindles pity and indignation, and being in its origin deeply intermixed with, and sprung from sensuality, it becomes the dominant counterpart of his soul. Yet in his awakening consciousness he is all purity; he prays:

> May heaven new-string my soul, and confirm me in the Christ-like feeling I first felt. May I, in all my least shapeful thoughts, still square myself by the inflexible rule of holy right. Let no unmanly, mean temptation cross my path this day; let no base stone lie in it. This day I will forsake the censuses of men, and seek the suffrages of the god-like population of the trees, which now seem to me a nobler race than man. Guide me, gird me, guard me, this day, ye sovereign powers! Bind me in bonds I cannot break; remove all sinister allurings from me; eternally this day deface in me the detested and distorted images of all the convenient lies and duty-subterfuges of the diving and ducking moralities of this earth. Fill me with consuming fire for them; to my life's muzzle, cram me with your own intent. Let no world-syren come to sing to me this day, and wheedle from me my undauntedness. I cast my eternal die this day, ye powers. On my strong faith in ye Invisibles, I stake three whole felicities, and three whole lives this day. If ye forsake me now—farewell to Faith, farewell to Truth, farewell to God—

IV

Isabel, as is fitting with her symbolic value, is living in a remote farm near a lake of "blankness and of dumbness, unstirred by breeze or breath." This lake is bounded by vast forests, out whose "infinite inhumanities came a moaning, muttering, roaring, intermittent, changeful sound . . ." Indeed all her surroundings and circumstance are clearly indicative of the approach to a supersensuous consciousness. When Pierre knocks at the door, she meets him in the typical attitude of a soul-symbol, illuminated by the rays of her own lamp, which she holds above her head. In innocence he would embrace her as a sister, but at the touch feels that there is more than a brother-sister relation between them.

This passage and the four chapters that follow are, in their vivid imaginative realism, in marked contrast to the deliberate artificiality of the earlier part of the book. Isabel tells her story. It is mysterious and supernatural, yet the symbolism is carefully precise. She tells of the birth and the growth of that enlarged consciousness which comes to life's initiates. It is the story of the birth of the conscious soul. She has known no mother, and the lips that speak "have never touched a woman's breast." She tells him how she seems not of woman born but that how her first dim life-thoughts cluster round a ruinous old house in the midst of a wood, how she had for companions mute or mumbling archaic figures, how these spoke to each other in a language different from her own and how they fed upon bread and wine, but did not share with her. There was a cat, also incomprehensible to her, softly scratching for some hidden thing amongst the litter of abandoned fireplaces.

She hints that after quitting that mysterious house she crossed the ocean, but her memories are dim; always in her the solidest things melt into dreams, and dreams into realities. "Never have I recovered," she says, "from the effects of my strange early life." And in this wise also speaks to him the soul of the initiate.

> This it is that even now—this moment—surrounds thy visible form, my brother, with a mysterious mistiness; so that a second face, and a third face, and a fourth face peeps at me from within thy own. Now dim, and more dim, grows in me all the memory of how thou and I did come to meet. I go groping again amid all sorts of shapes, which part to me; so that I seem to advance through the shapes; and yet the shapes have eyes that look at me. I turn round, and they look at me; I step forward, and they look at me.—Let me be silent now; do not speak to me.

She tells how, afterward, she came to be lodged in a lunatic asylum, how she was surrounded by strangely demented people, composed-of-countenance, but wandering-of-mind; soul-composed and bodily-wandering and strangely-demented. Thus it is that the awakening consciousness of the soul, is closely and dangerously beset, in its lonely infancy, by the undifferentiated and demented-seeming forms of the collective unconscious. She tells of the death of these undifferentiated forces, of the consciousness of death, which came to her, and of the increasingly tragic consciousness which is her being. And while she speaks, telling of these mysterious beginnings, there are all the while soft steps overhead, which, intermittent and pointing the emphasis of the story, pause and continue.

It is here that another and more subtle piece of symbolism is introduced. There is a girl called Delly Ulver, who, like Isabel, is also an outcast from society, and is a kind of earthly double of her. Delly was the mother of an illegitimate child, which died soon after it was born. She has been disowned and cursed by both her parents, though she still remains in their house, as the result of Isabel's pleading. It is she who is intermittently walking to and fro upstairs in distress and loneliness, while Isabel tells her story. The significance of Delly is difficult to understand, but if one reads carefully all that is said about her, and is familiar with the way in which Melville hides in a name the key to his meaning, it becomes evident that she is the primitive, quite innocent, but sensual, and unconscious counterpart of Isabel; she is that essentially primitive, *female* and innocently-sensual and suffering element in sex.

Here, in this symbolism of Delly Ulver and her relation to Isabel, Melville shows his genius. He is as courageous an explorer into the secrets of the soul as any man who has ever written. His greatness as a psychologist is not to be surpassed by any other writer. There are deep, far-away things in him, and his greatness is revealed not only in what he writes but in what he leaves unwritten. He suggests more than can be written; and as this world of Becoming is a symbol of God's vaster transcendental Universe of Being, so Melville's books shadow-forth and are themselves symbols of that same transcendental universe. His works indicate remote distances beyond actual expression, and of these distances we become increasingly aware as we go deeper into *Pierre*.

Isabel, while that related double of herself paces up and down in the room overhead, continues with her story. She tells how at last she left the asylum of those undifferentiated human figures, and hired herself to work in the ordinary domestic houses of men. One day she buys a guitar from a passing pedlar; this she has re-strung, and feeling an intuitive sympathy and relatedness to the instrument, takes it to her room and murmurs and sings to it. After a while, the guitar, of its own self and without being touched, answers her with a sweet and sudden sound. She sings and murmurs to it in a different modulation, and once more it answers her with a different string.

> The guitar was human; the guitar taught me the secret of the guitar; the guitar learned me to play on the guitar. No music-master have I ever had but the guitar. I made a loving friend of it; a heart friend of it. It sings to me as I to it. Love is not all on one side with my guitar. All the wonders that are unimaginable and unspeakable, all these wonders are translated in the mysterious melodiousness of the guitar. It knows all my past history. Sometimes it plays to me the mystic visions of the confused large house I never name. Sometimes it brings to me the bird-twitterings in the air; and sometimes it strikes up in me rapturous pulsations of legendary delights eternally unexperienced and unknown to me.

She bids Pierre bring her the guitar, and again in answer to her murmurings it plays to them. Isabel bends over her instrument, her long, dark hair falls over it and veils it, "and still from out the veil came the swarming sweetness, and the utter unintelligibleness, but the infinite significances of the sounds of the guitar."

> Mystery! Mystery!
> Mystery of Isabel!
> Mystery! Mystery!
> Isabel and Mystery!

> Among the waltzings, and the droppings, and the swarmings of the sounds, Pierre now heard the tones above deftly stealing and winding among the myriad serpentinings of the other melody;—deftly stealing and winding as respected the instrumental sounds, but in themselves wonderfully and abandonedly free and bold—bounding and rebounding as from multitudinous reciprocal walls; while with every syllable the hair-shrouded form of Isabel swayed to and fro with a like abandonment, and suddenness, and wantonness:—then it seemed not like any song; seemed not issuing from any mouth; but it came forth from beneath the same veil concealing the guitar.

Thus at their first meeting Pierre is overwhelmed by the supernaturalness of his strange sister. At their next meeting on the following night, she tells her further history; how she had found by the light of her own lamp her own name written, hidden inside the instrument. It must have been written there before the guitar was made. Intuitively she believes it to be the name of her unknown and dead mother, believes that the guitar was once hers.

Of the second meeting of Pierre and Isabel it is difficult to give any contracted account—every word contributes to that sense of mystery and suggestions of which Melville is a master. Pierre and Isabel explore the mystic environment of their awakened spiritual recognition, and most tenderly does Melville portray the communion between these interpenetrating portions of the human soul. They voice the innermost intuitions of mortal understanding.

> I am called woman, and thou, man, Pierre; but there is neither man nor woman about it. Why should I not speak out to thee? There is no sex in our immaculateness. Pierre, the secret name in the guitar even now thrills me through and through. Pierre, think! Think! Oh, canst thou not comprehend? see it?—what I mean, Pierre? The secret name in the guitar thrills me, thrills me, whirls me, whirls me; so secret, wholly hidden, yet constantly carried about in it; unseen, unsuspected, always vibrating to the hidden heart-strings—broken heart-strings; oh, my mother, my mother, my mother!

She speaks the tragedy, which is her being, and again the guitar answers. She seems to swim in an electric fluid, and as she bends over the guitar, sparks and phosphorescent glimmerings are in her hair, and again the melody breaks forth, only in a still more subtle and wholly inexplicable way. Pierre is swayed and tossed on supernatural tides, and again hears the mysterious calling of that awakening self, which brings, together with the rapture of new consciousness, a knowledge of the tragedy and evil of life.

It is impossible and would be most certainly undesirable to interpret the symbolism of the guitar in any definite or exact *formulæ*. It is to be comprehended by the soul rather than by the mind, but one might suggest that the guitar is to Isabel a more beautifully and profoundly-conceived symbol of what her bird and her shell are to Yillah, who in *Mardi*, is the impersonation of the glamor of Life and Love. Or, to approach from a somewhat different angle, one might say, in the terminology of Lao Tze, that the guitar is the Teh, namely the immanent manifestation within the individual soul of the transcendental reality of Life.

V

The intermediate period between the two stages of initiation between the first and second meetings with Isabel is emphasised by Melville as of considerable importance. In this period the consciousness is able to adjust itself to its new experience. It is now vaguely revealed to Pierre that every detail of the visible world, some of which had seemed common and prosaic, was now steeped in a mystery wholly hopeless of solution. He is aware at this moment that he stands between his angel of innocence and his angel of experience, between Lucy and Isabel; he must choose one or the other. Yet both seem his, and into Lucy's eyes has stolen half of the mournfulness of Isabel.

On returning to his mother's mansion, there is already almost an open hostility between them; his mother's pride will not suffer his new-found self to live within her dominion. Pierre goes out to be alone in the depth of the forest, for suddenly the thought of the proximity of man has become distasteful to him: only the most durable of all things, the forests and the seas, seem tolerable to his mood. With the deepening of life has come a whelming melancholy. Evil, injustice, cruelty and the scorn of an unheeding world weigh on his spirit; his growing consciousness does not only raise him to the heights, but takes him downward to the depths. He comes in his wanderings on a great rock, wedge-shaped, like a lengthened egg, which at some obscure point on its under side is balanced on a hidden lateral ridge. It seems at any moment about to crash downward, but has remained through the ages unmoved, held by an invisible support. Round it is the aboriginal forest. This stone, the object of wonder to Pierre, is to other men only a huge stumblingblock in the way of running a prospective cross-road through that wild region. There is a space beneath it where a man may crouch as though to court destruction. Here, beneath this Terror Stone, Pierre lays himself full length, and thus invokes his fate:

> If the miseries of all the undisclosable things in me, shall ever unhorse
> me from my manhood's seat, if to vow myself all Virtue's and all Truth's,
> be but to make a trembling, distrustful slave of me; if Life is to prove a
> burden I cannot bear without ignominious cringings . . . then do thou,
> Mute Massiveness, fall on me.
>
> A down-darting bird, all song, swiftly lighted on the unmoved and
> eternally ummovable balancings of the Terror Stone, and cheerfully
> chirped to Pierre. The tree-boughs bent and waved to the rushes of a sud-
> den, balmy wind; and slowly Pierre crawled forth, and stood haughtily
> upon his feet, as he owed thanks to none, and went his moody way.

In this Terror Stone, surrounded by the primordial forest, he meets
the Wisdom which is woe; on this stone he finds graved the initials of
Solomon the Wise. It is the wisdom which knows that in his lonely
journey of the soul's commanding, he is destitute and deserted of that help
that fellow men can give. He knows not yet that the gods can desert him,
and has not fully apprehended that non-benevolent wisdom of Ecclesiastes; he is only at the beginning of his descent into Hades, and has
barely passed the portal over which is written: "All hope abandon ye who
enter here."

As he goes on through the woods, all thoughts leave him but those in-
vesting Isabel. "He saw or seemed to see that it was not so much Isabel
who had by her wild idiosyncrasies mystified the narration of her story, as
it was the essential and unavoidable mystery of her history itself, which
had invested Isabel with such wonderful enigmas to him." He knows that
she is of earlier birth than himself, and knows, too, the eternal quality of
her youthfulness.

> Out of the infantile, yet eternal mournfulness of the face of Isabel, there
> looked on Pierre that angelic childlikeness, which our Saviour hints is the
> one only investiture of translated souls; for of such—even of little
> children—is the other world.
>
> Now, unending as the wonderful rivers, which once bathed the feet of
> the primeval generations, and still remain to flow fast by the graves of all
> succeeding men, and by the beds of all now living; unending, ever-
> flowing, ran through the soul of Pierre, fresh and fresher, further and still
> further, thoughts of Isabel.

And the more this thoughtful river ran, the more mysteriousness it
floated to him. In Isabel the qualities of both Hautia and Yillah are no
longer separated, as in earlier years in *Mardi*, he had more conventionally
portrayed good and evil separated and opposed to one another. In Isabel
they are merged, Good in Evil, and Evil in Good. These values no longer
exist as antitheses, but are one in mystery. The dark still balances and
gives significance to the light, and is as beautiful as the light, and, in the
first impulse of recognition, more overwhelmingly attractive. Isabel
reveals the night to him. She is a *strange*, and seemingly supernatural
light, illuminating the whole sky; and as Halley's comet, arching the en-

tire vault of the tropical heavens flings its vast tail in a fan of luminous ether, through which the accustomed stars shine with strange aspects, so the face of Isabel, close to the troubled sea of Pierre's awakening soul, covers the heavens of his vision with a diffuse and undefinable mysteriousness. One thought burns clear:

> Fate had separated the brother and the sister, till to each other they somehow seemed so not at all. Sisters shrink not from their brothers' kisses. And Pierre felt that never, never would he be able to embrace Isabel with the mere brotherly embrace; while the thought of any other caress, which took hold of any domesticness, was entirely vacant from his uncontaminated soul, for it had never *consciously* intruded there.

Melville, in his elaborate thoroughness, devoted a good deal of time to the whys and wherefores and reasonings which bring Pierre to the final resolution of establishing Isabel, not as his sister, but as his wife. The directing motive is Pierre's profound recognition of Isabel as a soul-image; and it is always with the soul-image in human form that the lover wishes to unite. Although Pierre, at this first stage of his ordeal, has no thought of an incestuous relation, yet he would, to justify the deepest springs of his being, celebrate a spiritual marriage with Isabel. This is his desire, and his reasonings lead him to this end. With the awareness of things unsuspected, all values are changing, and though at first from habit he may adhere to the conventions of good and evil, yet these values, too, are no longer set and definite. It is not long before he says: "Look: a nothing is the substance, it casts one shadow one way, and another the other way; and these two shadows are cast from one nothing; these, so it seems to me, are Virtue and Vice."

Therefore, all reasonings apart, the fundamental cause of his proclaimed marriage with Isabel is his profound desire for such a marriage. On this point the whole story turns. To understand what follows, the reader must make himself as emancipated from conventional thought as is Melville himself. He must not believe that Good is preferable to Evil, or Sanity to Madness; but rather recognise that Evil and Madness may be necessary and indispensable to certain phases of development. He must know, not only with his mind but with his heart, that the "sick soul" is just as relevant to life as the "healthy-minded" soul, and that many sick souls are spiritually far in advance of happier, healthy-minded souls. He must know, moreover, that such souls as are depicted in *Pierre*, though they go (together with all their lesser associated personalities) down into madness and death, are necessary and valuable contributions to the life of Man. We can see that if Pierre had not married Isabel, but had kept his consciousness of tragedy and mystery as something separate (though loved and recognised) from his directing soul, then madness and misery would not have inevitably followed, but we can not say it would have been *better* thus. Melville has given us the privilege of seeing another kind of happening, one which is rich in a transcendent beauty.

Pierre, is a rare, and a lovely creation. It is no book for idle readers. To understand it is an ordeal; and appreciating its strange, spiritual beauty, we should be purged of valuations, should perceive that all that can be ultimately said of life is this: *Life does what Life does;* that moral valuations are optical illusions, and that the force of life is beyond moral judgments.

At this critical period, Pierre must break, if need be, with all ties and affections of the past; he will proclaim Isabel as his wife, and accept the ordeal which will prove for him the transvaluation of all values: he is thus impelled by the facts of his experience. It is suggested that because fictitiously he had tried to put his mother in the domestic relation of a sister, so now he would make his sister into a wife. This is interesting to consider in its symbolic value. He does not know fully, though he apprehends vaguely the tragedies which lie in his path. He is impelled by the innermost forces in himself; and as the guitar answers to the voice and presence of Isabel, so he hears the deep voice of her being calling him from "the immense distances of the air, and there seemed no veto of the earth that could forbid her heavenly claim." Hers is "the unmistakable, unsuppressable cry of the Godhead speaking through his soul." And while he answers this call, his conscious self would guard the memory of his father. Thereby it is suggested that he would keep justified his vision of life, while realising that the acts and nature of life should be kept secret.

To Lucy he first makes known his changed condition. His words are short, merely announcing that he is married. He speaks, knowing that he must blast her and at this moment his earlier consciousness of a happy and innocent world falls, as does Lucy, into a swoon; she seems almost utterly to be destroyed. The vision of innocence fades before the rivalry of experience, and he is impelled to risk the death of part of his own soul.

He goes directly to his mother's mansion; in the same short words he tells her he is married. Mrs. Glendinning's pride and haughtiness rise to the rebuke. "My dark soul," she says, "prophesied something dark. If already thou hast not found other lodgement, and other table than this house supplies, then seek it straight. Beneath my roof and at my table, he who was once Pierre Glendinning no more puts himself." For Mrs. Glendinning, Pierre's wife, whoever she be, whom he has taken without her (Mrs. Glendinning's) consent, is a dark, *unknown thing*, as indeed the Spirit of Tragedy, awake within an individual soul is dark and unknown to herd-consciousness.

VI

Disinherited by his mother, he returns to Isabel, assuring her that all loss for her sake is gain, for "she is of that fine, unshared stuff of which God makes his seraphim." He goes together with her and Delly to the village inn. Delly he has also taken under his protection, for he perceives that she is indubitably associated with Isabel, and must from now on be her handmaiden. To the inn he brought all his private papers together with the betraying portrait of his father. These he now burns, that he may have no unnecessary weight from the past to burden his soul. This accomplished, he prepares for the journey to the city. Very early the next morning they enter the stage coach, and travel throughout the day. During this fateful journey they are all silent. Delly and Isabel sit with faces averted, and Pierre, plunged in gloomy contemplation of the bivalent nature of life, broods over the evils he has been forced to visit on Lucy and his mother in following what so clearly seems his best and most commanding impulse. In this mood of despondency his fingers close on a pamphlet, or rather on a fragment of a pamphlet, left by some former traveller. He looks at it at first unseeingly, but after a while begins to read with increasing interest.

This pamphlet is a lecture by one Plotinus Plinlimmon. It is the first of three hundred and thirty-three lectures and is entitled: *Chronometricals and Horologicals*. It is not possible to do justice to this pamphlet without giving it in full. It can not be curtailed, it exists as a whole, and to attempt to shorten its compacted significances would be to do an injustice. I can but indicate its argument, and leave its fuller understanding to those who shall read for themselves, assuring them that there is much to repay a fourth and a fifth perusal.

The writer contrasts those values which condition and rule in the universe of transcendental Being with those others, which in the practical way of life, are found convenient in the every-day world of Becoming; and he suggests that since we are willy nilly in the world of Becoming, we can not in practice live by the transcendental values of that greater universe which our souls apprehend, without doing evil to both ourselves and others.

Pierre reads and understands more than he is aware of at the time; indeed he carries the understanding of that pamphlet in his unconscious to determine his later acts. It is this that sets him a little bit aslant from his line of transcendental idealism, makes him a rebel against the destiny which is the guerdon of an enlarged and religious consciousness, inculcating a doctrine of exalted and aloof non-benevolence. Thus Pierre, under the influence of a philosophy which is not his by nature to fulfil, fails, both in the world of ordinary human values, and in that other universe of all-accepting, Christ-like love to which he has aspired. There are hints here, developed more fully in the following story, which throw interesting illuminings on Melville's psychology. He is a deep searcher into the ways of life, the purity of whose perception is in some way clouded. Men such as Meister Eckhart and Jacob Behmen, are mystics both by nature and circumstance. Melville seems rather to be primarily a thinker, who by the accident of deep experience has become a mystic. He is never quite content to be led solely by the inner light, and though he is enough of a mystic to know that he can not rely upon the conclusions of thought, there are always not far distant, even in his most mystic moods, conscious strivings which sometimes seem to further his search and sometimes to drive him the more recklessly into a region of oblivion. Of this region he writes:

> But the example of many minds, forever lost, like undiscoverable Arctic explorers, amid those treacherous regions, warns us entirely away from them; and we learn that it is not for man to follow the trail of Truth too far, since by so doing he entirely loses the directing compass of his mind; for arrived at the Pole, to whose barrenness only it points, there, the needle indifferently respects all points of the horizon alike.

This is not the mystic speaking but the baffled thinker, and it is the thinker in Pierre who understands the pamphlet of Plotinus Plinlimmon. This thinker is at variance with the mystic acceptance of either Isabel or Lucy. He does not accept the child-like and twice-born wisdom of either his dark or his bright angel; he *thinks*, continually he thinks, and will not rest from thinking; his thought would persuade him to the attitude of a man who would master space and time with an aloof non-benevolence; his mind persuades him of the possibility of such a mastery, and at critical moments he hesitates between the polite, non-benevolent and aloof masterliness of Plinlimmon, and the tragic acceptance of the *Untergang* that the embracing of the religious principle involves. This is the tragedy of a divided nature, and Melville, in writing *Pierre*, has set down a large portion of his own psychic history. In the end of this story, though neither triumphant nor serene but passionately grasping at despair and self-immolation, poor Pierre declares himself neuter; the twin angels of his soul have both of them fallen into decline.

VII

But many things happen before the end, and the complex events which follow are often not obvious of interpretation; yet the inner reality is always to be found, and, once found, is far more significant than the surface happenings of the story. These latter often seem wild and fantastic, crowded with continual use of symbolism; often the smallest details shine with significance. New characters are introduced; representing tendencies or complexes within the *psyche*. Isolated and individualised, they stand out the clearer, and can be the more easily grouped to show the intense inner conflict.

Glen Stanley is the respectable counterpart and worldly double of Pierre, just as Delly is the sensual double of Isabel. These seemingly separate personalities only amplify one human consciousness, and, as Glen is one aspect, so Charlie Millthorp is another; as Lucy is the angel of goodness, innocence and heavenly love, so her mother, aunts, and brothers are related adjuncts to that attribute of human identity. This may seem at first sight a far-fetched interpretation, but if examined without prejudice, such a reading will give significance to events, which, taken at their surface value as happenings in the world of actuality, will seem merely exaggerated.

In the city they meet with a terrible reception. Glen Stanley, Pierre's successful and worldly double, refuses to recognise him in his changed state. For the first time in unguarded contact with the brutalities of the world, Pierre not only tastes the bitterness of his new experience, but is assailed by tumult from within, the up-spewings of anger and disgust, and other half-recognised tendencies, which, symbolised in the rabble from a brothel, fight and claw one other. The crisis passes, and the travellers, after a roundabout drive, find a lodging for the night.

At this point of the narrative are inserted two long, satirical chapters on contemporary American literature. They have nothing to do with the main theme; the only (and inadequate) excuse for their insertion is that Pierre, who in his youthful inexperience had been a successful contributor to magazines, now imagines that, having entered on the path of experience, and having at last something to write about, he will be equally successful as a writer of more serious work. His hope is to sustain himself and his two companions by the creative efforts of the soul.

The individual reader can determine the symbolism of The Church of the Apostles, and the amusing account of the three rooms all heated by the one stove, where Pierre, surrounded on all sides by other mystically-minded philosophers, sets about his book. All this follows easily enough from what had gone before. Pierre engages on a book which, he believes, will bring neglected Truth to the world; all that he has before written he counts as unworthy and will not even glance at. He finds himself swayed to universality, and in his immaturity sets out to attempt a mature work. Already revealed to him are portions of the territory of the soul.

> But as to the resolute traveller in Switzerland, the Alps do never in one wide and comprehensive sweep, instantaneously reveal their full awfulness of amplitude—their overawing extent of peak crowded on peak, and spur sloping on spur, and chain jammed behind chain, and all their wonderful battalionings of might; so hath heaven wisely ordained, that on first entering into the Switzerland of his soul, man shall not at once perceive its tremendous immensity; lest illy prepared for such an encounter, his spirit should sink and perish in the lowermost snows. Only by judicious degrees, appointed of God, does man come at last to gain his Mont Blanc and take an overtopping view of these Alps; and even then, the tithe is not shown; and far over the invisible Atlantic, the Rocky Mountains and the Andes are yet unbeheld. Appalling is the soul of a man! Better might one be pushed off into the material spaces beyond the uttermost orbit of our sun, than once feel himself fairly afloat in himself!

And to this Melville significantly adds: "Still had he not as yet procured for himself that enchanter's wand, which but touching the humblest experiences in one's life straightway it starts up all eyes, in every one of which are endless significances. Not yet had he dropped his angle into the well of his childhood, to find what fish might be there." It is dropping this angle into the well of his childhood that Melville himself is attempting in *Pierre*; he is attempting an analysis which goes down to the beginnings of childhood's earliest associations, and which carries its subjective developments and dangers into the sensual and supersensual universes.

While Pierre is writing this book, he gets news of his mother's death, and knows that it is he who has killed her. He suffers remorse—and the knowledge that he is no longer husk-enfolded by the world. Neither his mother, the world, nor his father, the source of life, is there any longer to uphold him; he has dared to cut himself free from their support, and henceforth he must try to walk alone. It now seems to Pierre that "divinity and humanity are equally willing that he shall starve in the street for all that either will do for him." He works on doggedly in the bitter cold of winter, warmed only by that small angle of pipe that comes from the kitchen where Delly lives. While he is writing, the cold eye of Plinlimmon is upon him, and the coldness of that all-knowing look seems to say to him: "Fool, fool, fool, Vain, vain, vain, Quit, quit, quit, Ass, ass, ass!" Yet he works on, pouring out all his life in that effort of thought, which of its own will would hold at bay all other influences, and will even shut out, during his hours of work, the presence of Isabel. His relation to Isabel is changing, and if his power of thought, is strong and harsh enough to blast her, then, though he may still love her as his mother, as his sister and his bride, let it work its will.

> Pierre hath ringed himself in with the grief of Eternity. Pierre is a peak inflexible in the heart of Time. . . . He will not be called to; he will not be stirred . . . Here surely is a wonderful stillness. . . . In the heart of such silence surely something is at work. Is it creation or destruction? Builds Pierre the noble world of a new book? Or does the Pale Haggardness unbuild the lungs and the life in him? Unutterable that a man should be thus!

VIII

Into the midst of this terrible tension, where the thinker holds his thought inviolate against the influence of Isabel, who in the possessive role she is assuming, becomes the symbol of the seductive power of the unconscious, comes a letter from Lucy. This letter is the herald of the return to Pierre of that innocent consciousness which is a function of reality. Lucy announces that she is coming to his aid. Intuitively she knows that he is in need of her; she will ask no questions, she will come to serve him, not as his wife but as a nun-like cousin. This letter is created by Melville straight from the pure and transcendental realms of Being; in it is the beauty of the soul's innermost heaven, of God's sweetest sanctuary. Lucy is all Virtue; there is nothing of human weakness left in her; she, too, like Pierre, is being consumed by inward, heavenly fires. These fires make her almost too pure, too beautiful; she is the heavenly Aphrodite, without any touch of earthliness; her pallor, her fine-cut marble whiteness is a sign of her humility; she subjects herself to Isabel. Because of this heavenly sweetness and softness, the tension which in life is an earthly tension between the upper and under soul, is *not* sustained. Pierre inclines fatally to Isabel; Isabel, who seemed at her first recognition the angel who would *lead him to Truth*, contains, in the hidden depths of her mysteriousness, qualities which will destroy in the mind the *apprehension of Truth*.

Lucy arrives and takes up her abode at "The Apostles"; she, too, like Pierre, renounces all her past associations; she renounces all claim on Pierre; and comes willing to serve both him *and* Isabel. She seems so pure that she is unaware of the rivalry that she creates. Her mind is more alert than Isabel's, and it is she who offers to help by the creative act of her own artistry. Isabel, stung into a desire for action, passionately bids him take out her eyes to see with, if his own are failing, to use her heart's blood for his support. But acts are not for her; in her passivity lies her strength. "Thy hand is the caster's ladle, Pierre," she says, "that holds me entirely fluid. Into thy forms and slightest moods of thought, thou pourest me; and I there solidify to that form, and take it on and thenceforth wear it, till once more thou mouldest me anew." To this mood of Godlike indolence he answers: "The Gods made thee of a holyday, when all the common world was done, and shaped thee leisurely in elaborate hours, thou paragon."

Pierre continues to work on at his book. In this work, in his cold, isolated room, he is cut off from both Lucy and Isabel; their offered helps he refuses. Lucy, now occupying the empty room on the other side of the kitchen, works at a secret portrait. Isabel gives an involuntary homage to the heavenly virtue of her rival; even her guitar answers sometimes when Lucy speaks; and Delly, the almost mute, unconscious vital-dynamism of this strange trio, cooks for and waits upon them all.

The stage is set for the last and fatal struggle of these inner forces, and it were well to review our former analysis and carry it further. Pierre's mother is the world-substance which enfolds him: under her sway he is still in the womb. He must free himself, and with the coming of a larger, individual consciousness, burst the husk. In that act lies the cause of his mother's death. He would seem to discover an outlet for growth in Isabel, and with growth, freedom. She is for him, in that first contact, the consciousness of the tragic aspect of life, and also the channel of contact with all the mysteriousness of unknown forces. But she is more than this, and, if we look closely, we shall see an interesting relation between

Pierre's mother and Isabel. Isabel is, as it were, the complement, and not the opposite of his mother, and, as the complement, is of the same material. The incestuous relation is still retained, and in place of a mother Pierre has substituted a sister; his introversion in relation to the sister, and his espousing her as his wife, is a disguised incest-tendency towards his mother. Not only have we the incest-tendency shown clearly, but the incest-prohibition, for he renounces both Isabel and Lucy and with them the complete erotic experience, in order that he may remain a child. The mother-material which is in Isabel, namely the mysteriousness, the beauty, and the divine-seeming moods of indolence are of *danger* to Pierre. At the last, with the vial of poison in her bosom, she names herself, the murderer of Pierre.

But all this, it must be clearly understood, has no part in actuality. This is not intended as a simple story of the freeing from the physical mother, as perhaps some schools of psycho-analysts would name it. It is the story of a conscious soul attempting to draw itself free from the psychic world-material in which most of mankind is unconsciously always wrapped and enfolded, as a foetus in the womb. Melville would draw the history and the tragedy of a soul seeking freedom outside (or rather apart from) the world-substance. And here we find an analogy in the book which immediately precedes *Pierre*. In this comparison we see that, as the mysterious Isabel is a danger and a final destruction to the virtuous Pierre (Pierre, who is Melville's representation of the God-man), so the mysterious white whale in *Moby Dick* is a danger and an ultimate destruction to Ahab and all his crew (Ahab being the Man-god). Isabel is of the same world-substance (mother-substance) as Moby Dick; the aspect from which they are viewed constituting the difference. Their mystery, their attractiveness and their all-engulfing destructiveness is the same. If we have understood the books aright, we see them as complementary aspects of the same problem. And here again it should be emphasised that Isabel is no more a symbol of *evil* than is the white whale. In both these books Melville is dealing with life-values which are beyond good and evil. Only from the terrestrially human standpoint, and still enwrapped in that same mother-substance of the world, do these words have any meaning.

Lucy, with her heavenly love and her heavenly acceptance of the event, is an essence direct from the universe of transcendental Being; and although, as Pierre's innocence of conscience, she was framed to save him from the brother-sister incest relation, which, as we have seen, is reversion into the world-substance, she is of too heavenly a nature to offer adequate compensation to the lure of Isabel. She is too pure and too frail in her earthly manifestation. In actuality she has not earthly strength enough to portray him as he should be *in the flesh*; she draws him only in the skeleton. And, when at the crisis of his fate he bursts in to see the portrait, she sits mute and unmoving, allowing him to rush away *from her* to his destruction.

Attended upon each hand by these familiars (his heavenly and his earthly Aphrodite) Pierre still works at his book, seeking to find in thought a deliverance from his fate, his fate sealed already by his union with Isabel. His forces fail him; he can do no more. "A general and nameless torpor seems stealing upon him."

In this state of semi-consciousness he has a vision, in which are contrasted man's earthly household peace and the ever-encroaching appetite of God; here is given (symbol of Pierre as a thinker) the giant Enceladus, who would storm the heavenly heights, and regain his paternal birthright even by fierce escalade, but who is overthrown by the gods themselves, with a mountain heaved upon his back, and pinned to the earth. As Enceladus he sees himself battering the steeps of heaven with his bare, armless torso. And here Melville steps forward with an explanation. Pierre, he says, "did not wilfully wrest some final comfort from the fable; did not flog this stubborn rock as Moses his, and force even aridity itself to quench his painful thirst."

> Thus smitten, the Mount of Titans seems to yield this following stream:
> Old Titan's self was the son of incestuous Coelus and Terra, the son of incestuous Heaven and Earth. And Titan married his mother Terra, another and accumulatively incestuous match. And thereof Enceladus was one issue. So Enceladus was both the son and grandson of an incest; and even thus, there had been born from the organic blended heavenliness and earthliness of Pierre, another mixed, uncertain, heaven-aspiring, but still not wholly earth-emancipated mood; which again, by its terrestrial taint held down to its terrestrial mother, generated there the present doubly incestuous Enceladus *within* him; so that the present mood of Pierre—that reckless sky-assaulting mood of his, was nevertheless on one side the grandson of the sky.

From this vision Pierre rises and, on an impulse, offers to take his two companions out into the city. Isabel is overjoyed that he has left his "hateful book." She hates it as part of the realm of thought, and thus opposed to her. Pierre offers to take them out on the sea—a desire for further contact with the unconscious. This last passage is so tremendously charged with events and symbolic significance that it should be read carefully and in detail. Every detail counts, and not only what is written, but the great silent vistas between the words, these need all faculties to grasp their suggestiveness. The mysterious picture of a *foreigner*, that to Pierre resembles the portrait of his father, and to Isabel resembles her memory of her father, when he came to see her at the farm after she had left the asylum, this foreign picture clothes the image of the father in yet further ambiguousness; and this is further enhanced by Lucy's preoccupation with the copy of Guido's "Beatrice Cenci." These two pictures front one another on opposite sides of the gallery, "so that in secret they seemed to be pantomimically talking over the heads of the living spectators below." This, in the light of recent psychological research, is significant enough, and significant, too, Isabel's excitement at the motion of the boat, and her desire to plunge over the side and float away into the blue profound where sky and sea meet.

The end comes swiftly. Pierre, who has been wrought to the uttermost extreme of exasperation by the hostile gestures of his double, Glen Stanley, now ruthlessly murders that part of himself which Glen symbolises, and in so doing: "His own hand had extinguished his house in slaughtering the only unoutlawed human being by the name of Glendinning." After this action of inner violence he falls into a self-shut-in state of gloom and despondency, well symbolised by the prison. But even in prison he is attended by his two angels; Lucy, so long as sanity remains, will ever cleave to his soul, however great his despair, and Isabel is that deeper part which can not be separated even by death or madness. Enveloped by the uttermost despair, and surrounded by the ruin which has become his fate, he knows them, in a light of a newly-won wisdom, as the Fool of Virtue and the Fool of Truth. Himself, as the Fool of Fate, has already repudiated them both.

> Ye two pale ghosts, were this the other world, ye were not welcome. Away!—Good Angel and Bad Angel both!—For Pierre is neuter now!
> Oh, ye stoney roofs and seven-fold stoney skies! not thou art the murdered, but thy sister hath murdered thee, my brother, oh my brother!
> At these wailed words from Isabel, Lucy shrank up like a scroll, and noiselessly fell at the feet of Pierre.
> He touched her heart—"Dead!—Girl! wife or sister, saint or fiend!"—seizing Isabel in his grasp—"in thy breasts, life for infants lodgeth not, but death-milk for thee and me!—The drug!" and tearing her bosom loose, he seized the secret vial nestling there.

Yet at the end when they are both dying it is Isabel who claims the knowledge of his identity.

> "All's o'er, and ye knew him not," she gasps in dying. . . . her form sloped sideways, and she fell upon Pierre's heart, and her long hair ran over him, and arboured him in ebon vines.

IX

Melville was thirty-two years old when *Pierre* was published. The book was a complete failure; the critics were shocked, and there is no record left that any one understood the inner significance of the story. Soon after its publication the printing house where most of the copies of its one edition were stored burned down. By later editors of Melville's work it was considered "almost unreadable" and was not reprinted till long after Melville's death.

By those who are now able to obtain copies and who take the trouble to understand the inner symbolic meaning, it will be found to be the greatest of Melville's books. The high imaginative quality is quite as fine as the best in *Moby Dick*, and the style is less flamboyant. In *Pierre* a luxuriant imagination meets with an adequate controlling power and an artistic appreciation of reticence. The book is a far better artistic whole than *Moby Dick*; there is less matter irrelevant to the main theme, and the elaborate fabric in which Melville's thought and intuition meet and are interwoven, is a quality quite unmatched by any other work of his time.

The difficulty and profundity of his theme is adequately compensated for by the precision of his expression. One is again and again astonished at the suggestiveness and perfection of his symbols. These symbols, no doubt, came to him as inspiration; they are the transcending values, born of the conflict of thought and emotion, which made further discovery possible for him. They had their birth in the unconscious, but once in being, they were found to be adequate to the demands of the mind; Melville was never *lost* in the shadow-peopled universe of the unconscious. In him the conflict between thought and feeling was balanced and intense. If his anvil were some vast, primal outcrop of the soul's igneous matrix, his hammer was his mind, and the sparks which flew from the contact of the two, had thus a double origin.

Melville was both mystic *and* thinker. The center of Melville is *Pierre*; if one would understand him, one must understand this book before all others. Many critics have declared that *Moby Dick* is his greatest work because they have not taken the trouble to understand *Pierre*; and often in their appreciation of *Moby Dick* they have only skirted the interpretation. Some, to cloak their own indolence, have said that Melville did not understand the significance of his own writing, and that though certain passages probably have significance, Melville could not himself have explained them. Perhaps he could not have explained to the full; he was dealing always in life-values. But he did know the *significance* attached to every name and every suggestion. If anyone thinks that he did not know what he was doing in *Moby Dick*, and suggests that the symbols used there were the result of chance stumbling in the region of the unconscious, let him read *Pierre* and see that Melville himself understands what Melville has written, and that the Melville who created Pierre, Isabel, and Lucy, and built up their interactions into so closely a cemented and fool-proof structure—that this Melville was even profounder than he who created Ahab, Fedallah, and Moby Dick.

Pierre, as I have said, was the center of Melville's being, and the height of his achievement, and although his literary style and his artistic sense are seen to better advantage in *Piazza Tales*, *Pierre*, like a mountain, towers above the rest. It is a mountain that will need many explorers; and like *Hamlet*, *Lear*, and life itself, will remain largely unexplored. Psycho-analysts of future generations will no doubt make high picnic there. Like Spitteler and Goethe, Melville will provide them in *Pierre* with a path and a sign, leading to that Mount of Titans, where the catnip and the amaranth contend for ever on the hearth-stones of the human soul.

A Restoration

Malcolm S. MacLean*

Gratitude is due Professor Forsythe, specific editor; Bernard DeVoto, series editor; and Alfred A. Knopf, publisher, for restoring to the American reading public the first edition of Melville's fascinating novel. The format is fine; the printing a work of art; the editing masterly. The thousands who saw the revival of *After Dark* at Mr. Morley's theatre, the hundreds of thousands who through articles, biographies, movies, and college courses, find their interest in American life and literature of the last century quickened, will turn with sharp delight to this experiment in fancifully rhetorical, epical, melodramatic romance by the author of *Moby Dick*.

High satisfaction rises from the realization that the demand of this vastly increased reading public will be met by this edition, not by any other. For in Professor Forsythe's introduction there is, I think for the first time, a sane attitude, a truly critical appreciation, a balanced judgment of *Pierre*. What Professor Cross has done for Fielding, what John Drinkwater has done with almost as great success for Byron, Mr. Forsythe has done for Melville. He has not white-washed Melville's performance in *Pierre*; he has explained it reasonably and accurately. He has pulled the novel out of the slough of psychopathic self-exhibitions and given it its proper place among the experiments of great writers. He has shown, with the surefootedness of a scholar thoroughly familiar with the narrow paths, pitfalls, and crevasses of his own section of Parnassus, how utterly unreasonable it is to generalize the autobiographical element in the novel to cover all its incidents, characters, and especially the workings of the hero's mind.

The autobiographical influence, Mr. Forsythe has put in its right perspective by drawing forth in orderly progression other important influences at work on Melville during the time of his creation of this novel. These he has bolstered by documentary evidence which has been notably lacking in the work of those recent critics and biographers who have maintained that there was a fetid Freudian significance in the darker phases of plot and character. Dr. Forsythe demonstrates Melville's own

*Reprinted from *Quarterly Journal*, 21 (Fall 1930), 76–78. A review of the Knopf edition of *Pierre*.

happy childhood, his own bodily and mental health and vigor at the very time he was writing *Pierre*. He shows Melville's deep absorption in Shakespeare's melancholy Dane, his acute interest in the theme of disillusionment and doubt at war with idealism. Mr. Forsythe says, concerning the melodramatic close of the book, "Perhaps, in those last moments Pierre had gone insane—was or was not Hamlet mad?" I wish the editor had gone further and asked of other Melville critics, "Was Hamlet's disillusionment, his horror, his doubt, his despair, the result directly of his own guilty and incestuous passion for his mother? And did not this in turn reflect a similar passion on Shakespeare's part?" An answer to this absurdity would further support Mr. Forsythe's answers to the like absurdities of Melville critics.

The editor shows likewise Melville's over-accentuation of Fate, a weakness Shakespeare escaped. He analyses the close parallelism of the plot structure and that of good melodrama. He recalls Melville's marked tendency to disgress, and soundly defends these digressions for their ironic and satiric power. He makes patent the reason for the rich infusion of symbolism in *Pierre* by substantiating the influences upon Melville of those supreme symbolists, Hawthorne and Carlyle.

Even the highly mannered style of the novel is adequately explained in Mr. Forsythe's critique although he does not defend it. In effect he asks if any novelist, soaked in Hamlet, saturated with Carlyle, habituated to Hawthorne, an active disciple of Sir Thomas Browne, and fresh from a reading of DeQuincey's *Suspiria de Profundis*, and further writing in haste and careless of revision, could have avoided composing as Melville here composed. The answer is that of course he could not.

In fine, Professor Forsythe has restored to us Melville's *Pierre* for exactly what it is, an experiment of a great American writer. Not a great book certainly, but a book worth the reading. Not, as some would have it, the outpouring of filth and blood from a diseased mind, as though Melville had entered the enchanted forest and lopped off the head of his own Error, but as his attempt to express a philosophy, to write an American *Hamlet*. It is a good melodrama. It contains passages of a high irony and rich satire one should not miss. Guided by the introduction, the reader goes through the novel clear sightedly, never expecting more than he gets, often getting better things than he is led to expect. Thank the Gods of Scholarship for critics like Mr. Forsythe. May their tribe increase.

[A Literary Experiment and the Destruction of Certainties]

E. H. Eby*

Now that the text of *Pierre* follows that of the first edition of 1852 with the editorial emendations exactly recorded, scholars can turn with confidence to the more important considerations which the novel evokes. These problems Mr. Forsythe discusses briefly in his preface with solutions that take a sane middle course as opposed to the elaborate conjectures which have been offered as an explanation of *Pierre*. For instance, that it is largely an autobiographical novel is an assumption not proven by ascertainable facts. Although Melville did draw from the storehouse of his life as all artists must do, nevertheless, as Mr. Forsythe demonstrates, the novelist had no intentions of writing himself into the novel. He altered personal facts to suit his artistic intentions until, for example, one cannot say with accuracy that Mrs. Glendinning is Melville's mother, or that Pierre's father is a speaking likeness of Allan Melville.

With this granted it is still true that *Pierre* is the key to a knowledge of Melville's inner biography. Regardless of how he altered external facts, regardless of literary sources, it is still certain that the problems confronting the author, his feelings about life, are recorded in these pages. Mr. Forsythe in his effort to say only what the facts justify has been unduly reticent on this the most important aspect of the novel.

However, some of the editor's suggestions are so valuable that they need further investigation. The possible literary relations between Carlyle and Herman Melville both as to style and leading ideas may serve to clarify much that is puzzling in the latter. Again, Longfellow's *Hyperion*, as Mr. Forsythe points out, affords suggestive parallels, although in Longfellow's case the question of sources is a delicate one. Longfellow, as his literary contemporaries knew, was an intermediary, naturalizing European romanticism. In such a case it will be most difficult to decide whether an influence was by means of Longfellow or more directly from his original source. The stylistic similarities to DeQuincey also need more investigation.

Above all it seems obvious that Melville was consciously writing a modern Hamlet. Speaking of the Memnon Stone, Melville says:

> Herein lies an unsummed world of grief. For in this plaintive fable we find embodied the Hamletism of the antique world; the Hamletism of three thousand years ago: "The flower of virtue cropped by a too rare mischance." And the English tragedy is but Egyptian Memnon, Montaignized and modernized; for being but a mortal man Shakespeare had his fathers too.

*Reprinted from *American Literature*, 2 (November 1930), 319–21. A review of the Knopf edition of *Pierre*.

Now as the Memnon Statue survives down to this present day, so does that nobly-striving but ever-shipwrecked character in some royal youths (for both Memnon and Hamlet were the sons of kings), of which that statue is the melancholy type. But Memnon's sculptured woes did once melodiously resound; now all is mute. Fit emblem that of old, poetry was a consecration and an obsequy to all hapless modes of human life; but in a bantering, barren, and prosaic, heartless age, Aurora's music moan is lost among our drifting sands, which whelm alike the monument and the dirge.

With this in mind some of the problems of *Pierre* are cleared up. Melville, as did many of the romantics, felt the need of a new prose style more fluid, more rhythmical, an intermediary between blank verse and ordinary prose. With *Hamlet* so strongly in mind, Melville carried this experiment farther than he did previously. This accounts for the curiously inflated style, for the stilted dialogue of the "high" characters, for the contrasting realism of the "low." Here certainly Melville failed to modernize his *Hamlet*.

The symbolism, the unplausible web of circumstances are a resultant of the same tendency. It has not been recognized sufficiently that there was a demand particularly among the Transcendentalists that the novel be profoundly changed to suit the new point of view. In a sense Hawthorne was doing this with his pervasive symbolism, but a better though less known example of what they wanted done is found in Sylvester Judd's *Margaret; or, the Real and the Ideal*. In it is seen the same effort to enrich the prose with poetic feeling and rhythm, the same desire to reveal the symbolism which inheres in every object and event, the same carelessness of plot structure that comes from a shift in attention from the outer to the inner world. Somewhere in this stream of experimentation was Melville.

However, the chief importance of *Pierre* is in Melville's clearly marked attempt to show the "ambiguities" of motive which underlie the conventional and the conscious. Melville saw that motives to action are not simple but inextricably woven of confused and contradictory impulses, that more lies beneath the conscious layer than above. Brotherly feeling may be composed of tabooed sex impulses, self-sacrifice may be egotism, good arise from evil impulses, and bad from the good. This discovery destroyed for Melville his last refuge. *Moby Dick* records his knowledge that the external world is not the Emersonian Nature but at best an unmoral universe; *Pierre* records the finding that neither is the kingdom of the ideal within. Emersonian optimism turned out to be a whited sepulcher.

This destruction of certainties alienated Melville from his generation just as it brought him close to the moderns. The central idea of *Pierre* and probably that of Melville was not understandable to his contemporaries. It is expressed in Plotinus Plinlimmon's lecture on chronometricals and horologicals. Melville saw the disparity between the ideal (chronometrical) and the existent (horological) as none of his contemporaries did. "And yet it follows not from this, that God's truth is one thing and man's truth another; but—as above hinted, and as will be further elucidated in subsequent lectures—by their very contradictions they are made to correspond."

Certainly in *Pierre*, Melville never got to this subsequent lecture. In fact Melville's life was a search for the answer and a search in vain, for like *Hamlet* "the rest is silence."

[The Consummate Sorcery of Melville's Language]

Henry A. Murray, Jr.*

If one can swallow the unpalatable title of this series—*Americana Deserta*—with its flippant and smartaleckish pun upon Doughty's noble book, the present volume makes available for the first time to those who are not so fortunate as to have discovered and purchased a first edition of *Pierre*, the original text of Melville's *danse macabre*.

No alterations of the original have been made "except (1) in the correction of obvious typographical and grammatical errors; and (2) in the systematizing, according to Melville's own usage, of spelling, capitalization, hyphenation, and punctuation." These minor revisions have been most judiciously executed by the editor, Professor Robert S. Forsythe, who adds a scholarly introduction to the book.

In 1851, at the age of thirty-two, a few weeks after dispatching the manuscript of *Moby Dick* to his publishers, Herman Melville wrote to a neighbor in Pittsfield who had presented him with two books: "the Fates have plunged me into certain silly thoughts and wayward speculations which will prevent me, for a time, from falling into the reveries of these books—for a fine book is a sort of revery to us—is it not?"

He could not read these books, in other words, because he had submitted to "possession," a "possession" which drove him to the locked seclusion of his workroom on the second floor. Here it was he wrote for Fate, before the window facing Greylock up against the northern sky.

He was at it for a fevered year [probably only three or four months. Ed. note.] and then emerged, a shattered victim, with the diabolic manuscript of *Pierre*. He might himself defensively have spoken of the substance of his mysterious book as "silly thoughts and wayward speculations," but he was far too sensitive to accept with humorous offhandedness any such judgment from his fellows. He had written "what he

*Reprinted from *New England Quarterly*, 4 (April 1931), 333–37. A review of the Knopf edition of *Pierre*.

thought to be new, or at least miserably neglected Truth," and from the fact that he took pains to forespeak and everlastingly repudiate the anticipated censure of the critics, it may be surmised that when upon the publication of *Pierre* the critics to a man rose to denounce him each sneer was the lash of a whip across a face already scrunched up in pain.

The story of *Pierre* opens with an extravagant and sentimentally artificial account of the gifts and graces of the hero. He is a manly young aristocrat with a fortune, who lives like a Virginian blood with his queenly mother in the family manor house. His Victorian heart of gold beats with ideal pubescent affections—glowing enough to answer the demands of his devoted mother as well as of a charming girl to whom he is engaged. And to add to the perfection of the ensemble the gods have favored him with a touch of literary genius. Will he not marry and live happily ever after? No. The three ironic spinsters have arranged it otherwise. For quite by chance one day he meets the hauntingly tragic gaze of a mysterious girl—Isabel, the eternal Sybil. And at that instant the pair are seized by the unambiguous hand of destiny. Although Isabel turns out to be Pierre's half-sister, like Tristan and Isolde they have partaken, and no private wills can drive them asunder. Everything that follows: the desperate rending of old loyalties, the precipitous flight, the furious efforts to circumvent misfortune and all the hate, despair, and madness that result, are for Pierre the direct consequence of the predicament of having fallen in love—a fact which receives from him but tangential recognition—with the illegitimate daughter of his dead father. It is only later that Pierre apprehends the utter extent of his need: "Call me brother no more!" he says heatedly to Isabel. "How knowest thou I am thy brother? Did thy mother tell thee? Did my father say so to me?—I am Pierre, and thou Isabel, wide brother and sister in the common humanity—no more. For the rest, let the gods look after their own combustibles. If they have put powder casks in me—let them look to it! Let them look to it!"

All the morbid reasonings which derive from the underlying malistic sentiments to which Pierre as the story progresses gives eloquent and superb expression are engendered by the failure to surmount the obstacles which arise out of this situation. I can hardly see how there can be any disagreement about the fact that a compulsive socially-unsanctioned passion—in this case incest—is the nucleus of the book.

Professor Forsythe, however, in his accurate, thorough and most gentlemanly introduction does not mention the word incest. In fact he says: "The plot of *Pierre* itself can hardly be considered of especial interest or importance. It is sensational and unconvincing. The action is, however, only a necessary structure erected upon the foundation of Melville's ideas of life. To the reader of today, it is these ideas and the problems which arise from them that constitute the most valuable part of the novel."

To me the value of the novel is the consummate sorcery of Melville's language, particularly in certain portions of the book. The ideas, as such,

are not especially important—in fact, they are for the most part quite il-
logical—but taken as a series of overtones or intellectual orchestrations for
emotional states and permutations, they are as thrillingly rewarding as
anything in our literature. It is the logic of the passions, we might say,
rather than the logic of the ideas that absorbs us. Having heard others at
just this stage of affective development express similar opinions, and on
discovering *Pierre*, embrace it as a Bible, I am prepared to regard such
rationalizations as the outcome of a particular constellation of emotive
tensions. For instance, the marvelous ironic whimsy of the semiphilo-
sophical section on "Chronometricals and Horologicals," aside from its
acute observations of fact, is representative of a particular organization of
the sentiments. It is the product, one might say, of a dichotomized mind.

These facts, however, have little to do with the delight which we experience when at the critical moments of the story Melville gathers
together the widespread resources of his genius and compresses them to a
focus of intense experience.

It is to be granted that there are many dissonances in this pseudo-
morphic novel and that the treatment of the plot is in many respects artificial and melodramatic, but far from considering the plot itself as
unimportant, I should maintain that the ensuing sentiments are meaningless without it. It is not difficult to understand how Pierre came by
them if one keeps in mind the nuclear situation. But since it is probable
that at this period of his life the author himself was agitated by the same
emotions, it is at least permissible to advance the biographical query: how
did Melville come by them? For if, as Professor Forsythe believes, the plot
was constructed by Melville as a scaffolding for his ideas, we have yet to
explain the genesis of the latter—the blackest in the history of American
literature. In fact no bleeding man before or since ever hurled in the teeth
of society more eternally vitriolic words.

Professor Forsythe, furthermore, takes special pains to dissociate the
story of Pierre from the story of Melville. He so belabors this point that the
reader may suspect that he is practicing Melville's preaching; namely,
that "man, in the ideal, is so noble and so sparkling, such a grand and
glowing creature, that over any ignominious blemish in him all his fellows
should run to throw their costliest robes." As if Melville, that "mighty
pageant creature, formed for noble tragedies" needed any such cod-
dling—except perhaps to preserve a perfunctory reputation with tame
and sessile souls who never would understand him.

Pierre, like *Faust*, is rather to be taken as a spiritual biography, a
modern counterpart, let us say, of the *Confessions* of St. Augustine. For it
is clear that Melville's notion of a great book was much the same as
Dante's. A theorem which, stripped of its trappings, would lay stress upon
the poetical account of the states and transmutations of a man's central
and most profound feelings towards the varied aspects of the universe
taken as a whole._

In this sense *Pierre* is most certainly autobiographical, and Melville merely tells us the expected when he, looking over the shoulder of Pierre and reading what he has written, says "he seems to have directly plagiarized from his own experience." It was due to the compelling and unresolvable character of Melville's personal conflicts that he was never able during this period to achieve the desired state of aesthetic detachment.

In fact he gives us reasons to believe that his writing was of secondary importance to him; for instance, when commenting upon the effort which Pierre, a thin disguise for himself, is expending upon his transcendental book, Melville writes: "that which now absorbs the time and life of Pierre, is not the book, but the primitive elementalizing of the strange stuff, which in the act of attempting that book, was upheaved and upgushed in his soul." For in the last analysis "all the great books in the world are but the mutilated shadowings-forth of invisible and unembodied images in the soul; so that they are but the mirrors, distortedly reflecting to us our own things; and never mind what the mirror may be, if we would see the object, we must look at the object itself, and not at its reflection."

It is because in this instance Melville puts the soul of man first and its literary "shadowings-forth" second that some critics consider *Pierre* his best book, and others consider it his worst.

[Melville's Quest for the Ultimate]

Willard Thorp*

Melville's contemporaries dismissed *Pierre* as not only a dead failure but as a work so "repulsive, unnatural and indecent" that it might endanger one's mental health to read it. With his admirers of more recent times, enthusiasts over the neglected *Moby-Dick*, it did not fare much better. Only in the past half dozen years has it been studied objectively with the intent of elucidating its mysteries and determining what Melville thought he had accomplished.

Pierre is still a difficult book. To us of this generation who read with ease Meredith and James and Woolf, and think we fathom the expressionism of Joyce's *Ulysses* and Lawrence's *The Rainbow*, Melville's methods are not utterly confusing, as they were to an earlier generation. Our difficulty is not to understand the drift and significance of the story but to know how much of what we think we see was placed there by Melville, and how much we read into the text because we have lived through the Freudian era.[1] So startling is Melville's prescience about such

*Reprinted from *Herman Melville: Representative Selections* (New York: American Book Company, 1938), pp. lxxv–lxxx, lxxxi–lxxxiii.

subjects as adolescent psychology and the unconscious and so modern is his literary use of dreams and myths that one has constantly to remind oneself of the date of the novel.

As a barrier to our enjoyment of *Pierre*, and sometimes to comprehension, we cannot overlook the insecurity of its style. In *Moby-Dick* potentially dissonant passages of realism, rhapsody, instruction, humor, and tragedy are modulated to the universally heroic tone of the book. These various elements have one trait in common. In *Pierre* this is not the case. Time and again it is impossible without weighing and comparing to apprehend the intended tone of a particular passage. Two examples will sufficiently demonstrate this. The over-sweet Arcadian opening of the book, disclosing Pierre the Innocent in the center of his earthly paradise, is probably intended as satire and is artistically satisfying when read as such.[2] But it is so near to the style of the "thee-and-thou" school of sentimental fiction contemporary with it that one cannot be quite sure. For a second example consider Plinlimmon's pamphlet on "Chronometricals and Horologicals," advocating a "virtuous expediency" in moral actions, which opens Pierre's eyes though it does not affect his will. So unemphatic is Melville's attitude toward the pamphlet that some critics have been convinced that he sided with Plinlimmon, though if such were the case, the novel would contain insoluble contradictions.

In spite of these difficulties *Pierre* is a fascinating book. It possesses the vigor and promise of greater things to come which any primitive displays. André Gide has said that more interesting than the finished novel itself would be the journal of a great novelist like Stendhal or Dostoevsky showing the progress of the fight to achieve it. In *Pierre* we see Melville struggling, as M. Gide says of his central figure in *Les Faux Monnayeurs*, "entre ce que lui offre le réalité et ce que, lui, prétend en faire." The substance of the book is Melville's struggle to fathom the mystery of Pierre, who in turn is struggling to understand his author-hero Vivia, who is struggling to write a novel about his own "pursuit of the highest health of virtue and truth."

Melville knew that he would have to disrupt the confines of the conventional novel which laboriously spins veils of mystery, "only to complacently clear them up at last." His readers need not expect him to unravel his mysteries, because in human life there are no proper endings, but only "imperfect, unanticipated, and disappointing sequels," which "hurry to abrupt intermergings with the eternal tides of time and fate." He was about to descend into the heart of man by a spiral stair without an end, "where that endlessness is only concealed by the spiralness of the stair, and the blackness of the shaft." In two earlier books he had presented the tormenting dualism which is masked behind the inscrutableness of the universe, as it is embodied in the political and economic realm (*Mardi*) and as it may be discovered in the world of nature (*Moby-Dick*). He wished to work it out anew in the plane of metaphysical values. His search for the Ultimate here brought him, as it did Browning, into conflict with the dominant belief of the nineteenth century fostered by the scientist, that reality is to be found in the natural world.

Melville wished to show in *Pierre* that there are some men, "Enthusiasts to Duty," who will obey the highest behest of their souls, though they lose their worldly felicity and bring upon themselves a "not-to-be-thought-of-woe." They stake all on the good faith of God. The world casts them out and mocks them. Heaven gives no sign, either of having ordained their fall or of being concerned for it. They are befooled by Truth, Virtue, and Fate. This theme would be projected through the story, deliberately Hamletian in outline, of Pierre Glendinning, gently born and reared in innocence and piety. He reveres the memory of his father as the personification of a goodness which is almost divine. He adores his haughty, worldly mother and worships Lucy Tartan, to whom he is engaged, as if she were almost more than mortal. Suddenly there invades this heaven on earth a mysterious dark-haired girl (Isabel) who, he is convinced, is an unacknowledged daughter of his father. He faces a dilemma. Heaven-decreed Duty compels him to receive Isabel, yet to receive her as his sister will shame his father's memory and cast down his mother's pride. He cuts the knot by the fantastic device of a pseudo-marriage to her. Lucy nearly dies of the shock and his mother, after disinheriting Pierre, is killed by grief and anger. In the city whither the couple have gone, Pierre struggles to write a novel, which is a failure. Lucy follows him to the city, pursued by Glen Stanly, Pierre's cousin and former friend, who wishes to save her. Pierre is goaded into killing him. Lucy dies of shock. Pierre and Isabel end the tragedy with poison.

What Pierre learns in the boundless expansion of his life, how society judges the folly of men like him, what the philosophers have to tell the Pierres of the world about the disparity between heavenly and terrestrial morality, what Melville had concluded about the issue, were all to find a place within the plot of this *Hamlet raisonné*.

A few ludicrously melodramatic scenes in *Pierre* have induced critics to overlook the fact that Melville invented an external plot which could be excellently manipulated to embody his theme and was capable of appropriate symbolic elaboration. There is scarcely a situation in the story which is not sound psychological realism except the pseudo-marriage between Pierre and his half-sister Isabel. The exception is a large one, but Melville could not avoid the episode. The incest motive was symbolically indispensable to the development of the idea of the ambiguity and the terrestrial taint of heavenly truth. Yet Pierre, since he represents in the beginning absolute innocence (though he is soon made alarmingly aware of the inversions of Truth) could not be made a deliberate partner in a physically incestuous relationship, however much this might have enhanced the probability of the external plot. The solution of the pseudo-marriage Melville recognized as a weak link and he devotes most of Book

X—"The Unprecedented Final Resolution of Pierre"—to an analysis of the motives which induced his hero to take this way out. In the course of it he uncovers two psychological facts which nearly convince the reader. Isabel's mysterious nature had already begun to work an ambiguous charm upon Pierre so that the performance of his heaven-appointed duty was not single-motived; nor was the act, for another reason, entirely unprepared for. The artificial and ambiguous brother-sister relationship which Pierre and his mother had established between themselves was the preparative to this "nominal conversion of a sister into a wife.". . .

In *Moby-Dick* Melville stood outside the tragedy; though sympathizing with Ahab's feud, he believed the captain's thirst for revenge was not fated and that he might have avoided the woe that is madness. Melville is not Ahab. What is the circumstance in *Pierre?* Does Melville identify himself with his hero; are we permitted to suppose Pierre's tragedy is his also? Actually, Melville, even more directly than in *Moby-Dick*, cautions us against assuming that hero and author are one: "But the thoughts we here indite as Pierre's are to be very carefully discriminated from those we indite concerning him."

Commenting on the dangerous state to which "enthusiastic Truth" has brought Pierre, he goes so far as to declare that the "example of many minds forever lost, like undiscoverable Arctic explorers, amid those treacherous regions, warns us entirely away from them; and we learn that it is not for man to follow the trail of truth too far, since by so doing he entirely loses the directing compass of his mind; for arrived at the Pole, to whose barrenness only it points, there, the needle indifferently respects all points of the horizon alike."

These words do not prove, of course, that when Melville was at work on *Pierre* he had abandoned his speculations on the nature of ultimate truth. Though he would stop short of Ahab's madness and Pierre's self-destruction, he had still much to say, explicitly and by implication, on the quest initiated in *Mardi*.

There can be no doubt, in the first place, of Melville's disgust with the prudent materialism with which the world, represented by Mrs. Glendinning, her white-handed pastor, and Pierre's cousin Glen, views Pierre's agony, which these people would be quite incapable of comprehending. The desire to satirize their hypocrisy persisted with Melville until the writing of *The Confidence Man*. But there is another way of viewing the problem which obsesses Pierre, that offered by the transcendentalist philosopher Plotinus Plinlimmon, in his lecture on "Chronometricals and Horologicals." His comfortable doctrine proclaims a "virtuous expediency" as the best way for the heaven-conscious mortal to live on earth. When he goes to heaven it will be quite time enough to live by heaven's chronometrical time.

By introducing Plinlimmon and his pamphlet, which promised a later (unaccomplished) reconciliation of God's truth to man's truth,

Melville intended a satire on all shallow and amiable transcendental "reconcilers" of the "Optimist" or "Compensation" school. Their waving away of the problem he found quite as distasteful as the worldly hypocrisy of the Rev. Mr. Falsgrave.

To know at what position Melville had now positively arrived in his quest for the Ultimate, we must study a passage in Book XIV of *Pierre* where he sets down candidly his own conclusions. He testifies there to the conviction of divine origin which the beauty of the Sermon on the Mount carries to the heart of an earnest or enthusiastic youth. When he first looks about him in the world he cannot believe that the professed Christian can live so totally at variance with it. Unless his faith fades, or he fails to see the lying world around him or unless "he can find the talismanic secret, to reconcile this world with his own soul, then there is no peace for him, no slightest truce for him in this life." The talismanic secret has never been found, nor does Melville suppose it will be found. Philosophers pretend to have it—"Plato, and Spinoza, and Goethe,[3] and many more belong to this guild of self-imposters, with a preposterous rabble of Muggletonian Scots and Yankees, whose vile brogue still the more bestreaks the stripedness of their Greek or German Neoplatonical originals." They lie when they assert they have received an answer from the "Voice of our God." How can a man "get a Voice out of Silence"?

Here in 1852 ended, for the moment, Melville's quest for the Ultimate. His mood had changed from the reckless high adventure of Taji, not content with Serenia, to partial sympathy with the vengeful Ahab who longed to strike through the mask of whiteness and so lay bare the malice or the blankness which lay beyond, to the desponding and skeptical mood of *Pierre*. There seems to be no answer, least of all a transcendental one, yet for Melville there could be no truce in the war to wrest one from the silent heavens.

If Melville could have continued to objectify his quest in books like *Mardi, Moby-Dick,* and *Pierre,* he might have saved himself from the emotional collapse which darkened the next ten years of his life. But the story of his truceless war was told on all possible planes. Chaos was come again, but there was no further possibility of subliming it into another *Moby-Dick,* for the "fullness" was gone. He abandoned himself in private conversation to continued wandering over the deserts of speculation.

Notes

1. In this connection one may object to some of the terminology in E.L. Grant Watson's "Melville's *Pierre*" (*New England Quarterly*, 3, April, 1930). He is inclined to treat the novel as if it were the work of a contemporary whose symbolism shows him to be thoroughly familiar with the concepts of the Freudian school. In *Pierre* the story takes place in the realm where moral values are paramount, in society that is, and chiefly within the family. But the theme which the story embodies is metaphysical as well as moral and the symbols which Melville invents to add depth to it belong therefore to both orders of thought. When they seem

to be startlingly erotic as well, the presumption is that they are often so only by the accident that Melville's plot necessarily involves various sex relationships.

2. Braswell believes that the aberrances of style throughout the book are deliberate on Melville's part and reveal his satiric purpose ("The Satirical Temper of Melville's *Pierre*," *American Literature*, 7, 432–435).

3. The inclusion of Goethe here is illuminated by Melville's remark in a letter to Hawthorne: "In reading some of Goethe's sayings, so worshipped by his votaries, I came across this, 'Live in the all.' That is to say, your separate identity is but a wretched one,—good; but get out of yourself, spread and expand yourself, and bring to yourself the tinglings of life that are felt in the flowers and the woods, that are felt in the planets Saturn and Venus, and the Fixed Stars. What nonsense! Here is a fellow with a raging toothache, 'My dear boy,' Goethe says to him, 'you are sorely afflicted with that tooth; but you must *live in the all*, and then you will be happy!' "

[From "The Craft of Herman Melville"]

R. P. Blackmur*

A great author is of one substance and often of one theme, and the relation between his various creations is bound to be reciprocal, even mutual; each is the other in a different form. So with "Pierre" and "Moby Dick." If we wish to take up thinking of the two novels together in this way, the alert consciousness will be struck with the repetition of the vices of "Pierre" in "Moby Dick," or struck the other way round with the fact that the tragedy of "Pierre" fails to come off as well as "Moby Dick" only because it lacks the demonstrable extraneous interest of whaling. The efforts at plot in the two books are as lame; narrative runs as often offside. Dramatic motive on the subordinate level is as weakly put; Starbuck's tentative rebellion against Ahab and the threatened revenge of Glendinning Stanly and Frederick Tartan upon Pierre are equally unconvincing. The dialogue is by turns as limp and stiff and flowery in one book as in the other. The delineations of character are almost interchangeable examples of wooden caricature. And so on. More important, the force and nobility of conception, the profundity of theme, were as great in either book—not because of the dramatic execution but in spite of it; for they lay in the simple strength of the putative statement, and in the digressions Melville made from the drama in front of him, which he could not manage, into apologues or sermons, which he superbly could.

The strength of the putative statement is simple only when thought of abstractly and as appealing to the intellect—to the putative element in appreciation: as if we read lyric poetry solely for the schematic paraphrase we make of it in popular discussion. What we want now is to

*Reprinted from *Virginia Quarterly Review*, 14 (Spring 1938), pp. 274–82.

see what is the source of putative strength and how deeply its appeal is asserted; and in that pursuit we shall find ourselves instantly, I think, in the realm of language itself. Words, and their intimate arrangements, must be the ultimate as well as the immediate source of every effect in the written or spoken arts. Words bring meaning to birth and themselves contained the meaning as an immanent possibility before the pangs of junction. To the individual artist the use of words is an adventure in discovery; the imagination is heuristic among the words it manipulates. The reality you labor desperately or luckily to put into your words—and you may put it in consciously like Coleridge or by instinct as in the great ballads or from piety and passion like the translators of the Bible—you will actually have found there, deeply ready and innately formed to give objective being and specific idiom to what you knew and what you did not know that you knew. The excitement is past belief, as we know from the many myths of heavenly inspiration. And the routine of discovery is past teaching and past prediction, as we know from the vast reaches of writing, precious and viable to their authors, wholly without the conviction of being. Yet the adventure into the reality of words has a technique after the fact in the sense that we can distinguish its successful versions from those that failed, can measure provisionally the kinds and intensities of reality secured and attempted, and can even roughly guess at the conditions of convention and belief necessary for its emergence.

Melville is an excellent example for such an assay. We have only to relate the conception of the reality of language just adumbrated to the notion of the putative statement to see whence the strength of the latter comes; and we have only to relate the conception of language to its modifying context of conventions in order to understand the successes and at least excuse the many shortcomings and overleapings of Melville's attempts at the paramount and indefeasible reality that great words show. For Melville habitually used words greatly.

Let us take first an example not at all putative and with as little supporting context of convention as possible: an example of words composed entirely of feelings and the statement of sensuous facts, plus of course the usual situating and correlative elements which are the real syntax of imaginative language.

To a landsman, no whale, nor any sign of a herring, would have been visible at that moment; nothing but a troubled bit of greenish white water, and thin scattered puffs of vapor hovering over it, and suffusingly blowing off to leeward, like the confused scud from white rolling billows. The air around suddenly vibrated and tingled, as it were, like the air over intensely heated plates of iron. Beneath this atmospheric waving and curling, and partially beneath a thin layer of water, also, the whales were swimming. Seen in advance of all the other indications, the puffs of vapor they spouted, seemed their forerunning couriers and detached flying outriders.

This is the bottom level of good writing, whether in prose or verse; and a style which was able to maintain, at other levels and for other purposes, the qualities of accurate objective feeling which it exemplifies, could not help being a great style. The words have feelers of their own, and the author contributes nothing to the emotion they call forth except the final phrasing, which adds nothing but finish to the paragraph. It is an example of words doing their own work; and let no one think, because the mode is that of close description, that it is not imaginative work, or does not come to an emotion. Let us compare it, with achieved emotion in mind, with a deliberately "emotional" description taken from the chapter called "Enceladus" in "Pierre."

> Cunningly masked hitherto, by the green tapestry of the interlacing leaves, a terrific towering palisade of dark mossy massiness confronted you; and, trickling with unevaporable moisture, distilled upon you from its beetling brow slow thunder-showers of water-drops, chill as the last dews of death. . . . All round and round, the grim scarred rocks rallied and re-rallied themselves; shot up, protruded, stretched, swelled, and eagerly reached forth; on every side bristlingly radiated with hideous repellingness. . . . 'Mid this spectacle of wide and wanton spoil, insular noises of falling rocks would boomingly explode upon the silence and fright all the echoes, which ran shrieking in and out among the caves, as wailing women and children in some assaulted town.

This is, if I may insist on the term, putative description. It asserts itself to be description and passes for description until it is looked into, when you see that it is primarily the *assertion* of an emotional relation to landscape, and through effects of which landscape is incapable. Its force depends on the looseness, vagueness, and tumultuousness of the motion of the words. As a matter of fact, the words are so chosen and arranged that they cannot contribute any material of emotion beyond that which may be contained in a stock exclamation. The primary point of our comparison is that the second passage dilutes and wastes an emotion assumed to have existed prior to its expression, whereas the first passage built up and united the elements of an emotion which exists only and actually in the words employed. The first passages discovers its meaning in words, the second never reached the condition of meaning. The first passage reminds you of Gerard Hopkins, the second, of Ann Radcliffe; and this contrast brings up the secondary point of our comparison.

The spirit of the Gothic novel ran frothily through the popular literature of America in the first half of the nineteenth century, ending possibly with its own travesty in "The Black Crook." Melville, faced with the bad necessity, as it must have seemed to him, of popularizing the material of "Pierre" and "Moby Dick," adopted outright the Gothic convention of language with all its archaisms and rhetorical inflations. He thought that was how it was done. The effect in the two books was similar in fact though not quite the same in effect. Some of the soliloquies in

"Moby Dick" seem more like tantrums than poetry, but they were the tantrums of a great imagination fed with mastered material. In "Pierre," without any fund of nourishing material, the dialogues, soliloquies, and meditations get lost in the flatulence of words.

Now, the Gothic convention is not insusceptible of reality in itself, as we see in Beckford and Peacock and Emily Brontë—perhaps in Poe and occasionally in Hawthorne—but it requires on the part of the author unconditional assent to it as a convention. This assent Melville could not give; he used it, so far as I can see, as a solemn fraud and hoped for the best. In "Moby Dick" the fraud passed preliminary muster because the lofty "unreal" terror that rode the *Pequod* made it seem at least plausible, even in its greatest extravagance, as a vehicle of response. And there is the further defense, often made, that the worst excesses of language and sentiment are excusable because of the poetry they are supposed to hold. To this the answer is that the poetry would have been better without the excess; when Melville dropped the mode and wrote in language comparable to the passage first quoted above, as in Ahab's last soliloquy, better poetry was actually produced. But no one, so far as I know, unless it be Foster Damon, who writes *con amore* of anything both American and Gothic, has defended the excesses of "Pierre," of which the passage quoted above is a tame example.

It may be said in passing that what is often called the Elizabethan influence in Melville's prose might more accurately be called the Gothic influence heightened by the greatness of Melville's intentions. If I may have the notation for what it is worth, I suspect that in "the three boats swung over the sea like three samphire baskets over high cliffs," while the samphire baskets undoubtedly came from "King Lear," still they had got well spattered with Gothic mire on the long journey. Again, the sister-brother crux in "Pierre," while it may be found in John Ford, has a very different reality of expression from that in Ford's verse.

> "The menacings in thy eyes are dear delights to me; I grow up with thy own glorious stature; and in thee, my brother, I see God's indignant ambassador to me, saying—Up, up, Isabel, and take no terms from the common world, but do thou make terms to it, and grind thy fierce rights out of it! Thy catching nobleness unsexes me, my brother; and now I know that in her most exalted moment, then woman no more feels the twin-born softness of her breasts, but feels chain-armour palpitating there!"

These lines, spoken by Isabel in response to similar declarations on the part of Pierre on the occasion of their second conversation, could not have been matched in Ford, but they could be matched a hundred times in the popular Gothics. As for the minor effects of Elizabethan influence, although it has been said, by Mumford among others, that Melville's prose is Websterian—and perhaps it sometimes is—yet it far more often supplies us with Marlovian tropes. For every phrase such as "the cheeks of his soul collapsed in him," there are a dozen on the tone of the following: "With a frigate's anchors for my bridle-bitts and fasces of harpoons for spurs, would I could mount that whale and leap the topmost skies. . .!" This is the Marlowe of "Tamburlaine," and the unregenerate Marlowe letting himself go, not the Marlowe, remolded and compacted, of "Faustus" and "The Jew of Malta." Occasionally there is such a triumphant meeting of rhetoric and insight as the passage which contains the famous phrases: "To trail the genealogies of these high mortal miseries, carries us at last among the sourceless primogenitures of the gods,"—a passage more mindful of the "Urn Burial" than of anything in "The Duchess of Malfi," but most mindful of Melville himself.

If it was the Gothic excess that gave occasional opportunity for magnificent flashes, we should be grateful to it that much: it is at least a delight by the way; but it far more often produced passages like the speech of Isabel, which are perhaps collector's items, but not delights. Besides, what is most and finally illuminating, when Melville really had something to say, and was not *making* a novel, he resorted to another mode, which was perhaps the major expressive mode of his day, the mode of the liberal Emersonian sermon, the moral apologue on the broad Christian basis. There Melville's natural aptitude lay; when he preaches he is released, and only then, of all weak specifications. That the sermon was, to say the best of it, an artificial mode in fiction, mattered nothing, and emphasizes the fact that Melville was only a novelist betimes. He made only the loosest efforts to tie his sermons into his novels; he was quite content if he could see that his novels illustrated his sermons and was reasonably content if they did not; or so the books would show. He preached without scruple, and with full authority, because he felt in full command of the mode he used: he believed with all his heart in its convention of structure and the deeper convention of its relation to society. Father Mapple's sermon on Jonah and Plotinus Phinlimmon's lecture—it is really a sermon—on Chronometricals and Horologicals are the two sustained examples of self-complete form in his work. The doctrine might not have appealed to Channing or Parker; but the form, the execution, the litheness and vigor and verve, the homely aptnesses, the startling comparisons, the lucidity of presentation of hard insights, the dramatic and pictorial quality of the illustrations, and above all the richness of impact and the weighted speed of the words, would have appealed to them as near perfection.

The curiosity that needs emphasis here is that the vices of Melville's style either disappeared or revealed themselves as virtues when he shifted his mode to the sermon, and this without any addition of insight or eloquence, but simply, I believe, because he had found a mode which suited the bent of his themes, which allowed the putative statement to reach its full glory without further backing, which made room for rhetoric and demanded digression, and which did not trouble him, so great was his faith in it, with its universal lurking insincerity. Consider the following lines, which form the counter-sermon to Phinlimmon's lecture in "Pierre."

> All profound things, and emotions of things are preceded and attended by silence. What a silence is that with which the pale bride precedes the responsive *I will*, to the priest's solemn question, *Wilt thou have this man for thy husband?* In silence, too, the wedded hands are clasped. Yea, in silence the child Christ was born into the world. Silence is the general consecration of the universe. Silence is the invisible laying on of the Divine Pontiff's hands upon the world. Silence is at once the most harmless and the most awful thing in all nature. It speaks of the Reserved Forces of Fate. Silence is the only Voice of our God.
>
> Nor is this so august Silence confined to things simply touching or grand. Like the air, Silence permeates all things, and produces its magical power, as well during that peculiar mood which prevails at a solitary traveller's first setting forth on a journey, as at the unimaginable time when before the world was, Silence brooded on the face of the waters.

The author of these paragraphs was at home in his words and completely mastered by them; and he had reached in that language, what Pierre never reached, the "sense of uncapitulatable security, which is only the possession of the furthest advanced and profoundest souls."

[From "The Troubled Mind"]

F. O. Matthiessen*

In 'Benito Cereno' Melville built his effect out of ambiguity in the Jamesian sense. He made the tension depend on how the sinister situation on the Spanish ship slowly comes to penetrate the consciousness of the trusting and obtuse Yankee captain. The way the captain's mind sidles round and round the facts, almost seeing them at one moment only to be ingenuously diverted at the next, prefigures also something of Conrad's method in working up to a crisis. But at the time of *Pierre* Melville was incapable of manipulating any such studied device. He had already stated that there were depths in Ahab beyond the reach of his words; but he now realized more painfully that 'the strongest and fiercest emotions of life defy all analytical insight.' Yet no matter how hard it might prove to discern psychological causation, he was determined to 'follow the endless, winding way,—the flowing river in the cave of man; careless whither I be led, reckless where I land.' In *The Scarlet Letter* Hawthorne had spoken of how, 'at some inevitable moment, will the soul of the sufferer be dissolved, and flow forth in a dark, but transparent stream, bringing all its mysteries into the daylight.'

*Reprinted from *American Renaissance: Art and Expression in the Age of Emerson and Whitman* (New York: Oxford University Press, 1941), pp. 476–87.

The difference between the two images is symptomatic. It marks the divergence between Hawthorne's deliberate darkening of the shadows for the sake of intensified high lights, and Melville's involuntary horror at what he encountered as he penetrated the dark, and ambiguity dissolved into obscurity. The difference in emotional voltage behind the images, the difference involved in Melville's throwing himself helplessly open to the workings of his unconscious mind, accounts for the fact that it was in him and not in Hawthorne that Lawrence found expression of 'the extreme transitions of the isolated far-driven soul.'

Moreover, in spite of all wildness and incoherence, Melville was still grappling closely in *Pierre* with Shakespeare's 'contraries.' He may have been driven no less than his hero to the verge of collapse by the inscrutability of existence. He may have been sick with doubts not only about the world, but even about the divine element within himself. But he was still translating Shakespeare into his own language and time. And his oblique American approach enabled him to see and confront ambiguities in *Hamlet* which no Englishman was then facing, and which were not to be apprehended again with such dynamic fierceness until after Freud's investigation of the Oedipus-complex.

This is what gives coherence and significance to the many parallels between the novel and the play. These are to be traced through nearly all the characters: Lucy's pale innocence fails Pierre as Ophelia's did Hamlet; the well-named Reverend Mr. Falsgrave's cushioned voice of worldly policy is not unlike the platitudinizing of Polonius; Charlie Millthorpe plays a kind of Horatio; Glen Stanly confronts Pierre's seemingly mad violence with the decisiveness of Laertes. But the crucial relation here as in *Hamlet* is that of son and mother. Pierre's father has died when their only child was twelve, and his mother has grown to treat him more like a younger brother than a son. The current of tenderness between them, now that Mary Glendinning is 'not very far from her grand climacteric,' has unconsciously flowed almost into that of lovers.

Pierre's tragedy is caused by the shattering of the spotless image that he had preserved of his father. Isabel's arrival on the scene, her uncanny likeness to the sketch of his father as a young bachelor, her confused memories of her orphaned childhood are agonizingly pieced together by Pierre into the pattern of a liaison and desertion. Worse still, once 'the long-cherished image' of his father has been 'transfigured before him from a green foliaged tree into a blasted trunk,' once his youthful and middle-aged portraits are seen as unlike as those of Hamlet's father and uncle, every other image in Pierre's mind begins to fluctuate and alter. He knows without mentioning them to her that his mother will not endure the new facts; he sees her as no longer lovely, but haughty and selfish, determined to preserve privileged appearances at all cost. He has previously felt that Lucy's pure radiance was so unearthly that marriage with her would be almost 'an impious thing.' He can certainly tell her nothing about what has happened. He is thrown back entirely on his own resources, and quickly decides that he can take Isabel under his protection only by pretending that he has married her. But from that act results an ambiguity worse than all the others. Pierre has aspired to an inhuman ideal which he cannot sustain. Even at the outset he has felt that 'never, never would he be able to embrace Isabel with the mere brotherly embrace; while the thought of any other caress . . . was entirely vacant from his uncontaminated soul, for it had never consciously intruded there.' Yet, in spite of his belief that he is acting wholly unselfishly, he has broken away from a sister-mother to become involved with a sister-wife.

Since little is known about Melville's own childhood and youth, his biographers have drawn heavily on *Pierre*; and since Melville's father died when he was twelve, they have concluded that Mary Glendinning is to be taken as an exact likeness of Maria Gransevoort Melville. This interpretation neglects such items as that Melville was not an only child but the third among eight, that his mother was not left in sheltered affluence at her husband's death, that none of her sons killed her by marrying a half-sister or even by writing *Pierre*, in which she recognized no insulting portrait of herself, since she remained in correspondence with her son Herman until her death when he was beyond fifty. The travesty of trying to make fiction into autobiography is that it oversimplifies and thus distorts the creative process; it jumps without warrant from the life of the soul to that of outer events, for that is what is involved in the translation of symbolic fantasies into literal happenings. It is by no means impossible that Melville felt an incestuous attraction to one of his sisters, but we prove nothing by assuming that he did. It is apparent that the author of *Pierre* was tormented by the ambiguity of sexual relations as they revealed the impossibility of ideal truth. The search for certainty and authority may be understood as a phase of the search for a lost father. But since such connections are hard enough for a trained scientist to make when analyzing a living patient who furnishes him evidence for months, harder for even Freud with a dead man like Leonardo da Vinci, it is impossible for a literary critic to produce more than long-shot hunches in trying to get at an author's particular conflicts through his novels or plays. What the critic is in a position to know best are the complex transformations involved in any imaginative creation; and the slightest acquaintance with psychoanalysis should teach him how intricate is the technique required to interpret biographically the ambivalent symbols of even the simplest dream. This is not to maintain that a man's writing does not distill the essential qualities from his inner life; and it would be absurd to deny that a scientist could make a challenging, if hypothetical case-history out of what is known of Melville's biography and the indirect light cast upon it by his books.[1] But a generation of amateur efforts on the part of critics have served largely to explain away rather than to explain works of art. And in the case of Melville, it must be repeated, these have tended so far to deflect from any comprehensive study of the works, and to compensate with no reliable biography, owing to the loose liberties that have been taken with the known facts.

What a critic can gain from Freudian theory is a very comprehensive kind of description of human norms and processes, an incalculably great asset in interpreting patterns of character and meaning. What can be learned directly from *Pierre* is that much material had surged up into Melville's mind, of the sort that remains unconscious for most authors, and was not allowed to ripple the surface of Victorian literature. It is no longer shocking to observe Melville's pained awareness of an Oedipus-relation, or even of the latent homosexuality in Pierre's boyhood attachment to his cousin Glen, for we now know that such elements are usual in a human being's evolution. Why their hidden memories rose to plague Melville during the writing of *Pierre* is fairly clear from the text itself. When Pierre starts feverishly to write, Melville comments that he had 'not as yet procured for himself that enchanter's wand of the soul, which but touching the humblest experiences in one's life, straightway it starts up all eyes, in every one of which are endless significancies. Not yet had he dropped his angle into the well of his childhood, to find what fish might be there; for who dreams to find fish in a well?'

But that is exactly what Melville himself had now done. In his determination to penetrate the mask of appearance even more deeply than he had in *Moby-Dick*, to drive even farther down to primary levels of experience,[2] he had found himself surrounded by corridors of 'endless significancies' opening in all directions, with only hazy vistas at their ends. He had made the very dangerous discovery he was to proclaim in *The Confidence Man*, that to portray a consistent character in fiction is to be untrue to life; that no matter whether shallow critics declare that an author 'should represent human nature not in obscurity, but transparency,' nevertheless he who says of human nature what 'is said of the divine nature, that it is past finding out,' thereby evinces a better appreciation of its mysterious contrasts. To be sure, he went on to firmer ground in that discussion, for he added that the greatest 'psychological novelists . . . challenge astonishment at the tangled web of some character, and then raise admiration still greater at their satisfactory unravelling of it.' Thus they prove their rare mastery of the truth that, despite all twistings and apparent confusions, 'the grand points of human nature are the same to-day they were a thousand years ago.'

Melville insisted on that universality also in *Pierre*. He explicitly stated that the tragedy of Memnon, ' "the flower of virtue cropped by a too rare mischance," ' was an ancient *Hamlet*, and thus implied that *Pierre* could be a modern one. Yet he encountered great difficulty in objectifying his own sufferings. Especially when Pierre started to be an author, Melville could not keep the boy of nineteen separate from himself at thirty-two, from the man who was finishing his seventh book in as many years, and who, to judge from the texture of its thought and writing, was not only discouraged but nearly exhausted. While still engaged with *Moby-Dick* he had cried out to Hawthorne: 'Try to get a living by the Truth—and go to the Soup Societies.' Now he had no hesitation in saying that Pierre, in his lonely room, was embarked on 'that most miserable of all the pursuits of a man.' He added too what the general misunderstanding of *Moby-Dick* was just teaching him: 'He shall now learn, and very bitterly learn, that though the world worship Mediocrity and Commonplace, yet hath it fire and sword for all contemporary Grandeur; that though it swears that it fiercely assails all Hypocrisy, yet hath it not always an ear for Earnestness.'

Melville could not keep the contours of his hero distinct from this heart-knowledge of his own. What Eliot has remarked about *Hamlet* might be applied to *Pierre*, that it gives the impression of being full of some 'intractable' stuff which its writer could not 'manipulate into art.' Although the sexual problems have become more explicit in Melville's meditation over Shakespeare than in the play itself, further ambiguities are introduced by the contrast between Lucy and Isabel. This contrast corresponds to nothing in *Hamlet*, but goes back to the symbolic abstractions of Yillah and Hautia. Once again the difference between fair and dark is subjected to a variety of interpretations. The two seem to stand for ideal love and earthly passion, or as Isabel wretchedly says, they are Pierre's good and bad angels. But the contrast is not left so clear-cut as it is, say, in Shakespeare's *Sonnets*. For Isabel is obviously not evil. Pierre's presentiment at first seeing her is cast in the familiar Melvillian terms of the difference between the peaceful land in which Pierre has been living and the dangerous waters that lie ahead: 'He felt that what he had always before considered the solid land of veritable reality, was now being audaciously encroached upon by bannered armies of hooded phantoms, disembarking in his soul, as from flotillas of spectre-boats.' But Isabel is no Fedallah. She is a child of nature to whom the policy of the world is unknown. She feels rather than thinks, and it strikes her that she will always continue to be a child, no matter how old she lives to be. Yet there is an imploring anguish in her beauty, in her expression compounded 'of hell and heaven.' She has suffered desperately in being alone, and wants to absorb life, or rather, to be absorbed into it, for she feels that 'there can be no perfect peace in individualness.'

In the chaotic state of mind that led Melville to say, 'Let the ambiguous procession of events reveal their own ambiguousness,' the theme of 'Isabel and mystery' was diffused to insufferable lengths. Some of its less controlled elements may have been stimulated by Sylvester Judd's rhapsodic descriptions of his heroine Margaret, whose shadowy childhood memories are not unlike Isabel's.[3] But in spite of all such extravagant qualities as her preternatural 'magnetic power,' the crux of her relation to Pierre is unmistakable: she has bound him to her from the start by an attraction that is both spiritual and physical, and which will prove impossible for him to deny.

On the other hand, Lucy is all light. As Pierre tells her at the outset, she belongs 'to the regions of an infinite day.' But even in his inexperience before meeting Isabel, he senses something inhuman in such unrelieved whiteness, in the fact that Lucy is almost angelic in her lack of 'vulgar vigor.' The news of his supposed marriage throws her into a swoon, and then into a nearly mortal illness. But as she rallies, she is made still more unearthly by her grief. She determines to join Pierre and Isabel in the city, for she says that she can live only for him, that she asks no visible response, but trusts only that her love will triumph in heaven. A terrifying quality creeps into such virtue. She is sustained by her self-sacrifice, which is so complete that she does not even feel that she is making a renunciation. Her action, nevertheless, brings on the final tragedy. The very fact of her presence drives Isabel into jealousy and desperation. It also goads Lucy's brother to join Glen Stanly in taking drastic steps against Pierre, whom they now judge to be the worst of seducers. Moreover, when Lucy at last learns the secret, when she sees Isabel embrace Pierre and call him not husband but brother, she is killed by the shock.

It would be profitless to pursue all the ramifications of these symbols, since they are not really created into living characters, but are dispersed in metaphysical clouds. Melville came nearest to condensing his meaning into dramatic form through the dream of Enceladus, the dream that Pierre had during the state of debilitated torpor produced by his final unsuccessful struggles with his book. In this dream Pierre remembered how, in the purple haze of distance, the mountain at Saddle Meadows had seemed to live up to its old name of the Delectable Mountain; but that if he went near, its unexpected crags and savage precipices, its stark and ruinous desolation justified its being called the Mount of the Titans. In addition to this fit symbol for the differences between anticipation and the event, Pierre remembered too how among these vast rocks was one formation that had struck him as looking like Enceladus, 'the most potent of all the giants, writhing from out the imprisoning earth,' and, though armless, 'still turning his unconquerable front toward that majestic mount eternally in vain assailed by him.' But in the dream this form was no longer frozen into rocky stasis. He sprang as leader of the Titans in their assault upon heaven, and 'despairing of any other mode of wreaking his immitigable hate, turned his vast trunk into a battering-ram, and hurled his own arched-out ribs again and yet again against the invulnerable steep.' In the moment when Pierre saw this leader's anguished face, he recognized it as his own. 'With trembling frame he started from his chair, and woke from that ideal horror to all his actual grief.'

Melville's comment was that Pierre did not wrest the final comfort from the fable that he might have, that just as Enceladus was the incestuous offspring of Titan and his mother Terra, herself the incestuous wife of her son Coelus,

> even thus, there had been born from the organic blended heavenliness and earthliness of Pierre, another mixed, uncertain, heaven-aspiring, but still not wholly earth-emancipated mood; which again, by its terrestrial taint held down to its terrestrial mother, generated there the present doubly incestuous Enceladus within him; so that the present mood of Pierre—that reckless sky-assaulting mood of his, was nevertheless on one side the grandson of the sky. For it is according to eternal fitness, that the precipitated Titan should still seek to regain his paternal birthright even by fierce escalade. Wherefore whoso storms the sky gives best proof he came from thither! But whatso crawls contented in the moat before that crystal fort, shows it was born within that slime, and there forever will abide.

But such reflections could hardly have given much comfort to Pierre in his final headlong disasters. And though the meaning of the fable seems secure within its context, when you try to square its implications with the somewhat different incests in Pierre's life, or with the contrasting doctrine of Plinlimmon's pamphlet, you find yourself caught in multiplying the ambiguities still further. You can better discern what had been Melville's emotional center in his contrast between Lucy and Isabel through a minor passage in the dream. The pastures by the Delectable Mountain had been increasingly invaded by 'a small white amaranthine flower,' inodorous and sterile, and 'irreconcilably distasteful to the cattle.' It seemed to the disheartened tenants that this flower was immortal, since every year the pastures grew more glitteringly white. Only here and there you might still catch the sweet aroma of clumps of catnip, 'that dear farm-house herb.' Yet 'every spring the amaranthine and celestial flower gained on the mortal household herb; for every autumn the catnip died, but never an autumn made the amaranth to wane. The catnip and the amaranth! —man's earthly household peace, and the ever-encroaching appetite for God.'

Melville makes no clumsy parallel to Lucy's whiteness; and there are many guises in which Isabel, despite her longing for the immobility 'of some plant, absorbing life without seeking it,' is anything but a peaceful herb. Yet what had bothered Melville ever since he began to think about the differences between the sensuous instinctual life of the savages and the tortures of the aspiring mind and spirit became part of the contrast between the two girls. Pierre seems to need them both, but far below any conscious awareness, he is drawn most naturally to the dark life-giving forces of Isabel, the forces that were being so atrophied by the incessant pale American search for the ideal.

Although the Enceladus myth is one of the few symbols in the book that seem really under control, there is no denying the amount of extraordinary writing. It is hard always to be sure of its intention. Melville himself declared, 'I write precisely as I please,' and reiterated the conviction which had come upon him in *Mardi*, that genius is full of trash.[4] His manner is frequently so reckless that Shakespearean scraps get out of hand and go into hysterical seizures; and what may start as telling irony generally breaks down into facetiousness. The chief trouble is the lack of any norm. Beside one of Arnold's sentences, 'It is comparatively a small matter to express oneself well, if one will be content with not expressing much, with expressing only trite ideas,' Melville was to write 'G.W.C.' which would refer most appropriately to George William Curtis, one of the milder young men of Brook Farm, subsequently the author of *Nile Notes of a Howadji* (1851) and *Prue and I* (1856), who as editor of *Putnam's* once counselled Melville to study Addison in order to improve his work. As Arnold held, and Melville noted, 'The problem is to express new and profound ideas in a perfectly sound and classical style.' What Arnold observed in the English writers of the day was the lack of any such balance. He put it down to the unfavorable atmosphere, to the want of a clarified tradition, a state that tended 'to make even a man of great ability either a Mr. Carlyle or else a Lord Macaulay.' Melville marked that sentence too, as well he might; for he had labored with far less semblance of any tradition. At least Carlyle's mannerisms, however lugged-in from the German, were intentional; whereas Melville in *Pierre* was often obviously at a loss how to handle the radical material he wanted to express.

He was capable of producing passages of an electric intensity, the passages that testify to what Lawrence meant by saying that Melville gave him the sense of being almost played out in 'his human-emotional self,' of being 'abstract, self-analytical and abstracted,' almost over the verge into pathology; but that on that verge he could portray the full fierceness of anguish. Such a passage is the one where Pierre receives Lucy's letter saying that she is coming to join them: and the swiftly varying prose reaches into every interstice of his tangled reactions:

> He held the artless, angelical letter in his unrealising hand; he started, and gazed round his room, and out at the window, commanding the bare, desolate, all-forbidding quadrangle, and then asked himself whether this was the place that an angel should choose for its visit to earth. Then he felt a vast, out-swelling triumphantness, that the girl whose rare merits his intuitive soul had once so clearly and passionately discerned, should indeed, in this most tremendous of all trials, have acquitted herself with such infinite majesty. Then again, he sunk utterly down from her, as in a bottomless gulf, and ran shuddering through hideous galleries of despair, in pursuit of some vague, white shape, and lo! two unfathomable dark eyes met his, and Isabel stood mutely and mournfully, yet all-ravishingly before him.

Such a pitch could not possibly be sustained as a norm.[5] Melville was so helplessly open to his emotions that he sometimes could not find language distinguishable from that of the magazine-shocker: ' "Curses, wasp-like, cohere on that villain, Ned, and sting him to his death!'" cried Pierre, smit by this most piteous tale.' Harder to place is some of the diction in the opening section, the many clichés, the heaped-up jargon of such needlessly ugly inventions as 'diamondness,' 'amaranthiness,' 'descendedness.' It is even harder to be certain what Melville intended in the first passages between Pierre and Lucy. They read in part like a forecast of the ejaculative idyll of young love that Meredith was to handle between his Lucy and Richard Feverel half a dozen years later. But often they give the impression that Melville was so tormented by the thought of what lay ahead for his hero that he could not help mocking his own lyricism. The result, from the author of *Moby-Dick*, was incredible: confused insecurity of intention could reduce his voice to an impotent echo of the *Lady's Book*: 'Love is both Creator's and Saviour's gospel to mankind; a volume bound in rose-leaves, clasped with violets, and by the beaks of humming-birds printed with peach-juice on the leaves of lilies. Endless is the account of Love'—and so on, without undercutting, to the end of the chapter.

The most powerful section in the book, the first night of Pierre and Isabel's arrival in the city, may owe its greater steadiness to Melville's having had a partial model in the flight of Clifford and Hepzibah. That is not to say that Melville's effect is not peculiarly his own, the quality of a heart-breaking nightmare wherein trusting inexperience is shattered against the hardness of a world in which only money opens doors.

At the outset of his hero's trouble, Melville addressed him: 'Ay, Pierre . . . for thee, the before undistrusted moral beauty of the world is forever fled; for thee, thy sacred father is no more a saint; all brightness hath gone from thy hills, and all peace from thy plains; and now, now, for the first time, Pierre, Truth rolls a black billow through thy soul! Ah, miserable thou, to whom Truth, in her first tides, bears nothing but wrecks!' That imagery goes back not only to *Moby-Dick* but also to *Mardi*; and Pierre enacts the 'utter wreck' that Taji dreaded and yet challenged. It is impossible to write tragedy if you feel an ambiguity in all distinctions between virtue and vice, if in your hopelessness about human misery, you can take joy only in the fact that 'death is a democrat.' Nevertheless, if *Pierre* is a failure, it must be accounted a great one, a failure in an effort to express as honestly as possible what it meant to undergo the test 'of a real impassioned onset of Life and Passion.' The importance of such an effort may be grasped in the contrast between two variations on the same theme. To instance the inevitability of man's fate, Emerson remarked: 'I seemed in the height of a tempest to see men overboard struggling in the waves, and driven about here and there. They glanced intelligently at each other, but 'twas little they could do for one another; 'twas much if each could keep afloat alone. Well, they had a right to their eye-beams, and all the rest was Fate.' To those to whom such easy acceptance seems inhuman, Melville's surcharged words about Pierre come with the relief of uninhibited passion: 'For in tremendous extremities human souls are like drowning men; well enough they know they are in peril; well enough they know the causes of that peril; nevertheless, the sea is the sea, and these drowning men do drown.'

Notes

1. Such a study has been under preparation for some time by Dr. Harry Murray of the Harvard Psychological Clinic.

2. He wrote to Hawthorne in the fall of 1851: 'Lord, when shall we be done growing? As long as we have anything more to do, we have done nothing. So, now, let us add Moby-Dick to our blessing, and step from that. Leviathan is not the biggest fish;—I have heard of Krakens [the fabulous Scandinavian sea-monsters].' That harks back to his letter of the spring before, which had likened the miracle of his growth since his twenty-fifth year to that of 'one of those seeds taken out of the Egyptian Pyramids, which, after being three thousand years a seed and nothing but a seed, being planted in English soil, it developed itself, grew to greenness, and then fell to mould.'

3. Melville had borrowed *Margaret: A Tale of the Real and Ideal, Blight and Bloom*, from Duyckinck in the summer of 1850, when, incidentally, he had also borrowed Thoreau's *Week*.

4. He also checked, in *The Seven Gables*, Holgrave's remark, 'I begin to suspect that a man's bewilderment is the measure of his wisdom.'

5. Even more violent is the concluding sentence to Pierre's first verification of his presentiment of Isabel's identity: 'He could not stay in his chamber; the house contracted to a nutshell around him; the walls smote his forehead; bare-headed he rushed from the place, and only in the infinite air, found scope for that boundless expansion of his life.'

Out of its context another final sentence, that of the chapter in which Pierre struggles towards his decision to act, is so extravagant in its verbal action that it is almost over the border into burlesque: 'The cheeks of his soul collapsed in him; he dashed himself in blind fury and swift madness against the wall, and fell dabbling in the vomit of his loathed identity.'

The Early Love Scenes
in Melville's *Pierre*

William Braswell*

Ever since its publication in 1852, Herman Melville's *Pierre; or, The Ambiguities* has been a difficult problem for critics interested in judging it as a work of art. A major difficulty, of course, lies in the author's having been in such an extraordinary state at the time he conceived and wrote the novel that critics have been unable to determine just what he intended it to be. He apparently had a composite purpose. Judging from present critical opinion, however, it seems likely that much more criticism of the

*Reprinted from *American Literature*, 22 (November 1950), 283–89.

novel will be written before a generally satisfactory conclusion can be reached as to precisely what his intentions were and how *Pierre* should be ranked as a work of art.

The obscurity of Melville's purpose has, in my opinion, made some of his most distinguished and most sympathetic critics condemn certain features of the novel unjustly. Failure to appreciate the "wild, heroic sort of levity"[1] that was among factors influencing the conception and composition of *Pierre* has, I believe, led to misconceptions about Melville as an artist.

Many critics, for instance, have deplored the peculiarities of language in *Pierre* as indicative of a sudden lapse in Melville's power as a writer, saying that the genius with words which contributed so greatly to the majesty of *Moby-Dick* here often manifested itself in oddities and excesses that mar the style. With no desire to appear the chivalric defender of Melville's eccentricities as a writer, and certainly with no desire to make faults appear virtues, I am constrained nevertheless to argue that the peculiarities of style are due not to a loss of skill that prevented his doing what he wanted to do, but to his consciously and deliberately giving free rein to an ebullient and assimilative inventive faculty, to his putting the tall style of *Moby-Dick* on stilts, as it were, when it suited his strange mood to do so. There is no norm, complains one critic.[2] Perhaps it would be more precise to say that Melville's norm was too elastic to please most readers. I feel sure that he consciously changed his technique and tone to accord with his intentions: hence the occasional overtones not only of Shakespeare, Carlyle, DeQuincey, and other masters of English poetry and prose, but also of melodrama, the penny dreadful, and *Godey's Lady's Book*. Passages in *Pierre* have been praised as among Melville's "finest utterances";[3] the skill he showed in such passages alone is enough in itself to suggest that some of the so-called "lapses" of power elsewhere in the book may possibly appear to be so merely because of the reader's failure to understand the author's purpose.

To cite a specific instance, that part of the novel introducing the youthful Pierre and Lucy in love has been called deplorably bad by critics who, it seems to me, merely failed to perceive Melville's intention in that section. Three of Melville's ablest critics, Lewis Mumford, F. O. Matthiessen, and Henry Murray, have singled out this part of the book for particularly adverse comment. Mumford says that the "mawkish" style becomes "perfumed silk" with the appearance of the two lovers. A sentence quoted from the novel about love's being "a volume bound in rose leaves"—the sentence will be given in full in a moment—prefaces his remark that in style Melville "had suddenly lost both taste and discretion."[4] Matthiessen comments on the difficulty of ascertaining Melville's intention in various places in the novel, and especially in the first passages about Pierre and Lucy. He comes close to discerning Melville's purpose when he says that often these passages "give the impression that Melville was so tormented by what lay ahead for his hero that he could not help mocking his own lyricism"; but he adds that the "result, from the author of *Moby-Dick*, was incredible: confused insecurity of intention could reduce his voice to an impotent echo of the *Lady's Book*," and then he quotes as evidence the same sentence Mumford chose.[5]

Murray, who gives more space to the problem, offers an explanation. He avers that Melville's deficiency in this part of the novel resulted from his voluptuous imagination's being "steeped in the erotic literature of his day"; "the origin of most of the repellent elements in the first two acts of *Pierre*" is the "pitiful religion of the heart that was being promiscuously propagated by novelists of the second and third order during the sentimental decades." He praises two later chapters of *Pierre* as showing Melville to be "the first satirist" of this same literary school: "He deserves first prize for having been eighty-odd years ahead of Branch and other critics even though it is clear that he himself was not wholly free of the tastes and dispositions he was ridiculing."[6]

This judgment raises a disturbing question. How could Melville have discerned the spurious quality of the sentimental romances of his day and have satirized them so mercilessly, and still have been so uncritical as to write in the same novel the same kind of trash? Careful reading shows, it seems to me, that he wrote something quite different. Although he may appear superficially to have been writing like the conventional romancer, there is really a vast difference in his manner. Instead of showing a sudden and inexplicable loss of taste, or the debilitating influence of cheap, sentimental fiction he is known to have thought ridiculous, his style reveals a satirical purpose. One who considers the symbolism of the novel can see that in his highly mannered presentation of the fantastically idyllic love affair at the beginning of the story Melville mocks the cloistered innocence of his own early spiritual life.[7] Here, one might say, is some of the "laughter of self-derision" that William Ellery Sedgwick perceived in the novel.[8] But apart from the inner story, there is ample evidence that Melville found perverse amusement in writing some of these passages.

Exaggeration was one of his favorite humorous devices at that time. In a letter to Mrs. Hawthorne written during the composition of *Pierre*, he jested in an exaggerated manner about Hawthorne's dislike of visiting, saying: "Does Mr. Hawthorne continue his series of calls upon all his neighbors within a radius of ten miles? Shall I send him ten packs of visiting cards?"[9] A similar tendency to overstate characterizes much of his satirical technique in the novel.

Just as he elevates Pierre's social status by way of contrast for the degradation to come, so he exaggerates the felicity of the romantic Eden from which Pierre is to go out into a world of hatred and violence. Consider the description of Pierre's beloved. Now Lucy as a character has fine qualities, and symbolically she plays an important role; yet Melville amuses himself in describing her loveliness. The world, he says, will never see another woman to match her beauty. "Her cheeks are tinted with the most delicate white and red, the white predominating. Her eyes some god brought down from heaven; her hair was Danae's, spangled with Jove's shower; her teeth were dived for in the Persian Sea."[10] After three paragraphs in the same vein on the queenliness of beautiful women, he remarks on the "merry dance" on which he has taken the reader, and then virtually asks the reader to share the fun while he tries to outdo the conventional romancers; the mock-serious tone is heightened by his rising to the cadence of the Psalmist:

> this may seem rather irregular sort of writing. But whither indeed should Lucy Tartan conduct us, but among mighty Queens, and all other creatures of high degree; and finally set us roaming, to see whether the wide world can match so fine a wonder? By immemorial usage, am I not bound to celebrate this Lucy Tartan? Who shall stay me? Is she not my hero's own affianced? What can be gainsaid? Where underneath the tester of the night sleeps such another?

But he despairs of giving an "inventory" of all her charms. "Who shall tell stars as teaspoons? Who shall put down the charms of Lucy Tartan on paper?"[11] With the basis of logic the author's peculiar and somewhat perverse delight, it is quite reasonable that a character described in such extravagant terms should speak in an extravagant manner: hence the fantastic nature of some of the dialogue. When Pierre chides Lucy for not bidding him good morning, she is quite in character when she replies, "That would be little. Good mornings, good evenings, good days, weeks, months, and years to thee, Pierre;—bright Pierre!—Pierre!"[12]

Murray asks to be excused from the mortifying task of quoting the more repellent passages about Lucy and Pierre, saying that Mumford has already done so, but he does cite one offending specimen: "When love is in ascendancy we are offered pretty filagrees of fancy, such as the image of sailors at sea tying 'love-knots on every spangled spar' when they feel 'ineffable distillations of a soft delight' in the morning's breeze."[13] He thereby condemns what the context shows to be an admirable bit of irony.

When Melville flashes this little gem before the reader, he is just getting under way in a long ironical discourse on love. One soon perceives that he is using the word *love* in a very broad sense, so as to include not only the affection of lovers, but also the spirit of beneficence reputed by some philosophers and divines to be an animating principle of the universe. When reading the passage, the reader should keep in mind the agonizing concern shown in *Mardi, Redburn,* and *White Jacket* over the evil in the world, and the diatribe in *Moby-Dick* against the Christian conception of a God of Love. One should also keep in mind that no American author then living, not even Dana, knew better than Melville what a rough, uncouth class of men sailors were. One should remember in particular such characters of his as the mutineers and chief mate in *Omoo*, Jackson in *Redburn*, and the "heathen crew" whelped "by the sharkish sea" in *Moby-Dick*.[14] It is in his description of the lovely day on which Pierre and Lucy ride forth together that Melville lets himself go and, choosing as ridiculous an image as he can visualize, represents hard-boiled sailors as unable to tie any knots but love-knots. As Lucy stands out among women, so this day among days. It is not just *a* beautiful morning:

> That morning was the choicest drop that Time had in his vase. Ineffable distillations of a soft delight were wafted from the fields and hills. Fatal morning that, to all lovers unbetrothed; "Come to your confessional," it cried. "Behold our airy loves," the birds chirped from the trees; far out at sea, no more the sailors tied their bowline-knots; their hands had lost their cunning; will they, nill they, Love tied love-knots on every spangled spar.[15]

One would perhaps appreciate more readily the mockery of the paean on the beauty of the earth that follows this passage if he recalled, together with the total import of *Moby-Dick*, such phrases from the novel as the "horrible vulturism of earth" and "God's great, unflattering laureate, Nature."[16] Again Melville falls into the rhythm of the Hebraic poet: "Oh, praised be the beauty of this earth, the beauty, and the bloom, and the mirthfulness thereof!" He is so pleased with this mock-hosanna that he repeats it at the beginning of the next paragraph. He comes back to Pierre and Lucy long enough to say that "That morning, two bay horses drew two Laughs along the road . . . ," and to present a choice bit of dialogue:

> "Smell I the flowers, or thee?" cried Pierre.
> "See I lakes, or eyes?" cried Lucy, her own gazing down into his soul, as two stars gaze down into a tarn.

Fascinated by the possibilities of farfetched conceits on lovers' eyes, Melville contrives a number of them, such as: "There are not so many fishes in the sea, as there are sweet images in lovers' eyes. In those miraculous translucencies swim the strange eye-fish with wings, that sometimes leap out, instinct with joy; moist fish-wings wet the lover's cheek."

He has not yet finished defining love, however. Now he uses the floral motif in an image that would have appeared precious and saccharine even in a gift-book of that day; this is the sentence that Mumford and Matthiessen unfortunately read as a serious attempt at beautiful prose: "Love is both Creator's and Saviour's gospel to mankind; a volume bound in rose-leaves, clasped with violets, and by the beaks of humming-birds printed with peach-juice on the leaves of lilies." The author who had just created Ahab could not, I submit, have written such a sentence without satirical intent. Anyone who has difficulty understanding the irony of Melville's heaping up of rose leaves, violets, lilies, peach juice, and beaks of hummingbirds in this ludicrous tribute to the Creator's and Savior's gospel of love should turn to a prison scene at the end of the novel, for there he will see the hero blaming the Savior's gospel of love for his own disastrous fall and breathing flames of defiance at the unloving Creator:

> Had I been heartless now, disowned, and spurningly portioned off the girl at Saddle Meadows, then had I been happy through a long life on earth, and perchance through a long eternity in heaven! Now, 'tis merely hell in both worlds. Well, be it hell. I will mold a trumpet of the flames, and, with my breath of flame, breathe back my defiance![17]

Though it is obvious from much he had written earlier that Melville did not share the optimistic Emersonian belief that good is ousting evil from the universe, he says in the opening pages of *Pierre*, with an air of innocence and simple faith: "All things that are sweet to see, or taste, or feel, or hear, all these things were made by Love; and none other things were made by Love. Love made not the Arctic zones, but Love is ever reclaiming them. Say, are not the fierce things of this earth daily, hourly going out?" His delight in this cherubic posturing is indicated by the ridiculous evidence he offers to prove his argument: "Where now are your wolves of Britain? Where in Virginia now, find you the panther and the pard? Oh, Love is busy everywhere." The betrothal of his young lovers suggested another amusing figure to him for presenting the same idea: "All this Earth is Love's affianced; vainly the demon Principle howls to stay the banns. Why round her middle wears this world so rich a zone of torrid verdure, if she be not dressing for the final rites?" And on he goes to other ludicrous conceits.

One hopes, however, that enough has been said to indicate that certain passages which have been criticized as insipidly sentimental are rather mock-romantic, and that there is more irony in the opening chapters than has generally been recognized. Melville's humor in such passages might with some justice be criticized as too esoteric to be generally effective—certainly it has failed to delight some extremely perceptive readers. Furthermore, the appropriateness of his satirical intention might well be questioned: is it fitting that a novelist go so far in mocking a hero to whom he is obviously devoted and for whom he ultimately desires the reader's deepest sympathy?

But censuring Melville on such points would be very different from censuring him for not writing conventional romance in an acceptable manner. Though he might justly be condemned for a perverse use of his undeniably great power as a writer, he should not be condemned for failing to do what he had no intention of doing.

Notes

1. The quoted phrase is from *Israel Potter*, p. 198, where Melville wrote admiringly of the courageous spirit that Ethan Allen showed in adversity. References to Melville's works other than *Pierre* are to the Constable Edition (London, 1922–1924).

2. F.O. Matthiessen, *American Renaissance* (New York, 1941), pp. 484–85.

3. Lewis Mumford, *Herman Melville* (New York, 1929), p. 196.

4. Mumford, pp. 207–08.

5. Matthiessen, p. 486.

6. *Pierre; or, The Ambiguities*, ed. Henry Murray (New York, 1949), pp. xlii–xliii. All subsequent references to *Pierre* are to this text.

7. See William Braswell, *Melville's Religious Thought* (Durham, N.C., 1943), pp. 93–95.

8. *Herman Melville: The Tragedy of Mind* (Cambridge, Mass., 1944), pp. 157 and 163.

9. This letter, dated Jan. 8, 1852, is reproduced in part in a catalogue of an American Art Association sale at the Anderson Galleries, Inc., New York, 1931. [The full text of the letter is reproduced in *The Letters of Herman Melville*, eds. Merrell R. Davis and William H. Gilman (New Haven: Yale University Press, 1960), pp. 145–47. Ed Note.]

10. *Pierre*, p. 26.

11. *Pierre*, pp. 27–28

12. *Pierre*, p. 2

13. *Pierre*, pp. xlii–xliii

14. *Moby-Dick*, I, 211.

15. *Pierre*, p. 26. The remaining quotations on love are from pp. 36–39.

16. *Moby-Dick*, II, 34; I, 236.

17. *Pierre*, p. 424.

[The Growth of the Mind]

Warner Berthoff*

So it is in just these late stages that *Moby-Dick* moves most deliberately toward the mode of allegory. This mutation was not on the whole a happy one for the best exercise of Melville's narrative talent. It appears, however, to have pleased the Hawthornes. Melville was lucky in having two such first readers for *Moby-Dick* as Nathaniel and Sophia Hawthorne; their appreciation was indeed, as he wrote them, a "glorious gratutity." But insofar as they "intimated the part-and-parcel allegoricalness of the whole" to him, and mentioned approvingly the various "particular subordinate allegories," they in effect gave their blessing to what was shakiest in the book's ad hoc structure, and thus to the direction in which its author's ambitions were now carrying him. The terms of their

*Reprinted from *The Example of Melville* (Princeton, N.J.: Princeton University Press, 1962), pp. 46–53.

approval must be acknowledged as having contributed at least indirectly to the overweening misadventure of *Pierre*—upon which Melville now embarked almost without catching breath.

About this misadventure, which was decisive in the progress of his career, there is a certain air of inevitability. We have a few revealing glimpses into Melville's state of mind at this time, at the end of his intense and engrossing labor on *Moby-Dick*—as he talks through the night with Hawthorne of "all possible and impossible matters," or writes Hawthorne the strained, soaring, not wholly coherent letter of mid-November 1851, with its unanswerable questions and its inadmissible assumptions of some extraordinary intimacy or "infinite fraternity of feeling."[1] To Mrs. Morewood in Pittsfield, his condition was very simply a "morbid excitement which will soon injure his health." Her letter to George Duyckinck of December 28, 1851, gives us a symptomatic picture of Melville during the writing of *Pierre*: "now so engaged in a new work as frequently not to leave his room till dark in the evening when he for the first time during the whole day partakes of solid food. . . ."

At this climax of his explosive inward growth, two apprehensions took command of his thought—first, that he now fully understood the order of the world's existence, and had therefore some power of imaginative ascendancy over it; but, also, that he now fully understood the accidental, contingent nature of his own particular being, his profoundest mind and soul, and therefore had no real independence of action at all. The first apprehension made him bold to strike harder and probe deeper than ever yet at the very "axis of reality," in the way that seemed to him to define the special genius of Shakespeare. The second taught him that he had no real position to strike from, or at least none from which he could gain the one kind of hearing that now seemed worthwhile—among that "aristocracy of the brain" to which he confessed to Hawthorne his own sense of a calling, or in "that small but high hushed world" which he had made Ishmael declare himself "not unreasonably ambitious of." His will to create and control was eroded by self-doubts; his confidence in his powers as a writer was beset by all the "thousand inconceivable finicalnesses of small pros and cons about imaginary fitnesses, and proprieties, and self-consistencies" that much of *Pierre*, in just this overwrought idiom, is exhaustively devoted to.

Yet not even in *Pierre* did the rush of Melville's presumption, or the anguish of doubt, overset his imagination's fundamental honesty and objectivity. He held as doggedly to "truth" in piecing out this most confessional of his books as he had in documenting the naval service or the whaling industry. "With no son of man," he truthfully enough told Hawthorne, "do I stand upon any etiquette or ceremony"—and least of all with himself. The determining subject of *Pierre* corresponds to his own most pressing personal history, for it is "that maturer and larger interior

development" within his hero which is predicated in so many words at the
outset of the main narrative.[2] In composing *Pierre* Melville laid his hand
to various means of emphasis and elaboration—analogies with the history
of Christ, allusions to the *Inferno* and *Hamlet*, intimations from transcendentalist philosophy and the myths of Memnon and Enceladus, not to
mention a dreary assortment of stock Romantic emblems (mirrors and
portraits, a mystic guitar, fair and dark female angels, and so on)—and
all of this has resulted in as many philosophical, allegorical, and psycho-
biographical interpretations as may be imagined. But his main theme is
Pierre's development in natural consciousness and insight, and the good
writing in the book is never far off it. For literary history, then, the
significant fact is simply that at this extremity of personal crisis Melville
plunged, in his first essay outside the form of first-person narrative, into
the prime Romantic subject of the "growth of the mind." And though his
inward agitation and his inordinate personal stake in the undertaking
wrecked the book formally, they also were what gave it its almost saving
virtues—the "force and subtlety of thinking and unity of purpose" praised
by the *Graham's* reviewer, and intermittently a passionate exactness of
psychological notation which can bear comparison with its great Romantic prototype, *The Prelude*.

From a secure base in first-person narrative Melville had improvised
for most of *Moby-Dick* a spectacularly effective formal solution. But the
apparatus of Romantic melodrama that he now turned to proved un-
reconcilable with his deeper purposes in what he chose to call "this book
of sacred truth." The odd divisions and sub-divisions of the novel speak
for Melville's difficulties. There are twenty-six "Books," so-called, of
which several run to fewer than ten pages, while others are broken into
half a dozen or more sub-sections; also, there is an immoderate use of
short-winded, discontinuous paragraphing, as if the narrative was
repeatedly gathering itself for some radical new departure. If anything
good can be said of this structure, it might be of the abrupt transitions it
makes possible into exploratory metaphor and analogy, such as in long
stretches of *Pierre* wholly supersede narrative incident. By these inter-
polations Melville seeks, as it were, to canvass the surrounding possibilities, and to generalize the meager and usually implausible events of the
story and assert their participation in some broadly significant order of
things. I am not thinking here of set-piece digressions like the Enceladus
passage or Plinlimmon's pamphlet on "chronometricals and horologicals." I have in mind rather the fitful, tangent-following succession of
short metaphoric paragraphs, or of overloaded single sentences and
clauses, in which themes and ideas never quite satisfactorily embodied in
the fantastic action of the novel come boiling up from below.[3] But this
kind of structure, and the style that carries it forward, would at best be
suitable only to some other genre, such as the long Wordsworthian narra-
tive-reflective poem, in which the job would be to represent a uniform

series of moral and psychological incidents with sensuous force and precision, rather than to round out a coherent story. The organization of *Pierre*
is really not dramatic at all, but at once lyrical and expository. The book
proceeds by strophe and antistrophe—Melville was in fact to grow so im-
patient of his plot that at one late juncture a new sequence of "most
momentous events" is simply dropped onto the page in outline form (xxi,
ii). Even the grotesquely inventive vocabulary of *Pierre*, with its par-
ticipial nouns and adverbs and its bizarre coinages ("slidings," "slopings,"
"overlayingly," "perennialness," "universalness," "smilingness," "trans-
mittedness," "vacant whirlingness of the bewilderingness," and the like),
is a poet's vocabulary, aimed at some ideal denomination of its subjects
according to their determinative mode of being. The effect of this
vocabulary is mostly disastrous. But it is fair to note that magnificent
precedent for at least one of its idiosyncrasies may be found, again, in
Wordsworth:

> . . . those obstinate questionings
> Of sense and outward things,
> Fallings from us, vanishings,
> Blank misgivings. . . .

With a work as freakish as *Pierre*, comparisons may be helpful. It is
instructive to put beside it another novel of the period. Meredith's *Ordeal
of Richard Feverel* (1859), in which, too, the organization is essentially
discursive and lyrical rather than narrative or dramatic. Like Melville the
young Meredith was undertaking to be something more than a story-
teller; and he used the gross scheme of romantic melodrama as an instrument of truth-telling and moral indoctrination. When near the beginning
of *Pierre* we find Melville opposing "the demon Principle" to an idyll of
youthful summer love, the resemblance appears very close indeed. Both
novels have much to say about the equivocality of worldly affairs and the
distress that results for fine spirits—Meredith's, it must be granted, with a
steadier humor. But this resemblance is mostly between what is weakest
or most commonplace in the two books, both of which lean too readily,
when imagination is slack, on a kind of poeticized wisdom-mongering.
"All round and round does the world lie as in a sharp-shooter's ambush, to
pick off the beautiful illusions of youth, by the pitiless cracking rifles of
the realities of the age": it perhaps will take a discriminating ear to say
with confidence which one this sentence is taken from. But in a round
view, differences in temper and direction are immediately apparent. The
confessional and meditative intensity of Melville's narrative is quite absent from Meredith's, which condescends to its materials, and is altogether less curious about them. Where *Richard Feverel* stays fastened to a
set of a priori moral precepts which the particulars of the novel are merely
allowed to illustrate, *Pierre* is exploratory and introspective, at whatever
cost. In Meredith's handling, romantic love, or the first love of the young

and healthy, is an absolute virtue. The agency by which other healthy virtues are released, it is itself whole and uncontingent. But for Melville the action of love belongs to the natural history of the developing soul, and must participate in the ambiguity of that history, though standing for a time at its vital center. And insofar as love is thus the force by which the human person grows into his main life and emerges, if ever he does, out of "empty nominalness" into the "vital realness" of unsheltered experience, it must be for him a deepest pain and torment.

At the center of Melville's conception of his hero's life-history is this natural sequence of inward growth. The insistence on explaining in minute detail every inflection of motive in Pierre's mind, and every new position and rhythmic phase in the mechanics of his responsiveness, follows from this conception—though when the method resulting is applied to a character's most casual or merely prudential decisions, it becomes grotesque. At its most effective, however, it gives us with considerable cogency something like an affective, not to say dramatic, theory of knowledge; it provides, that is, a working display of the process by which thoughts are formed and the commitments of feeling actually entered into within the human mind. At this level of demonstration *Pierre* is an extraordinary performance.[4] Its delivered strength is not in its ideas-as-such but in this central rehearsal of the organic life of the soul, or what others in Melville's day were calling the natural history of intellect. Even the sensational plot serves chiefly for demonstrative emphasis; so the situation of incest, curiously underplayed, is principally a sign of the fearful tautologies of consciousness as it goes its natural course, and especially of its bottomless capacity for self-violence. The universal distrust that breaks on Pierre; the sense of "the ambiguities" of existence (or of "the tragic convertibility between truth and falsehood, good and evil" which Charles Feidelson, I think misleadingly, has called the backbone of the novel); the vivid projections of nervous disorder and of the insanity produced by the encroachments of ungoverned memory—all come as the consequence of a natural and irreversible growth of mind, in the "boundless" expansion of its single life. And if we say that in themselves the assertions of philosophical opinion in *Pierre* are not deeply impressive, holding our attention only as they happen to speak for this main action, we are simply being consistent with the book's strongest "philosophical" intuition: "For there is no faith, and no stoicism, and no philosophy, that a mortal man can possibly evoke, which will stand the final test of a real impassioned onset of Life and Passion upon him. . . . For Faith and philosophy are air, but events are brass. Amidst his gray philosophizings, Life breaks upon a man like the morning."

Notes

1. "Whence come you, Hawthorne? By what right do you drink from my flagon of life? And when I put it to my lips—lo, they are yours and not mine."

2. This phrase occurs in the first of a series of carefully worded sentences of foreshadowing explanation, in section ii, Book I.

3. A passage in Book xxv, section ii, is typical of the way in which most of *Pierre* gets itself told. Here Pierre's cousin Glen and his prospective brother-in-law Frederic have come into the field against him: "What then would those two boiling bloods do? Perhaps they would patrol the streets; and at the first glimpse of lonely Lucy, kidnap her home. Or if Pierre were with her, then smite him down by hook or crook, fair play or foul; and then, away with Lucy! Or if Lucy systematically kept her room, then fall on Pierre in the most public way, fell him, and cover him from all decent recognition beneath heaps and heaps of hate and insult; so that broken on the wheel of such dishonor, Pierre might feel himself unstrung, and basely yield the prize.

"Not the gibbering of ghosts in any old haunted house; no sulphurous and portentous sign at night beheld in heaven, will so make the hair to stand, as when a proud and honorable man is revolving in his soul the possibilities of some gross public and corporeal disgrace. It is not fear; it is pride-horror, which is more terrible than any fear. Then, by tremendous imagery, the murderer's mark of Cain is felt burning on the brow, and the already acquitted knife blood-rusts in the clutch of the anticipating hand.

"Certain that these two youths must be plotting something furious against him; with the echoes of their scorning curses . . ."—and so on through half a dozen more intricately specifying subordinate clauses, after which the main statement—"Pierre could not but look forward to wild work very soon to come"—is fairly ludicrous.

4. Particularly striking in this respect are two long sequences painstakingly analyzing the impact upon Pierre's mind of a single new transforming apprehension, in both instances of the knowledge of dark Isabel and what she portends for him (iv, i to v, ii, and ix–x).

[Chronometricals and Horologicals]

Brian Higgins*

In the pamphlet on "Chronometricals and Horologicals," Melville draws on a number of common satirical strategies, developing them in his own original manner. His primary device is the familiar one of the mask or persona, in which the author presents to the world, as if his own, the views he wishes to satirize. The particular persona he chooses to adopt—that of the rational, pragmatic man engaged in addressing himself, for the benefit of others, to a distressing problem—is also common. It is that adopted, for example, by Defoe in *The Shortest Way with Dissenters*, and by Swift in *An Argument Against Abolishing Christianity* and *A Modest Proposal*. As a satiric device it can be most effective; it can also easily leave the author open to misinterpretation. Defoe's *The Shortest Way* is a well-known case. Intended to satirize an extreme Tory view of how to deal with Dissenters, it was hailed by the Tories as a forceful expression of their case; it was denounced by the Dissenters, whose cause it aimed to serve.[1] Plinlimmon's lecture has often been similarly

*Reprinted from "Plinlimmon and the Pamphlet Again," *Studies in the Novel*, 4 (Spring 1972), 27–38.

misunderstood. Plinlimmon teaches that adherents of absolute Christianity are likely to become involved in "strange, *unique* follies and sins,"[2] a point of view which the rest of *Pierre* supports. The Pamphlet, nevertheless, does not represent Melville's own considered wisdom, as many critics have assumed:[3] while Melville agrees with Plinlimmon that absolute Christianity is impracticable, he by no means endorses the rest of Plinlimmon's teaching.

Like the analogies in *A Modest Proposal* between men and women and breeding animals and between human offspring and animals for slaughter, Plinlimmon's analogy between souls and chronometers and horologes (by which Christ too becomes a chronometer, his teaching "his bequeathed chronometer," and heaven "the Central Greenwich") is clearly enough a false one.[4] But Plinlimmon's limitations as thinker and teacher are exposed in less obvious shortcomings, such as the circularity of the Pamphlet's argument. Plinlimmon presents the heavenly wisdom of God—or the chronometrical wisdom of Christ—as earthly folly to man: "Nor does the God at the heavenly Greenwich expect common men to keep Greenwich wisdom in this remote Chinese world of ours; because such a thing were unprofitable for them here" (p. 212). In other words, God expects men to reject the wisdom of Christ, which insists on the nothingness of this world, insists that the world and the things of this world be renounced for heavenly treasure (as we are reminded in the section of the novel previous to the Pamphlet), because "such a thing [or wisdom] were unprofitable" in this world! Christ teaches that he who would save his life must lose it. Plinlimmon teaches that a man "must by no means make a complete unconditional sacrifice of himself in behalf of any other being, or any cause, or any conceit" (p. 214) (as Christ would have him do), because such a sacrifice would not accord with "his own every-day general well-being," though his own mere instinct for the latter will teach him to make "certain minor self-renunciations." Christ teaches in the Sermon on the Mount:

> Blessed are they which are persecuted for righteousness' sake: for theirs is the kingdom of heaven.
> Blessed are ye, when men shall revile you, and persecute you, and shall say all manner of evil against you falsely, for my sake.
> Rejoice, and be exceeding glad: *for great is your reward in heaven:* for so persecuted they the prophets which were before you
> (Matt. 5: 10–12, italics added).

Plinlimmon teaches that if a man "seek to regulate his own daily conduct" by chronometrical truth, "he will but array all men's *earthly* time-keepers against him, and thereby work himself woe and death" (p. 212; italics added). The teaching designed to help men reach heaven is invalid because so far as *practical* results are concerned—*regarded in a purely earthly light*—the only great original moral doctrine of Christianity (*i.e.* the chronometrical gratuitous return of good for evil, as distinguished from the horological forgiveness of injuries taught by some of the Pagan philosophers), has been found (horologically) a false one; because after 1800 years' inculcation from tens of thousands of pulpits, it has proved entirely impracticable (p. 215; italics added).

Critics who accept the Pamphlet as representing Melville's own wisdom are missing the irony of Plinlimmon's overlooking the purpose of Christ's teaching—to get men to heaven, something they cannot achieve by following the ways of the world; "the history of Christendom for the last 1800 years" can be "just as full of blood, violence, wrong, and iniquity of every kind, as any previous portion of the world's story" (p. 215) and Christ's teaching still be practicable in terms of individual salvation.

Plinlimmon's reasoning elsewhere is suspect and comic. He argues that "for the mass of men, the highest abstract heavenly righteousness is not only impossible, but would be entirely out of place, and positively wrong in a world like this. To turn the left cheek if the right be smitten, is chronometrical; hence, no average son of man ever did such a thing" (p. 213). Two points need to be made here. First, Plinlimmon again misses the purpose of heavenly righteousness, which does not seek to be right in "a world like this," but seeks a higher approval and can only be irrelevantly judged by the standards of "a world like this." The New Testament is constantly explicit in its condemnation of the wisdom of men and the world. Second, the proposition that the *highest abstract* heavenly righteousness is impossible to the mass of men might be a reasonable one (it is hard to say exactly what this "highest abstract" is), but in the next sentence this "highest abstract heavenly righteousness" is equated with the chronometrical turning of the left cheek after the smiting of the right—which no average son of man ever did, Plinlimmon avers. Yet clearly there is a difference: chronometrical turning of the cheek is not impossible, even for the average son of man, though it may be hard. A confusion like this between the impossible and the difficult is perfectly consistent with a philosophy which sees a "virtuous *expediency*" as "the *highest desirable* or *attainable* earthly *excellence* for the mass of men" (p. 214; italics added).

Plinlimmon several times uses this strategy of introducing an acceptable premise then following up with a more questionable one. The Pamphlet begins: "Few of us doubt, gentlemen, that human life on this earth is but a state of probation." Then comes the insidious follow-through: "which among other things implies, that here below, we mortals have only to do with things provisional" (p. 211). The following question and premise are perfectly reasonable: "of what use to the Chinaman would a Greenwich chronometer, keeping Greenwich time, be? Were he thereby to regulate his daily actions, he would be guilty of all manner of absurdities:—going to bed at noon, say, when his neighbors would be sitting down to dinner" (p. 212). Plinlimmon's chronological conceit enables him to exploit that reasonableness in drawing his false conclusion: "Nor does the God at the heavenly Greenwich expect common men to keep Greenwich wisdom in this remote Chinese world of ours" (p. 212). By several years Plinlimmon anticipates Melville's Confidence Man.

The satire of the Pamphlet is directed at the vast majority of mankind who (like Plinlimmon) are unable to judge the unworldly wisdom of Christ except in worldly terms and so resort to that virtuous expediency which Plinlimmon lays down as that which "the best mortal men do daily practice" (p. 215). Highly individualized as it is, Plinlimmon's thinking is representative of the devious rationalizing with which nominal Christians reconcile their ways with the ways of Christ. The tone of the passage in which Plinlimmon outlines his "virtuous expediency," his behavioral standards for men, reinforces the satire against him. The mixture of lip-pursing judiciousness ("if a man gives with *a certain self-considerate* generosity to the poor; abstains from doing *downright* ill to any man; does his *convenient* best *in a general way* to do good to his whole race") and easygoing tolerance and virtue ("is perfectly tolerant to all other men's opinions, *whatever they may be*; is an honest dealer, an honest citizen, *and all that*") is surely calculated by Melville to amuse (p. 214; italics added). The tolerance is too easy and general, the virtue too vague, the benevolence too undirected and diffuse. Plinlimmon's last condition is fine-sounding: "and more especially if he believe that there is a God for infidels, as well as for believers, and acts upon that belief" (p. 214). But what does it amount to other than another case of easy acceptance? The final clause ("and acts upon that belief") is comfortably vague; and, according to Plinlimmon, acting upon belief should in any case be limited to a "virtuous expediency." Inadvertently comic, lapsing into easy sentimentality, Plinlimmon is advocating in this passage nothing more than a conscience-salving tokenism.

Even without reference to Christ's warning against anger in the Sermon on the Mount,[6] and his injunction to love thy neighbor as thyself, which Plinlimmon is blandly ignoring, the tolerance is again too easy, simply by humanitarian standards, when Plinlimmon writes that a man who is

> sometimes guilty of some minor offense:—hasty words, impulsively returning a blow, fits of domestic petulance, selfish enjoyment of a glass of wine while he knows there are those around him who lack a loaf of bread . . . . need never lastingly despond on account of his perpetual liability to these things; because *not* to do them, and their like, would be to be an angel, a chronometer; whereas, he is a man and a horologe (p. 214).

The absolution is too nonchalant and too generous—a *perpetual* liability is allowed, not only for the listed offenses, but for their "like"; the requirements for being angel-like are surprisingly low—simply not to commit these "minor offenses" "would be to be an angel" (but then Plinlimmon's estimate of the moral stature attainable by an "average son-of-man" is correspondingly low). There is a moral sleaziness about Plinlimmon's thinking that fits well with the physical sleaziness of his pamphlet, a sleaziness nowhere more apparent than in the smugness of the attitude not uncommon to nominal Christianity: "When they go to heaven, it will be quite another thing. There, they can freely turn the left cheek, because there the right cheek will never be smitten. There they can freely give all to the poor, for *there* there will be no poor to give to" (p. 214). In this continual ignoring or tempering of Christ's teaching, in counseling men in effect not "to aim at heaven, and attain it, too, in all his earthly acts," Plinlimmon is again being set up by Melville as a butt. He is one more impostor philosopher purporting to have got a Voice out of Silence.

Notes

1. See J. T. Boulton, ed. *Daniel Defoe* (New York: Schocken Books, 1965), p. 87.

2. *Pierre; or, The Ambiguities*, ed. Harrison Hayford, Hershel Parker, and G. Thomas Tanselle (Evanston and Chicago: Northwestern University Press and The Newberry Library, 1971), p. 213. All subsequent parenthetical page references in the text are to this edition.

3. See, for example, William Braswell, *Melville's Religious Thought: An Essay in Interpretation* (Durham: Duke University Press, 1943), pp. 81–85; Newton Arvin, *Herman Melville* (New York: William Sloane, 1950), pp. 221–22; James E. Miller, Jr., *A Reader's Guide to Herman Melville* (New York: Farrar, Straus and Cudahy, 1962), pp. 132–38, 238; William Van O'Connor, "Plotinus Plinlimmon and the Principle of Name Giving," in *The Grotesque: An American Genre and Other Essays* (Carbondale: Southern Illinois University Press, 1962), pp. 92–97; and Floyd C. Watkins, "Melville's Plotinus Plinlimmon and Pierre," in *Reality and Myth: Essays in American Literature in Memory of Richard Croom Beatty*, eds. William E. Walker and Robert L. Welker (Nashville: Vanderbilt University Press, 1964), pp. 39–51.

4. See Henry A. Murray's discussion of the falseness of the analogy in his "Introduction" to *Pierre* (New York: Hendricks House, 1949), p. lxxi. A further correspondence with Swift can be found in *An Argument Against Abolishing Christianity*, which, like the Pamphlet, argues for a nominal as opposed to a real Christianity, casually accepts the impracticability of real Christianity, and lists the unfortunate consequences to society were it to be generally adopted.

5. The "character and fate" of Christ support this lesson, Plinlimmon considers (p. 213), overlooking the fact that Christ intentionally sacrificed himself for mankind—a sacrifice he overlooks later when he asks, "does aught else completely and unconditionally sacrifice itself for him?" (p. 214).

6. "But I say unto you, That whosoever is angry with his brother without a cause shall be in danger of the judgment: and whosoever shall say to his brother, Raca, shall be in danger of the council: but whosoever shall say, Thou fool, shall be in danger of hell fire" (Matt. 5:22).

[Conscious Idealizings and Unconscious Sexuality]

Richard H. Brodhead*

Pierre inhabits the sort of world Ishmael perceives in "The Gilder" and Ahab in "The Symphony." His is, in each of its manifestations, a world formed in love, calling forth a sense of joyous oneness and sustaining a confident, comfortable feeling of human identity. At the same time, the nature of this Eden is from the first somewhat questionable. When cattle become "brindled kine . . . followed, not driven, by ruddy-cheeked, white-footed boys" (3), the golden haze is, we must feel, being laid on rather thick; when horses are "kind as kittens" (22) we can suspect that nature has been too thoroughly domesticated, too easily humanized. This place is too soft a pastoral; like the paradise of Blake's *Book of Thel*, it seems overripe, its very lushness a symptom of unresolved and unrecognized problems.

Indeed the collapse of this world formed in love has already begun when the book opens. Pierre has seen a face which, with its combination of "Tartarean misery and Paradisaic beauty" (43), gives him a glimpse of heaven married with hell. Even before he hears Isabel's story her face gives him a presentiment that grief and gloom, which he has never known, may be realities profounder than pleasure. And even before he learns, through her, of his enshrined father's concealed sins he recognizes her face as having the power to call into question all the gentle beliefs that his loving existence has sanctioned. The face whose "fearful gospel" can thus "overthrow . . . all foregone persuasions" (43) begins to overthrow, as well, his sense of selfhood. He feels something pushing up in himself to respond to Isabel. "Bannered armies of hooded phantoms" (49) disembark in his soul. He discovers "infernal catacombs" (51) beneath the calm surface of his conscious mind. The vision energizes his own unconscious, forcing him to see in himself what Ishmael calls "the horrors of the half known life."

Pierre struggles to resist his experience of revelation. He vows to be Lucy's protector, and to fit himself for this role he undertakes a strenuous program of physical exercise. By this instinctive tactic of self-preservation he attempts to work off the terrific psychic energy Isabel has awakened in him and to channel that energy back into the relationships that compose his familiar world. But this tactic can be only temporarily successful. Isabel's letter, with its revelation of her identity and of Pierre's father's sexual transgressions, breaks down his defenses and completes the process of estrangement from his earlier life that his first sight of her had ini-

*Reprinted from "The Fate of Candor: *Pierre; or, The Ambiguities*," in *Hawthorne, Melville, and the Novel* (Chicago: University of Chicago Press, 1976), pp. 166–75, 177–79, 183.

tiated. The letter uncovers for him the evils on which the apparent goods of his world have been based, and in its light he rejects all natural and familial pieties to embrace a darker faith:

> "Thou Black Knight, that with visor down, thus confrontest me, and mockest at me; Lo! I strike through thy helm, and will see thy face, be it Gorgon!—Let me go, ye fond affections; all piety leave me; I will be impious, for piety hath juggled me, and taught me to revere, where I should spurn. From all idols, I tear all veils; henceforth I will see the hidden things, and live right out in my own hidden life!"
>
> (65–66)

In this speech the heroic Pierre is born. He discovers his own inscrutable foe and resolves to strike through its mask. He sees himself now not as at one with his world but as separate from it and in opposition to it. He exchanges reverence for the right worship of defiance and chooses as his true self the potentially infernal power in him that he had previously attempted to shun.

The accession of consciousness that leads Pierre to see the falsity of the human relations and values on which his youth's pastoral is based also leads him to perceive the natural world in a new way. Pausing on his way to Isabel's cottage he sees the pasture elms as shivering "in a world inhospitable" (109). The mountain masses that formerly inspired him with lyrical thoughts now seem to him "black with dread and gloom"; the slidings and crashings of their rocks suggest the "infinite inhumanities" (110) of raw natural processes. The lake reflects the sky, but this is no longer evidence of joyful reciprocity: "only in sunshine did that lake catch gay, green images; and these but displaced the imaged muteness of the unfeatured heavens" (109). He is discovering the alienness of nature that obsesses Ahab, and the final blankness that fills Ishmael with dread.

Isabel's tale reinforces these insights. In her autobiography she recalls not the memorial ring of Pierre's horizon but a ring of stunted pines whose shadows seemed to snatch at her and a ruinous house containing no tokens of a human past, no "memorial speaking" (115). The differentiation of human and nonhuman is as minimal in her world as it is in Pierre's, but for the opposite reason: nothing in it helps her to define her own human identity by offering a reciprocation of her love. In place of Pierre's fiancée and mother she remembers two grim figures who would not speak to her and who seemed "just like the green foundation stones of the house to me" (116). In place of horses kind as kittens she remembers a cat that responded to her tendered sympathy with a terrifying hiss. This figure of a consciousness stranded in a totally alien world does come to experience love and to recognize herself as different from her environment, but this increases, not alleviates, her sense of isolation and dread; she is left with the perpetual feeling of "my humanness among the inhumanities" (123). And her tale extends for Pierre the vision that her letter had opened up for him; in *Moby-Dick*'s terms, it inducts him into a world whose spheres are formed in fright.

The terrifying inhumanity and indifference of nature is only one aspect of the new vision Isabel gives Pierre access to. She leads him, as well, from the reality of a "visible world" that has seemed "all too common and prosaic to him; and but too intelligible" to a reality whose every facet is "steeped a million fathoms in a mysteriousness wholly hopeless of solution" (128). Since she cannot give an objective location to the scenes in her tale or an objective account of how and why she was moved from one to another, the course of her life's history admits of no external explanation. And even if it did, this would tell nothing essential about who or what she is. Her "vague tale of terribleness" (121) can tell only how she experienced and became conscious of the strangeness of her being; it renders mystery as a permanent condition of existence.

The realm of mystery she inhabits is also one of magic. Her tale, unfolding according to the urgings of her unconscious mind, has the dreamlike organization of romance, and since it has no independent reality-principle it freely includes apparently supernatural events—a guitar comes to her with her own name written in it, and when she whispers to it, it responds with the voice of her mother. Her own mode of being in the novel is that of a creature of wild romance. She scarcely seems to exist within the contexts of manners, dress, family, and social station in which the "all-understood" (129) Lucy has her being; her appearance and position as a dairymaid are an incongruous disguise through which the electrical power of her "dark, regal being" (152) occasionally flashes forth. Nor is she bound by the laws of ordinary causality. In the weird rituals in which she conjures voices from her guitar and glows with phosphorescent light she operates, in effect, as a witch. In her presence Pierre is literally "enchanted," sitting motionless as a "tree-transformed and mystery-laden visitant, caught and fast bound in some necromancer's garden" (128). She is his passport to a spirit-ridden realm, to the invisible spheres that elude comprehension but arouse powerful emotions of wonder and terror.

Pierre's discovery that what he has taken to be "the solid land of veritable reality" (49) is a surface concealing a deeper reality, one that is inhuman, inscrutable, and supernatural, marks his initiation into an Ahabian sense of the world. In *Pierre* the process of discovery presented in Ahab's case in the foreshortened form of flashback is stretched out so that we can observe all its stages. It becomes not a necessary prelude to the novel's action but the novel's action itself. In addition to this difference in presentation, Pierre's initiation takes place in a context that is in important ways different from that of *Moby-Dick*. Both Ahab and Pierre receive a "wound" (65; cf. *MD* 182) that is, for them, a revelation of the dark, Hindoo half of things, of truth with malice in it. Pierre's learning of his father's sexual transgressions is his equivalent to Ahab's loss of his leg;

in this book the cause of the hero's wound is not a natural creature but a human sin. And where Ahab generalizes from Moby Dick's cruelty by seeing a principle of evil within the beauty of nature, Pierre generalizes from the specific sin by seeing such a principle within the beauty of conventional social morality and religion. The evil he perceives is not natural but moral.

For both Ahab and Pierre this insight yields a new condition of selfhood. They find their identities now in a resolution, an unwavering determination to perform an act that will assert once and for all the primacy of benevolent human values against a malevolent world. In this respect Pierre's upholding of a Christlike ethic of sacrificial love in his acknowledgment and rescue of Isabel is akin to Ahab's assertion of personality against the impersonal in his hunt for Moby Dick; certainly the spirit of aggressive idealism and energetic absolutism that informs their quests is the most striking bond between them. But again, the dimension and direction of Pierre's quest are in important ways different from Ahab's. Ahab's adversary is in nature, Pierre's in society. Where Ahab seeks to achieve metaphysical justice through a physical act, Pierre aims at a much more specifically human and moral justice, to be achieved through an act of pure ethical choice.

This crucial shift in focus helps to explain Melville's change of fictional genre from *Moby-Dick* to *Pierre*. The action of the latter requires a social, not a natural setting. The form of sentimental romance enables Melville to create such a setting, to unfold a world of parents, sisters, fiancées, and clergymen. Further, in a way that no other genre Melville has worked in does, this one emphasizes human interaction: it establishes its characters' experience as lived within a complex web of loves and duties. Thus in *Pierre* the hero's wound is given concrete embodiment as a product of his specific relationships to others and to the framework of value he has inherited from them. He makes his discovery and works out his resolution in terms of these relations. His vision of evil is particularized as a discovery of his father's true nature, of his mother's pride and propriety, of Reverend Falsgrave's ethical trimming; his commitment to the cause of Holy Right is particularized as a choice to go to Isabel's aid, and the specific form that his aid takes proceeds from his sifting of his conflicting bonds of emotion and obligation to his sister, to Lucy, to his mother, and to his dead father. However unsuited they may seem to his talents, the characteristic figures and conflicts of this literary genre serve Melville as the means he needs to deal with what most interests him in Pierre. They enable him to construct a dramatic action in which he can explore the operations of good and evil in a social and moral context.

There is, then, a serious purpose behind Melville's adoption of this fictional form. This fact needs to be stressed; but as soon as it is admitted, we must add that his use of the form is anything but straightforward. In a provocative essay R. P. Blackmur writes:

The deadest convention was meant for life—to take its place. . . . [But] Melville either refused or was unable to resort to the available conventions of his time as if they were real; he either preferred or was compelled to resort to most of the conventions he used for dramatic purposes not only as if they were unreal but also as if they were artificial.[1]

In relation to the rest of Melville's novels this contention is highly debatable, but *Pierre* illustrates Blackmur's point. The materials that sentimental romance offers Melville for the construction of a dramatic action never get fully realized or dramatized. The pairings of genteel hero and genteel heroine, or of light and dark lady, are not transmuted into living relations among the characters but remain visible as stylized formulas. A close look at *Pierre* indicates that Melville's emphasis on the conventionality of the conventions he resorts to may be the product not of his disabilities but of conscious preference on his part.

His presentation of Lucy in "Love, Delight, and Alarm" demonstrates this most clearly. What is finally noteworthy about his description of her is how little complexity of individual being it confers on her. Melville shows her as an exemplum of "lovely woman," a "visible semblance of the heavens" (24), and instead of becoming more specific as he proceeds he simply reiterates in increasingly vigorous hyperbole the fact of her angelic loveliness. But there are also odd dissonances here. To the reader who quibbles with his paean to beauties Melville replies: "By immemorial usage, am I not bound to celebrate this Lucy Tartan? Who shall stay me? Is she not my hero's own affianced?" (25). This sounds like Ishmaelean mock-heroic puffing, but taken at face value it is, really, a declaration that his celebration is an obligatory performance, that his idealization of his heroine meets the strictures of a generic requirement. Other passages reinforce this suggestion. "It is needless to say that she was a beauty" (23), the narrator tells us, because handsome, well-bred youths always fall in love with beautiful girls—as every novel reader knows. Lucy's "eyes some god brought down from heaven; her hair was Danae's, spangled with Jove's shower; her teeth were dived for in the Persian Sea" (24). If we want to know who Lucy is we must find such descriptions as this increasingly frustrating, and this seems to be their point. The narrator is dramatizing his inability to present her as anything but a compendium of all the idealizing clichés that the "immemorial usage" of sentimental romance forces him to perpetuate.

Melville's irony here is directed not at Lucy but at the literary form that engenders such pallid heroines and at the readers whose demands make it the "proper province" of novelists to deal exclusively with the "angelical part" (25) of their female characters. As the chapter continues, he hints that the problems involved here extend beyond the realm of literature, that the procedures of such fiction are themselves symptoms of a more fundamental difficulty in the relations of the sexes in America.

His wildly chauvinistic hymn to American chivalry ends on a surprising
note:

> Our Salique Law provides that universal homage shall be paid all
> beautiful women. No man's most solid rights shall weigh against her
> airiest whims. If you buy the best seat in the coach, to go and consult a
> doctor on a matter of life and death, you shall cheerfully abdicate that
> best seat, and limp away on foot, if a pretty woman, traveling, shake one
> feather from the stage-house door.
>
> (25)

This is what the idealization of women means in practice, and the extremity of the passage's hyperbole makes the basic cruelty of this situation
all the more apparent. The novelist compelled to idealize his heroine is
only a special case of man subjected to the whims of women, trapped in a
ritual of deferential worship that works to deny the complex personal
natures and needs of both parties.

Melville's description of Lucy both involves us with and distances us
from her. He presents her as a character who can figure in his dramatic
action, but at the same time he asks us to recognize her as a stock figure
from a certain sort of fiction, covertly inviting us to see as well the emotional problems that underlie this fiction's idealizations. His scenic art
complicates our perception in a similar way. The scene in which Lucy and
Pierre become engaged is as charged with exemplary sweetness and innocent love as any popular lady novelist could wish. The narrator dilates on
the heavenly origin of earthly matches; he decks out his setting with all
the paraphernalia of idealized courtship—copies of Moore's Melodies,
swatches of bridal veils, the sheet music to "Love was once a little boy."
But as the scene unfolds, it becomes clear that its sentimental setting is a
cunning contrivance. Mrs. Tartan has made Lucy into a heavenly
creature and surrounded her with props alluding to love's consummation
in order to seduce Pierre's imagination. Lucy is simultaneously "angel"
and "bait," and she is keenly humiliated at the prospect of being "tasted
in the trap" (28). Lucy and Pierre are in effect victims of Mrs. Tartan's
sentimental art; she constructs a scene that arouses and plays upon sexual
desire without, however, letting it be frankly acknowledged or fully
expressed.

In this respect she is not unlike Mrs. Glendinning, and in showing
Pierre's relation to his mother Melville again presents his scenic action in
such a way that a concealed sexual drama can be discerned beneath a sentimental surface. Describing how Pierre helps his mother complete her
morning toilet, he insists on the wonderful tenderness of their relationship; Pierre's courtly bow, he says, shows how "sweetly and religiously
was the familiarity of his affections bottomed on the profounder filial
respect" (14). But later in his narration he makes it clear that this scene

too is a product of manipulation, noting Mrs. Glendinning's cunning in using such "merest appearances" as her becoming state of "dishabille" to play upon "the closest ties of the heart" (15). And then he steps back still further to indicate the unconscious needs that motivate her manipulations, to show how her "subtlest vanity" and her emotional condition as she nears her "grand climacteric" (16) makes her son's adoration necessary to her.

At the end of this chapter the narrator readopts the voice of a bright celebrant:

> this softened spell which still wheeled the mother and son in one orbit of joy, seemed a glimpse of the glorious possibility, that the divinest of those emotions, which are incident to the sweetest season of love, is capable of an indefinite translation into many of the less signal relations of our many chequered life. In a detached and individual way, it seemed almost to realize here below the sweet dreams of those religious enthusiasts, who paint to us a Paradise to come, when etherealized from all drosses and stains, the holiest passion of man shall unite all kindreds and climes in one circle of pure and unimpairable delight.
>
> (16)

He sees Pierre and his mother as proof that the kind of tender affection felt in courtship can spread out from an individual object into other relations, thus raising all modes of relationship to the level of its own purity. But in light of the rest of the chapter this blissful conclusion is somewhat ironic. After all, it is not that Pierre's feelings for Lucy have been translated into his feelings for his mother. He *is* his mother's suitor; she has ensnared him into a courtship that allows her to feel as gratified as "the most conquering virgin" (16). And to say that in their relationship love is "etherealized from all drosses and stains" tells only half the story. It is not that there is no sexuality in their relation, as Mrs. Glendinning's use of a becoming dishabille shows, but rather that it is based on a sexual attraction that can never be consummated or even recognized as such. In these terms the etherealization of Pierre's love is less a glorious possibility than a psychological problem.

Melville's language in this passage is calculatingly deceptive, and the nature of its deception is appropriate to its occasion. Like much of the style of *Pierre*, it conspicuously idealizes what it represents. It hints at sexuality only obliquely and euphemistically, pointedly averting its eyes from the elements of sexual cunning Melville has previously alluded to. The rhetoric here is sentimental, and in a sense the nature of sentimentality is the real subject of the passage. The etherealized passion of reverential affection purged of sexual dross is what the sentimental religion of love worships. But what Melville's concealed analysis of Pierre suggests is that this passion not only ignores sexuality but is itself energized by a sexual interest that has been suppressed and that the idealizing fiction that subscribes to this sweet vision operates in the same way.

The separation of sex and sentiment, and the way in which sentiment is exaggerated by the suppression of sexual awareness, is the essence of Pierre's predicament. The sight of Lucy's bedroom kindles an almost fetishistic impulse in him, and the stronger his wish to see her "secret thing" (40), the more he feels her room to be a sacred place, a saint's holy shrine. His "extreme loyalty to the piety of love"(39) here, like his "reverentialness" toward his mother earlier, is made all the more extreme because the energy of his suppressed desire is transferred into it. Lucy is an "invoking angel" to Pierre *because* he feels masculine desire to be "profane" (4). Every bridegroom leading his bride to the marriage bed is, to him, a new Pluto leading Proserpine to hell. And however much he may come to see the falsities on which his life at Saddle Meadows is based, Pierre cannot escape from the cycle of repression and idealization that he has learned in that life. When, for example, he considers Isabel's avoidance of his embraces and realizes that it will never be possible for them to express affection as brothers and sisters customarily do, Melville writes that the thought of other than brotherly embraces "never consciously intruded" in his mind; instead at this impasse "Isabel wholly soared out of the realms of mortalness, and for him became transfigured in the highest heaven of uncorrupted Love" (142). He is making angels again, and in the same old way. Because he remains committed to this cycle of repression and idealization he is compelled to see himself as living in a world divided between good and evil, heaven and hell, without realizing that his own images of the heavenly are fueled by what he considers hellish in himself.

Melville's sentimental mode creates and responds to its fictional world in the same way that Pierre does to his actual one. Like Pierre in Lucy's bedroom the book's style surges with exaggerated reverence and holy awe whenever it presents a scene with a sexual dimension. Its consistent use of the word "nameless" to refer to sexual feelings parallels Pierre's inability to recognize such feelings in himself. Its light and dark ladies, its angelic Lucies and potentially demonic Isabels, are its own versions of Pierre's emotional projections of the heavenly and the hellish. The sentimental romance of *Pierre* allows Melville to re-create in the texture of his own fiction the processes of seeing and feeling that are its subjects at the dramatic level. This mode repeatedly calls attention to itself as a kind of fiction in *Pierre*, but it does this, finally, not to discredit its own worth, but rather to engage us in a consideration of the psychological dynamics out of which this kind of fiction is created—in novels and in life. . . .

Pierre is the first of Melville's novels in which he adopts the narrative stance of an omniscient outsider instead of a first-person speaker-participant. His new commitment to psychological investigation accounts for this major change in procedure. In this book he needs a narrator who can know all the important determinants of his characters' lives, one who can both follow the involutions of their feelings and comment from without on the quality of their experience and on the inner processes that, unknown to them, give shape to their experience. He needs a narrator who can see where—and why—his characters are blind, one who can understand the workings of their minds even when they are most confused or self-deluded.

The narrator of *Pierre* is not totally omniscient, and he insists that he cannot be so.

> In their precise tracings-out and subtile causations, the strongest and fieriest emotions of life defy all analytical insight. . . . Idle then would it be to attempt by any winding way so to penetrate into the heart, and memory, and inmost life, and nature of Pierre [as to show why he responds so strongly to Isabel's letter].
>
> (67)

His words here recall Ishmael's, who concludes his depth analysis of Ahab by alluding to continuing mysteries that "to explain, would be to dive deeper than Ishmael can go" (*MD* 184). Like Ishmael, this narrator is careful to keep his fiction from seeming to make an inscrutable reality too comfortably comprehensible. But, given this as a final qualification, he does affirm the possibility of presenting a suggestively adequate account of the "subtile causations" of his characters' feelings. He can, thus, select the items in the inventory of Pierre's memory—his father's deathbed ravings, Aunt Dorothea's tale of the chair portrait, his repressed reflections on his mother's aversion to this portrait, and so on—that show how his life had prepared him to accept Isabel's revelations as being true. The narrator can reveal elliptically, if not totally, the past that determines this response in the present. Pierre resolves to go to Isabel's aid, and only afterward realizes that this choice entails his abandonment of Lucy. But the narrator can observe a causal relation at work, can note the way in which the conscious choice of Isabel is also an unconscious choice to reject Lucy, so that "in the more secret chambers of his unsuspecting soul" Pierre willingly binds Lucy over as "a ransom for Isabel's salvation." While Pierre can only become conscious of the "subtler elements" at work in him "in their ultimate resolvings and results," the narrator can see at least in part the "concocting act" (105), the interaction of hidden psychic forces by which what is "foetally forming" (106) in Pierre develops. And by emphasizing that his method does not make mental reality totally knowable he guarantees the validity of the kind of knowledge he can possess and communicate.

As his handling of the sentimental mode prepares us to expect, what Melville most often uses his qualified omniscience to show is the relation between Pierre's conscious idealizings and his unconscious sexuality. As Pierre debates whether or not to destroy the mysterious letter without reading it his antagonistic impulses appear before him as two angels, a bad one urging selfish self-protection and a good one appealing to his unselfish magnanimity. When he rejects the counsels of the bad angel the good one defined itself clearer and more clear, and came nigher and more nigh to him, smiling sadly but benignantly; while forth from the infinite distances wonderful harmonies stole into his heart; so that every vein in him pulsed to some heavenly swell.

(63)

In this moment of ethical ecstasy the good angel takes on the mournful beauty that is Isabel's, and she awakens in Pierre the sense of supernatural music that Isabel always arouses in him. This strange metamorphosis suggests the existence of an antagonism besides that of selfishness and altruism. It hints that his inner conflict is also between his powerful dread of the possibilities Isabel offers and his even more powerful attraction to her dark beauty. An ethical and a sexual logic are inextricably entwined in his decision, but he masks this ambiguity by presenting his sexual ambivalence to himself solely in ethical terms.

What is hinted in this episode is made explicit later. When Pierre makes his final resolution to go to Isabel he experiences a "Christ-like feeling" (106) and he urgently prays to be sustained in this exalted condition, to be bound "in bonds I cannot break" to "the inflexible rule of holy right" (106–7). But when his rhapsodic prayer is over, the narrator steps forward to "show how this heavenly fire was helped to be contained in him, by mere contingent things, and things he knew not"—by his attraction to Isabel's "womanly beauty" (107). The point here is not that his holy feeling is simply a sexual desire in disguise but that it is, unknown to Pierre, amplified by such a desire and that it is his suppression of his awareness of this desire that causes him to exalt his own ethical intentions into holy crusades. His feelings are both genuinely disinterestedly noble and genuinely sexual, but because he cannot recognize this doubleness he is bound to think of his sexual desires in terms of ethical imperatives, to conceive of his private wishes in the language of public duties, and to do so in such a way that the stronger his desire is, the more idealized his sense of his mission must be.

In uncovering the sexual logic that is hidden to Pierre the narrator becomes extremely self-conscious about his own role. He dramatizes himself as an intrepid psychic explorer: "I shall follow the endless, winding way,—the flowing river in the cave of man; careless whither I be led, reckless where I land" (107). And he insists that we understand his revelations as evidence of his special commitment as a novelist, his commitment to write nothing less than a "book of sacred truth."

So let no censorious word be here hinted of mortal Pierre. Easy for me to slyly hide these things, and always put him before the eye as immaculate; unsusceptible to the inevitable nature and the lot of common men. I am more frank with Pierre than the best men are with themselves. I am all unguarded and magnanimous with Pierre; therefore you see his weakness, and therefore only. In reserves men build imposing characters; not in revelations.

(108)

His exposure of his character requires from us a delicate respect, and also, he suggests, a measure of self-recognition. Pierre's condition, we are asked to see, is the human condition, the inevitable and common lot—"men are jailers all; jailers of themselves" (91). In affording us the privilege of seeing through his character's self-deceptions he asks us not to judge him but to see ourselves as *hypocrites lecteurs*. His psychological analyses, he implies, are an act of honesty designed to create a community of candor. They work against the habitual concealments of ordinary fiction and of the human mind itself, ours as well as Pierre's, for the sake of releasing a recognition of the real nature of human character. . . . Instead of steadily unfolding the drama of Pierre's individual personal experience Melville converts his experience into a parabolic exemplum of a philosophical and cultural problem. And as these new orders of meaning begin to pile up, we come to suspect that they may be designed less to enrich than to replace the sense that his psychological narrative has made. Melville pointedly ignores the "mere contingent things" in Pierre now, and he collapses the distance from his character that his awareness of these psychic complexities had required of him. Increasingly he comes to see his hero in the terms in which his hero sees himself. Pierre becomes artistic Earnestness and Grandeur assailed by Mediocrity and Commonplace, Christlike moral man besieged by immoral society; "the wide world is banded against him; for lo you! he holds up the standard of Right, and swears by the Eternal and True!" (270). By shifting his attention from conflicts of sexual and ethical impulses within the self to conflicts between virtuous self and external evil Melville dispenses with his need for irony, moving to resuscitate as an absolute value the idealism that he had previously shown to be at least partially a product of sexual repression and self-deception.

When a sexual drama does surface in the second half of *Pierre*, it does so with the luridness of a return of the repressed. The movement from the early dissections of Pierre's hidden feelings to the scenes of the *ménage à quatre* at the Apostles' is a movement from finely controlled psychological analysis to wildly compulsive fantasy. Isabel's "am *I* not enough for thee?" (312) and her intense sexual rivalry with Lucy—"she shall not get the start of me! . . . I will sell this hair; have these teeth pulled out; but some way I will earn money for thee!" (333)—threaten to inaugurate a new genre of hilarious, maniacal pornography. In its alternations of metaphysical and cultural philosophizing and such fantastic melodrama *Pierre* itself comes to act out the dynamic split between urgent abstraction and sexual wish that it had begun by taking as its dramatic subject.

Note

1. R. P. Blackmur, "The Craft of Herman Melville: A Putative Statement," *The Lion and the Honeycomb: Essays in Solicitude and Critique* (New York: Harcourt, Brace, and World, 1955), pp. 127–28.

[New Crosslights on the Illegitimate Daughter in *Pierre*]

Amy Puett Emmers*

An intriguing letter hinting of unsavory secrets in the life of Herman Melville's father has been uncovered in the Lemuel Shaw collection at the Massachusetts Historical Society. Were this find merely titillating, it would remain unannounced. In fact, though, the story behind this letter from Melville's Uncle Thomas to Chief Justice Shaw, Melville's father-in-law, seems to supply the crux of a central incident in *Pierre; or The Ambiguities*—the hero's discovery of his late father's illegitimate daughter. More importantly, Melville's use of such autobiographical detail very likely contributed to his acknowledged, but largely unexplained, disquiet during the decade of the 1850s.

It happened that Herman's grandfather, Major Thomas Melvill, Sr. (Herman's mother added the final "e" after her husband's death), asked Lemuel Shaw, Sr., to be an executor of his will. Judge Shaw had of course been intimate friend and legal adviser of the Melvill family long before he became Herman's father-in-law. Following the Major's death in 1832, Shaw processed matters relating to the estate, and in doing so he several times wrote Herman's uncle, Thomas Melvill, Jr., about two women who had claims against the interests of Herman's father, Allan Melvill, in Major Melvill's estate. (Allan Melvill had died a bankrupt only a few months before his father's death, and any claims against him would have been referred to his interest in his father's estate.) It is the second reply of Thomas Melvill, Jr., to Shaw about this demand for payment which is extant and which seems relevant to *Pierre*. It should be noted that while the proliferation of identical first names in successive generations of Melville's family is sometimes baffling, the Allan mentioned in this letter is clearly Herman's father, not his brother by the same name. The complete text of the letter follows, literatim:

> Dr Sir
> In the letter written you, as within alluded to, I wrote you allso [*sic*] in answer to the first one you wrote me in relation to Mrs. A.M.A.—
> As therein stated, I feel confident that my good father *never saw*,—or at least *never knew*, or *conversed*, either with *her*, or *Mrs B.*—
> They called at the house, if I remember right, twice—just before my arrival in Boston, (after Allans decease,) and saw only my *Mother* & *Helen*—
> The circumstance was made known to me—& it was concluded that I should call on them, which I did, and suceeded [*sic*] in dispelling the erroneous ideas they had formed of *claims*, on my father—as well as the condition of my late brothers affairs—

*Reprinted from *Studies in the American Renaissance*, 1 (1977), 339–43. (Originally titled "Melville's Closet Skeleton: A New Letter about the Illegitimacy Incident in *Pierre*.)

I well remember having paid some money to Mrs B—what the amount of it was, I do not remember,—nor, if it was a *part*, or *the whole* of what she may have claimed as due.—

Mrs. A.M.A.—must be mistaken in stating that I *"gave her some encouragement"*.—On what foundation could I give her encouragement? I had no means of my own. My brother left none—and I had strong reasons to think, that it would not be done, by those members of my own family who might have means, should the case be made known to them;—All of whom, except Helen, are to this day, as I presume, ignorant of her existence—

From the little I saw of her, I thought her quite an interesting young person,—that it was most unfortunate she had not been brought up different—and I most deeply regret that she too, has been called to feel the disappointments & sorrows, so generally attending our earthy sojourn—

Very respectfully & cordially, Th Melvill[1]

While Thomas' letter does not conclusively determine the nature of the relationship between Herman Melville's father and the two women designated as Mrs. B. and Mrs. A.M.A., it does clearly establish that he had a recognized obligation to them. The fact that Thomas Melvill gave Mrs. B. any money at all indicates that he virtually accepted the justice of her claim. Further, Allan's association with the women was obviously disapproved of by the members of his family who knew about it. Interestingly, they appear to wish to protect other members of the family from the knowledge, and Thomas assumes that his other relatives would not sanction the situation should they learn of Mrs. A.M.A.'s "existence." His very use of initials as the sole means of identifying the women throughout the letter underscores his desire for concealment. Had Thomas' concern been only for secrecy, Allan's association with the women might be dismissed as an unfair business transaction, even though women of that era generally did not engage in business. However, the letter clearly implies an unacceptable personal involvement. It might be argued, therefore, that both women claimed to have been Allan's mistresses, perhaps one or both with illegitimate children. But had both women been mistresses, what legal ground would they have had for claims? Further, had both women professed to be mothers of illegitimate children, would they have been likely to associate with each other, as the initial paragraphs of this letter suggest that Mrs. B. and Mrs. A.M.A. do? Above all, it is Thomas' defensiveness about the manner of Mrs. A.M.A.'s rearing, the woman he calls that "interesting young person," that implies a kind of concern not usually accorded mistresses. His concern, linked as it is with his shame and regret, tacitly acknowledges an obligation for Mrs. A.M.A.'s personal well-being, an obligation that would logically be felt toward a late brother's illegitimate offspring. It would appear, then, that Mrs. A.M.A. was Allan Melvill's illegitimate daughter by Mrs. B.

Herman Melville was twelve years old when his father, Allan, died.

It was another twenty years before he would publish *Pierre*, and just what, in the meantime, he learned about his father's life and incorporated into his novel cannot be precisely ascertained. However, almost everyone admits the autobiographical nature of much of that novel, which Melville originally thought would be a "rural bowl of milk."[2] The work evolved rather into a scathing portrayal of a young man consciously bent on doing right—honoring an obligation to support a girl he believes to be his late father's illegitimate daughter—but unconsciously driven by his incestuous love for this same girl. Various scholars have drawn parallels between the novel and its author's life; even more to the point, family members made the same connection. In an unpublished letter now in the Harvard College Library, Melville's daughter, Mrs. Frances Thomas, asserted:

> Cousin M—[Maria Morewood, daughter of Melville's brother, Allan] wrote me that she was pretty sure she had a copy of 'Pierre' & thinks it must be at Arrowhead[.] Will [Morewood, Maria's husband] had read it & said it seemed to refer to 'family matters'[3]

Further, Melville's granddaughter and biographer, Mrs. Eleanor Metcalf, apparently found the same enjoyment other scholars have in enumerating details from Melville's life also found in the novel. In her copy of the Constable edition of *Pierre*,[4] now in the Berg Collection of the New York Public Library, Mrs. Metcalf noted that the description of Glen Stanly's house in New York (p. 332) was like the Shaw home in Mount Vernon Street, Boston. And she also scribbled on her copy that Mr. Falsgrave's delicate hands (p. 137) resembled those of Judge Shaw's and his son Samuel's. In a novel thus acknowledged as autobiographical, it now seems likely that Melville took the incident of illegitimacy from his family history. Significantly, at one time he had thought of publishing the book anonymously or under an assumed name, perhaps partly to spare his family embarrassment.

The reaction of Melville's family circle to *Pierre* provides an important clue to the tantalizing enigma of Melville's health during the several years following the book's publication in 1852. The cryptic allusions about him in various family records of this period are all too scarce, but there is a family account of an examination for insanity about this time. An indication that his relatives were displeased with *Pierre*—and with Melville himself—comes from an uncle of Melville's, Peter Gansevoort, unable to understand an incivility on his nephew's part and thus driven to complain: "Oh Herman, Herman, Herman truly thou art an 'Ambiguity.' "[5] Further, Melville's brother-in-law, Lemuel Shaw, Jr., learning that *Pierre* had been refused by Melville's English publisher, wrote that he wished "very much he could be persuaded to leave off writing books for a few years."[6] Notably, too, after *Pierre* Melville's mother was especially determined that he should give up writing, stating as her reason that her son's health could not bear the strain of a literary career. The subject matter of *Pierre*, with its implications of illegitimacy and incest, would have been shocking to Melville's family regardless of how closely they identified with particular events and characters. Since they acknowledged that the book was about "family matters," it is probable that their embarrassment about *Pierre* made them shudder to think what he might write next. Their embarrassment, coupled with their inability to appreciate or understand the pitch of excitement into which Melville had worked himself after seven years of intensive writing, probably made them overly concerned about his health.

Thomas Melvill's letter, published here for the first time, seems to explain some of the tension that existed between Melville and his family in the 1850s. If Melville had disclosed a family skeleton in *Pierre*, as this letter strongly suggests, then his family might reasonably have wished to dissuade him from continuing along these lines. Unfortunately, their uneasiness about what he might write or do next would only have aggravated rather than alleviated any particular stress Melville experienced during this decade.

Notes

1. No date or place of writing for this letter is indicated, MHi; quoted with permission.

2. Melville to Mrs. Nathaniel Hawthorne, 8 January 1852, *The Letters of Herman Melville*, ed. Merrell R. Davis and William H. Gilman (New Haven: Yale University Press, 1960), p. 146.

3. Mrs. Frances Thomas to Mrs. Eleanor Metcalf, 16 November 1919, MH; quoted with permission.

4. *The Complete Works of Herman Melville* (London: Constable, 1922–24), vol. 9, *Pierre*.

5. Peter Gansevoort to Maria Melville, 9 October 1852; quoted in Jay Leyda, *The Melville Log* (New York: Harcourt, Brace, 1951), 1:461.

6. Lemuel Shaw, Jr., to Mr. and Mrs. Lemuel Shaw, Sr., 13 May 1852, MHi; quoted with permission.

The Flawed Grandeur of Melville's *Pierre*

Brian Higgins and Hershel Parker*

Pierre was not conceived as a lesser effort, a pot-boiler like *Redburn*, which Melville disparaged as something he wrote to buy tobacco with. His response to Hawthorne's praise of *Moby-Dick* in mid-November, 1851, makes plain that Melville intended his next book to be as much

*Reprinted from *New Perspectives on Melville*, ed. Faith Pullin (Edinburgh: Edinburgh University Press, and Kent, Ohio: Kent State University Press, 1978), pp. 162–96.

grander than his last as the legendary Krakens are bigger than whales.[1] Never a novelist or romancer within the ordinary definitions, Melville in *Moby-Dick* had attempted to convert the whaling narrative, a flourishing division of nautical literature, into a vehicle for the philosophical and psychological speculations a pondering man like him was compelled toward. *Pierre* is his comparable attempt to convert the Gothic romance (in one of its late permutations as sensational fiction primarily for female readers) into a vehicle for his speculations, the psychological now looming larger than the philosophical. The technical sea-knots he untied in *Moby-Dick* are grappled with again in the lacy toils of *Pierre*. In the earlier book, certain obligatory scenes, the staple of any whaling story, had to be converted into chapters which would retain their sturdy informativeness while advancing Melville's higher purposes. At best, as in 'The Try-Works', routine exposition was transformed into intense philosophical drama. Much the same way, Melville in *Pierre* inherited a Gothic toybox stuffed almost as full as Poe's with mysterious family relationships, enigmatical recollections of long-past events, suspenseful unravelling of dark, long-kept secrets, and landscapes symbolical of mental states, but once again in the best passages the trivial subgenre bore up under the weight of intense psychological and philosophical drama.

While *Moby-Dick* succeeded for many of its first readers, even if only as a reliable source of cetological information, *Pierre* failed disastrously on all levels. Yet Melville's basic preoccupations are almost identical in both, except that in *Pierre* he shifted considerably from metaphysics toward psychology. Many of the themes of *Moby-Dick* recur, among them the determinant power of wayward moods over human destiny and the tragic necessity that loftier souls hurl themselves against the unresponsive gods in order to assert their own godhood; many of the images recur, especially the sliding, gliding aboriginal phantoms which link Fedallah and Isabel as embodiments of the Unconscious.[2] Stirred by these or other powerful elements, whether or not related to *Moby-Dick*, the best readers of *Pierre* have paid tribute to the heroic intellectual tasks Melville undertook in it. Yet of them only E. L. Grant Watson thought those heroic tasks had been successfully accomplished,[3] while others more often admired the endeavour, whatever they construed it to be, but praised only one aspect or another of the performance. This critical ambivalence toward *Pierre* is captured in the concluding assessment of the Historical Note in the Northwestern-Newberry Edition: 'none of Melville's other "secondary" works has so regularly evoked from its most thorough critics the sense that they are in the presence of grandeur, however flawed'.[4] But scholars and critics have not been able to define the precise nature of the book's grandeur or the precise nature of the flaws which prevent it from being the masterpiece which *Moby-Dick* indisputably is. The problem of how *Pierre* fails can be answered only by rigorous attention to both biographical and aesthetic evidence. Our answers derived from documentary evidence are presented elsewhere[5]; here we focus on evidence from within the book itself.

To understand Melville's achievements and failures in *Pierre*, especially the unusual complexity of its plottedness, the air it initially breathes of being all worked out in advance, requires going backwards beyond *Moby-Dick*. Though real-life adventure dictated the simple, suspenseful outline of *Typee*, the book is marred by confusing shifts in narrative attitude, and several late-written chapters betray Melville's pragmatic necessity to overlay useful information onto his slim set of personal actions and perceptions. *Omoo* is much more of a piece, but its secure point of view does not wholly disguise the tinkering process by which Melville added chapters or parts of chapters as he gained access to certain sourcebooks or became absorbed with a particular topic. The first chapters of *Mardi* reveal far greater literary control than *Typee* and *Omoo*, but much of the book is notoriously 'chartless.' Far from being written consecutively according to a well-designed plan, the book reflects Melville's altering interests, as when the lengthy section of political satire was plumped down into a manuscript already thought of as completed. The latter half of *Redburn* is less unified than the first, despite the power of individual scenes. Most critics agree that an alteration in the point of view blurs the distance between Melville and his narrator and between the narrator and his younger self. As with *Mardi*, Melville seems to have drafted an ending of *Redburn* before inserting lengthy sections of new material, and possibly before adding a major character. In *White-Jacket* Melville skilfully deals out through the book little sets of chapters concerning the Jacket, flogging, places visited or passed in the voyage, and chapters anatomizing the man-of-war and its inhabitants. His narrator this time is close enough akin to himself to speak the most profound thoughts Melville could think on subjects such as human societies, and even shares his own lesser crotchets and compulsions. Still more ambitious than *White-Jacket*, with epic and tragic drama the models rather than a somewhat perfunctorily allegorical anatomy, *Moby-Dick* triumphs over its grabbag qualities. Melville's narrator is once again all but indistinguishable from the author in his patterns of thought, and as much more complex than White Jacket as Melville himself had become during the intervening year or two. Still, Melville's letters to Hawthorne show that however strong the 'pervading thought that impelled the book', the completion of *Moby-Dick* involved last-minute patchwork. After the first half or so had gone to press, chapters or parts of chapters were inserted here and there in the latter parts of the manuscript. Unlike his first three books, *Moby-Dick* triumphantly sustains its power to the end. By *Moby-Dick*, however, an ominous pattern had emerged: when Melville failed, it was not at the outset of a book, but later on, when the initial impulse had faded.

For a several-week period of almost uninterrupted concentration after he began *Pierre*, Melville exerted an intellectual power which he had previously manifested only in *Moby-Dick* and a sustained control over his plot which was new to him. Very possibly that power and control carried him through to the conclusion of *Pierre* as a short novel, the shortest book he had written since *Typee*. Since the Harpers had rebuffed him the last time he had negotiated concerning a work-in-progress, the manuscript of *Pierre* which he took to them around New Year's Day of 1852 was probably complete or almost complete. The publishers accepted *Pierre* promptly enough, estimating it to take up some 360 pages, but their terms were ungenerous: rather than the usual 50¢ on the dollar after expenses Melville was to receive only 20¢. Stung by the implications for his career (the terms meant he might have to give up any hope of supporting his family by his writing), Melville was further distressed by reviews of *Moby-Dick* in the January magazines, for among them were scathing attacks on him personally as well as on his books. Brooding over the ironies of his literary career—initial fame with *Typee* from little effort or merit, financial failure from the ambitious *Mardi*, new condemnation for *Moby-Dick*, ill omens for his latest brainchild, Melville seems to have done what he did with *Mardi* after it was 'finished'—worked a previously unplanned plot line into the latter part of his manuscript. Almost surely, as Leon Howard and others have assumed, what Melville added to make *Pierre* swell by some 150 or 160 pages was the plot involving *Pierre* as a juvenile author and a young author immaturely attempting a mature book.[6] The first half of *Pierre* as we know it probably survives pretty nearly intact from the original phase of composition, while the second half consists of more or less altered remnants of approximately the last third of the original version intermixed with sections written in January and February 1852. Signs of Melville's careful initial planning remain evident throughout the first half: to the end of Book XIV, 'The Journey and the Pamphlet,' action taking place in the novel's present occupies just four days, with Pierre and his companions leaving Saddle Meadows early on the morning of the fifth; lengthy flashbacks to different periods in the past illuminate developments in the present. Some signs of such careful planning survive even later, the heavy emphasis on the first and third nights in the city, for instance, suggesting that Melville may have originally written that section with a similarly controlled time scheme. A few awkwardnesses can be adduced, aside from those which are due to the insertion of the new plot,[7] but by and large the plotting in *Pierre* is intricate and accurate and of a novelistic expertise new to Melville, extending to consistency of detail, just where he had never manifested anything approaching a compulsive tidiness.[8] Care in plotting is especially obvious—indeed, deliberately over-obvious—in the elaborate predictions of events to come and in the complex set of cross references which lace parts of the book together.

The predictions come thick and fast at the outset, where they would naturally come if they are going to come at all. We are led to expect that the lives of Pierre and his mother will divide (5), and that after Pierre's interior development he will not prize his ancestry so much (6). His aspirations clearly will be thwarted by Time (8), and his 'special family distinction' will be important to his singularly developed character and life career (12). Fate will very likely knock him off his pedestal (12), he will become philosophical (13), and will become a thoroughgoing democrat, even a Radical one (13). The predictions continue: Nature will prove ambiguous to Pierre in the end (13); Lucy will long afterwards experience far different 'flutterings' from those at Saddle Meadows (26); Pierre will never regain his lost sense of an undisturbed moral beauty in the world (65); his crawling under the Memnon Stone will later hold immense significance for him (135); in aftertimes with Isabel, Pierre will often recall his first magnetic night with her (151); Pierre, Isabel, and Delly will never return to Saddle Meadows once they leave (203). After the departure from Saddle Meadows the predictions diminish, as they naturally would past the middle of the book, when predictions are being fulfilled, not made. The pamphlet which Pierre reads in the coach may influence his conduct (210); he will later understand the utility of Machiavellian policy though not have the heart to use it (222); his ties to Glen will involve in the end the most serious consequences (224); and he will learn that the world has fire and sword for contemporary grandeur (264). On reflective scrutiny a few of these predictions seem a trifle misleading, as when the reader may gather (5) that Pierre's and his mother's lives will divide then continue apart for longer than actually happens. Still other predictions (such as those at page 135 and page 151) seem to promise a more patient following of Pierre's river of mind than occurs after he arrives at the city and becomes settled at the Apostles'. But the predictions usually come true in unambiguous fashion. If the early chapters now stand roughly in order of their composition, they indicate that Melville had much of the basic plot well outlined from the beginning. The rather thick-strewn predictions do not, however, prove that no radical new elements were introduced into the plot. Curiously enough, despite all the fulfilled predictions there is nothing which conclusively proves that Melville intended from the outset to have Pierre become a writer once he was exiled from his home. In fact, the pattern of predictions makes it seem most likely that if Melville had had any such plan he would have signalled it at intervals throughout the Saddle Meadows section. Moreover, Melville may not have let stand some of the city episodes in the ways he had once intended. These limitations aside, the predictions do furnish at least some evidence as to the unusual degree of Melville's control over his material.

Equal care in plotting is revealed in the way much of the book is tied together by cross references such as those to Nature's bounty toward Pierre (13–14, 257); what Pierre and Lucy believe about lovers' secrecies

(37, 81, 309); Lucy's easel (39, 318); the will of Pierre's father (55, 179); the first paragraph of Isabel's letter (63, 175); Pierre's promise to protect Isabel (66, 113, 205); the chair portrait in the chintz-covered chest (87, 196); Isabel's one outburst of aggressive enthusiasm (160, 174); Lucy's fainting words (183, 206, 308); Mrs Glendinning's words of banishment (185, 206); the military cloaks which Dates packs (187, 301); the fire at the Black Swan Inn (198, 217, 255–6); Pierre's interest in the pamphlet attributed to Plotinus Plinlimmon (209, 293); Pierre's youthful sonnet 'The Tropical Summer' (245, 263, 306); and Pierre as a toddler (296, 305). The number and aptness of most of the cross references indicate that sometimes Melville was planning ahead for such details with what was, for him, remarkable thoroughness, and that at other times he was making an unusual effort to tie some of what he was writing to particular passages already written; and while writing some passages he may even have gone back to introduce forward-looking references.

Unusual though it was for Melville, control of such details obviously does not of itself lead to great fiction. Indeed the excessive emphasis on predictions early in *Pierre* reflects Melville's satirical playing with one of the routine conventions of popular fiction. His real triumph of control in *Pierre* is the way he leads the reader into fascinated engagement with his remarkable thematic preoccupations. At the outset he risks failing to achieve any such engagement at all, for he strangely idealizes the social rank and superior natures of the characters, who feel extraordinary emotions and speak an extraordinary language. In Book I, 'Pierre Just Emerging from His Teens', the first words of dialogue are ludicrous, by realistic standards, and there seems some fairy-tale quality about the whole situation. The style is often pseudo-Elizabethan bombast, often near the cloying romanticism of female novels of Melville's own time. Yet rapidly the reader begins to feel the tension created between the idealization of the characters and the constant predictions of disaster: the novel is to be a grand experiment in which Fate will take a hand in the life history of a rare specimen of mankind. With daring and often outrageous stylistic improvising Melville is in fact mocking Pierre's adolescent heroics, his unearned sense of security, and his unwillingness to face those dark truths that are to be the burden of the novel. The reader is led to view Pierre with amused, objective condescension and even slight contempt at the same time that he feels concern for the approaching crash of Pierre's illusions. After the early sense of impending calamity, Melville moves into another way of engaging his readers, by giving his hero unbidden inklings of a darker side of life. Events within and without impel Pierre toward maturer thought, yet he is reluctant to become philosophic (which in this novel means to awaken to a tragic sense). At the end of Book II, 'Love, Delight, and Alarm', Grief is still only a 'ghost-story' to Pierre (41). He resists the 'treacherous persuasiveness' (42) of the mournful pine tree and curses his reading in Dante (42), rejecting even imagined, not felt, ex-

perience of the darker aspects of reality, thinking, in juvenile pug-
naciousness, that deprived of joy he would find cause for deadly feuds
with things invisible.

In Book III, 'The Presentiment and the Verification', as Melville
begins to develop Pierre's deeper side, his narrative voice becomes more
restrained and sombre. He portrays the stirrings of Pierre's Unconscious,
from which 'bannered armies of hooded phantoms' (49) disembark and
attack his conscious mind. Yet Pierre still shrinks 'abhorringly from the infernal catacombs of thought' when beckoned by a 'foetal fancy' (51); he
fights against his new sensations as a 'sort of unhealthiness' (53) when
stirred 'in his deepest moral being' (as he thinks) by the sight of Isabel's
face (49). But after receiving Isabel's letter his reluctance to face Truth
when he does not know what he is evading turns into overeagerness to
face Truth when he does not know what he is inviting (65). Hereafter
Melville continues to trace the process of Pierre's mental growth, so that
the reader becomes privy to the seemingly 'boundless expansion' (66) of
the young hero's life. Previously engrossed and perhaps intermittently
baffled by the stylistic virtuosity with which Melville reveals Pierre's absurdities, the reader is now impelled to follow the murky courses of
Pierre's mind through all the ambiguous consequences of his absolute
behaviour.

Book IV, 'Retrospective', as the title suggests, interrupts Melville's analysis of Pierre's current mental state. Now Melville announces explicitly a
major theme present from the beginning but not emphasized before: that
of the supersubtle complexity of psychological motivations and indeed of
all psychological processes. We had been told (7) that tracing out 'precisely the absolute motives' which prompted Pierre to partake of the Holy
Sacraments at the age of sixteen would be needless as well as difficult;
merely, Pierre seemed to have inherited his ancestors' religion 'by the
same insensible sliding process' that he inherited their other noble personal qualities and their forests and farms. But the stress had been more
on Pierre's immaturity than on the subtlety of the processes by which he
behaved as he did. Post-adolescent love-extravagancies are associated
with 'subterranean sprites and gnomes' (34), but Melville does not then
reveal that these quaint monstrosities emerge from the same Unconscious
whence hooded phantoms are soon to embark (49). Early in the novel
various images of mental processes as gliding and sliding prefigure
Melville's full portrayal of the oblique workings of the mind, but not until
the first chapter of 'Retrospective' does he confront the theme directly: 'In
their precise tracings-out and subtile causations, the strongest and fieriest
emotions of life defy all analytical insight. . . . The metaphysical writers
confess, that the most impressive, sudden, and overwhelming event, as
well as the minutest, is but the product of an infinite series of infinitely involved and untraceable foregoing occurrences. Just so with every motion
of the heart' (67). The rest of Book IV uncovers the extremely complex

combination of suddenly recalled events and stories and unbidden night-thoughts which leads to Pierre's immediate conviction that Isabel is his father's daughter. Hereafter, treatment of Pierre's inward development is inseparable from the theme of the shadowiness of all human motivation, the 'ever-elastic regions of evanescent invention' through which the mind roams up and down (82).

Moreover, by the end of Book IV Melville has gone beyond the super-subtlety of all human psychology to assert the *autonomy* of those subtler elements of man, as we first see in the description of the adolescent Pierre sometimes standing before the chair portrait of his father, 'unconsciously throwing himself open to all those ineffable hints and ambiguities, and undefined half-suggestions, which now and then people the soul's atmosphere, as thickly as in a soft, steady snow-storm, the snow-flakes people the air' (84). The imagery suggests an evanescence of thought which the individual no more controls than he does the snow-storm, and Melville distinguishes these 'reveries and trances' from the 'assured element of consciously bidden and self-propelled thought' (84). With similar intimations of forces beyond Pierre's control, Melville refers to the 'streams' of Pierre's reveries over the chair portrait of his father which did not seem 'to leave any conscious sediment in his mind; they were so light and so rapid, that they rolled their own alluvial along; and seemed to leave all Pierre's thought-channels as clean and dry as though never any alluvial stream had rolled there at all' (85). In Book V, 'Misgivings and Preparatives', Fate irresistibly gives Pierre an 'electric insight' into 'the vital character of his mother' so that he now sees her as unalterably dominated by 'hereditary forms and world-usages' (89). As Melville says, 'in these flashing revelations of grief's wonderful fire, we see all things as they are' (88). Such use of images of natural phenomena to suggest the involuntary processes of the mind continues with added intensity after Pierre has had time to reflect on the letter from Isabel, when the thought of Lucy 'serpent-like . . . overlayingly crawled in upon his other shuddering imaginings' (104). These other thoughts, we are told, would often 'upheave' and absorb the thought of Lucy into themselves, 'so that it would in that way soon disappear from his cotemporary apprehension' (104). The serpent image and the image of upheaval imply, once again, an independent vitality in the thought, free of Pierre's conscious control. Natural imagery now becomes more complexly elaborated as Melville portrays an expansion of Pierre's interior dimensions during the mental turmoil into which his reading of the letter has plunged him: 'Standing half-befogged upon the mountain of his Fate, all that part of the wide panorama was wrapped in clouds to him; but anon those concealings slid aside, or rather, a quick rent was made in them' (105). Through the 'swift cloud-rent' Pierre catches one glimpse of Lucy's 'expectant and angelic face', but 'the next instant the stormy pinions of the clouds locked themselves over it again; and all was hidden as before; and all went confused in whirling rack and vapor as before'. Yet while thus 'for the most part wrapped from his consciousness and vision', the condition of Lucy 'was still more and more disentangling and defining itself from out its nether mist,[9] and even beneath the general upper fog' (105). This passage portrays a rapidly expanded mental terrain but still a chaotic and uncontrollable one.

What Melville has achieved is an extraordinary conversion of Gothic sensationalism—mysterious face prefiguring revelation of dark family secrets—into profound psychological exploration. Isabel, Pierre's presumed half-sister, is identified either as his Unconscious or as a product of it, so that his closer involvement with her parallels his gradual opening to incursions from the Unconscious. His after-reveries on her face (41) are associated with his dawning half-admission that Grief may be more than merely a 'ghost-story'. Without 'one word of speech', her face had revealed 'glimpses of some fearful gospel' (43). Within an hour of first seeing Isabel, Pierre felt that 'what he had always before considered the solid land of veritable reality, was now being audaciously encroached upon by bannered armies of hooded phantoms, disembarking in his soul, as from flotillas of specter-boats' (49). After reading Isabel's letter, Pierre 'saw all preceding ambiguities, all mysteries ripped open as if with a keen sword, and forth trooped thickening phantoms of an infinite gloom' (85). Prior to his first interview with her in Book VI, 'Isabel, and the First Part of the Story of Isabel', Pierre gives himself up to 'long wanderings in the primeval woods of Saddle Meadows' (109); formerly sunny and Arcadian, the landscape now mirrors his new sense of the world: in the 'wet and misty eve the scattered, shivering pasture elms seemed standing in a world inhospitable'. The landscape also mirrors the depths and terrors Isabel has opened up in Pierre's psyche:

> On both sides, in the remoter distance, and also far beyond the mild lake's further shore, rose the long, mysterious mountain masses; shaggy with pines and hemlocks, mystical with nameless, vapory exhalations, and in that dim air black with dread and gloom. At their base, profoundest forests lay entranced, and from their far owl-haunted depths of caves and rotted leaves, and unused and unregarded inland overgrowth of decaying wood—for smallest sticks of which, in other climes many a pauper was that moment perishing; from out the infinite inhumanities of those profoundest forests, came a moaning, muttering, roaring, intermitted, changeful sound: rain-shakings of the palsied trees, slidings of rocks undermined, final crashings of long-riven boughs, and devilish gibberish of the forest-ghosts. (109–110)

When Pierre at last meets Isabel at the red farmhouse, what she recounts concerns her childhood process of individuation, a process Pierre is undergoing only now, after first seeing her. She reveals that her constant psychological state is one in which the Unconscious impinges upon the Conscious: 'Always in me, the solidest things melt into dreams, and dreams into solidities' (117); only now has Pierre's own soul begun to be opened to the same integrative and disintegrative mental processes. But Isabel embodies the Unconscious in ways still alien from the awakening Pierre, even to the point of learning 'new things' from the thoughts which 'well up' in her and come forth on her tongue without the intervention of any conscious process, so that the speech is 'sometimes before the thought' (123). Bursting from the 'sorceries' of the interview (128), Pierre at the beginning of Book VII, 'Intermediate between Pierre's Two Interviews with Isabel at the Farm-house', for 'an instant' almost wishes for a reversion to his earlier vision of a simpler, unmysterious world and to ignorance of his own newly-opened, threatening depths: 'he almost could have prayed Isabel back into the wonder-world from which she had so slidingly emerged' (129). Yet the lure of these new depths is more powerful than their threats, for he again withdraws to a forest where his eye pursues 'its ever-shifting shadowy vistas' and where there come into his mind 'thoughts and fancies never imbibed within the gates of towns; but only given forth by the atmosphere of primeval forests' (139). Formerly the unconscious processes of Pierre's mind were imaged as a stream; now, indicative of his greater depths, from the 'thoughtful river' of his mind run 'unending, ever-flowing', thoughts of Isabel (141). But Pierre's process of yielding ground in his soul to the invading Unconscious continues to involve occasional checks or reversals. In the interval after his second interview with Isabel, during which he had made the most binding pledges, there comes a moment when, fain to disown his memory and mind, Pierre dashes himself against a wall and falls 'dabbling in the vomit of his loathed identity' (171). As the narrator warns, the human soul is 'strange and complicate' (176). Pierre's final resolution to champion Isabel by pretending to have married her is arrived at only by 'nameless struggles of the soul' (181).

Moreover, Pierre's 'infinite magnanimities' (177) from the outset are inextricably linked with appalling self-delusion. From the opening pages Melville has set forth, in scenes which initially baffle the reader, the chivalric artifice of Pierre's ideals and intimate relationships—a habit of mind that makes him uniquely vulnerable to the particular appeal Isabel makes. In our first glimpse of Pierre with Lucy he idealizes her as an 'invoking angel' while idealizing himself as a soldier marching under her 'colors'. She participates in the role-playing, crying ' "Bravissimo! oh, my only recruit!" ' when he fastens her flower to his bosom (4), and both of them speak in what seems an absurdly heightened rhetoric. From this depiction of Pierre as romantic cavalier Melville immediately moves to the depiction of 'romantic filial love', Pierre's benignly presented but ultimately unhealthy habit of treating 'his pedastaled mother' with a 'strange license' under which 'they were wont to call each other brother and sister' (5). Any suitor who might dare to propose marriage to this youthful-appearing widow 'would by some peremptory unrevealed agency immediately disappear from the earth', dispatched by her jealous chivalric protector (5). Pierre's dead father, we learn, had left him a legacy of idealistic maxims, one of which was that no one could claim to be a gentleman unless he 'could also rightfully assume the meek, but kingly style of Christian' (6). Thus at sixteen Pierre, playing the role of young Christian gentleman, partakes of the Holy Sacraments. To Pierre's exalted view 'the complete polished steel of the gentleman' was thereby 'girded with Religion's silken sash' (7). In this atmosphere of ideality he longs for a sister, someone whom he 'might love, and protect, and fight for, if need be' (7). He repeatedly images himself as would-be champion: 'It must be a glorious thing to engage in a mortal quarrel on a sweet sister's behalf!' (7). Predisposed toward such a self-image by both his parents, Pierre finds another source of chivalric notions in Nature herself, who in the beginning did 'bravely' by him (13): 'She lifted her spangled crest of a thickly-starred night, and forth at that glimpse of their divine Captain and Lord, ten thousand mailed thoughts of heroicness started up in Pierre's soul, and glared round for some insulted good cause to defend' (14).

For none of these chivalric impulses is there a normal outlet. There is no real likelihood that Pierre will need to fend off suitors from his mother, despite his playful-earnest role of her knight-in-waiting. With Lucy, Pierre's chivalric notions must be reduced merely to the courtesies of courtship, since she hardly needs his defense, what with two youthful brothers themselves overeager to fulfil their own chivalric obligations toward her. The first true appeal to his chivalry comes with his earliest glimpse of Isabel's face, on which 'he seemed to see the fair ground where Anguish had contended with Beauty, and neither being conqueror, both had laid down on the field' (47). The narrator's language reveals the intensity of Pierre's chivalric obsession. Beyond the bewildering allure of the beauty and the anguish of the face, Pierre is aware of a special effect, 'the face somehow mystically appealing to his own private and individual affections; and by a silent and tyrannic call, challenging him in his deepest moral being, and summoning Truth, Love, Pity, Conscience, to the stand' (49). Until he receives Isabel's letter, Pierre resists this appeal to his heroism, since his other chivalric obligations, his duty to his mother and his fiancée, forbid any response and since there is no reasonable course of action he can take. Her letter finally gives him the heroic good cause he has been looking for: suddenly he has the sister on whose behalf he can engage in a mortal quarrel. After the first devastating shock, the letter arouses all his would-be heroic, chivalric impulses: he will 'comfort', 'stand by', and 'fight for' Isabel (66).

Yet Pierre is woefully ill-equipped to set out as a Christian Knight-Champion, most obviously because the pattern of chivalric, romantic idealization has developed simultaneously with—and at the cost of —dangerous sublimation of his sexual feelings. His glide toward physical maturity, we are told at the outset, was accompanied by ambiguous feelings aroused during his reading in 'his father's fastidiously picked and decorous library' (6). There the 'Spenserian nymphs had early led him into many a maze of all-bewildering beauty' that created 'a graceful glow on his limbs, and soft, imaginative flames in his heart' (6). When first mentioned these nymphs seem to be summoning courtly, aesthetic impulses, but later it becomes clear that Pierre is unconsciously responding to them with the stirrings of puberty. For most of the novel, in fact, Pierre idealizes his sexual impulses, failing to recognize them for what they are. Latently incestuous, his courtly 'lover-like adoration' of his mother (16) is deceptively suffused with religious sentiment: the spell which wheeled mother and son in one orbit of joy seemed 'almost to realize here below the sweet dreams of those religious enthusiasts, who paint to us a Paradise to come, when etherealized from all drosses and stains, the holiest passion of man shall unite all kindreds and climes in one circle of pure and unimpairable delight' (16). At the time the novel opens, Pierre is still unprepared to recognize his sexual feelings, despite his engagement to Lucy. During their outing in the phaeton he alternates between mysticalness and merriment, unaware of the strength of his own sexuality, for he does not acknowledge the erotic nature of the 'subterranean sprites and gnomes' and 'naiads' that surround him (34). Lucy instinctively shrinks from him in 'Fear and Wonder' (35) when he bursts 'forth in some screaming shout of joy', the 'striped tigers of his chestnut eyes' leaping 'in their lashed cages with a fierce delight'. But even after holding Lucy's hand, 'feeling, softly feeling of its soft tinglingness', Pierre still idealizes his sexuality, diffusing it into an exalted response to nature, so that he seems like someone 'in linked correspondence with the summer lightnings', by 'sweet shock on shock, receiving intimating foretastes of the etherealest delights of earth' (36). Later, as he fetches a portfolio from Lucy's chamber, we learn of more mental contortions which he undergoes in order to sublimate and generalize the feelings aroused in him:

> He never had entered that chamber but with feelings of a wonderful reverentialness. The carpet seemed as holy ground. Every chair seemed sanctified by some departed saint, there once seated long ago. Here his book of Love was all a rubric, and said—Bow now, Pierre, bow. But this extreme loyalty to the piety of love, called from him by such glimpses of its most secret inner shrine, was not unrelieved betimes by such quickenings of all his pulses, that in fantasy he pressed the wide beauty of the world in his embracing arms; for all his world resolved itself into his heart's best love for Lucy. (39)

Thus predisposed, Pierre's mental processes betwist themselves anew at the sewing circle in order to let him feel that the mysterious face he has glimpsed is somehow tyrannically challenging him 'in his deepest moral being' (49). Characteristically, he manages to tame and prettify the profound experience, safely Spenserizing it into a 'delicious sadness' so that some 'hazy fairy swam above him in the heavenly ether, and showered down upon him the sweetest pearls of pensiveness' (54).

One immediate aftereffect of reading Isabel's letter is that Pierre suddenly sees his father as morally corrupt, although he had always idolized him to the point of sacrilege (68), and the narrator emphasizes that the extreme of Pierre's idealization was possible only because at the age of nineteen he 'had never yet become so thoroughly initiated into that darker, though truer aspect of things, which an entire residence in the city from the earliest period of life, almost inevitably engraves upon the mind of any keenly observant and reflective youth' (69). To be sure, during the four years that he had possessed the chair portrait of his father, Pierre had felt 'ever new conceits come vaporing up' in him (83), so that the portrait seemed to speak with his father's voice: 'I am thy father, boy. There was once a certain, oh, but too lovely young Frenchwoman, Pierre'. Then, 'starting from these reveries and trances, Pierre would regain the assured element of consciously bidden and self-propelled thought' (84), promising never again to fall into such midnight reveries, suppressing suspicions of his father even as he begins to diffuse his own sexual feelings. In his agonized hours following the reading of Isabel's letter, Pierre feels that 'his whole previous moral being' (87) has been overturned. But though he is no longer free to worship his father, he still does not apply to himself the lesson earlier intimated by the chair portrait and apparently confirmed by Isabel's letter, that 'Youth is hot, and temptation strong', that beneath seeming innocence sexual impulses may be stirring (83). His sense of his own immaculateness is chronic. In sublime delusion he feels Christlike, as if 'deep in him lurked a divine unidentifiableness, that owned no earthly kith or kin' (89). While the narrator offers us 'hell-glimpses' (107), reminding us that Pierre was championing 'womanly beauty, and not womanly ugliness', Pierre himself is asking heaven to confirm him in his 'Christ-like feeling' (106).

More mental contortions follow as the deluded Christian knight begins to respond to Isabel's attractiveness. Accustomed from adolescence to a certain falseness in the relationship of mother-son, and more recently exposed to the new artifice by which Mrs Glendinning had converted Lucy into her little sister, Pierre blames Fate for his bewildered feelings about Isabel: 'Fate had done this thing for them. Fate had separated the brother and the sister, till to each other they somehow seemed so not at all. Sisters shrink not from their brother's kisses' (142). Pierre begins 'to seem to see the mere imaginariness of the so supposed solidest principle of human association'—an incipient discrediting of the taboo against incest—yet feels 'that never, never would he be able to embrace Isabel with the mere brotherly embrace; while the thought of any other caress, which took hold of any domesticness, was entirely vacant from his uncontaminated soul, for it had never consciously intruded there' (142). In this state of mind, and just because his latent incestuous feelings are now stirring, Pierre is compelled, all ignorantly, to sublimate: 'Isabel wholly soared out of the realms of mortalness, and for him became transfigured in the highest heaven of uncorrupted Love' (142). Even as Lucy's bedroom had represented Love's 'secret inner shrine' for Pierre, at his second interview with Isabel the 'deep oaken recess of the double-casement' seems to him the 'vestibule of some awful shrine' (149), though Isabel's power over him is by now more obviously erotic: Pierre feels himself (150) 'surrounded by ten thousand sprites and gnomes, and his whole soul was swayed and tossed by supernatural tides'. (Here the narrator's word 'soul' merely reflects Pierre's own self-protective instinct toward sublimation.) Aware of an 'extraordinary physical magnetism' in Isabel, Pierre nevertheless generalizes his sexual attraction by associating it with a 'Pantheistic master-spell, which eternally locks in mystery and in muteness the universal subject world' (151). Just as he had pledged to Lucy 'the immutable eternities of joyfulness' (36), Pierre now makes extravagant lover-like declarations to Isabel, wishing that his kisses on her hand 'were on the heart itself, and dropt the seeds of eternal joy and comfort there' (154). In egregious delusion of immaculate magnanimity, his pledges to Isabel become as extravagant as his recurrent threats to the gods: 'we will love with the pure and perfect love of angel to an angel. If ever I fall from thee, dear Isabel, may Pierre fall from himself; fall back forever into vacant nothingness and night!' (154). By reinforcing his sense of his own Christlikeness, calling him a 'visible token' of the 'invisible angel-hoods', and praising the 'gospel' of his acts (156), Isabel aids Pierre in sublimating the passion increasingly evident in his words.

Yet both Isabel and Pierre use the licence of their supposed brother-and-sister, champion-and-damsel, relationship to indulge in verbal love-making. In language that appeals to Pierre's religious-chivalric impulses, Isabel describes her reluctant surrender to him at the sewing circle: 'Once having met thy fixed regardful glance; once having seen the full angelicalness in thee, my whole soul was undone by thee . . . till I knew, that utterly decay and die away I must, unless pride let me go, and I, with the one little trumpet of a pen, blew my heart's shrillest blast, and called dear Pierre to me' (159). In his own imagination Pierre still sees himself as Christlike knight. When Isabel fears that he might be hurt by any public or secret relationship with her, he lies—denies what he has so recently learned about his father—in order to keep his heroic cause from slipping away: 'Is Love a harm? Can Truth betray to pain? Sweet Isabel, how can hurt come in the path to God?' (159–60). He swears by heaven that he 'will crush the disdainful world down on its knees' to Isabel (160). As she exultingly responds, her 'long scornful hair' trails out like a 'disheveled banner' before the would-be knight, who acknowledges 'that irrespective, darting majesty of humanity, which can be majestical and menacing in woman as in man' (160). (A part of Isabel's allure for Pierre is her fleeting resemblance to his mother, whose 'stately beauty had ever somewhat martial in it' [20].) As a culmination to the emotional self-indulgence which increases throughout this interview, Pierre and Isabel partake of what Pierre blasphemously calls 'the real sacrament of the supper' (162).

Miserably deluded, Pierre thinks, even after his second interview with Isabel, that he is responding to 'the unsuppressible and unmistakable cry of the godhead through her soul', a cry which commands him 'to fly to her, and do his highest and most glorious duty in the world' (174). By the time he has reached his final resolution his formula, sublimated once again, has become: 'Lucy or God?' (181), though soon afterward Pierre speciously claims that he and Isabel will act deceitfully for the 'united good' of themselves and those they deceive (190). Just after insisting that he is 'pure' (191) and claiming that he and Isabel reach up alike to a 'glorious ideal' (192), Pierre whispers his plan as 'his mouth wet her ear' (192). Then comes an immediate and appalling descent from the exalta-tion: 'The girl moved not; was done with all her tremblings; leaned closer to him, with an inexpressible strangeness of an intense love, new and inexplicable. Over the face of Pierre there shot a terrible self-revelation; he imprinted repeated burning kisses upon her; pressed hard her hand; would not let go her sweet and awful passiveness. Then they changed; they coiled together, and entangledly stood mute' (192). For the first time in the book Melville's deluded idealist acts—and knows that he acts—out of undisguised sexual passion.

But Pierre's capacity for evading unpleasant self-knowledge is far from exhausted. Shortly afterwards, at the Black Swan Inn, he decides that his memorial gold pieces must be spent now 'in this sacred cause' (196), an obvious denial that Isabel had 'become a thing of intense and fearful love for him' (197)—fearful precisely because of his terrible self-revelation at the dairy. Yet that sundown at the Inn Pierre burns the chair portrait of his father out of an unconscious need to free himself of the strongest visible reminder that his passion for Isabel, whatever else it is, is incestuous. In the coach next morning his 'still imperfectly conscious, incipient, new-mingled emotion toward this mysterious being' (206) appals him, to the point that he feels 'threatened by the possibility of a sin anomalous and accursed'—perhaps the unpardonable sin itself. Though he has learned much about his mother's and his father's character, he is still in the first stages of reluctantly learning about his own. Just as he had destroyed the reminder of Isabel's paternity the night before, now in the coach Pierre refuses to recognize the applicability of the strange pamphlet on 'Chronometricals and Horologicals' either to his own situation or to Christianity in general: he can admit neither that an absolute attempt to obey Christ is apt to involve ordinary mortals 'in strange, *unique* follies and sins, unimagined before' (213) nor that Christianity has flourished for two millennia only by systematically diluting the edicts of its founder, rather than taking them literally, as he has tried to do.

Nowhere in the book, moreover, does Pierre see that for all his efforts to be Christlike he has never been a true Christian. Despite his partaking with his mother of the Holy Sacraments, he has in fact been only nominally a Christian, drawn to the Church as a family responsibility laid down by his father, whose maxim linked gentlemanhood and Christianity. The super-human powers Pierre invokes are ill-sortedly Christian or pagan; consistently he images his relationship with such powers as an antagonistic one: demons or gods, they are to be threatened and, especially, bargained with. The language he uses again and again threatens what he will do 'if' the powers do not act as he wishes. He conjures the 'sovereign powers' that claim all his 'leal worshipings' to lift the veil between him and the mysterious face; if they abandon him to 'an unknown misery', his faith 'may clean depart' and leave him 'a railing atheist' (41). If 'deprived of joy', he feels he would 'find cause for deadly feuds with things invisible' (41). He feels he has a 'choice quarrel' with the Fate which had led him to think the world was one of Joy, if in fact the night which wraps his soul after he reads Isabel's letter is genuine (65). In the interval before his first interview with Isabel he prays that heaven 'new-string' his soul (106), confirming in him 'the Christ-like feeling' he first felt on reading her letter; yet in the same speech he simultaneously invokes and threatens the 'sovereign powers' (106-7) if they betray his faith in them:

> I cast my eternal die this day, ye powers. On my strong faith in ye Invisibles, I stake three whole felicities, and three whole lives this day. If ye forsake me now,—farewell to Faith, farewell to Truth, farewell to God; exiled for aye from God and man, I shall declare myself an equal power with both; free to make war on Night and Day, and all thoughts and things of mind and matter, which the upper and the nether firmaments do clasp! (107)

Pierre's new Christlikeness is a most ambiguous one, since it leads instantly to threats against God. Then, between the two interviews with Isabel, Pierre slides under 'the very brow of the beetlings and the menacings of the Terror Stone', named by him for the temple of Memnon. Not threatening the Stone, he nevertheless promulgates a series of conditions in which the 'Mute Massiveness' is invited to fall on him (134). When the Stone fails to act on the implied challenge, he adolescently assumes a new haughtiness and goes his 'moody way' as though he 'owed thanks to none' (135).

The threats and bargains with the gods culminate in the scene with Pierre and Isabel at the Apostles' the third night after their arrival in the city. Once again Pierre makes pledges, inviting the 'high gods' to join the devils against him if he deceives Isabel (272). Once again he invites instant punishment if he fails in Virtue: 'then close in and crush me, ye stony walls, and into one gulf let all things tumble together!' (273). Once again he warns the gods, this time to 'look after their own combustibles':

'If they have put powder-casks in me—let them look to it! let them look to it!' (273). But in a crucial difference from earlier scenes Pierre now suspects that man himself, instead of the gods, may be a 'vile juggler and cheat' (272). Incapable now in Isabel's presence of denying to himself her erotic appeal, he fears that 'uttermost virtue, after all' may prove 'but a betraying pander to the monstrousest vice', and finally declares that the 'demigods trample on trash, and Virtue and Vice are trash!' (273). Declaring that Virtue and Vice are both nothing, and having already rid himself of the chair portrait, the most tangible reminder of Isabel's link to his father, Pierre is now free to commit incest, though whether or not actual sexual intercourse occurs that night at the Apostles' remains ambiguous but hideously possible.

Up to Pierre's arrival in the city with Isabel and Delly, everything has worked together to enhance the attentive reader's sense that he is in the hands of a profound thinker and innovative craftsman who will convey him through yet more hazardous regions of psychological and aesthetic experience. Melville has not only managed to put sensational Gothic plot elements to the service of an acute analysis of a tortuously complex mind; he has also managed to convert analysis into very vivid action, repeatedly portraying Pierre's psychological states and processes in extended metaphors and images, passages that are short, graphic, and frequently intense narratives in themselves.[10] In these highly-charged passages, Melville combines penetrating analysis of his hero's states of mind with the enunciation of general truths, so that the record of Pierre's particular experience is continually expanding to include human experience at large.[11] By the beginning of Book XVI, 'First Night of Their Arrival in the City', the reader wants nothing more than to follow 'the thoughtful river' of Pierre's mind through all the ambiguous consequences of his sublimely absolute and miserably deluded behaviour. Yet despite the brilliance of the scene on the third night at the Apostles', the wish goes mainly unfulfilled. Melville's primary concerns in the first half of the novel only intermittently engage his attention in the second half, and at times he seems lamentably unaware of the direction the first half was taking.

Symptomatic is the flaw in the first paragraph of Book XVII, 'Young America in Literature':

> Among the various conflicting modes of writing history, there would seem to be two grand practical distinctions, under which all the rest must subordinately range. By the one mode, all contemporaneous circumstances, facts, and events must be set down contemporaneously; by the other, they are only to be set down as the general stream of the narrative shall dictate; for matters which are kindred in time, may be very irrelative in themselves. I elect neither of these; I am careless of either; both are well enough in their way; I write precisely as I please. (244)

Earlier Melville had talked bluntly about his demands on the reader: 'This history goes forward and goes backward, as occasion calls. Nimble center, circumference elastic you must have' (54). He had called attention to his apparent disregard of rules in a passage that might strike the reader as 'rather irregular sort of writing' (25), and had announced that he followed 'the flowing river in the cave of man' careless whither he be led, reckless where he land (107). In these instances he had been in superb control, knowing exactly what he was doing with his stylistic absurdities in Books I and II, then knowing that his simultaneous exploration of Pierre's mind and his own might lead him into unknown winding passages (even as he kept to the outline of his plot), but confident that he could bravely follow that flowing river wherever it ran. Not reckoning where he landed was a way of proclaiming his determination to tell everything 'in this book of sacred truth' (107); he was not abandoning a point of view but asserting his determination to hold to it. The beginning of 'Young America in Literature' marks a drastic change in Melville's authorial purpose, a deep draining off of his control over the relationship between narrator and reader. The change is due to what happened in Melville's life between the last days of 1851 and the first days of 1852, but our concern here is with the effects on the manuscript, not the biographical causes.

After his claim to write precisely as he pleased, Melville continues with this remarkably inexact passage: 'In the earlier chapters of this volume, it has somewhere been passingly intimated, that Pierre was not only a reader of the poets and other fine writers, but likewise—and what is a very different thing from the other—a thorough allegorical understander of them, a profound emotional sympathizer with them' (244). On the contrary, we had been told, by Pierre himself in a moment of insight, that he had *not* been that sort of reader: 'Oh, hitherto I have but piled up words; bought books, and bought some small experiences, and builded me in libraries; now I sit down and read' (91). Furthermore, Melville had also asserted that before Pierre was enlightened by the flashing revelations of Grief's wonderful fire, he had *not* been a thorough allegorical understander of the poets:

> Fortunately for the felicity of the Dilletante in Literature, the horrible allegorical meanings of the Inferno, lie not on the surface; but unfortunately for the earnest and youthful piercers into truth and reality, those horrible meanings, when first discovered, infuse their poison into a spot previously unprovided with that sovereign antidote of a sense of uncapitulatable security, which is only the possession of the furthest advanced and profoundest souls. (169)

When he began Book XVII, Melville had simply forgotten this crucial aspect of his characterization of Pierre.[12] But even in the process of crediting Pierre with being 'a thorough allegorical understander' of and 'a profound emotional sympathizer' with poets and other fine writers,

Melville seems to have recognized his blunder and attempted an immediate recovery:

> Not that as yet his young and immature soul had been accosted by the Wonderful Mutes, and through the vast halls of Silent Truth, had been ushered into the full, secret, eternally inviolable Sanhedrim, where the Poetic Magi discuss, in glorious gibberish, the Alpha and Omega of the Universe. But among the beautiful imaginings of the second and third degree of poets, he freely and comprehendingly ranged. (244–5)

In these rapid second thoughts Melville ends up saying quite another thing from what he had just said: in fact, he reverts to saying something very like what he had denied at the outset of the paragraph, that Pierre was no more than a normally alert reader. The bitter fun Melville has with his mockery of the rules of writing comes at the considerable cost of jeopardizing the reader's trust in the narrative voice.

Deflected into preoccupation with his own literary career, Melville in Books XVII and XVIII let absurdities intrude upon what he wrote of Pierre, as in his analysis of the phenomenon of young writers who win instant success with a book original in subject matter although not the product of a genuinely original mind. In this passage (259) Melville plainly has begun to write about the reception of his own *Typee* six years before, not about Pierre. From his new vantage point Melville was honest in his self-assessment, sure that *Typee* was, after all, original—the first eyewitness account of Polynesian life with the readability of fiction—although he had unoriginally cannibalized his source-books and employed a second or third hand style. The satire in Books XVII and XVIII is acute, but only as applied to Melville and his own critics, not to Pierre, in whose history it is distractingly out of place. Pierre, of course, has never 'embodied' any experience at all in a book, much less 'some rich and peculiar experience' (259), although the reader is belatedly apprised of his authorship of 'little sonnets, brief meditative poems, and moral essays' (248). In suddenly determining to take satiric revenge upon his own reviewers and his literary competitors, Melville is indulging in a 'lamentable rearward aggressiveness' at least as unwarrantable and foolish as Pierre's toward the Rev. Mr Falsgrave (166). The reader was well prepared for Pierre's folly, but the narrator's own mature wisdom throughout the Saddle Meadows section, especially his cautious distance from his hero, had left the reader unprepared for this new and unwarrantable authorial recklessness.

Even before the disastrous Books on literature in America ('before' in final placement though not necessarily so in order of composition), Melville had begun dissipating much of the accumulated tension by introducing lengthy narrative and expository passages largely or wholly irrelevant to the central concern of Pierre's commitment to Isabel. Book XV, 'The Cousins', which is devoted to the intense adolescent love-friendship between Pierre and Glen, might be defended as an essential part of this ruthlessly honest history of the soul in which no taboo in Melville's society can be left unviolated, and indeed the analysis of the stages in that relationship are interesting in themselves. However, the Book seems too long and distinctly anticlimactic, coming immediately after the pamphlet: it is not focused on major issues and the analysis does not impel the book forward, does not tell the reader things he needs to know or prepare him for highly significant things to come. Even the most comparable passage in the early part of the novel, the account of Aunt Dorothea's reminiscences, does not seem so relaxed, because there the reader is in suspense, actively putting things together as he absorbs and meditates upon her story rather faster than she tells it. Books XVII and XVIII have even less to do with the central issues of the first fourteen Books. By contrast, in Book XIX, 'The Church of the Apostles', the history of the building and its inhabitants is potentially relevant, since the Apostles can be seen as versions of Pierre, thwarted idealists, and since the building itself at least casually symbolizes the transfer of power from Christianity to something akin to Transcendentalism. Not enough is made of these points, and the 'gamesome' banter which Melville adopts (267) is distinctly out of keeping with the high seriousness of most of the early part of the novel. The satiric grotesquerie of these pages goes, if not for naught, at least for less than it might have gone in another novel, where other expectations had been set up. Book XX, 'Charlie Millthorpe', seems even more extraneous, since it begins by explaining something which had already been accepted without explanation—Pierre's being at the Apostles'. Now, after the fact, and after the intense scene between Pierre and Isabel which hints at actual physical incest, the reader is told much more than he wants to know about details which are not strictly relevant. Unlike the earlier Books ('Presentiment and Verification' makes a good contrast), Book XX does not significantly add to our knowledge of Pierre's motivation or to our understanding of the main themes. There is considerable verve in the portrait of Charles Millthorpe, just as there had been in the account of the Apostles, but none of the intensity the reader has come to expect. Later, the jocular account of the Apostles' eccentricities (298–301) is jarring, especially when the narrator is led into this commentary upon idealistic behaviour:

> Among all the innate, hyena-like repellants to the reception of any set form of a spiritually-minded and pure archetypical faith, there is nothing so potent in its skeptical tendencies, as that inevitable perverse ridiculousness, which so often bestreaks some of the essentially finest and noblest aspirations of those men, who disgusted with the common conventional quackeries, strive, in their clogged terrestrial humanities, after some imperfectly discerned, but heavenly ideals: ideals, not only imperfectly discerned in themselves, but the path to them so little traceable, that no two minds will entirely agree upon it.

These observations, offered as if they had just occurred to the narrator, had already formed some of the darkest implications of the pamphlet.[13]

Throughout the second half of the book Melville continues this sort of generalizing tendency, making observations on such subjects as 'boy-love' and the change to love of the opposite sex (216–17), the advisability of converting 'some well-wishers into foes' (221–2), the advantages of simplicity (224–5), the need for 'utter gladiatorianism' in dealing with some reversals of fortune (226–7), the 'dread of tautology' (227), the nature of coach-drivers (232), and 'the *povertiresque* in the social land-scape' (276–7). Earlier in the novel Melville's generalizing commentary had been a major source of power, dealing as it had with the motivation and states of mind of Pierre and the social, moral, and metaphysical problems he exemplified. In the second half the authorial commentary largely creates the impression of improvisation and redundancy, an impression emphasized when the narrator compares himself to one of the 'strolling improvisatores of Italy' (259) and when he carelessly concludes one Book with the mention of something 'by way of bagatelle' (294). The reader who has paid alert attention can only feel cheated by this casualness and laxity in authorial commentary.

Bad as these lapses are, by far the worst failure lies in Melville's altered treatment of Pierre. In the first half of the book, one of the most remarkable features had been the scrupulous and often brilliant presentation of the hero's motives and states of mind. In the last Books, Melville not only fails to provide certain contemplative scenes which were earlier implied if not directly promised (such as scenes in which Pierre thinks about the episode of the Memnon Stone after reaching the city or in which he remembers his first evening with Isabel), he also fails to devote sufficient analysis to Pierre's present states of mind, especially as they involve Isabel. Pierre had vowed to cherish and protect her, to treat her as an artisan handles 'the most exquisite, and fragile filagree of Genoa' (189). But he does not fulfill his pledges; instead, in a few days after reaching the city he becomes almost entirely preoccupied with the book he suddenly begins to write. Isabel is not allowed to participate in his labours (except much later to read aloud proofs to him) and is no longer at the centre of his thoughts. After the arrival in the city, in fact, Isabel is absent from the narrative for long periods. Apart from the scene on the third night at the Apostles' (271–4), she scarcely figures in the story at all until the reintroduction of Lucy. Henry A. Murray aptly comments: 'Pierre, having devoured what Isabel had to give him, is withdrawing libido (interest, love) from her as a person and using it to fold, and warm, and egg round embryoes of thought and to feed a precipitant ambition'.[14] Such an outcome is perhaps credible enough, considering the trauma and the 'widely explosive' mental development Pierre has experienced, but it does not receive from Melville the close analytical scrutiny that is typical of the first half of the book.

Markedly, what we do learn of Pierre and Isabel—sexual arousal, deceit, insincerity, and unease on his part, suspicion, jealousy, and hysteria on hers—is presented dramatically for the most part, without the earlier omniscient commentary. We are told that, on the news of his mother's death and Glen Stanly's inheritance of Saddle Meadows and rumoured courtship of Lucy, Pierre curses himself for an 'idiot fool' because 'he had himself, as it were, resigned his noble birthright to a cunning kinsman for a mess of pottage, which now proved all but ashes in his mouth' (289). We also learn that he feels that these are 'unworthy pangs' and resolves to hide them from Isabel (289). But otherwise Pierre's feelings for her are scarcely explored. His awareness or unawareness of the extent to which the relationship has deteriorated, his attitude toward that change, are not examined. Pierre's incestuous passion, once central to the book, becomes the subject of offhand allusion: 'Not to speak of his being devoured by the all-exacting theme of his book, there were sinister preoccupations in him of a still subtler and more fearful sort, of which some inklings have already been given' (308). When late in the novel we learn of Pierre that the 'most tremendous displacing and revolutionizing thoughts were upheaving in him, with reference to Isabel' (353), the only such thought we actually learn about is the question of whether she is truly his half-sister. The crucial information that Pierre's virtuous enthusiasm in behalf of Isabel has declined comes in an aside; his 'transcendental persuasions' that she was his sister, we learn, were 'originally born, as he now seemed to feel, purely of an intense procreative enthusiasm:—an enthusiasm no longer so all-potential with him as of yore' (353). Melville's exploration of Pierre's problems as an author tends to disguise his failure to explore Pierre's changing attitude toward Isabel, but the careful reader cannot help but be aware of it.

The more emotionally involved Melville becomes in his portrayal of Pierre as author, the more he loses his grasp on the implications of other parts of his narrative. As Pierre's suffering and degradation in his attempt to be a profound writer worsen, Melville's rhetoric starts to exalt him: 'In the midst of the merriments of the mutations of Time, Pierre hath ringed himself in with the grief of Eternity. Pierre is a peak inflexible in the heart of Time, as the isle-peak, Piko, stands unassaultable in the midst of waves' (304). Implicitly approving Pierre's commitment, in spite of the self-destructiveness of his attempt to write a great book, Melville speaks of the 'devouring profundities' that have opened up in his hero: 'would he, he could not now be entertainingly and profitably shallow in some pellucid and merry romance' (305). In the next passage on Pierre as author, it is in his 'deepest, highest part' that he is 'utterly without sympathy from any thing divine, human, brute, or vegetable' (338). The mental distance between author and character diminishes appreciably: 'the deeper and the deeper' that he dives, Pierre perceives the 'everlasting elusiveness of Truth' (339), an elusiveness that Melville as narrator had postulated

earlier (at page 165 and page 285). Pierre's scorn of the critics now is
clearly Melville's: 'beforehand he felt the pyramidical scorn of the genuine loftiness for the whole infinite company of infinitesimal critics' (339).
As the distance between author and hero narrows, the hero is increasingly
exalted, and Melville speaks of Pierre in the same terms as Pierre sees
himself. Pierre begins to feel 'that in him, the thews of a Titan were
forestallingly cut by the scissors of Fate' (339); Melville comments:
'Against the breaking heart, and the bursting head; against all the dismal
lassitude, and deathful faintness and sleeplessness, and whirlingness, and
craziness, still he like a demigod bore up' (339). Shortly afterwards
Melville writes that the 'very blood' in Pierre's body 'had in vain rebelled
against his Titanic soul' (341). In focusing on his hero as author, Melville
loses sight of Pierre the young man attempting to be Christlike but undone
by human flaws. Now he portrays Pierre the embattled demi-god, whose
degradation is an inevitable part of his Titanic greatness: 'gifted with
loftiness' he is 'dragged down to the mud' (339), even literally (341).
Pierre is identified with Enceladus, 'the most potent of all the giants', one
with 'unconquerable front' and 'unabasable face' (345). Melville approves
the 'reckless sky-assaulting mood' of both Enceladus and Pierre: 'For it is
according to eternal fitness, that the precipitated Titan should still seek to
regain his paternal birthright even by fierce escalade. Wherefore whoso
storms the sky gives best proof he came from thither! But whatso crawls
contented in the moat before that crystal fort, shows it was born within
that slime, and there forever will abide' (347).

But Pierre's increased stature as 'deep-diving' author and admirable
'sky-assaulting' demigod works against the logic of much of the novel's
development. For despite Melville's preoccupation with the hardship and
misery of Pierre's attempt to write profoundly, the last Books still bring to
a climax the disaster entailed in his attempt to be Christlike. A number of
events forcefully recall the pamphlet's warnings of calamity for the
chronometrical idealist. Lucy writes to Pierre that she intends to join him,
that she is commanded by God (311), and that in her 'long swoon' (after
Pierre told her he was married) 'heaven' was preparing her for a
'superhuman office', wholly estranging her from 'this earth' and fitting
her 'for a celestial mission in terrestrial elements' (310). Pierre is 'sacrificing' himself, she writes, and she is hastening to 're-tie' herself to him
(309). Obeying this impulse, she arrives at the Apostles' imitating Pierre's
chronometrical self-sacrifice, thereby compounding the possibilities for
disaster. In these last Books we are reminded more than once that Pierre is
sexually attracted to Isabel, that he may have committed incest with her
(308, 337, 351). But after the arrival of Lucy's letter, his relationship with
Isabel is seen to deteriorate rapidly and his relationship with Lucy becomes dangerously ambiguous. In the final pages, Pierre bitterly rejects
both Isabel and Lucy, and murders Glen; in his prison-cell Lucy dies on
hearing Isabel call herself Pierre's sister; Pierre and Isabel commit suicide.

Melville does not comment directly on much of the action in the last four Books of the novel, but these events clearly appear to illustrate the pamphlet's lesson that 'strange, *unique* follies and sins' are to be expected from one, like Pierre, attempting 'to live in this world according to the strict letter of the chronometricals' (213).

Yet for all Pierre's status as a profound, deep-diving author, he never consciously understands the relevance of the pamphlet to his life, though he has glimmerings of understanding (and Melville says that unconsciously he understood its application by the end of his life). He does not recognize the danger of Lucy's imitation of his sacrifice of self for another, in spite of his own experience. He reads Lucy's letter and is certain that 'whatever her enigmatical delusion' she 'remained transparently immaculate' in her heart (317), without even recognizing the possibility of a sexual motive in her decision to join him, as in his own deluded resolve to protect Isabel by living with her. He naively admires Lucy as 'an angel' (311), unmindful of the insidious sexual element in his earlier worship of Isabel as 'angel'. He later feels that 'some strange heavenly influence was near him, to keep him from some uttermost harm' (337–8), once Lucy is ensconced at the Apostles', though to Isabel's 'covertly watchful eye' he 'would seem to look upon Lucy with an expression illy befitting their singular and so-supposed merely cousinly relation' (337). Even in the death-cell he sees his predicament as merely the result of his refusal to disown and portion off Isabel (360), just as earlier he tries to accept his grief at the news of his mother's death as a part of the cost at which 'the more exalted virtues are gained' (286). After belatedly recognizing the incestuous nature of his attraction to Isabel, Pierre copes with the knowledge by shutting it out of his consciousness and continuing to deceive himself about his motives. In earlier Books Melville frequently comments on and analyzes Pierre's lack of awareness and his self-deception; now in the last four Books such commentary is notably lacking. Instead, Melville exalts his hero as consumed with devouring profundities, the result of his recent momentous experiences, even while Pierre is revealing a lack of profundity, a lack of perception, and an inability to face the truth of what he has actually experienced—limitations that are as dangerous as ever. While earlier Melville had commented incisively on Pierre's 'strange oversights and inconsistencies', he now fails to recognize a major contradiction in his characterization. He also forgets the origin of Pierre's book. Pierre announces to Isabel that he will 'gospelize the world anew' (273), but his new gospel is delusive, merely the result of his inability to accept himself as anything less than immaculate. Rather than recognizing that he is no longer virtuous, he proclaims that 'Virtue and Vice are trash!' (273). Melville makes no attempt to reconcile Pierre's initial evasion of truth as an author with his later supposed profundity. Nor does he make any attempt to explain the incongruity of Pierre's writing a blasphemous new gospel yet feeling protected by 'some strange heavenly influence' when

Lucy joins him, though the incongruity makes Pierre seem more a simpleton than a man of profundity.

Still other parts of the novel are in conflict with the ending. In *Pierre* Melville sets out to demonstrate, among other things, that chronometrical altruism leads inevitably to catastrophe. His self-renouncing hero, as the pamphlet predicts, arrays 'men's earthly time-keepers against him' (212), falls into a 'fatal despair of becoming all good' (215), and works himself 'woe and death' (212). Yet near the end of this progression Melville endorses his hero's 'Titanism'. Thus, in *Pierre* Melville is sceptical of a world-rejecting Christian ethic because it destroys the individual who holds to it, but finally advocates a world-rejecting Titanism equally destructive of the individual who holds to it. Through many Books he prepares the reader to expect a catastrophic ending, a disaster that will be the inevitable result of Pierre's chronometrical sacrifice for Isabel and of his being merely human. But when the disastrous end comes, Pierre's state of mind is a 'reckless sky-assaulting mood' that Melville admires as evidence of demi-godliness. As he goes out to meet Glen and Fred, Pierre proclaims: ' "I defy all world's bread and breath. Here I step out before the drawn-up worlds in widest space, and challenge one and all of them to battle!" ' (357). In the prison-cell after the murder of Glen, Pierre is like Enceladus with the mountain thrown down upon him: 'The cumbersome stone ceiling almost rested on his brow; so that the long tiers of massive cell-galleries above seemed partly piled on him'; Pierre's 'immortal, immovable, bleached cheek was dry' (360). His defiance in the prison-cell is again Enceladus-like, again implicitly approved, it would seem, by Melville: 'Well, be it hell. I will mold a trumpet of the flames, and, with my breath of flame, breathe back my defiance!' (360). In a sudden reversal, the chivalric posturing ('challenge one and all of them to battle', 'mold a trumpet of the flames', 'breathe back my defiance'), earlier indicative of Pierre's adolescent delusions, is now associated with a 'heaven-aspiring' nobility (347).

These conflicting attitudes toward Pierre's behaviour are not final, meaningful ambiguities Melville has carefully worked towards, but abrupt, confusing contradictions, the ultimate results of his excessively personal sympathy for Pierre's frustrations as an author. The decision to make the hero an author, whenever it was made, led to some powerful writing in the second half of *Pierre*, particularly in the Enceladus vision. It also deprived Melville of a full sense of what he was doing, in the second half and in the novel as a whole. 'Two books are being writ', said Melville (304), referring to the bungled one Pierre is putting on paper to offer to the world's eyes and the 'larger, and the infinitely better' one 'for Pierre's own private shelf', the one being written in his soul as the other is written on paper. In *Pierre* itself two books were also written, the one up through Book XIV (and intermittently thereafter) which examined the growth of a deluded but idealistic soul when confronted with the world's conventionality, and the later one which expressed Melville's sometimes sardonic, sometimes embittered reflections on his own career. There was no successful fusion of the two. As the new obsession drained off Melville's psychic and creative energies, the original purpose was blighted. Under the circumstances, it may be wrong to think of what *Pierre* might have been: behind Melville there was no educated literary milieu, no available models, no shoptalk with other literary masters, no rigorously critical friend, no one to assure him of ultimate glory—nothing, in short, to help him hold to the pervading idea that impelled the first half of the book. Yet he had accomplished so much in this book that one becomes anguished as Melville's genius goes tragically to waste. The great epic of metaphysical whaling came tormentingly close to being succeeded within a few months by a Kraken-book, one of the finest psychological novels in world literature rather than merely the best psychological novel that had yet been written in English.

Notes

1. When he wrote this letter to Hawthorne, Melville had just begun work on *Pierre* or else was at the point of beginning it. The fullest timetable of the composition of the book is in our "Introduction" to this volume, pp. 4–19.

2. Furthermore, ways of conceiving and organizing passages recur, as in Book IV, where Melville as narrator announces the ultimate futility of 'all analytical insight' (67) and instead resorts to subtler conjurations to convey his meaning, just as he has Ishmael do in 'The Whiteness of the Whale'.

3. 'Melville's *Pierre*', *New England Quarterly*, 3 (April 1930) 195–234).

4. 'Historical Note', p. 407, in *Pierre*, ed. Harrison Hayford, Hershel Parker, and G. Thomas Tanselle (Evanston and Chicago: Northwestern University Press and the Newberry Library, 1971). Page references are to this edition. The 'Historical Note' is by Leon Howard (365–79) and Hershel Parker (379–407).

5. Our 'Introduction' to this volume, pp. 1–27, largely supersedes previous accounts of the composition and publishing history of *Pierre* by Hershel Parker, "Why *Pierre* Went Wrong," *Studies in the Novel*, 8 (Spring 1976), 7–23, and "Contract: *Pierre*, by Herman Melville," *Proof*, 5 (1977), 27–44. The latter article is still valuable for its photographic reproductions of draft passages and the final contract. Our "Introduction" also supersedes Leon Howard's account cited in the previous footnote as far as dating the composition of *Pierre* is concerned but does not supersede his discussion of literary influences.

6. "Historical Note,' pp. 375 ff. See also our "Introduction" to this volume, pp. 12–18.

7. In 'Retrospective' Pierre may be portrayed as rather more infantile than a lad of twelve or more should be, for instance. Some apparent awkwardnesses, such as the uncertain age of Isabel, may well be deliberate ambiguities.

8. Melville had recently concluded in fact that 'There are some enterprises in which a careful disorderliness is the true method' (*Moby-Dick*, chapter 82, 'The Honor and Glory of Whaling').

9. The word 'nether' is Parker's recent emendation for the first edition's 'nearer'. The emendation will be incorporated in subsequent printings of the Northwestern-Newberry edition. See Parker's "Conjectural Emendations: An Illustration from the Topography of Pierre's Mind," *Literary Research Newsletter*, 3 (Spring 1978), pp. 62–66.

10. Page 65 provides a clear example: 'now, for the first time, Pierre, Truth rolls a black billow through thy soul! Ah, miserable thou, to whom Truth, in her first tides, bears nothing but wrecks!' The passage continues: 'as the mariner, shipwrecked and cast on the beach, has much ado to escape the recoil of the wave that hurled him there; so Pierre long struggled, and struggled, to escape the recoil of that anguish, which had dashed him out of itself, upon the beach of his swoon'. See also the accounts of the 'shrine in the fresh-foliaged heart of Pierre' (68); the 'choice fountain, in the filial breast of a tender-hearted and intellectually appreciative child' (68); the 'charred landscape' within Pierre (86); the 'billow' that had 'so profoundly whelmed Pierre' (104); the things 'fœtally forming' in Pierre (106); the 'electric fluid' in which Isabel seems to swim (151-2); the 'Hyperborean regions' into which strongest minds are led (165); and the 'vulnerable god' and 'self-upbraiding sailor' (180-1).

11. See, for example, the passages explaining that 'From without, no wonderful effect is wrought within ourselves, unless some interior, responding wonder meets it' (51); that 'in the warm halls of the heart one single, untestified memory's spark shall suffice to enkindle . . . a blaze of evidence' (71); that the 'inestimable compensation of the heavier woes' is 'a saddened truth' (88); that 'when suddenly encountering the shock of new and unanswerable revelations . . . man, at first, ever seeks to shun all conscious definitiveness in his thoughts and purposes' (92); that the soul of man 'can not, and does never intelligently confront the totality of its wretchedness' when 'on all sides assailed by prospects of disaster' (104); that the 'intensest light of reason and revelation combined, can not shed such blazonings upon the deeper truths in man, as will sometimes proceed from his own profoundest gloom' (169); that 'on the threshold of any wholly new and momentous devoted enterprise, the thousand ulterior intricacies and emperilings to which it must conduct . . . are mostly withheld from sight' (175); and that 'There is a dark, mad mystery in some human hearts' (180).

12. Also, the section of 'Young America in Literature' (250-1) on the flirtatious young ladies who entreat Pierre to 'grace their Albums with some nice little song' (and who live within easy walking or riding range, judging by the way his servants deliver the albums back to their owners) seems out of keeping with the portrayal of the maidens of Saddle Meadows in Book III (p. 46, especially). Until Book XVII there is no hint that Pierre has been sought out by any of the local girls, or that he has had social exchanges of any significance with any of them besides Lucy Tartan (who resides only part of the year in Saddle Meadows). Perhaps an even clearer example of Melville's forgetting his earlier characterization is in Book XXI, 'Plinlimmon', where he declares that a 'varied scope of reading, little suspected by his friends, and randomly acquired by a random but lynx-eyed mind' in the course of 'multifarious, incidental, bibliographic encounterings' as an 'inquirer after Truth' had 'poured one considerable contributary stream into that bottomless spring of original thought which the occasion and time had caused to burst out' in Pierre (283). But earlier Pierre's reading was said to have brought him 'into many a maze of all-bewildering beauty', not Truth (6). These examples are conspicuous; probably some other improvised passages are consistent enough with the rest of the book to escape notice.

13. There is always the possibility that this passage was written before the pamphlet and left uncancelled; similar redundancies were created by late additions in *Typee*. However, Melville's forgetting and improvising elsewhere in the second half of *Pierre* tends to cast doubt on this possibility.

14. *Pierre* (New York: Hendricks House, Inc. 1949) p. lxxxiii.

Prospects for Criticism on *Pierre*

Brian Higgins and Hershel Parker*

Even so large and wide-ranging a collection as this cannot claim to contain the last word on *Pierre; or, The Ambiguities*. For all the power of some of the essays from the Melville Revival—E. L. Grant Watson's tribute to the book in 1930, to name our own favorite—and for all the perceptiveness of some of the later academic criticism, important essays remain to be written.

This is true partly because great literature is, as the axiom has it, inexhaustible. It is also true because the discovery of *Pierre* by brilliant literary men (rarely professors of literature) during the Revival, a period notable for new interest in Melville's biography (especially as facts or rumors about his life could fuel Freudian speculation) was rapidly followed, in the 1940s, by the rise of academic criticism as an industry for the manufacture of New Critical interpretations. As a result, the initial scholarly investigations were never zealously pursued. We still have scant knowledge of the relationship between Pierre's family history and Melville's own, despite such recent illumination as that afforded by Amy Puett Emmers's evidence that Melville's father may have sired an illegitimate daughter, as Pierre's may have done. Possessing only a vague sense of the book's literary precedents, we talk of the Gothic novel and of British and American sentimental fiction as sources or analogues, but we rarely read the books that we suspect Melville read. Conspicuously, we have not pursued all of the parallels the early reviewers pointed out in writers such as Jean Paul Richter, Eugene Sue, and Martin Farquhar Tupper; the parallels that critics of the Revival discovered—seriously or whimsically—in writers such as Horace Walpole, Laura Jean Libbey, and Sylvester Judd, as well as in major writers such as Shakespeare, De Quincey, and Carlyle; and the parallels that Henry A. Murray, in the Explanatory Notes to his edition of *Pierre*, pointed to in writers such as Godwin, Scott, Disraeli, and Thackeray. Only with a clearer sense of such contexts can we begin to locate *Pierre* more precisely in that "stream of experimentation" E. H. Eby sketchily charted in 1930, and, particularly, to distinguish those passages where Melville was imitating from those where he was parodying debased forms of language, characterization, and plot. We have scarcely begun to explore the relationship of *Pierre* to the rest of Melville's writings. Once again, the strongest attempts were made in the 1920s and 1930s, by readers who identified a trilogy of great, closely related books: *Mardi*, *Moby-Dick*, and *Pierre*. Only recently have critics begun to explore the obvious topic of the relationship of *Pierre* to *Moby-Dick* in any detail. Not until 1980 was there a reliable chronology of the tales Melville wrote after the publication of *Pierre*[1], although they are,

---

*This essay was written specifically for this volume and appears here by permission of the authors.

along with *Moby-Dick*, the starting point for study of the book's relationships to the rest of the Melville canon. Good readers, good scholar-critics, can still hope to illuminate even the oldest of these topics, and to open new topics for discussion.

Old approaches, then, need to be pursued again, with new vigor. But new approaches need to be taken, notably an approach which seeks to show the aesthetic implications of textual and biographical evidence and to write criticism in the light shed by such evidence. Good critics of the future, we dare to hope, will discard the prevailing assumptions inherited from the New Criticism, so that they will not automatically feel compelled to define Melville's "intention" in *Pierre*, as if he had had a single intention, one "pervading thought that impelled the book," but rather will acknowledge and analyze his dual or multiple intentions which shifted as a result of the blows dealt him by his publisher and by the reviewers of *Moby-Dick* and as a result of other, perhaps still identifiable, forces in his life. Such critics, we further hope, will attempt to locate the value of the book by a standard other than formal "unity"—a quality Melville sacrificed as he enlarged his manuscript. Without necessarily discarding favorite concepts of the New Criticism such as irony and ambiguity (certainly not in writing on a novel so subtitled), scholars and critics may humanize the vocabulary of aesthetic discussion by analyzing the flaws and achievements of *Pierre* in the light of what we know and can learn of the always hazardous and seldom totally triumphant creative process.

The most heartening words for those awestruck as they read *Pierre* for the first time and begin to think about their responses in relation to responses of earlier readers are in the book itself: "Something ever comes of all persistent inquiry; we are not so continually curious for nothing."

Note

1. Merton M. Sealts, Jr. "The Chronology of Melville's Short Fiction, 1853–1856," *Harvard Library Bulletin*, 28 (October 1980), 391–403.

INDEX